AMANDA R. HOWLAND

Beasts and Creature

First published by Erie Oak Moon 2022

First edition

ISBN: 979-8-218-02255-6

Cover art by David Russell Stempowski

This book was professionally typeset on Reedsy.
Find out more at reedsy.com

For Mitchell, my Angel,
for my family, and my noise family,
with love always.

Contents

1

Dry Eyes

Down the hallway again. Most walls in apartment building halls are white, maybe grey or tan or cream, but those walls were *red*. The hall stank like eucalyptus and apartment cooking, other people's cheap meat and noodles. I knocked and stood back with my hand at my throat, annoyed by the deranged pulse. Waiting at the door. I looked out the black window. There was a tree in the dumpster below, silver tinsel shivering on the edges. It was cold but there was no snow.

The door opened, not on Lizabeth, but on her nephew, called Matt or Mike or something. He slumped with a bowl of ramen noodles, eyebrows slightly raised.

"Hey, man, where's the old woman, she home?" I said.

"Come on in, Margot." He swiveled. I followed him into the heat, hoping the human smells wouldn't be too close. Steam heat filled every pore with the smell of the old woman: scalp and powder. Mildew and medicine. I'd become intimate with her nest. Piles and piles of papers and magazines. The long living room was dark with shades drawn against streetlights and just two dim lamps on. It was quieter than usual, and I realized it was because Lizabeth's oxygen machine wasn't on. "She's not here. Where is she?"

Matt or Mike pushed some dusty *Ladies Home Journals* and *Us* magazines off the couch and onto the floor and motioned for me to sit while he went over to the old woman's La-Z-Boy and reclined with his noodles. "Oh, do you want to share my noodles, Margot?"

"No, thanks." I sat in the dust.

"She's at Giant Eagle." He twisted up a fat wad of noodles on his fork. "She should be back soon."

"I'll wait."

"I don't know, maybe she won't be."

"Right on."

He looked too free and easy up on her throne. It made me a bit sick. This young man with his product-laden hipster hair and white belt, so happy to be lounging all day in a stale low-level drug den in Cleveland's west side, lapping up his aunt's product and sucking on Save A Lot noodles. He reminded me of my ex-husband.

Lizabeth had been sitting in that chair for so long that it had contoured to her twisted mass like a worn glove. The old woman had told me the La-Z-Boy had once been her husband's chair, from which he bossed her around the apartment. He died from a heart attack in 1982, and she took over his chair and his business. She took back her maiden name *Vickers*, and got her younger brothers working for her. Her husband had sold heroin for a bigger family in the seventies, and she came in and started her own crew just in time for crack. Business started to slow in the late nineties, at least that's what she told me. Liz was a bullshit artist, sitting back in her chair, smoking Kools and hacking into a tin garbage bin, tissues all over her lap. She lied about things she didn't have to.

Now this boy crossed his legs and set down his noodles, and *motherfucker*, if he didn't pick up a carton of her Kools, pull out a pack, tap out a cigarette and light up.

Liz's lapdog playing house.

I squirmed.

He said, "Do you want to get high?"

I said no fast.

He picked up a blown glass pipe and packed it with buds, using an expired Easy-Whip canister to ground the weed down into the bowl. He packed in a little extra shake to make it super dense.

"Then why are you here to see old Crackerpants? She's like your best friend or some shit?" The little punk would never have the stones to use Lizabeth's nickname to her face

"I don't want to get high *now, here, with you.*" I didn't have much to do the last few months, so I'd come by after work to sit and talk with Liz, watch the assholes come and go. Her brothers worked for her, but the few times I'd seen the nephew, he'd been loafing on one of the two couches with a Nintendo DS. We'd never really talked before.

My eye twitch had grown worse. I knew he couldn't see it, but I was afraid he could smell it. What was wrong with my heart: too hot, too fast. It distracted me, running my blood too fast, and I was pretty much not into talking with people anyway. I wanted out.

He pressed his lips together. "You like Obama or Hillary?"

"What? Oh." The Ohio primary was in about six weeks.

The kid looked at me, licked his lips and let his mouth hang open.

I squeezed my left forearm with my right hand. "I don't care, man. I'll just be glad when Bush is out. I wouldn't be surprised if he started another war in October or something so he could declare martial law or something to postpone the election."

"I don't vote—blood's on your hands either way." He exhaled smoke through his teeth.

My toes curled in my sneakers. "They shouldn't have cut Kucinich from the debates. He should have stayed in, anyway. He's the only one who's really on the left, he wants single-payer and gay marriage and to get us out of these wars, and free college...the rest of the democrats are just republicans, and the republicans are fascists."

"Yeah, but didn't Kucinich get probed by aliens or some shit? People are never going to go for that Kucinich, Nader stuff. I am not interested in politics."

"You brought it up, Mike."

"Mark. You're funny, Margot."

Watching him smoke the menthol cigarette made me feel the burn of freebased cocaine hitting my lungs. I couldn't take it. I would have to leave, wait outside for the old woman or something.

Mark looked like a kid, but his voice was deep. He didn't take his eyes off me, just smiled, and rubbed his chin. "She doesn't sell as much as she did back in the day, I guess. Mostly weed, but I guess you don't like weed. Sometimes she gets e or mushrooms, never acid. But you're too keyed up to be looking for heady stuff anyway, right Red? Anybody ever call you Red?"

"Look-it, man, I just want to be cool and relax, okay, let's not play, okay." I picked up a magazine. There was the tv actress from the nineties with her wheaty-clean grin and razor-straight part—would I always have to look at that face?

He said, "She doesn't mess with meth anymore, too much drama for too little bread. You gotta have a little breathing room to cook. Too much competition from those fucking crazy people out in Medina."

"Maybe I'll just wait for Liz out in the hall." I picked up a magazine with bald Brittany Spears on the cover, baring her teeth just before attacking a car with an umbrella.

He smiled wide. "You look too poor for coke, wearing those broke-ass ratty sneakers. So it must be bread and butter, it's mostly bread and butter stuff around here, crack or oxy, oxy or crack. Crackerpants is smart. Bread and butter."

"Whatever. I mean, rock, whatever. So why are you asking, anyway?

Are you holding this shit or what." I fingered the container in my pocket. I felt better with the little rose case on my person. Panic shot through me as I tried to remember if I still had Chore Boys left at home. But yes, yes. I went through the ritual in my mind of picking them up at Fred's Deli and sticking them in the kitchen drawer.

I just wanted to get home and get high alone and hang out with my cat. The thought of my cat's wise owl face made me desperate to get home. Home was my room and my cat and my paintings and my music.

Strange coincidence was, I used to live in this very building with my ex-husband on the floor below, but I didn't know Liz then. It's a nice building, 1920's Deco, built for Rockefeller's executives, right by the lake. So, all this drug shit was happening right above us, and we had our completely separate unhappy marriage shit going on below. I longed to be away from this creep and get back to my room and my cat. That's all I needed.

"Ah, sick. Crack. You are a nasty girl, Margot. I guess that's a perennial favorite. It comes from Guatemala, did you know that?"

I opened the magazine. I closed it. "That's what she told me. She was talking about Mayans and stuff." I was dry at the mouth for the want of it. *What a piece of shit I am.* I stood up, ashamed, hoping it was dark so he wouldn't see cold drops of sweat clinging my scrubs to my torso. He stood up too.

"Whoa, be cool. I know. It sucks not having a tv in this shithole. Makes things edgy. Have a seat, Margot, she'll be back soon. I'll get you a drink."

"Okay, good idea." I sat down. It must be this *shit* making me so nervous, this isn't how I've felt before, in life before. You do something for some fucking peace of mind and then it robs you of any peace forever. Just like anything you do I guess, like marriage. First it's sweet and easy, then irritating, then a tragic disaster. I felt sick and

5

leaned back into the stinking couch to breathe and relax a little. He handed me a small amber glass.

"Right," I smiled. I drank. I let the Remy Martin warm me, slow me, loosen my chest. He was sitting close now on the couch. "I'm surprised you drink this stuff," I said and laughed.

"Well, it was the old man's favorite, she keeps it around for clients, but she never drinks it." He tossed his back and poured us each another.

The cognac went straight to my *Svadhisthana* chakra. He put his hand on my leg. "Oh, no, kid, I'm dirty from work, too old for you." My tongue felt thick. His heavy brown eyes sunk into mine, and I liked it. I felt flustered again, but warmer, hot and dizzy. I stood up, and he stood up next to me quickly. I was surprised to see panic in his eyes and hands, his cheeks pink and lips full, his eyes sleepy.

"Lizabeth will be home soon, please stay." His voice went soft. "I have been alone all day."

"Solitude, Matt."

"Mark." He smiled. I felt my knees falling out beneath me. My desire turned to deep confusion, and he put his hands on my arms. It felt like we were dancing. Then we fell into the dark.

I woke up lying on a bed in a strange room. I squinted my eyes shut against the awful overhead bulb. A woman—Lizabeth—was stroking my face, my hair.

"Ah, that's my girl, hey Margot." She said my name wrong like "Mar-goat".

I rolled onto my side and she spooned me. Her rotten peach smell caught in my nose and throat. But the feeling of her hand in my hair was the best thing I'd felt in a long time.

"Margot, sh, I'm so sorry. My brothers are dealing with Mark."

My limbs were gone like when you meditate, but my chest was caving in. "Liz."

"You want some milk? Is your stomach okay?" She shouted at the door, "Jeff. Draw Margot a bath."

"No, no milk, I need to smoke, Liz. I need to wake up." The room sweltered with steam heat, and the itchy red blanket woke up my skin in a bad way.

"I know baby."

Coming out of a twilight sleep. The next minute I was in a salmon-colored bathroom, sitting on the closed toilet, Lizabeth towering over me. The walls were papered in busy angels.

My eyes were new and far off, my lips numb, and my cheeks gone.

"I'll fix you up, Margot, don't worry." Big old crone, her neck was as wide as her shoulders. I was glad to see her grisly face and shock of canary yellow hair. She lunged down and cupped my face in her hands. *Ow*, everything was loud.

"Were we just lying down, Liz?"

She nodded.

Her youngest brother Billy leaned in the doorway. He was breathing fast, his close-set eyes contorted in rage. "Margot, baby. I'm gonna disembowel that little bitch—are you hurt?" Billy and I had had a fling last summer that had been hard to get out of.

My stomach rolled at any distraction from getting high. I could only glance at him.

Everything was electrical soft edges, just awful. Then Lizabeth carefully fitted together a makeshift pipe from a Love Rose tube. The sight was like a slap inside my brain. I was awake. An insect with all eyes fixed on gnarled old hands. I didn't even ask if Mark had roofied me, of course he had. Liz smiled and handed me the rose to hold onto

7

while she prepared my fix.

She bumped her hip on the sink. "Shit." Old guilt festered for a moment when Billy made an animal sound and tore from the room. On a dusty shelf sat ancient perfumes, and something called Artificial Tears.

I looked up at Liz like any baby mammal looks at its mother. I whispered *thank you*. She lit the foil. Liquid god burning. Ah god, lost in blazing electrical whiteness. Out of the darkness and into the light stuff. Stupid stars, I could care less, no, not at all.

Then I was on. I pushed past her and knew to go back into the rotting spare bedroom down the hall. The overhead light cast flat yellow light into a room with crusty red blankets covering the windows. Billy and middle brother Jeff had Mark on the floor, and they were kicking him quietly. Beefy Jeff with the green Mohawk was Mark's father.

Electric balls of crack flicked up my spine and I pushed the men away hard with a squeeze and looked down on Mark. Panting, Billy put his hand on my forearm. "I'm so sorry this happened, girl. Get a kick in if you want.

Jeff stood aside and nodded at me so I could kick. Mark's body was lurching from the blows, but even with blood running down his face, his eyes were still and calm, his mouth gently shut. He was a sedate motherfucker. Even blazing, I couldn't kick this broken animal. I just spat without any spit and said, "You didn't have to drug me ass—hole, I would have fucked you right there on the fucking magazines!"

I copped a little stash that would last me a few days, at least until Thursday. I'd walked to Liz's apartment. She had Billy drive me home. The nights were still so long, but it must have been close to dawn. Billy followed me up the stairs and into my rented room.

Clarence hopped from the top of the mini-fridge and padded over to me. I bent down and touched his cheeks. I scooped him up and held him like a baby and then pressed our faces together. Clarence looked into my eyes. I buried my face into his neck for a deep whiff, *ah cat*.

I set him down and walked over to the mini-fridge and pulled out cans of Pabst, wishing for liquor.

"God, I was so numb back there, I couldn't tell, but I think he had sex with me, but everything feels okay." I forced a little dry laugh. I wanted to sit, but there was only one chair and my low air mattress, and I didn't want to draw Billy's attention to the bed. I leaned against the counter instead, willing my body to stop shaking.

"Margot. You've been raped. That psycho raped you."

"No, god, don't say that." I waved for him to please sit down in the chair. I closed the blinds against the cold wind and impending sun. I'd checked in the bathroom. It was sore but not too wet. Mark must have used a condom, or maybe he didn't come.

"Jesus, Margot." He sat down fast. "When we got there, you were passed out on the couch, and he was rubbing your legs. I hoped maybe nothing happened."

"Nothing happened."

"What the fuck, girl." Billy opened a beer. "I've always hated that shitty kid. *Vickers don't rape!* Goddamnit. When Marky was five he tried to set Jeff's feet on fire! I mean, he *poured* lighter fluid on his dad's fucking feet!"

I liked Billy. He'd spent his life in and out of prison for petty things, so he was like a time traveler. In his mid-forties, with a compact muscular body and foxlike face, he kept his hair in a blond mullet with sharp bangs, he wore muscle shirts, he listened to Twisted Sister, Pink Floyd and Ozzy, and he lived to party. A memory flashed of riding in a truck with him last summer. I had directed him to go

9

straight, and he'd said, "No girl! Forward! Never *straight!*"

I said, "I'm sorry, Billy. It's a shit night. I've been thinking, though, lately. It's time to go to a show."

"What?"

"Music, I want to get back in." I smiled and smashed my beer before scooping up Clarence again. I pressed my face into his feathery shoulder and felt his purr.

"Good, sure, but right now I don't care. You got to stop with the crack."

"You smoke it."

"I don't have an *addictive personality.*"

"Neither do I. It's not as bad as meth. My mother told me that shit puts holes in your brain, and I've never touched it. Crack is just cheap coke, all that stigma surrounding it is racist."

"I like to party. I like to party with you, girl. But I never let partying get me into a situation like the one you got yourself in back there. Plus, I never smoked rock daily, not for more than a week-ten days at a shot I guess."

He shifted in the chair, crossed his arms and frowned up at me.

"Billy. It wasn't the free-based cocaine that I was there to purchase from your sister that got me in 'that situation'. It was the roofie your nephew put in my drink."

I put my hand on his arm. "But look. I'm doing okay. I go to work. I take Milk Thistle for my liver. I do yoga. I was going to create a quitting ritual this night actually, but the night's shot now." I laughed. "I keep it pretty rationed actually. I have rules. I only get high after the sun goes down, and soon the days will be getting longer, so. I'll think about it tomorrow night. I'm spent and pissed now. And I want to focus on straight chilling now. Let's listen to some noise." I put on Skin Graft, hoping to banish Billy from my room. I'd fucked up reminding him where I lived.

Skin Graft blasted harsh abstract waves of electronic dissonance, but Billy just talked louder. "I blame Simon—he should never have turned you on to the stuff. Just stay away from him, girl, if you got to do it, at least get it from Liz. She's good people. Mark won't be around anymore. But, really, you should just quit for a while."

"I don't talk to Simon." Simon was the young dealer I'd dated for a minute. I thought Simon and Billy were friends. No more, apparently.

"Good. Back there—you said you would have fucked Mark anyway…"

"Billy, I don't know what the fuck I'm doing."

"It's okay girl, sorry to bring it up."

I wished Billy would leave. I wished he'd rub my back, but I'd never ask. I sat down on the floor across my crate table from him and picked up the Modern Lovers album with "Roadrunner" and pretended to read the back. "Why would someone buy tears, *artificial tears*—is it a theater thing? Was Liz an actor?"

He said nothing but made noises with his crushed can. Skin Graft filled the room with sickening high pitch.

I just wanted to be free all the time. I missed my friends. I closed my eyes and saw the red desert out in Arizona where my family was.

I poked his knee with my toe. "You can go on, Billy, I'll be okay."

He looked at the small stack of 7-inches on the blue crate and nodded. "I don't see any new paintings, you still paint?"

"It's too dark."

"Margot."

"Yes, Billy."

"Margot—you are getting too passive. I don't feel like it's your true nature. I don't buy it. Stop letting stuff happen to you and do something!"

"I got sick of doing things, Billy. I wanted to see where the Tao took me, and here I am."

"There you are. Well. Sometimes in life, girl, you got to choose something! Fight for something!"

"Now I need to sleep."

He stood up. "Well. I still don't get this noise music, girl. Too harsh!" He smiled, lingered for a minute, trying to find my eyes. "Take care, now. Maybe I'll see you at Liz's. But not for crack, please. Liz's been like a mother to me, but she's a businessman first. Don't care how people get fucked up by this shit."

I stood up and we had a long hug. I was glad that he left then, that he didn't try to stay. I wanted to be alone with Clarence.

I got drunk on cans of Pabst and slept like death.

That night it finally started to snow.

2

Independent Living

A few days passed. I realized I was out of crack before I opened my eyes. Clarence slept with his soft black back against my face. I sat up and looked out the square window next to my air mattress. Groundhog Day. Two planes let out billowing white lines that crossed. Get up. Got to go to work. I had no hangover. I'd been waking up feeling like I hadn't slept: bruisy all over, foggy headed, dry eyes. My own voice racing through my head all night. I got into the shared shower in the hallway, then into my scrubs and sat in my chair drinking a Monster energy drink. It was big and black with neon green writing. Clarence fell on his side against my left foot, purred and turned his face up to me. I offered my finger, and he pressed his tiny cheek against it.

I worked first shift cleaning rooms in the assisted living section of Autumn Villa Senior Center. Better than the nursing section, not as good as the independent living section. I drank these energy drinks, one first thing, then two more at work. I needed to feel keyed up to stay calm until I could get home and smoke. The energy drinks made the day go faster, and if I relaxed too much, that's when I got really nervous and started wanting to get high. I was okay. I was 33.

I made shit money, but I didn't need much. I lived in a room above a mechanic's garage on west 79th and Madison that only charged $85 a month. The lady who owned it, owned it outright. The two rooms above the garage were afterthoughts.

Before my ex-husband left Ohio a year before, I'd saved up a little over three grand, so that helped for a while. I'd worked as a hairdresser a long time, hated it, and quit as soon as I didn't have to carry his sorry ass anymore. Housekeeping suited me much better, mostly because you get to work alone.

My building was a hundred years old and shook. The garage was slow. The small room was fine for Clarence and me. It smelled bad when they had work downstairs, like wallpaper glue and burning plastic and metal on fire. I hated gasoline the most, though, man, was I sick of gasoline. Liz's building, where I'd lived with Georgie, was just a mile north of where I lived now. It was a nice apartment, but Georgie was a slob, man, his side of the bedroom was piled with fast food bags and cups with cigarettes floating in the melted ice. I didn't miss the mess, but I missed the oaks and the lake and the safety.

I didn't miss my ex-husband. Georgie was far away now, back in his strange hometown of Jerome, Arizona. Jerome was a tiny town nestled on a remote little mountain called Cleopatra Hill. Jerome was a revived ghost town, a tourist spot, but it had originally been a copper mining town. When I first met Georgie, I thought he was Latino, but he was Irish, descended from Irish people who moved to Jerome to mine copper for the First World War. Now his family owned a gallery and coffee shop.

I still woke up in the night, my heart slamming, images of his beetle-black hair fading slowly. I had to say out loud that he was not in Ohio anymore.

I was used to being poor, but I missed walking to the lake, the feel of my bare feet on soft grass. I was only twenty minutes farther away by foot, but I wouldn't walk that alone just for fun. I lived in one of the roughest neighborhoods in Cleveland, statistically. I hadn't really been fucked with, though.

I had a few things. I had books and records and a player and a mini-fridge and an air mattress and a cat-box and a self-portrait of myself as a lion with a mane, red and gold and orange, a lady lion, but she has a mane anyway, with my eyes and mouth and nose. I spent most of my time in that room. The landlady's pregnant niece lived in the room across the hall. She was quiet. If I wasn't in my room, I was at work or at Lizabeth's.

Bleak months.

I had been part of a noise/experimental music community, but I'd lost touch with my friends. I did bad things. I didn't want to see my friends. Sometimes I went to the library and got online and watched them on Facebook, but I didn't post. I hadn't checked MySpace in months.

Years ago, my brother and I moved to Cleveland from Canton, Ohio, where we grew up. Canton is a small industrial city an hour south of Cleveland. Canton has its own thing going, but we had to see what else was going on.

We came here to play music. My brother and I both played noise guitars, and we went through various drummers. Then my folks moved out to Flagstaff, Arizona ten years ago, and my brother followed them a couple years after that. I'd already made tight friends with the musicians here.

I only visited my family once. On that trip, I met Georgie. My brother and I drove down to Tucson in 120-degree heat to visit the San Xavier Mission where everything went white: the sky and the ground and the church all bone white in the heat. Georgie sat a few pews up. He turned back as we came in. His eyes were liquid night.

We were married for a few years, then shit went down, and Georgie finally left last winter. Then I just didn't want to go to shows anymore. Ironic, because Georgie was always trying to keep me in, to keep me from going to shows, but some plaque had formed over my brain, and I didn't want to go out anymore.

I only liked crack now. I kept trying to read *A Language Older than Words* by Derrick Jenson, but I couldn't focus on it. It was the fucking crack cocaine, made reading hard, the lines blur, and the book made me suck the insides of my cheeks. Jenson says it was legal in the U.S. to hunt Indigenous people just over a hundred years ago, he writes about scientists torturing baby chimps, he writes about how our mega-culture, the culture of Civilization and Corporation, is just a violent anomaly in the vast human experience. That our culture moves against and over nature through coercion, how progress is nothing more than the extermination of wildness: destroying the organic complexity of life itself.

I threw the book at the mini fridge. Then, I picked it up again. I made ugly faces, but my tears were dried up and I couldn't make myself cry anymore. I couldn't take it. I had to get to work.

I flashed on an hour of my life, years ago, somewhere between two and three in the morning. A noise friend dragged me to the freezer section at the Giant Eagle on 117th street to share with me the rushing sound it makes, the massive sound 24 hours a day. We stood breathing in the roar.

Another flash as I pushed into my shoes, pushed my heart into my shoes. Yearning for another night, long ago, when I stood barefoot on a golden wood floor warm with peach candles listening to The Velvet Underground...

But now I was running to work with stiff legs in the cold, my bag was heavy, I didn't need this shit, the umbrella, the Jensen book, lunch, I didn't want lunch, I opened and closed my mouth, opened and closed my hands in the cold.

Memories flashed like slides from different-colored years. Listening to Nico's strange dirgy solo albums, kissing a friend. Him with thick dry lips, lanky body and devouring eyes. "Chelsea Girls" swelled up but then began to skip, but we kissed, we didn't stop kissing all night, grls'grls'grls'grls...I needed a friend like that.

I needed a close *friend* like an arrow in my brain. I needed a deep-eyed soul lover, an angel to pull out my guts and make them shimmer again.

I felt good riding the rapid to work. My favorite show: roots and brown trees and dirt running past the train windows.

Clawed up fields of concrete, winter weeds tearing through twisted iron, loopy orange painted graffiti, the word NOSTALGIA written large, harsh yellowed grasses lunging out at the tracks. Moving fast past a wall of dirts, a trench Cleveland that can only be seen from the tracks. Then we shoot over the industrial flats, the river valley, towards downtown. We were in the air, over the whipped curves of the Cuyahoga, riding high over ancient-modern squat buildings used for manufacturing or storage, drinking and prostitution, the lake hanging like a sea in the north. Forests and factories and streets winding down the valley.

I loved housekeeping: the constant movement, the cycles of cleaning and returning. I also loved the building where we worked on the west bank of the Cuyahoga just southwest of downtown, old and scary, full of long hallways.

We worked eight to four, so our first break was at ten. That's another thing I liked about the gig. There were more regular breaks than anywhere else I'd ever worked. I like a good rhythm. I poured two Dixie cups of cold water and went to sit down by my janitor friend Keith in the yellowed break room. He sat in the corner, engrossed in Scene Magazine. It had been cool in decades past but was now owned by one of the two corporations that owned most of the "local" alternative papers these days. He nodded and smiled at me, "Hey bud," and then adjusted his center part and pushed his glasses further up his nose. Keith and I were in a barely active cover band together.

His wife Carrie sat down next to us.

"Hey Margot, how's Mrs. Paffe these days?" She said.

She spoke to me but ignored her husband. A housekeeper for life, she viewed janitors as nothing more than trash collectors. Even her husband, who had started after being laid off from a car paint factory. She wore boxy flowered scrubs and had dyed her hair permanent brown over and over again so that the ends were dull black and the roots bright orange-sand. A slight know-it-all quiver to her smile. Carrie had trained me when I started here. I took over her route in assisted, and then she moved up to independent living.

"Yeah, same old."

I returned her smile, glad to have some bullshit to sling around. Keith raised his eyes at her. "It's trashy to talk about the residents you guys."

"Ha. What else is there." Carrie pressed her fat little hand into the table and pulled her glasses out of a little cigarette purse. "It's bullcrap that we can't smoke in here anymore, used to be nice, you know, when it's cold like this to sit in this warm room to smoke. Frickin' politically correct whatever." She shook her head at her own partial insight. She gave me a sideways smile, "Mrs. Paffe is nice. She's a nice lady, Margot."

"She is."

We call most of the residents by their first names, though some less sensitive housekeepers and aides call them *Gra*-ma! Pearl Paffe was one of the few surviving members of the Greatest Generation who still insisted on formal address. That's where the formality ended with Paffe. Her deal was she somehow got feces wedged under her fingernails and wanted to tell you about it. She claimed it was from her dogs. Then she asked you if there was some way you could help her with this.

"Nice lady. But for the *dog shit!*" Carrie boomed. Hahahaha. I smiled, Keith picked up the paper again. "I'd say, MISSUS PAFFE, WHERE IS YOUR DOG?" Carrie looked at me expectantly.

Carrie said the same shit all the time, and Paffe's was also a routine Keith and I had both experienced first-hand.

"I mean, she says, 'Girl, I've got dog shit under my nails, can you help me get it out? *Girl,* do you have a toothpick or something?' So sweet, she says it so sweet, but man, there ain't no dog shit smell in there, all human shit, so what I want to know is, when she's digging shit out of her asshole, does she like, fricking disassociate and think she's digging in the ass of a dog, or what? Hahahahah."

Carrie looked at me, then at the Keith for approval.

I groaned and let my head drop into my hands, feeling sick.

Carrie poked my head. "Seriously though, Sharon's doing checks, soon. You might be off that crap route and over in independent with me!"

I told her that would be good.

"When McCain *kills* Clinton or, *what's-his-name*, in November, we'll be doing better. Bush is a dummy, but McCain can get crap done. I know it, honey." She winked at me. "Oh. Hey. I think my cousin knows you. Liz? Over on West Boulevard?"

"I don't, maybe."

"Sure! She said you'uns were over the other night, says you mentioned working here, wanted to pass on her regards."

Paranoia flickered through my belly. My two little worlds were colliding.

"She didn't tell me *you* worked here. Did she say anything else?"

"Just she knew you from the neighborhood, said you was sick the other night, for me to look out. But Vickers is trouble, honey, I love them. Liz seems like a nice old lady, but she's got..."

Keith leaned forward, "It's freezing in here."

"Oh, not you! With your baby fat!" She pinched him in his belly and sat back laughing.

He jerked his skinny arms over his soft spot. "Okay, that's. Okay. I've got to get back to the storage room I think."

"No, honey," Carrie patted his arm and he flinched a little, "No you just sit there, honey, you'uns still have seven minutes of break left, I'm going outside have a cigarette. At least while that's still legal! To smoke outside!" She stood up and pulled out a cigarette. "Margot. I'll put in a good word with Sharon, but watch out for Liz!" She swayed out of the room.

Keith stood up. "Margot. Shit. I forgot what I was going to say." He put down the paper

"That's okay. It'll come back."

Soon, he ambled off to his scrub work and I to mine.

The Patients' Bill of Rights states that we have to knock before we enter their rooms. The mauve hallway hummed with deeply controlled air. They couldn't always give consent, but at least they knew we were coming in.

So many Maries. I knocked and entered the room of one of

my favorites, and she was sitting on the bed, paper white skin disappearing into white springy hair matted in the back from sleep just like a small child. Black eyes shining against all that white. Her hands folded on her lap. Red dress and black shoes. She turned toward me with a half-smile, knowing blank eyes, made a low affirmative sound and then turned back to the grotesque opening music of her soap opera.

Normally I liked it when they were out of their rooms so I could clean without their eyes on me. Asking me every three minutes "What are you doing in here!" as I run around the room wiping things down with hot rags. But I loved this Mary and the Mary next door. This Mary had a strong body, but her memory and much of her ability to talk were gone. Her eyes saw things, I could tell.

Being around these Maries sent a tingle up my spine for some reason, like when my grandmother stroked my hair as a child. They offered free-floating affection. They didn't notice that they couldn't hold onto my name. But the affection was present.

Our routine started by spraying Scrubbing Bubbles on all the surfaces of the bathroom, and then we sprayed some into a bucket and filled it with hot water from the tub faucet. We sloshed the hot soapy water on the mirror with a rag and then polished it with a dry towel. I held the sink as things went grey for a minute—how long could I pull this off. I looked into the wet mirror. I wiped. I needed noise.

I said loud enough for her to hear in the other room, above the soap, "Mary, how are you today? Do you need anything?" I wasn't allowed to give her anything.

"What about the orchard." She surprised me by appearing in the doorway as I was wiping the bathtub. I'd never seen her on her feet. She towered above me. I'm not a short woman, and most of the residents have lost a few inches. It was a little shocking.

21

"Orchard?"

She held up her hands and swayed a little on heavy black dress shoes. "No no, the orchid. You know, garden. The roots…like cinders." Her hands fell down. "Five cinders long, three su-cinders…" she held up three fingers, instructing me.

I went back to the tub, rinsed it, and moved to the toilet. "Right, I heard it's good to plant flowers and vegetables together to attract bees… and something about parasites."

She smiled and leaned in the doorway as I finished, flushed, and squirted more blue stuff in the bowl to sit.

"Okay Mary, you want to step back into the room? I've got to mop in here. I don't want you to slip."

She stepped back while I finished. When I returned to her living area, she was sitting on the edge of her bed, facing the tv, staring at a helmet-haired brunette in red who shook her head, wrinkled her forehead and accused someone of faking something.

Gummy toothpaste, clean metal. I didn't really have much of a desire to go to the independent living side. The rich healthy folks were a bunch of paranoids with dozens of dusty nick-knacks. Over here the surfaces were simple and waterproof. Mary's only visible possession was a mauve bedpan full of costume jewelry on the surface of her simple dresser.

Dusting the dresser, I felt a sick grumble in my gut, my body processing the caffeine, sugar, cocaine, alcohol. I thought for the first time, maybe I could work for Liz.

Mary bolted up, and I turned fast. She nodded her head and smiled with that look she always had, as if she had a secret. She had high cheekbones like my grandmother and me.

"You okay, Mary? You seem pretty active today."

She held up a crooked index finger. "Chrt Chrt, uh, huh. Huh." She gave out a dry laugh.

I used a rainbow duster to get the cobwebs in the corners that came back fast each week, and in the corners of the one small window that looked out over grey sky, bare trees, the roofs of warehouses.

Mary shook her finger at me and sat back down. I felt a spasm at the thought of working for Liz. I couldn't do that, I wouldn't want to do that, I don't even know what that would be... selling rock to my Maries? My heart seized, and I tried to pump it with the Ganesh mantra to banish the craving.

Next door, my other Mary's room was dark. The blinds were drawn and just a simple lamp by her bed. She looked at the blank screen. I'd never seen her outside of her chair. When I walked in, she turned and said, "Well, hi there, who are you here to see?"

This building was built a hundred years ago as a secondary school. Some of these residents may be spending their final years back in their very own high school, a nightmare I wasn't going to clue them in on. The interior had been re-done in the early nineties, all mauve, violet and cream, the walls and halls resurfaced, many of the windows filled in. But now, some of that ice cream-colored paint was fading, pealing, scraped away.

This Mary had a square face, thick Sicilian steel-colored hair, a moustache, and wore soiled housecoats with heavy prints. She had the aids keep the room cold. Even now, in early February, cold air quietly shot up from the vents under the window. Boiled broccoli and sour milk smell had settled in the room.

"Not here to see me. No one comes here to see me."

"I think your sons were here the other day, Mary..." I dawdled a little before starting up. The cold air felt good.

"Couldn't prove it by me."

Several minor strokes had transformed her consciousness into screens that were constantly being refreshed into nothing but the room in front of her.

"So, who are you here to see?"

It was soothing, like being alone but not alone. I took my time in her room because there was a hole in my schedule after her room since last month when the old man next door died. I just had to keep the dust from piling up too much on the windowsill in his empty room. He had one of the few single rooms. It was small. He'd been kind and handsome, healthier than most, fully dressed, walking the halls. Henry Weston.

Sometimes I looked at Mary's photo album with her. She showed me pictures of Edgewater beach, on the shore of Lake Erie not far from me, right by where I'd lived with Georgie. There once was a menacing three-story bathhouse on the beach that was torn down in the forties. I never tired of looking at pictures of the bathhouse, the beach, the willow tree that still stands. Souls drifting in and out of long-lost passages on the beach I've walked hundreds of times.

She'd laugh, lick her thumb to turn the soft black pages of black and white photos. She told me about old twentieth century Cleveland in its glory days, when it was the seventh biggest city in the United States. She was born in the 1920's and hinted that her father and uncles may have been somehow involved with the Cleveland Mafia. If I asked for details, she'd shake her head, wave her hand, and say, "I don't know anything about that stuff, I don't know. No such thing as the Mafia."

On other days I'd come into her room, and she'd be sitting with her whiskered chin in her palm, saying her husband is missing, that no one will tell her where he's gone. I never tell her that he's been dead seven years.

When I first started, I didn't understand. I went to the nurse's station to ask after her husband.

Babies all look the same. By the time we get old, we grow into such individualized physical beings, like twisted century-old trees of different species. I knew each of these old folks. They had their haunts: a tall young-faced black woman in a wheelchair padded herself back and forth along A wing, Christopher and Margaret were parked near the elevator by aides, he with twisted hands in his lap staring at the wall, she murmuring into her armpit. The aides pretended they were friends, wheeling them together with a loud, "Well, look who's here today!" It was okay, the pretending was better than if they'd been left in their rooms.

I didn't want to go back to Liz's. My stomach knotted. I had to go back.

My boss Sharon walked into the room, catching me sitting on Mary's bed next to her in her chair, our gazes into nothing perpendicular to each other.

I stood up, put on a smile.

"Margot, I just wanted to make sure you were on schedule, and I see you are. 302 looks good. It's okay to take a breather, hon."

Sharon was one of those two-pack-a-day ladies with tanned skin and hair cut close in the nape blooming into a hard perm on top. She was like a dry pumpkin muffin.

I said something friendly and went to my cart.

"Yes, oh, and I'm sure you'll be fine, but I should let you know..." Sharon lowered her voice as Mary's chin fell to her chest, followed by a quick snore that made her jerk her head back up and smile at us. "Corporate says they're going to extend random drug testing to the nonmedical staff soon. Don't worry about it, just thought I'd give you guys a heads up. See ya!"

Sharon had barely left the room when Keith poked his head in.

"Margot! Hey bud!" He sniffed and put a hand to his hair.

I jumped and knocked the heavy can of generic lemon dusting spray off Mary's table. It clattered and flew under her bed.

"Oh, hun, I didn't mean to startle you! Hey, remember about

practice after work today? I totally spaced earlier, reading "Top 20 Bands to Watch This Year". Good stuff. Founding Fathers, Uno Lady..."

"Oh yeah, I know them."

During a brief mania I experienced the June before, I'd joined up with his cover band, *Cheap Kiss*, thinking it would be good to stretch myself. Now I wished I could tell these guys to fuck off, but I'd feel guilty. *Cheap Kiss*. After weekly practices in the summer, and one abbreviated BBQ gig, we somehow didn't get together all fall. But since Christmas, Keith had been hitting me up at work and sending group emails about "getting the band back together!" He was the only one enthusiastic about the project, but he had enough enthusiasm to maybe pull us together.

"Shit, man, I'm sorry, I totally forgot, I got to go somewhere after work."

"Aw, Margot, man, that's okay—are you good for Sunday?" He had thick smoky frames on his glasses, and the way he pushed his hand through his thinning light brown hair was endearing. Poor dude had to go to bed with Carrie every night. They'd been together since high school.

"Sure man, I'll be there."

Soon I stood in Henry Weston's empty room. The air was clean and still. I looked out his small window. I could still see the river, but condos would be built in the space between soon, I'd heard. All there was to do was wipe down the windowsill.

Heading across the parking lot to catch the train, I spied someone I used to know in a little red car that stood out like a cardinal in the snow. It was Lucy, an old music friend. Sitting in the passenger side talking to someone. I recognized her by the way her black bob jerked around. I ducked my head, shame sneaking up my neck. She wasn't here for me, I knew. But I didn't want her seeing me like this. She was ten years older than me, maybe one of her folks lived at Autumn Villa. I looked back once more, still just ten feet away and caught sight of the driver. He looked familiar.

I stopped, forgetting my fear of being seen, captivated by trying to place him. He watched her talk with a serious cast to his face, his mouth set, his eyes not leaving her face. He wore glasses. His hair was dark cool gold, waves. She put her hand on his thigh. I looked away, but not before he looked my way, and just for a second, our eyes met. I walked fast so Lucy wouldn't see me.

3

Honest Weather

T he weather in Cleveland shows up. It hurts with the city. I rode the rapid. The honest weather made dark come in the four o'clock hour when things should still be light. I thought *well, I'm not going back to Lizabeth Vickers's house anyway. I'll be clean by the time they do the drug test.* A knot in my chest.

I put Lucy out of my head. I'd known her for ten years, a big organizer in the experimental music scene. Seeing her and her striking man reminded me of a life I'd lost. I wasn't ready to think about that.

What happened with Mark—it was a good time to quit.

To just—be cool.

The lights flicked on in the train. It made it hard to see outside, but I did see two big black birds muscling their outlines across the air above the flats before we were submerged into the doomy vegetation waiting on the west side of the river.

I couldn't believe I'd considered working for Liz. I thought of Mark, looking into his scared eyes before I blacked out, his dead eyes on the floor while he was kicked. I wouldn't go back there. But I squirmed, I couldn't keep the panic down. I needed to get high.

A guy in front of me wore a bandanna covered with crude factory prints of dull brown brass knuckles. It reminded me of a picture I'd seen on a flier years ago with a woman sleeping on a train in China, wearing a mask to ward off the bird flu, and a baggy sweatshirt with the word *FUCK* on the front. I didn't dare smile, though, because he was sitting sideways, nervously looking around at everybody on the train, sucking his upper lip over a missing tooth.

I only smoked crack after dark, measured out. It's been five months now. It was time to stop. The guy with the bandanna turned and looked at me with his rat eyes. "You married?"

"Yes."

He turned away.

There was Simon, I could call Simon.

Simon had been the one to turn me onto crack. I swore I wouldn't call him again, but I still had his number in my phone.

My stop. I exited the rapid like a machine, and before I was out of the station and back down to the street, I was texting Simon. My pride would have to wait.

Last June, Georgie had been gone a few months. I was working at Autumn Villa and had my room. I'd spent the second half of my twenties and into my thirties in an oppressive marriage from which music had been my only escape. Georgie was the kind of guy who, if he thought you were talking too much, he'd slap the back of your hand *hard* and then laugh and tell you you liked it. He told me I liked it. He told me I liked things I did not like.

On days I had a show, he'd spend hours wearing me down, trying to get me to stay in. It was a mind-fuck, and by last June I was free and feeling like a kid. I was feeling good. I was celebrating. My life. On my own—without any hang-ups or Georgie grubbing at me, keeping me on the edge of his attention. In fact, I didn't want to see *anyone* I knew, most of my old friends probably didn't even know we'd split up. He'd succeeded in wearing me down after all, keeping me away from them, and I felt like a coward. Thinking of my old friends felt heavy, weighted with conversations I didn't want to have. I was free alone. I could stay up all night reading if I felt like it, drink a box of wine, entangle myself with strangers and retreat to my room.

I did yoga in the early blue hours while Clarence was bewitched within the wildcat hour of latest night, cat-dancing around balled up bills, bottle caps and pistachios I couldn't get out of the shell. I painted my portrait. I planned my return to noise music. I'd be ready soon. This was when word got out at work that I played guitar, and Keith tracked me down. I tried to explain to him that I didn't play regular guitar, that I played more like abstract expressionist guitar, but he didn't give up, and I thought then that I could do anything, and that anything was fun.

I made friends with Tasha. I cleaned her granddad's room, and she and I would bullshit while he ate pureed broccoli and beef. She liked me. Georgie took our car when he moved to Arizona, so Tasha picked me up and took me places I'd never been, a late-night Chinese restaurant with dark booths and free-flowing booze, a comedy club on the east side where I was the only white person. I started hanging out at her apartment complex. She lived southwest of me, in a newer part of Cleveland built in the fifties. It was a police and firefighter neighborhood with stout little houses and clipped square lawns. City workers had to live in the city and chose this farthest tip of Cleveland. The generically Brutalist apartment complex accepted section eight and was considered the ghetto of the cop neighborhood.

The complex had a swimming pool. That's all I could ever want.

It was a hot summer, filled with pleasure from drinking beer before solar noon on a Saturday and slipping into the sleazy water, beats pumping from a box, meat grilling… even to a lifelong vegetarian, this was the smell of summer. Melon and grapes, sexy strangers. Spanish vocals popping and sliding. Hiding behind sunglasses. Jokes and raucous laughter, the bright life that burned away winter.

Tasha laughed the loudest. She loved to party. She was a full, fleshy woman who floated around the complex in flowery robes and animal print swimming suits. She shaved her head and wore primary color wigs and smart glasses. She was the apartment manager, which meant she could get into the pool after it was supposed to be closed. She had a master's degree in education, but the schools were hell, so she got by in other ways.

She got by with help from her friends, handsome friends who visited her in the night, and in the day. The men brought mango malt liqueur and high-quality steak, cartons of Newports and money and weed and heavy drugs to her cool apartment. She was a long-term resident of the complex. Her walls were painted dark blue, the space was filled with potpourri, mango-scented candles, and plastic blue flowers.

She got by stealing from corporate retail stores with Billy Vickers. I met the whole crew through Tasha. Liz Vickers's little brother Billy got out of jail a week after I started hanging out with Tasha. She and Billy would sell the stuff to whoever wanted it in the apartment complex, and other older west side neighborhoods. Electric drills, diapers, beer. They provided the party stuffs. They were Robin Hood bringing diapers into the parking lot, calling out the mothers.

I'd sit at her feet as she played with my hair and fed me mango malt liqueur. Videos played through her stereo with the bass up. Faces became familiar as the endless party revolved around the long days and short nights.

It was in the bathroom of her apartment that I fucked Simon for the first time. Blind drunk, I thought it was night because the lights in the bathroom were off. It was a party. We'd been drinking Carlo

Rossi Burgundy and hitting a gravity bong made from an empty two liter of Orange Crush in a sink full of water. This was one of the few times I'd smoked weed in recent years. I couldn't resist the danger as the water came up.

Simon smiled as he took my hand and walked me to the bathroom. I hadn't had sex with anyone since Georgie. On the linoleum floor, I realized I was with a stranger, and I felt afraid. I asked him if we were safe, if this was okay. He didn't say anything, just pressed his forehead into my forehead and breathed, our lips almost touching.

Last summer felt stars and planets away from here. The other side of the year. Tonight, I walked to a certain corner. Lucky for me, I *lived* in Simon's territory. Walking woke me up. The destination took my shakes and itches away.

I ran on the short stretches of shoveled sidewalk. I climbed over the mounds of snow packed on the longer stretches of un-shoveled sidewalk. My throat burned from cold air, and I was terrified that Simon had come and gone, and I would be out there dying alone waiting. I couldn't really tell how long it had taken me to get there.

But when I got to the corner I had to wait. I knew he might have come and gone, but I had nothing to do but wait. I waited in front of a tall dark house with a sign: "No Copper".

I wore a grey sweatshirt over my scrubs. The wind was awful on my legs. My feet had been wet and cold all day from walking through knee-deep snow that morning. I moved from side to side.

We only saw each other a few times after hooking up in Tasha's bathroom. Drinking more reasonably, having sex more consciously. Tasha had given me his number—he lived in the complex, too. He told me straight up that he was a crack dealer. He said it was just to save up a few years and then he wanted to start a day care in his old neighborhood. A good one with certified Montessori teachers and murals based on the art of Bryan Collier. I had to write down the artist's name and look him up. Simon said he never smoked himself.

I'm an anarchist, I said, *drugs should be legal anyway.*

He was a few years younger than me. But he was sharp and self-possessed in a way that made him like a peer. Short with skinny muscles, he had sad old eyes that could draw you in just so far. There was a wall behind those eyes. His laugh was sexy, it made him feel nicer than maybe he was.

I tried rock the next time I saw him.

I was glad Georgie was gone—but—still it felt like someone had been murdered. Being suddenly alone like that. I had nightmares. July flashed by in a mango malt liquor blur and the days would soon be clipped by growing night. I needed something more electric than alcohol to purify my body and mind and memory.

I was talking to myself in sleep all night long and then just before dawn finally falling into a deep sleep, so I was getting up too late to do yoga, barely making it to work on time. My paints sat. I had no money for canvas, and the art supply store was far away for someone without a car. I felt a million miles away from music and the purification it offered. Nowhere to make noise. I needed to purify myself now.

The next time I saw Simon was during a late, late summer pool party: nice cold cans everywhere, grilled stuff, loud R&B and seventies soul. I'd brought over some vegan sausages, the pool was full, kids were running around, Simon was bragging that his niece looked like a baby Beyonce. The complex was filled with old folks and babies, all kinds of black and brown people and a few white people. Lots of sexy folks to flirt with drunk and daytime bright.

Simon's cousin Johnny was there. Johnny Maker was older than

Simon, younger than me, and quiet. Tasha crushed on him, but she could never make any time. He was always ghosting early. He was taller than Simon but shared the same premature lines in his forehead. He wore thin baggy sweaters and mostly kept to himself. Sometimes he and Simon would stand together whispering and he'd let out a deep long laugh. Johnny loved Simon, but Johnny was the straight one. He'd gone to college but dropped out because his parents, both nurses who lived in Fairview Park, wanted him to study something in medicine or computers, but he just wanted to draw comic books. He lived by himself near the bar where I last played a show, in the border neighborhood between Cleveland and Lakewood. He'd grown up with Simon, and you could tell Simon admired him.

Johnny Maker was shy but liked to stand in the middle of a bunch of laughing people, listening with an easy smile while nursing his tallboy. I liked him, and I felt a little stab of something cold in my gut when he waved Simon off that night, saying something about not wanting to "mess with that shit." He walked off with his hands in his pocket and his head down.

"What's that about?" I asked Simon.

"Aw, I don't know—Johnny can get awful high and righteous sometimes. An old friend's coming by, just out of the joint. He was like an uncle to us growing up, and Johnny doesn't even want to say hello."

Just after sundown, a few of us were hanging out in Simon's cool, dark one-bedroom. I felt like a kid on vacation with wet chlorine hair cold on my shoulders in the air conditioning. Simon had put some cable tv fight on, but it was muted, as we all drank rose box wine and listened to Al Green. Tasha perched on the couch listening to a friend's hushed story, laughing: *NO you* didn't *take that bike from that dancer! Oh my GOD.*

There was a knock on the door.

A diminutive old man with a shaved head in a white linen suit came in. He was Sig, whose name I'd heard with reverence around the complex. He was just out of prison. *Sig's back, Sig's back.* A crew came in with him. He was the boss, I could tell, but no one said so. They left the fight on mute but turned the music low and we all sat around in a loose circle. Sig spoke gently and everyone's voices went quiet. The only light came from the tv, some fat pink candles on Simon's cheap black coffee table and the low light above the stove.

Sig turned to me and asked if I minded if they smoke. I don't know why, it wasn't my apartment. I thought they meant weed, even though I knew what Simon sold. I guess he asked me because I was a stranger, because I was a white woman stranger, I guess. I said, *of course not.* They passed it around. It was strange to see after growing up in the eighties and nineties with all the nightmare anti-crack tv images. Simon smoked, Tasha smoked. I smoked, even though Simon and Tasha each gave me a look. I'd watched carefully so I wouldn't look like an idiot when I lit it and hit it. It felt okay, nothing so deranged, just a nice lift.

Simon came over to my room a few days later and reluctantly brought some rock for me.

He didn't smoke, though. He said it wasn't his thing. "A little powder is good, *zesty.* But shit girl, I don't smoke *crack.*"

I asked him why he'd smoked with Sig. He said that when Sig offers, you smoke with him. He said Sig only ever had the best stuff, not like street crack. And sometimes he'd bring hash and stuff that you didn't see around much.

I asked about Tasha. He said, "Are you kidding me? Woman's a hound for that shit, but you know she'll gobble up anything tasty..."

But by then I was *gone.* It was that second time that felt better

35

than kissing at fourteen or drinking Jim Beam while listening to The Cramps in my first apartment.

"...corndog with hollandaise sauce. Kanye's rhymes, these nuts. You know—anything tasty. Can't blame her."

Crack was light and the giver of light.

Simon smiled quickly and snapped his fingers in front of my face. "Damn girl, I fucked up bringing you this shit. I fucked up."

Oh shit! That second time I was happy! Simon sat on my only chair talking with me, and I put my hands up, palms facing him, and he seemed to fade and waver, and the sounds out the window of rushing cars and clanging bugs took over, and I jumped but fell back into the deepest smile of my life.

He put his finger to my lips and laughed a deep, salty laugh. "That ass-flavored Mad Dog she likes, peachy-beachy-what-the-fuck. On ice. Yeah, Tasha gobbles it *all* up. Ha. You like that, Margot? You know I'm funny. Ha."

I thought I was in love with him for an hour! I walked around my room, showed him my books, my music, pictures of me and my brother when we were kids. I always heard crack only lasted a few minutes, but I felt good for a long hour, I never remember a whole hour of my life feeling so good.

The let-down was real. After he left, I sat on the floor looking at the wall under the small window. I wanted more. I wanted to have it on hand just so I could feel that good sometimes. I guess I hadn't truly experienced happiness before. No wonder I married a jerk. Being truly in love with the right person must feel more like crack.

I could try blending all kinds of things with crack! Like painting, or meditating! I held out a week and then he picked me up, we went back to his place, and I asked him for some, and he got me some, and I smoked again.

The third time was less powerful. And over so fast!

But I needed it more. I wanted to catch that second time again.

I only saw Simon occasionally after that. I was fucking up, but I knew enough to keep sex and crack and love separate. Simon had become crack to me, it overshadowed him, it ruined him for me, and it wasn't fair to him. I started buying from Liz Vickers. Crack was cheap, and I had rules. Life had been easy enough to control until the other night.

My feet still ached, even though the cold made them half numb. Could I stand on fully numb legs?

Simon pulled up in a burgundy Grand Marquis, an old one, from back when cars like that were bigger.

I hopped in so quick.

"Margot, what is this. You know, you calling me *now*. For *this*."

"I know. I know. I'm sorry. My phone was shut off for a while." Come on, come on.

He paused to note my desperation before pulling out a little sack.

"How many, baby?'

"Four. No, six."

"OKAY, hope that'll keep it back for a little bit. One-fifty. Okay, for you one-twenty."

"Shit, isn't that the normal price?"

"Maybe for that trashy shit you get from Liz."

"Whatever."

"Watch it, Margot. Damn girl, you're hard off. I should have known you'd go to Liz. Look, you can't be smoking in my car, but here, take a little taste."

He tapped a tiny bump of his stash of high-quality power onto the back of his hand and held it to my nose. Then he rubbed the excess on my gums.

"Look out, Margot. I'll get you out of those funky work clothes."

"Ha, yeah. God Simon, thanks, man. I feel so much better."

He handed me a Vicodin. "Swallow this. Whenever you decide to quit, they help take the edge, just let me know, I'll get you some."

I leaned back.

He took one, too.

He said, "Been a while since I actually seen these streets up close. I was out here when I was fourteen, you know? I was a foot soldier for four years. Most of them quit, go to prison, or get killed. You don't know about that. It was like a war, especially ten years ago when I started, it was still bad. Shit money. Most guys on the street get nothing. But I stuck it out, got my own franchise a few years back. That's this neighborhood. Remember Sig? He's like the regional operator, runs the west side of Cleveland. It's like McDonald's, you know? Ha." His laugh had changed.

"What about Liz?"

"Liz is like, it's like she was running the west side way back, like her family was big in the 70's heroin thing, but then she got absorbed into Sig's thing in the 80's. She's like me, I guess, a franchiser. She has her territory. Not a lot of street guys, though. She's sort of like an old weed dealer, but with other stuff, too. Don't you remember me laying this out when we were seeing each other?"

"I was fucked up. I'm fucked up." Details like this had been invisible to me in the rush of summer. Now my winter brain was waking up to the patterns and systems that crystallized around us.

"Shit Margot, are you a fucking cop? Is that what this is?" His hands were on my chest, feeling for a wire, no desire, all fear. "Fuck, fuck, you got to get out of here, woman."

I took his arms and shook him. "Simon—shit, man! No, Jesus, fuck."

He believed me and sat back in his seat, his cool lost for the moment, hands on his face. "Sorry baby, there's been a lot going on lately."

"I believe that."

"You got to get out of this shit, Margot. What the fuck are you doing. Don't you have a family?"

"See how we forget the things we tell each other?"

He laughed the sad slow laugh more familiar to me and let his hands fall to the wheel.

I felt settled but sad. "How do people afford this stuff, man? Everybody's poor. I'm about at the end of the only savings I've had in my adult life, right at the end of it, and then it'll be my rent. How do people keep it up?"

My chest still tight, I needed to *smoke* it to breathe right.

The heater was on full blast. It brought blood to my face. The car smelled of jasmine incense and spearmint gum.

"Don't be stupid. You know how people keep it up. See? There's some women over there right now, on that other corner, see, down on eighty-seventh. They do a little work for twenty, then they call up one of my soldiers for a rock. They're all over the place but no one sees them. Unless they're looking for them."

"I knew that was the regular price, you just wanted me to think you were doing me a favor without having to."

He laughed.

The cold women stood on Madison Avenue, waiting in the dead air.

Growing up in Canton, there was a place called Cherry Street, which was where the kids said all the "hookers" worked. One fall night when I was eleven, a bossy friend with brassy hair and a cleft in her chin pulled me out onto the sidewalk in front of my house. It was a busy street, the sidewalk always covered in pebbles and soot, wrappers tossed from cars. She wanted to play hooker. Stick our hips out at the cars moving so fast they shook us. I felt awful. I'd lost a dog to those fast cars. She laughed, baring her teeth, baring her leg.

Not long after that I got a call on my phone, new and dark pink with a long curly cord and stickers of grapes and lightning bolts. A man said he could see me, see into my window. That he watched me walking around my room naked. My hands went cold with shame and blood lost to my heart. I closed the heavy gold curtains. I was ugly. No boy in school would look at me. But this man still saw my body and wanted to hurt me. I still had the shame there like an arrow in my gut. I was careful in front of windows after that, and the care wore into resentment over time. But nothing happened. The man never called again.

"Get off this shit now, or you might end up out there. Margot."

"Yeah." I looked at the women standing in between piles of hard grey snow. Puffy starter jackets and bare legs. One of the women stepped into the street and back up onto the sidewalk. The other one cupped her hand to light a cigarette in the wind.

"I mean, it's mostly oxy and meth these days, but crack's still big in this city. News just doesn't care anymore. I guess meth is worse. But, what you doing, Margot. You think trash likes being trash?"

My calm was starting to thin. His voice was too loud.

"Are you listening to me?" He snapped his fingers in my face.

I cringed. "Simon, I am sorry for..." Who am I to him?

He smacked my thigh hard. "But you know, you could be a *dancer,* you could make some good money dancing, you want me to hook you up?"

I laughed, touching the door handle. "Oh, no, I'm too shy to pull that off. I'm sure my body isn't commercially viable."

He laughed. "Not you, Margot!" He shook his head and held my hand. Simon squeezed my thigh, "No baby, you're fine, you're *healthy.*"

Right. "No, I'm not. I'm not healthy, I'm sick."

"Margot, the only strippers you've ever seen are probably on the *Sopranos.* You are real-life hot."

40

"That's a relief."

"Don't be self-deprecating. Be grateful. Life is not easy for ugly women."

The windows were clouding up.

I hated talking about the way I looked. Why did insults and compliments feel the same? "So, for a while I worked at Pizza Hump with my brother. Our manager was a dumbass and real mean. Her pervert-moustache boyfriend hung around the Hump all day. If it was slow, he'd tell her she should have us clock out, and she would! We'd be clocked out, sitting at that stink-ass counter. Anyway, you know what the boyfriend's *real* job was?"

"I'll bite."

"Clean the poles at a strip club."

"The poles! No shit, man. Oh man. Ah. Margot." It felt good to make someone laugh.

"It's true. One time Noam, my brother, walked past him, looked him dead in the eye and whispered, 'Coward'. It was great." Why was I telling him this. I was smiling so hard it hurt.

Out. I had to get out, get home, smoke. I tried to think of a way to say good-bye without pissing him off, offending him, etc.

Simon and Tasha and Billy Vickers had all been friends that summer. That's how I met Liz. I'd been with Simon and Billy one time when Simon had to score from Liz because his supplier was hot and had to move all his product to some other place on the east side for a while or something. She lived close to me. I just went to her from then on. I ignored Simon's sugary texts.

The feeling of fall bled into August as golden light lingered long in the sky and blended with the smell of fire. I had a little crack-fueled fling with Billy that was fun but heated up too fast. I tried to end

41

it, but he followed me to work, he banged on my door, he left dirty yearning letters in the bathtub of my shared bathroom, which baffled the woman across the hall.

I was relieved of Billy's pursuit when he and Tasha were busted stealing clothes. For me. They'd always teased me about wearing the same black cotton dress over and over again, so they found the brightest, flounciest, fluffiest stuff they could at a local thrift chain, and they had some routine where she caused a distraction, and he would slip the clothes out, but they were busted. They'd wanted to surprise me—I felt sick about it, and I still feel sick about it.

I should have said something about it to Billy when I saw him. He didn't seem to hold it against me. He was easy and kind that way.

Poor Tasha was still in. They'd both gotten a year, but he was released at six months, even though Billy had spent most of his life in prison. She was black, he was white. I wrote with her a couple times. She actually seemed happy. She'd flipped to women and Jesus quick in Marysville.

I'd felt guilty about blowing off Simon, so I tried to go on a proper date with him sometime around Halloween. I smoked before he picked me up. He took me out to a steak place in the suburbs. I got potato, broccoli and salad, and he felt shitty because he'd forgotten I was a vegetarian. I was happy to have that hot potato, but he wouldn't believe me.

I was ready to get high by the time he got me home, but I tried to hide it. I kissed him quickly and bullshitted myself out of his car. He'd grabbed at my wrist, wanting me to stay, but let go when he maybe saw the sickness in my eyes. I don't know if that was the last time I saw him or not. Time moved strangely last fall and into this new winter. How could it be February?

"Margot. Why do you spend time with that inbred Vickers clan?"

"I thought you all were buddies."

"Territory out here's getting too thin. They don't respect our crew. You are a thrill-seeking creature. I know your type. You want action, but then you crawl up in your alabaster shell. Just remember, those Vickers are acid, Margot. They tear up soft organic material like you."

A long minute passed.

"Margot. Didn't I do right by you? I took you out, hooked you up." He turned toward me and put on an awkward posture that suggested planned spontaneity: caring, and not caring.

My heart jerked. It felt like a side effect. My eyes went to his chest. "Yeah. I really liked hanging out with you, I've just, done too much, damage. I guess." My eye twitch started up. I pressed my eyelid still with my right middle and ring fingers, hoping he wouldn't see.

He turned back. "Yeah, well. You got to get off this stuff, girl, it will eat you, I see it every day."

"Are you a DARE officer or a crack dealer?" I shuddered at the risk I'd taken to lighten the mood. Blowing off his concern, defining him. I winced as if about to be hit.

He just smiled. "Okay, Sugar. If that's how you want it."

He offered me a ride, but I declined.

Shut the door. Home.

My tongue felt grey, and my eyes were buzzing grey, and my limbs shook, and I sat in my green chair with my back to the window, and I didn't know what the light was like, and Clarence came up to me, opened his mouth into a long *mew*, and I was flat glad my folks were in Arizona.

I fiddled together my cheap metal makeshift pipe out from under my seat, tore a tiny bit of copper wool off the chewed-up Chore Boy

43

and stuffed it into the end of the glass tube and tapped the rock inside. I lit it up with a steady flame.

Feeling good again. A flash in the sinus cavities slapping the back of my eyeballs. I leaned back into backlessness. A knock at the door. I was burning myself pure. With light, but that other light, not solar but chemical, inside lighting up blue and crackle like those worms or breaking a flame. Ah march in and eat all the sick out, jump all over me and eat all the sick out, I could hear the laughing man die, not a man but a jackal.

Another knock. Panic cut in.

It was a soft knock. I crept over to the door, keeping my eyes on Clarence, pooled up inside the blue coffee table crate.

Yes. I whispered.

Louder: "Margot. It's Alicia. You there?"

I opened the door. Glad to see my pregnant neighbor, so pregnant I winced.

"Come in, oh man, it's good to see you, you look great. Come in."

"I just wanted to know if you had noticed how *loud* it's been lately? It's giving me migraines, you know, those machines banging downstairs or whatever." She looked like the young girl she was with her flat-ironed black hair and straight bangs and deliberately bored teenage face. Always alone, and so quiet.

"Sit down, look-it, I know you're pregnant, but I have to tell you what I'm thinking, okay? Getting high is something, okay? I know you're pregnant, but. High is like getting the art without having to make it, better, making it without having to have it, it feels like I made this big thing, like I made a big Work."

"Okay. Thanks, but I better go."

"Rest your tendons! Pop a squat!"

"If I sit down, I'll never get back up. I was just saying, she's my aunt. She won't listen to me, but you're a paying tenant, I know you get coffee downstairs in the mornings sometimes, if you see her working on a car or whatever, could you just mention—-"

"Oh yes. I will, Alicia! Oh god. You are so beautiful, your black eyes, your long golden hands…" I looked at her belly "… Can I paint you? But it's like I'm painting you now, as we speak, just by looking at you, it's more pure, more pure than painting with all those heavy materials. It's like crack pulls the fear residues out the back of my head and shimmer. Sh-shakes them into tender coming shadows just behind my eyes. It's like coming. Becoming. Coming. Becoming." I pulled at my hair, knew I was awful, but tried to convince her with my eyes.

"Did you say crack? Oh my god, never mind. Forget it."

"I'm sorry—I know I'm being weird. I just want to have fun."

Then she was gone. But I wanted her to stay so bad that I thought for a minute she was still in the room.

Sleep never really came that night. But I vowed to find a way out of my shitty head.

Because after the burning was gone, there was no bright place. No lasting purification. Only putrefaction, and stinking jackals gnawing on my feet.

4

Give Life

I texted Simon one more time, because I was less afraid of him
than of the Vickers. He said he was busy. He asked if I could
meet him at the Burger King on 117th and Madison in a couple
hours. He said he'd send his cousin Johnny to meet me. He said,
"You'll like him, he reminds me of you, you gonna be in the area?" It
was just one train stop past mine.

"Yeah, I remember John. I met him last summer at a couple of the
parties."

"Damn. Last summer feels like a hundred years ago."

I got off the train across the street and crossed. The fast-food place
the color of mustard and shit smelled the way it looked. There was
Johnny Maker on the far side, blowing into a cup of coffee. I was
grateful I wouldn't have to order anything.

"Hi, Johnny."

"Hi, Margot." He smiled a shy smile with just a flash of eye contact
before he looked away. He was too handsome and sweet in his powder
blue pullover sweater. I was embarrassed to be sitting across from
him, but he didn't judge. He had a canvas bag on the seat next to him.

"What's that?"

"Ah, some nerd shit. Latest Batman."

I told him I'd loved Batman as a kid, and he opened up, telling me all about what DC was doing. The window was made opaque by early night, so I couldn't watch for Simon. I wanted to smoke so bad I could cry. I wanted to concentrate on this man weaving the Batman mythology. I wanted to listen, but my addiction had taken everything.

Johnny told me about Roman Sionis. Johnny's long brown hands swayed slowly as he talked, like trees. "Roman Sionis, he was this rich guy, he was a counterpoint to Bruce Wayne, but see, instead of revering his murdered parents, he hated his parents because they were hypocrites, and so he killed them. He put them in the ground. But... he went to the ground to touch them. He... "

"Hey, man!" Simon walked over and Johnny stood up to hug him. They clapped backs. Simon glanced at me. He was proud of his older cousin.

Johnny said, "I was just telling her about Black Mask."

Simon scooched next to me and pulled out something from his bag. "Now get the bullshit coffee off the table, cousin! I've got something for you." He laid out his own new stash of comics.

"Don't worry, I got you, too, Margot Jones."

Then the rent-a-cop came up and asked if any of us would be eating. Simon said, "Oh, are you our waiter? Officer McBurger?"

I smiled but did not laugh when I saw the hard fear on Johnny's face.

The cop said we needed to clear out. Simon stood up and, though he was shorter than the cop, looked up into his face and said, "Can't you see my cousin has a cup of coffee?"

Johnny started packing up both their sacks of comics.

"I said, can you see my cousin's coffee? Can you see that?"

The cop had thin red hair and a loose face. He looked past Simon to the glare on the dark window, figuring out what he wanted out of

47

this. "Just go on and have a seat with your cousin, then. Go on, sit down. Sit down."

Simon wouldn't sit, but we were up and walking out anyway. Johnny pulled Simon's arm as he stayed planted looking at the cop, wanting something else to happen. Finally, he went with us and the cop waddled over to the counter. Simon's voice stayed cool, and with a soft flip of his hand, "I would not eat this food. Never would I eat this garbage. No."

Johnny said under his breath, "You do this shit, man. You're going to get us killed one day."

As we were near the door the cop said to the cashier, a middle-aged black woman, "I guess they're cousins. You're all cousins, right?"

Simon took the bait, he started to say something, but Johnny was a head taller, and he pulled him out of the burger place and tossed him on the ground, his brown paper bag of comics sliding on the ice.

They took our urine samples sometime after Valentine's Day. I didn't notice the holiday come and go, and I'm not sure how much time had passed, but I knew I was taking down the doilies and cheap cardboard hearts and cupids when I was summoned by a nurse aid. An old music friend's voice played in my head, "Piss for enjoyment, not for employment!"

When I was a hairdresser, I had nothing but contempt for my pathetic middle-class clients working at corporations that demanded they submit their body fluids for inspection. They thought they were doing right with their cog jobs and weekends filled with yard work, their nights filled with reality shows. They'd watch me in the mirror as I used my back and eyes and fingers to outline their ears and faces, and they'd say things like, "Can you really make a living doing this?" But I was the superior and smug one. I hadn't fallen for the con, keeping me a slave to some medical devices company where I'd have to submit my urine. I never thought I'd have to get a piss test as a housekeeper, either. Now here I was, urinating in a cup so I could keep my minimum wage job cleaning toilets.

Sharon had given me that heads up, but the weeks slipped away from me, everything slipping.

I kept seeing a blue line. Dash a blue line across a canvas, and then, whatever. Maybe gold, and then lots of black lines, charcoal. Photograph leaves, print them out in cheap black and white, cut them up and paste them into the painting. Drip water over the paper leaves and press cheap watercolors into them with my fingers.

I'd get so I'd forget whether or not I cleaned someone's feeding tray, and then, do I do it again to be safe, or skip it to stay on schedule?

I was distracted by their faces. I had memorized each face: Mabel with the half-frozen mouth who made eye contact and nodded each time I passed to make up for her inability to smile or talk. Ethel M. with dark grey curls and enormous eyes who smacked her lips and mumbled an old song about a cherry tree.

I touched their forearms as I made my rounds. I wanted to touch them more, to rub their shoulders, I wished that was my job, to touch them.

One night at home, I took out a black board I'd picked up on the tree lawn and started with a blue line. Okay, I felt like I'd crossed into something, an unknown space opened. I added red. Loud. Then, I took yellow and drew an animal with its mouth open.

But then, it just looked like a bunch of busy stupid crap and I put it back in the garbage.

I took a bus instead of the train to get to Liz's apartment after work. She'd texted me a few times to please come see her, she'd been texting me her deepest regrets. I deleted Simon's number from my phone after copping from him at Burger King. I felt ashamed buying from him because I liked him and Johnny Maker, and I cared what they thought of me.

Lizabeth herself opened the door and embraced me. I was hit with flashes of waking up here after Mark knocked me out. I went sick thinking of Sharon getting my drug test results. I hugged Liz and inhaled her deep melon rot.

She pulled me into her mess by my hand. Her awkward hallway was clogged like an artery with towering layers of magazines and papers.

When she'd settled back in her chair and set me on the couch across from her, she clasped her hands together, looked into my eyes with her deep crone's eyes, and said that from the bottom of her heart, she apologized, on behalf of her family, she apologized. She said that Mark had been exiled back to his mother's house in Brook Park.

I nodded. I said, "Okay, I know it wasn't your fault, there are plenty of screwball douchebags in this world." As the withdrawal seized my chest, so did something else, and, ridiculous, but it was hard for me to speak, as if I might cry.

She got me high, guaranteed me a free ration for a month—not all at once! That could be dangerous. But she felt the need to make amends.

"Margot, girl, you could work with me. Now that that little shit is out of here, I need an assistant." She coughed and butted out her Kool 100. Picked up a box of Saltines.

"Liz, how is it you can smoke in here with that oxygen machine?"

"It's ridiculous how much direct-dealing I do—I need more distance from my clients, like the old days. I can't have people coming here anymore. For a long time, my clients were mostly just Billy's friends, but they've multiplied. I need more people on street sales." Her hair looked freshly dyed dirty yellow, the roots were neon like a

50

highlighter. She nervously bounced her right knee, her housecoat slipped, revealing white and blue flesh.

"Okay, okay, yeah."

"Sure, we used to have a bunch of street dealers, back in the eighties, nineties. But as meth and oxy got more popular, we stuck with the other stuff, mostly weed and just a trickle of crack and heroin. So business dwindled. I was glad of it. Just a little here and there. I got some real estate, you know, so I didn't really *need* to be in the game. And his pension. I wanted to shift to more ethical merchandise. Weed is fine. Two years ago, mushrooms were everywhere, remember? DMT, then that new cheap ecstasy? Everywhere. But there's been a crackdown. Fuckers. You go to *prison* for having a couple caps."

"So—would you want me to..."

"Anyways, it slipped up on me that crack and h are bigger again, due to crackdowns on meth and oxy, et cetera. Cheap heroin coming through Michigan. So, suddenly, business is booming."

"Bread and butter."

"Potheads are okay, but I don't want a bunch of crackheads and junkies in my apartment. No offense. You're okay. Margot, I'm going to go make you a mimosa." She heaved herself up out of her chair and returned a few moments later.

"Here you go, hon! Happy Belated Balentine's Day!" She gave a little bow, and we clinked our giant blue plastic glasses of gold.

Crack and mimosa—now, that's class.

"Margot. You know the original in-*hab*-it-ants of this land were called the Erie people?" Liz leaned back and pushed her grinchy eyebrows together and her chin out.

"No... I thought that they were those mound people, I thought no one knew."

"You are referring to the Adena people, Margot. They were a civilization south of here, maybe living somewhere between one and two thousand years ago. Now the Erie were right here on the coast. The Dutch ran into the Erie a little, but it was the brutal Iroquois that killed them off or ran them west before Moses Cleaveland ever set his ass down there on the east bank of the river on July 27, 1796."

"AH. Okay. I see." I eyed the machine. Liz set her cigarette in an amber colored tray and put the oxygen up to her nostrils for a minute. She wore a faded navy-blue housecoat with a red stripe around the bottom. It was open at her knees, knees like punched around volleyballs. Her feet were bare and blue. I couldn't stop taking her in, in, in. God—fuck. I pressed my palms into my eyes.

"Means *long tail.*" She stopped for a little coughing fit, spit into an empty taco bell cup. "Long tail. As in the *eastern puma.* They were called the 'cat people'. Can you believe there were pumas here, too? Beautiful creatures, golden fur. Not too big, bout yay big," she stretched her arms wide, "Peaceful people, the Erie. Shit, Margot, and the whole lake, Lake Erie, that's why we're here, right? And they're the ghosts. To be honest, I hear their ghosts all the time. I do." She sat up, hands on knees looking at me. I saw past her, through the solid wall, to the lake blue, into the night sky, into the Moon. "I like to think some of them made it out west somewhere. Could be." She sat back.

I shook my head. And then rocked it slightly to the drone of her oxygen machine.

"Margot. What are you doing hanging out with that Simon, that little shit."

"Ah, Liz, after what happened here."

"You didn't think I would make amends."

"No, I just—" I couldn't figure out her angle, why she cared so much about me?

"Well, look, Margot, you stay away from Simon—he'll sell you out for sure."

I drained the mimosa. What the *fuck* is she talking about. I smelled cold cat shit—reminded me of a high school boyfriend's basement bedroom.

"Liz, what the *fuck* are you talking about."

She held out a sleeve of Saltines, I shook my head and she sat back.

Liz grunted out a tale of Simon the Pimp. The story of his purple-haired girlfriend from Akron with the three little kids, the fake breasts Simon gave her, the job at Lido Lounge he gave her, the habit he gave her, the private jobs after she got fired from the Lido lounge, the purple-haired girl's quick decline, how he dumped her when she was on the streets and couldn't get by, and now the little guys are stuck in foster care. *"That purple-headed girl is my cousin's daughter."* She said, "You think when me and my cousin were girls on swings swinging around, we were dreaming of a world like that for our little girls?" It might have all been true, but the way she told it made it sound like bullshit. At least one-sided. Sometimes Liz lied and it sounded true, sometimes she told the truth and it sounded like bullshit.

"Carrie? That cousin? You got her spying on me at work?"

"Don't be a paranoid. Carrie grew up in West Virginia, anyway. Cleveland's a small town, that's all. Vickers all over the west side, some on the east side, too. Different cousin"

"Simon's not a pimp. He's not even a dealer, he's some kind of local boss, right?"

"Boss? He has kids selling for him, girls working for him. He's no boss. You need *time* to be a boss, a *name*. He's got some territory, I've got history. He is a pimp, Margot, don't be stupid."

"Liz, those things happened. Doesn't mean Simon did those things, maybe they just happened." *What the fuck am I doing here, Jesus, I've got to get out of here*—but my thighs felt magnetically trapped on her couch, her broad aquiline face locked me down.

"I'm just saying, he's an opportunist. Don't be surprised if he gives you some buffed product. It's the filler that's dangerous, Margot. And don't let him talk you into any dancing or escorty type of situations, okay? Ever been to the Lido Lounge? It's all lit up in trashy black light, trust me when I say it would do nothing to complement your pale skin."

"Look—I know, I deleted his phone number even. How did you even know..."

"The kid's trying to move too fast. He doesn't have any family, real connections. He's desperate. And I don't approve of the flesh trade, generally." She coughed. "He's trying to move on Sig, okay? Between you and me. Billy's done with him even—Billy knows bad dynamite when he smells it."

I wanted to talk about working for her. After getting high, the idea helped me feel better since I'd been down about the piss test all day. Yeah, I wouldn't sell, I could never sell anything, and I'd isolated myself from everyone I knew. I could just be her assistant. Help her get organized. The first thing I would do would be to clean this place up.

Bang-bang-bang on the door.

Liz furrowed her brows, not expecting anyone. She nodded at me to answer, and I obeyed. I didn't want to hear any more banging while she hefted herself out of the chair for ten minutes anyway. Once I was up, I felt springy and knew I could get out soon.

I opened the door and SHE blew in. Flew past me straight to Liz.

This electric woman. Hands on her hips in front of the old woman, giving her: *What the fuck Liz, Simon's not fucking around*, etc etc. I watched.

The woman had strong bare arms, even though it was winter. She had weird shoulder tattoos in plain letters: **Give Life, Be an Organ Donor.** Another: **Food not Lawns.** She wore a red do-rag over white-blond hair. She let her pretty face get mangled and red while she pushed heavy, ugly words out with her mouth and her hands. She

54

didn't seem like anyone's bitch to me. She was beautiful.

Liz hefted herself up, swaying slightly from side to side, her mouth open.

I wanted to leave, but I couldn't stop watching. I felt loyal to Liz, but there was something sickly satisfying about listening to this sexy tough woman give it to her.

"Listen to me *Crackerpants*, you need to keep your stank ass back up out of our neighborhoods. You got Lakewood, we got the northwest side of the city. You keep your greasy brothers and nephews *west* of 117th, you hear me, old girl?" The woman's face was close enough to Liz's for her to feel her breath.

Liz closed her mouth, cocked her head, stepped back into the mess and stumbled a little.

I felt shame seeing Liz cowed like that. Nervous, I laughed. My eye twitched.

The woman looked at me, and I held out my hand for no reason. She took it and shook it. "Hey sister, what you doing sitting with this old worm? My name's Wendy." Then she smiled wide and toothy. I went faint looking into those wild blue eyes rimmed in thick black lashes, her hair like blown snow, her mouth full and expressive. Wendy radiated heat and power.

In her wake, we sat. Liz and I.

"What the fuck was that?" I said.

"Oh, that's Simon's new gal Wendy. She thinks she's some hard ass bitch, but she'll burn out quick. Or else quit. She's a *house painter* for shit's sake. I don't mean that euphemistically. I mean she's a fucking house painter. She's all over the place. Her cover is that she's an activist or something, but she's just some sleazy enforcer wannabe." But Liz's hands and head were shaking a little bit. "He's getting territorial. See? Don't mess around with him, Margot, he runs a tough crew. Me, it's just me and my brothers, family, you know?"

"Liz, I want to work for you."

She sat back, eyeing me and working her mouth. "Ah." She tapped out a Kool.

"I could clean. I could clean this place up, make it nice. I could meet people for you, at a coffee shop, or the park when it's nice."

She laughed. "Oh honey."

I felt a surge at the thought of working off the clock, cleaning up, maybe sitting down with that woman, Wendy, to try and make peace for Liz. I could be a diplomat. "I could be a mediator, between you and Simon. I used to love helping my friends work out their problems, translating their feelings to each other, finding common ground, in a gentle way..."

Liz got a phone call and waved me away, laughing a little, blowing a kiss, mouthing, *see you soon, honey.*

5

Winter Rites

The sky gave me a headache. Saturday. White and dull for days on end, the sun diffused into opaque cloud, oppressive and unattainable. I had neglected the winter rites for several years. My room was flattening: the cube was becoming a square with my things painted on the walls, and the walls were bumping up against my hips, shoulders. Clarence even, seemed far from touch in the flatland. I had to get out. I had nowhere to go.

I thought of Lucy. I flipped open my phone. She kept coming back to mind after seeing her in the parking lot at work that day. I had still had her number. *440*, must live in the suburbs. But her and my other old friends... my throat caught thinking of calling them. My own voice, awful.

I hated the weekends. My feet were always cold, my fingernails blue. Only at work did I feel warm. Saturday and Sunday stretched out, and it was harder to control the crack, it was harder to not do something.

I slipped down to the garage to get some burnt coffee. The mechanics, just my landlady and her sister, mostly worked weekday mornings, so I didn't often see them. They came in some Saturdays, and they were there that morning. They didn't acknowledge me as they worked together on an old Cadillac. They wore wool coats, and their breath was visible. No one worried about conversation. I couldn't remember what my pregnant neighbor had wanted me to ask them.

I braced against the bitter air and headed out to the library. It was warm there. The library was a small building with a metal detector and flat dark orange carpet. The computer hummed and made me feel sick fast. The computer's radiation felt like the grey sky. Both chewed at my brain and hurt my stomach.

I checked MySpace, nothing was happening. I'd just gotten on Facebook and was kind of grossed out by its preppy layout, but also intrigued. It was fascinating to have a growing registry of people from my past. High school boyfriends I'd occasionally dreamed of or googled without result were still in existence, strangely appearing in Cleveland Browns hats holding babies, and they were all mixed up with my noise friends and old co-workers in this flat blue and white world. I looked up the Erie people and the eastern puma on Wikipedia but jumped to back Facebook despite myself. My heart jumped. I didn't want to be caught by anyone on there.

Liz's brother Jeff was the only Vickers on Facebook, and he'd sent me a friend request. My ex-mother-in-law had "poked" me. Gross. I was still invited to events, even though I hadn't been to a show in over a year. There was a cool-looking noise show tonight at a new DIY warehouse space called The Cat. I wanted to go, but it seemed impossible. I exhaled. Desire, then shame.

Georgie was now on Facebook. We weren't friends. In his picture, he looked away, black hair grazing his eyes. He was looking into the sun. The *Sun*. He'd put in a friend request. I was surprised. My heart going again, and I'd have to leave soon, the computer making me sick, I accepted his request.

I never felt right anymore. I had to get clean, but after that night with Mark somehow, I couldn't figure out or remember how. I couldn't imagine tapering off—the thought of it made me want to smoke. I googled "how to get off crack". Pages came up, and I clicked on one, scrolling past the intro until I saw the list of hairy withdrawal symptoms that included heart attack, hallucinations, seizure, and oddly, hypersexuality. I kind of understood, though: there was a woozy itchy feeling to withdrawal that was kind of like an awful sexy feeling.

I felt panicky, but I kept going—the page said people needed to go to a rehab place, that it wasn't safe to go cold turkey, and that quitting slowly was too hard.

This was the first time it occurred to me that I couldn't just stop.

I googled "how to quit crack at home" and got more of the same. But all these pages were sponsored by rehab places. I googled "how to pay for rehab" and I saw stuff about Signa, Blue Cross, etc. I'd never worked anywhere that offered health insurance - except one of the salons. But I only took home 800 there and the insurance cost 350... Sometimes Medicaid was mentioned, like maybe it would pay for part in some states, but I couldn't get on Medicaid anyway because, you couldn't get on Medicaid if you didn't have a kid or a disability...

I jumped back to the puma. I looked at my hands, things were going a little grey, but I'd figure it out. I looked at the face of the puma.

Then back to Facebook to log out, but there was a message. Georgie asked if he could call me. I logged out of everything.

Later, I smoked crack in my room. A little dirty white sunlight slipped in though my shoebox-sized window. OKAY. I just couldn't wait till dark that day. I stood up and turned up the Misfits record when "Horror Business" came on. I was psyched up. I thought of that woman, Wendy, who worked for Simon. She was mesmerizing. I had to get out. I had to do something.

The record ended, and I dialed Lucy's number. It was a landline, strangely solid and clear.

"Hello?"

"Hi, this is Margot Jones, how are you?"

"Margot. Jeez, what's up?"

"I know. I've been out for a..."

"No kidding—are you okay?"

"I saw you, the other day... in a car."

"Where?"

Suddenly I had to urinate.

"Oh, I don't know, but hey, I was wondering if you were going to the show at The Cat tonight? If you are, can I go with you?"

"Oh yeah, can you get out here? I'll give you my address. Just park in the driveway and we can ride out together. Fun!" Lucy was an underground writer who covered experimental music in Northeast Ohio. She also played and curated shows. I'd met her a few years back when the noise stuff started bumping. Aside from glimpsing her in that red car, I hadn't seen her in over a year, since that strange season before Georgie's leaving when I stopped going to shows.

I took the rapid to a bus out in North Olmsted where she lived. I don't know why she hadn't offered to pick me up, The Cat wasn't far from my place anyway, but I didn't want to ask for anything. A ride home, maybe. The RTA is shit on the weekends, so I had to leave before six to get to her place by eight.

I didn't often ride the train at night, and I hardly ever rode it west. The lights were awful. They came from above and made the windows opaque. I couldn't see outside, just my face, pasty but also red, my foundation concealing nothing.

Out in the suburbs, I got off the train and walked a mile to Lorain Avenue for the bus that would take me a few miles up the road closer to her neighborhood. The wait for the bus was bad when the biting wind picked up, there was no bus shelter at this stop. Cars screamed past me and the other woman waiting for the bus. Pedestrians were considered an error out in the suburbs. There was no sidewalk, just packed snow. It was a long forty minutes waiting for the bus. I must have just missed one. I thought of walking, but I wasn't quite sure how long it would take, or even quite where to go, and for all I knew a bus would pull up any minute. I could have asked the other woman. As my feet went numb, we both craned our necks hopefully, looking the long length of the suburban drag, seeing mirages of busses that congealed into trucks or vans as they got closer. My nose ran.

Finally, the bus pulled up, and soon I was on Lucy's street. Ranches, all the same. Streets named after dales and things. My mouth had been sealed shut since I'd talked with her a few hours back, and now I felt shy. I'd made a mistake.

Down the street a light was on in front of a ranch with a rainbow flag. I felt like a trick-or-treater. The warmth of the bus faded fast and soon I was shaking again. My head went dull.

I couldn't do this, I'd be going through withdrawal at the show, people would be asking about me, what I'd been doing, coming up to me, getting in my face. This addiction was turning me into a nervous fucking coward.

I could go home. Drink the rest of the wine. Smoke the rest of the crack. Quit tomorrow: Sunday. What ritual...

My phone vibrated. I stopped. My heart—jumped—maybe Lucy was canceling. I could slip off, and she'd never know I'd come all the way out here. I flipped open my phone.

"Margot." It was Georgie. We hadn't spoken since last spring when the dissolution went through.

"Oh. How are you?" I stumbled. My toes were numb from the cold. I paced in the middle of the street.

"I dreamed about you, Margot, I dreamed about you being here on the mountain with me." His words were clipped by the shitty phone. I had to brace myself against his voice. I had the weakness of believing what he said about me, and about me and him. Away from him, I saw things as they were. Which had been petty, mean and dry.

Now there was no desire. I just felt trapped in the street, in the cold, the dark.

"Georgie. We loved each other, but it was bad."

"How can you say that? We were happy until, you know, the last few months, how can you say that Margot?" I'd forgotten his voice, how it thickened when he was pretending to love. In my bad dreams, I heard his voice coldly directing me to *pick up this. Put down that. Read on your own time.*

"We were *only* happy the *first* few months. I can't do this, I got to go."

His voice shifted. "Wait. Okay. Listen—I need to get the marriage annulled."

"What. But it's already been dissolved."

"Margot—my family's Catholic. If I want to get married in the church again, I can't get married unless my first marriage is annulled."

"Null. As if we were never married."

"Don't hang up."

"No, forget it, we were married, and we aren't married anymore. We can't annul that paradox."

I clipped the phone shut. My hands shook, but I took off my gloves. I blocked his number. I made a sound like a dog squeal. My body was hot liquid. I took off my hat.

I stepped back from Lucy's house. How loud was my squeal? How loud had I talked? I turned. The street was silent, the air frozen.

"Margot?"

Caught, I turned, and there stood Lucy on her concrete front stoop.

"Lucy—I got to go."

"What? Wait—where's your car? Margot?" She looked shiny and fit.

"I got to go." I turned and walked. It took all my courage to hide my fear, to stand upright and walk rather than put my head down, stick out my ass and run.

When we'd found him, when my brother and I found Georgie that day in Tucson, Arizona... down inside the four-hundred-year-old church, white-flame stucco in 120-degree dry heat, and the sanctuary was filled with candles—when we found him—in that white-fire moment—anything was possible. The candles, the heat, the church and the sky. Georgie was beautiful. The sky was unpunctuated with cloud, endless blue, the white stucco burned the eyes, and inside, the sanctuary was a cave with its own low fire. All heat, all *potencia*. I held that day, and the lucid blue night that followed and soothed away the brightness, a night with real stars. I held that day and that night though the rest of the years of our marriage. I held them like two stones. I just wanted us to be good. I wanted our lives to be beautiful.

My husband ended up just being, not evil, but compulsively selfish, that's all. And mean. Annul. To nothing.

I walked to the bus stop. At least the clouds had cleared. Most Cleveland winter nights the sky was flat harsh pink. The sky was black and soft now. I even saw stars. Now it seemed tears might come.

I didn't miss Georgie. I missed my brother. I remembered riding the rapid with him to the airport years ago when he left Ohio for good. When we were kids, I could just wiggle my fingers across the room at him and he'd laugh because he so knew the feel of me tickling his belly. As an adult, I'd save up funny things to tell him. I never got more of a rise than when I could make him laugh. The rapid ride to the airport was too short, there were things I forgot to tell him, dumb things my boss said, an artist I read about that I can't name.

Watching his plane take off, I felt like I'd dropped something. Keeping my eyes on the plane getting smaller, I frantically searched my bag and pockets for keys, bus pass, wallet. Everything was there.

Now, I was shaking down the street, *where* was the bus stop, this was past the point of sickness, I had to get off, I had to get off it soon. I just needed to get to Liz's one more time, then get away for a while, somewhere, I don't know where, there's no one no one here. I looked back. Lucy hadn't followed. I wanted her to forget she saw me. Ah, but fucking sober people remember everything!

Death shawls crept on my skin, no getting right again, fucking bus was long off from this icky development. Vivid thoughts came at me: my sexy dentist from the dental school above my face flashing down and drilling, holding my mouth stretched rubber open, tooth dust and mouth water, holding down a bird. He played Indian pop music while he drilled. I walked and my left foot kept crunching like it was in a bear trap. I didn't know if I should walk faster or slower, my body didn't know how to respond, if I should step deeper or shallower.

Vibration. Simon: [beginning to think you forgot me Margot – i got what you need].

My belly rumbled with confusion. I couldn't let him see me sick like this.

The trees were bare and brittle. My skin was wet, my armpits hot, my nipples frozen. I ran for the bus. If I didn't get there in time I'd have to wait an hour, if I had to wait an hour I would die. I was coming up to the stop on Lorain Avenue: I could see the white low buildings across the street. I held my arms and whimpered, I called a little for my mother, soft as rose scented toilet paper, but not dusty at all, my mother, was she dusty now in the desert?

I needed to get to Liz's. I just had one rock left. She'd *promised me* all I need for the month.

A young tree walked into the street.

I jumped. It was deer. Four deer. Twelve deer. Young deer walking across the slow street in front of me, crossing with no fear, half a block beyond them was busy Lorain Avenue, I lurched for fear of seeing the bus coming ahead, but it didn't come. The deer moved in front of me, black eyes, soft nose, fluid fur. This was *their woods* and the cars on Lorain tore dead behind them.

Lizabeth only responded to my text when I was outside her apartment door. [dry]

Everything went grey. It was cold. It had been a long ride from Westlake.

Twitches pulled my body, the kind that comes when you can't sleep. My eyes went grey then shot with tears. I held my fist from knocking and put my cheek to the door. Her oxygen machine hummed.

I moaned and knocked softer, then louder.

Oh, oh come on, Lizabeth!

Squatting, whimpering with my head between my knees. My hands asleep, I needed in.

The red wallpaper of the hall stood tall and angry. I put my hands on it. I had to put my hands on the red wallpaper. I knelt down and pressed both hands into the wall, looking into the red for an answer.

I hadn't heard the two men come up the stairs behind me. One turned and briskly walked toward an apartment down the hall. The other one said to him, "Wait," then to me, "Okay, I've had enough of you weirdo druggy specters. You need to get up off your knees, get your dirty paws off our wallpaper and get out of the building, m'kay?"

I staggered up to standing. "Oh, I was just trying to make sure it had a smooth texture, I'm thinking of putting up some paper in my place." Only cowards lie.

He looked at me with raised eyebrows. Then gave me a once over and walked toward his apartment, saying over his shoulder, "*It* looks like it used to be something sexy. Good cheekbones. Too bad."

The other guy started to ask if I needed help but was pulled by the other guy and their door shut. I looked at the wallpaper wishing I had lipstick that color to ward off the shame.

I went back to Liz's door and whispered, "Please, don't you have something?"

The door directly across from hers opened and an old man stuck his head out. "Hey, girl, come on, I know you don't want me to call the police, okay? Come on." He came over to me.

I stepped back. "What." I felt faint. I pulled my breath to the bottom of my belly, then tried to open the top of my chest. This could turn into a panic attack if I couldn't soften my chest.

"Honey, shh…" He held his hands up flat to me. He whispered. "Honey, what you need? Is it rock?"

My breath came rushing back. Salvation.

I nodded.

He smiled as if he'd just tamed a wild dog to take meat from his hand.

"Okay girl, now I ain't done this for none of the others come by today, but I'll do this for you. I got a little stash of my own, come on in."

The thing was—I didn't have any money—I was counting on Liz to supply me for free. I followed him in.

The tv was on. SyFY channel. Commercials for Whoppers and soap. I sat on the couch as he went into the other room. It was hot with steam heat like Liz's, which felt good for a minute, but then suffocating. The only light came from the cold florescent ceiling light in the kitchen, and the tv. Liz's place had hardwood floors, like most apartments around here, but this guy's had thick green shag carpeting like I hadn't seen since early childhood. The muppety hide of garbage monsters.

Also, unlike Liz's place, although it was a mirrored version, the place was mostly empty, just one leather couch, and a large wooden television across from it.

The old man came back and I jumped. He seemed quite old, but it was hard to tell. He sat next to me on the couch. He had a black plastic bag, which I guess had his stuff in it. He set it on the floor. I went faint again, the grey wave of lightheadedness. I reached for his bag.

"Wait, honey," he said, "Here, let me get you out of that coat."

I couldn't even talk. I looked at him. His hair was thin and white, parted on the side, his face was clean and pink like a baby's, his pale eyes bugged out, no depth at all. He was a small man, but his red flannel shirt bulged a little at his belly. He wore blue shorts and no shoes and had one leg bent on the couch so he could face me better, flexible for such an old man, but his feet were hooked and calcified.

"I need these rocks honey," he said as he put one hand on the back of my neck.

"I know."

"So, I know the regular price is twenty per, but I need to sell them to you for thirty per, okay? So how many you want? Two? Three?"

He started rubbing my neck.

I hiccupped. "I don't have any money."

"Okay, listen. I just washed my hands."

"Liz owed me, so…"

"It's okay honey, don't worry, I just want to touch." He swallowed.

On tv a semi-professional athlete jumped out of bed in a dark hotel room because the closet door opened by itself. He was a ghost hunter.

"No, look, I don't do that… I haven't been on, this stuff, very long, I just do it, take it, at night, but I'm not a prostitute, okay, no, I don't suck dick for rocks." I didn't look at his shorts, I was sweating, but I knew if I stood up I would faint.

"Such words from your mouth! Honey, sh, it's okay, relax, I won't make you do anything like that, I just want to touch you, let me touch for a few minutes, just your front and then I'll give you a couple rocks, and you can, go, okay?"

I said nothing as he gently turned me by my shoulders toward him. He hopped closer and I closed my eyes.

His hands were eager. He made little grunting sounds to slow himself down. He touched my breasts on the outside of my t-shirt, gently grazing over my nipples. I kept still, I kept my eyes closed. And then, the fear and shame I felt flipped into sudden overwhelming pleasure.

He reached under my shirt, pulling it over the top of my bra, and then gently pulled my breasts out of my bra. I hadn't been touched in a long time. His breathing was heavy. I stopped holding my breath, but I kept my eyes closed.

He softly searched my skin with the pads of his fingers and I felt my nipples hardening. This soft touch was what I liked, and not the way my husband had touched me. My chest and my heart and my breathing were all offered up to this touch. My eyes closed, I didn't picture anyone else. I just stayed with the darkness.

68

All the withdrawal itching and compressing funneled into this profound desire. His hands were cool and smooth. He gently started kneading my breasts. My mouth opened.

His breathing turned into a kind of humming sound and then he started talking. His voice was awful and I had to close my eyes harder. "You know you're a bad girl who likes it too much..." His hands moved faster and I tensed. The strange ecstasy of just seconds before vanished. "You know you need punished."

Then he grabbed my left breast hard with one hand and pinched the nipple hard with the other. I opened my eyes.

His eyes were closed. I pulled away. He pinched harder. Drool escaped his mouth and landed thoughtlessly on his thigh. His voice was quiet: "Bad girls who like it too much need to be raped into place—deserve to be—deserve to be...."

"No!" I grabbed his wrists and pressed my thumbs into the soft parts so he would let go. He did. I covered my breasts with my hands, my left nipple throbbed. "Why!" Hot tears came out of my eyes and my nose stuffed up.

(Georgie used to hurt me. He said, *It's your fault I hurt your nipples! If you hadn't pulled my hands off—I wouldn't have had to pinch so hard!*)

The old man sat back, eyes open but looking at the tv, blinking, seemingly surprised to find himself here, unaware of the tiny erection poking out of his shorts.

I was shaking so bad, pulling my clothes back over me, struggling to stand.

He looked at me, confused, then ashamed. "I'm sorry, honey, I don't know what came over me. I just wanted to—be..."

I stood up, doubled over and dry-heaved nothing onto his shag carpet. Lucky I hadn't eaten that day. The floor blurred like paint.

He picked up the black bag, with his head down, he fumbled for this thing we need.

I stood up and clasped my hands behind my back and stretched my heart to the ceiling.

I held out my hand.

He dropped two rocks into my palm.

I looked him in the eye.

He dropped a third.

I was out the door as he was going on with his pervert singsong, going *Sorry honey,* and *I think you'll be back again. I'll make it up to you next time.*

6

Waxing

Monday. I made it to work, but I had to bring a rock with me. Fuck waiting for nightfall. What happened with the old man played over and over. I had to drink a little just to keep cool. Vodka would have been better, but all I had was a jug of red wine, so I poured some in a travel coffee mug just in case I needed something to calm my nerves. I was late, but I made it.

I just couldn't figure out how to get off this ride.

And *The Price is Right* on all morning. Every morning. But I felt safest at Autumn Villa.

I worked in Mrs. Paffe's room. She didn't say a word about feces or anything else, just stared at the tv, pursing and unpursing her lips, stealing quick glances my way. She had clown hair. My hair wasn't much better. It was getting long and hot. I had to keep it up in an ugly little bun all the time. My face wet with sweat. They kept it hot in there. I vacuumed. I saw Keith walk past, but he didn't see me. I staggered out to the hallway—an interior balcony on the third floor. Styrofoam music washed all around us every day at work.

A housekeeper on the balcony across the atrium with diarrhea hair and bad eyes looked up at me and then away fast. My neck itched. I felt like a resident, *I should stay here*, I thought, I need a walker. I need the vitamin milkshake meal replacement, thickened with starch, *Ensure.*

I leaned forward and put my hands on my knees. I did some deep belly breathing. I felt better. I let shit fall to the sides of my brain.

I focused on the heart of the flower pattern in the carpet, tightening my glottis to practice *ujjayi*: psychic breathing.

My shoes were broad and medicinal. I gripped the railing.

"Margot." Sharon's gravel voice. I jerked back to standing. "Paffe said you left her room." She chomped her nicotine gum, how you're not supposed to. We were always finding the empty little packets. Her face looked nicotine stained, smelled like fake tan.

"Oh, I just needed to get some air for a minute, feeling kind of dizzy today, maybe it's a cold or something, but, I'm just about to go back in."

She looked at the gorgeous little watch she wore around her neck. She told me I was an hour behind. I had no idea, I'd thought I was ahead, coming up on my first break, when really, I'd worked through my first break, but very slowly and was in fact coming up on lunch.

"I'm sorry, Sharon, like I said, a cold or something is coming on, I'll work through lunch to catch up."

"The *schedule* honey, that's the thing. That's everything in this business. These old folks cherish their routines." She smiled at me and walked off.

I worked through lunch and time went slow, so slow that I caught up and then had nothing to do. Several hours went by and I ran into Sharon again. This time she looked pissed and had a clipboard.

My phone vibrated, but I ignored it.

I was sitting on a round stone bench rubbing pieces of ivy, trying to determine whether they were real or plastic. I was wondering if anyone would notice if I left.

"Margot. I just did checks and there was another complaint about you. From Mrs. Paffe."

"Ah, Sharon, you know Mrs. Paffe, I didn't shit in her room."

"What? I know, and, what are you doing?"

"Cleaning the ivy. It won't get enough sun from the skylights with all this dust on it."

"It's plastic, honey." She took my chin in her hand, "Margot, corporate's getting uptight about things, so no cocktails at lunch, okay?"

"What?"

"You smell like Wild Irish Rose, honey. Look, I used to take a nip here and there before I was promoted to Director back in '96—I know how it is, one room, then the next. Tedium." She was now sitting next to me on bench, pushed up close and whispering in my ear. I had the feeling that she still took nips. If I had an office, I would take nips, and naps, too. The ivy tickled my neck. The light was high and grey, distant sunlight, like in a mall, sanitized and impotent.

"I think this ivy is alive. See the dead spots?"

"Mrs. Paffe said you cleaned her room twice today. And the chart says she's not due till tomorrow."

"Well, her room needed some extra work."

"Well, once a week is the deal, Margot, you know they get paranoid that the 'help' is stealing if you come when you're not supposed to. Steal *what* I don't know, bedpans or Tv Guides...did you say that you 'didn't take a *shit*' in Paffe's room?"

"I was just kidding, you know, how she is? Kind of a, fecalphiliac? Or scatophile, maybe? You know what I mean? No. Anyway, sorry

73

about the profanity. I have had a bit of a cold lately, Sharon, like I said. My sinuses." I didn't want to lose this job—I wanted to get clean. Working for Liz would be hell—I needed to get clean and keep this job.

My cell vibrated again.

Sharon pulled her head back. Then she laughed, laughed, laughed, sounding like an animal made from paper bags. "Go on, honey, go out and take a break for Christ's sake."

I went outside. It was a rare bright day, but the ground was covered in sludgy grey slush, so my feet went wet in my sneakers as I crossed the parking lot over to the little patch of trees. My heart constricted when I saw a pigeon dead on her back.

I remembered my texts and looked at my phone. Simon again. [cant get you out my mind – even in the shower girl –im givin it to you in my dreams] and [I know you not blocked me so you get these – start to think you don t like me lol – hit me up i got yr ride]. I felt a chill—I'd ignored the last dozen and he just kept texting more. I had blocked him, but the phone only blocked calls, not texts. I couldn't avoid him. I'd have to see him.

I faced the back of an ash white flat painted wall, the same color as the Cleveland sky, and felt almost giddy with gratitude for the coverage. The skyline was there like a dead shattered Moon, peaks scattered over bare trees. My whole body pulsed as I fiddled together my pipe, stuck the rock in and took a deep hit. I could swallow it. I felt less high and more just normal. Still pissed even. I took another hit, sucked deeply, but it was going out. Shit.

Why did I have to see Simon, deal with Simon. Why couldn't I just be left alone. I tried to light the rock again.

"When you start smoking, Jones?"

I jumped and turned around to see Carrie, her overly dyed hair especially dull in the flat February light. I curled my kit into my hand, burning the palm.

"Ah, just stepped out for a minute. Get some air."

"You sure?" She eyed me as she lit her cigarette.

"Is it the two o'clock break already? Shit."

"Well, sure or we wouldn't be out here, right, Jones? I've been wondering about you. Keith says you are totally spaced. One of the girls said you looked sick outside Paffe's and that you been acting weird with the ivy and whatnot today... what's going on with you?"

"I don't know, maybe some kind of new swine flu, bird flu, some shit."

"Okay. Heard you cleaned Paffe's room two times. Early. So. Maybe you did catch something."

"Well, I gotta go back in," I ducked away, out from the trees.

She called after me, "Margot Jones, I know *why* people visit my cousin Lizabeth. It's not for the company.

I looked back at her. "Actually, she's good company, a real autodidact. You can just shove whatever you think you know about me." The pigeon lay like a dove.

"We'll see."

My blood was on fire as I came back into the building. Ever since the other day *...deserve to be punished...* I was on the edge of a rage. I went into the single stall public bathroom, so I could fucking be alone for a minute, and I slapped myself in the face three times...*done with you...* No tears came out. I felt better. But my jaw ached, and I felt sorry for it, as if it were a separate creature from me.

I splashed my face with cold water to cool the redness. Uneasy out in the hallway, I went to get my cart and start the last ninety minutes of this awful, ugly day.

"Margot Jones! Oh my god is that you!" A woman came out of a resident's room and embraced me. It was Lucy. "Margot, what happened the other night? You came to my house, but what happened?"

My mouth was clumsy. "A friend called, it was an emergency."

"Okay. Well. You *really* need to come out to The Cat sometime. For real. You'll love it."

She looked so healthy. Tall, thin and dry, shiny black hair in a chin-length bob, blunt bangs, no makeup. She wore a tan suit. With no effort she wore it, even as my skin stuck and bulged in the shapeless scrubs.

She wanted me to come into the room. It was a resident I didn't know, an uncle of hers. I peaked in the room and saw an old man with a greased black pompadour watching television. Beyond him was the striking man I'd seen in the red car with Lucy. He was reading. I stepped back into the hallway. I told her I had to get back to work. I tried to stay in the shadows so she couldn't see my dull hair, the naked acne on my chin, my puffy eyes

"Okay, okay, but look, I can't let you go! You've got to… do you still play?"

"Sure, Lucy, I'm a lifer. But this last year's been rough. I've been on hiatus." I kept my distance so she wouldn't smell the cheap wine on my breath.

"Okay. I'm sorry about you and Georgie. He was so *handsome*! But controlling. Margot. Honestly, you're better off. You need to get back in the game! Cut loose a little! Anyway, you've *got* to play the Spider Moon Fest!" This was a fourteen-hour-plus noise fest she'd hosted around the summer solstice for the last five years or so.

"Okay, yeah. Sorry I missed the last one."

"I'm so freaking glad I ran into you! Gosh. I was worried about you, but couldn't find your number!" She hugged me again. She smelled like clove cigarettes.

"I can text it to you."

"Margot. I don't *text*."

I wrote it down. Lucy said they still had shows all the time at Bela Buda, that I should come by. I said I would and meant it. ...*girls who want it deserve to be torn*...No, but I meant it. I wanted to play again. And I would play again.

I went to Liz's. The building made me sick. I'd once loved it—beautiful 1920's stone and brick facing northeast toward the lake ringed by a family of thick oaks. When I'd first moved there with Georgie years ago, I thought it was the beginning of a beautiful life. Then came his pinching and fast-food stink, Mark taking off my clothes in the dark while I was essentially dead, and the old man and his hands. Going into the building was like going into a sour mouth.

"Come on in, Mar-goat, how are you honey?"

"Not well, Liz. I've got to quit, I think. But not today."

We sat down. I got high. She poured herself a vodka and Red Bull. What if the man who shared the wall saw me come in? What if he tells Liz what I let him do?

"Liz, I got to get off this stuff soon, you know? Mostly because I'm running out of money, ha, I know you don't want to hear that, right? Don't get me wrong, I like it, I like it, it solves more problems than it causes in a way, but it's just dangerous to run out of money, you know? With a habit like this? Like, how do people you know get off of it?"

"Honey, you don't want to quit. Just think, you'll get fat. It's not bad for you, really. It's not like meth, it's *natural*. My stuff is clean. You just let me know when you run out of bread and I'll get you some *clean* side work. If you still want to quit, well, you know, call a hotline or something."

She brushed the cracker crumbs off her shorts in angry little bursts. I threw my hands up.

"Listen Margot. I'm not really serious. Sure, you need to get off it. I don't know how you do it, honestly. I'll admit it, crack cocaine built this house, figuratively, but it's no good."

I didn't feel high. Just low normal. Just the lift you get from a moment's respite from profound depression.

Liz went on. "I don't know how you've kept your use so low, really, most people, you've been smoking now for, what nearly six months! My god, most people would be in the street after two months of daily use. You're strong."

"You've got to be kidding. What do you want from me."

"What magical power are you holding onto, Margot?" Liz furrowed her brows, then let go and laughed.

"My paycheck is gone. It's almost the first of March. I *will* be on the streets if I don't get my rent somehow! Look, I just did it on the weekends the first few months, then every fucking night, now the day." My skin crawled.

"Margot. I'll help you. Let's do something wonderful. I've got some money saved up, and I own some real estate. I got some buildings. Simon's taking over the west side. I'm trying to avoid him, but—"

"Okay, I hear you."

"Where's your people, anyway, Margot?" The yellow cobwebs hanging from the corners of her walls ceiling were driving me mad—I actually thought of bringing my magnetic rainbow duster from work the next time I came.

"Arizona. Out in Flagstaff."

"Damn. Sun belt. Dry heat. Why the hell are you here and not there?"

I thought I heard a banging from the other side of the wall, but maybe I didn't. "Uh, I don't know, Liz."

"Falling out?"

"Naw. It just worked out that way."

I counted to ten in my head and stood up.

"Wait. Margot," I watched as she pushed and groaned and rocked herself out of the chair. Her hair was splayed flat in the back exposing a white part between yellow.

"Yeah." We stood in the ruins of her living room.

"I mean it. I have some business to wrap up, like you said, soon's the first of the month. I get a lot of business then. So, I'll give you enough to last a few days, *just keep it to* nights, keep getting your ass to work every day. My cousin Carrie says you're acting weird, I told her to leave you be, but please keep your head down. Carrie's a busybody *cooze*. She hasn't been cleaning up other people's dirt for twenty years because she's *not* attracted to dirt. Let's meet up later in the week, and I've hooked onto something good, something real. My brother Jeff's wife is a beautician. Now between you and me, she works in this upscale spa out in North Olmsted. Her boss has cancer of the bladder. He wants to sell. So, Jeff and her and I are thinking of getting in on it. Didn't you tell me you once were a beautician?"

"Attracted to dirt? I don't appreciate your insult to housekeepers, okay? But I see what you mean about Carrie. I like your idea about the spa, but could I teach yoga instead? And, or, therapeutic painting? I don't have my hair license anymore. I hate hair."

"Hmph, well. We'll have to get you in shape and certified, but yes, that's the right idea! It's going to be great! I'll sell some off some properties, and we'll just get the *eff* outta dodge. If nothing else, maybe we can sell some weed out of the spa. I wish mushrooms, but they're too big a risk. Legally risky for us, but they come down on us because of the *bigger* risk to the *status quo*. It's because if every

American had access to entheogens there would be a revolution, or an evolution, I mean people would drop the shit out of the capitalist game."

"Yeah. Liz. What about that woman who was here—Wendy."

Her face went hard. "What? Simon's girl."

"I mean, it'll be good for you to get out of this business, with people getting aggressive. Right?"

Her mouth made a smile, but her eyes stayed still. "Yes, Margot, I told you. Simon's pushing, pushing. Yes, get out and leave it to the young bucks. He can keep it."

Leaving this haunted building. Simon and Liz at odds. Getting out. Getting off. Wendy lightning. The old man's hands. The old woman's breathing machine. The Spider Moon Festival. *Let's do something wonderful.*

I just had to get Simon off my back and keep cool for a little while longer.

The next day after work, Simon picked me up in the parking lot of the boarded-up CVS close to my place. I'd never been good at setting boundaries with hungry men. It was time to learn.

I didn't want him to come to my room. I could hear the ice melting, but even with the taste of spring in the wind, it was still wind, and I hugged myself to keep warm. The late winter sun was melting fast into dark gold. I hoped he'd get here before dark. The empty lot left me and the winter weeds alone and exposed.

I smiled at his black car with the dark windows, glad to be out of the cold, but worried about him trying to get me back to his place. I told him I wanted to go to the park, to the beach. He'd worn me down

80

with the constant texts, so I believed I had to meet him face-to-face, that I owed him or something, that it was the only way he'd leave me alone. I was confused, easily pushed around, and I hated myself for it. At least I didn't need to ask him for any rock.

I thought he'd kiss me when I got in, but he just gave me a business-like hug.

"So, do you have people working these corners?"

"Baby, don't worry about it—all that is up to my employees and me."

"Oh. Like Wendy."

"*Wendy*. That girl *likes* you, Margot. She told me she met some fine red-headed freak over at Crackerpants's. I knew there could be none other."

"She came down on Liz—what's going on between you and her?"

"Come on girl, I didn't pick you up to talk business. I had some dreams about coming up on you and some girl, mm. Not Wendy, though. She... I can't see her that way. You go both ways, Margot?"

"Ah, Simon, I don't know which way I'm going."

"I could hook you up with a beautiful woman, so long as I get to jump into it with you all."

I touched my hand to my forehead and looked out the window.

Simon lit a cigarette. It didn't take long to get to the beach. I felt antsy. I couldn't put off seeing him again, but I didn't want to have sex. I felt sick thinking of sex. What did I think: I could just *hang* out with him? Then he'd leave me alone?

We parked in the oval lot carved into the top of what was once probably a hill. We sat for a minute while he finished his cigarette. The lake was choppy and grey, the sky grey, the trees, the buildings of downtown Cleveland in the background, all grey. Simon kept his distance, looked into the lake thinking, then he looked at me. "It's Liz who's pushing things. Crackerpants need to get her shit straight."

"I think Liz wants to get out of this shit actually." Maybe I shouldn't tell him that, maybe she wanted to appear strong while she was still in the game.

"Damn Margot, you are silly. She knows I'm looking to expand. She's got Lakewood, I want it, and she is not looking to give it up, believe me. Lizabeth Vickers is a compulsive liar."

He jerked out of the car, the door yelping like a kicked dog, and headed toward the wooded path down to the beach. He stopped and looked at me. I was still getting out of the car, slow, unsteady. "That old cracker-ass," he jerked a gloved hand, "*knows* I'm trying to move in on Sig, and she's telling me. She's been sending her trashy redneck brothers or cousins or whatthefuckever out telling people I cut my shit, that they'll take out my people if they're seen on certain streets. Stupid bar rumor stuff, try to get me scared. It's so old-school west side. She's saying, 'keep in your neighborhoods little boy'. Motherfucking pierogi-gobbling ghoul. *Crackerpants.* I bet she's trying to turn you against me. Telling you shit about women, right?"

"No—look, she wants me to work for her, I might do it, then maybe you all could sit down and—"

"Oh, living god. She's hiring more peddlers and you're telling me she's scaling back?"

"No man, she's talking about opening a spa in Fairview. Or Olmsted, some suburb. I'll work with her to make the transition, so keep things peaceful. I just want to keep things peaceful."

"Margot. That just means she's expanding her shit to the outer fucking suburbs. She told my boy Tonio that she doesn't like seeing a *little black kid* making himself big on the west side, she obviously didn't know that Tonio works for *me*, told him she was going to have to send a *message*—come on girl, you don't want me to wait around for that message, right? …See, damn. You believe what your drug dealer tells you. How'd you get full-grown being so stupid, Margot. See, traditionally Sig's people had the east side, and her people, the Vickers and other hick dummies had the west side. Now that was years ago, seventies, it was all about heroin back then. Then in the eighties Sig became the boss of both sides, of *all* Cleveland. And Vickers cut back anyway, so they always got on okay. Now Sig's in Chicago, he's regional, you know? But now that I'm making it bigger, she's getting antsy."

We walked the narrow lane in the side of the hill side-by-side, elbows bumping occasionally. The lake's waves lapped the cold hard rocky beach below.

He put his hand to his forehead. "Sorry for getting so hot. I'm under a lot of pressure, baby."

"It's just her and her brothers. They've done less the last fifteen years or so, she says." As soon as I said it, I wondered if it were true, or if the Vickers were part of a larger network. Or if Simon was just confused.

"I think she may even have my place bugged… or maybe trying to get in with some of my people. Wendy's the only one I can trust. She's a hardass. I've got her out getting my boys drunk, trying to test them about Liz, about if perchance Liz asked them to put little mics on or some shit."

"Oh Simon. I don't know."

"No, you don't, but come here, baby, you've helped me figure out what needs done. Shit's pissing me off." He stopped and pulled me in for a hug. His slim leather jacket felt cold. We were alone. No one went to the beach in late winter. The grey waves crashed small against muck on the sand. The trash was lonely. We were alone with the pigeons and the sea gulls, maybe a feral dog watching from the woods.

"Maybe just send Wendy over to talk to her some time." As much as I wanted to get away, I suddenly wanted to feel his hair, which was longer now and so soft. He smelled sexy—his cologne had a violet, earthy pit below the blue-green top.

We walked up the wooded path toward the circular parking lot and stopped for a minute to look at the lake from the top off the cliffs.

"You said a minute ago you were moving on Sig. Simon, please be careful. I don't know anything about your business, but from here it seems like it would be best to make peace and have a healthy, honest system in place to build from. You could change things, make things better. Like you talked about last summer. You could do anything you want. You have power, Simon."

"Okay, don't worry about it, Margot, come here to Papa. What're we doing in this fucking park anyway… let's go back to my place. I got some Rayme Ritchie over there, I'll make you a spritzer." He pulled me in for a hug, but then his smile, scent and everything felt far away, fake.

"I can't… I've got to go to band practice."

"Look—why are you jerking me around girl?" He gripped my shoulders and held me at arm's-length. His face changed. His eyes flashed contempt that had been there all the time, just under his joking and flirting.

"Simon, I just, you know I just divorced, I need time."

"Oh I get it. You're working for Liz already, come here to get information on me! Looks like I'm the dumbfuck." He got up in my face. For a second, I thought he'd push me down the hill to the rocks below.

"Shit! No. no. I just, look I'll soften her up, just send Wendy over some time, you'll see, Liz doesn't even want to do this anymore."

"Why'd you fucking meet me, Margot?" His hand shot up and yanked at my hair hard.

I stepped back. "Don't touch me. Look, I didn't want to keep blowing you off—you kept texting and…"

"Oh, well. I won't make that mistake again." He jerked my arm as the wind picked up, water in my eye, and I thought again that he was going to push me off the cliff. But he just turned me around like a child and gripped the back of my arm while walking me back to the car.

I told him I'd walk home. He said, "Get in the fucking car."

I tried a smile because I was scared of him. "Simon, I can't *date*—anyone."

"I never understood how bitches say, 'this isn't a good time', you like someone or you don't, and you clearly think you're too good for me. Which is far from objective reality. Where you stay now?"

"I got to walk."

He tore out the lot and through the red light on Lake Avenue and West Boulevard.

7

Worm

Twenty minutes later, I turned left on Madison and saw Keith parked in front of my building. I hopped in feeling too sober. It was already dark.

"Hey man, I hope you weren't waiting long."

"What's up, dude? You didn't show up that one Sunday." He sniffed and pushed his glasses as he pulled into the street.

"I'm sorry, I know."

"I emailed a *reminder.*"

"I haven't made it to the library in a while."

"Well, anyways. You left your guitar over last time, so it's just waiting for you. Let's go. Don't worry, dude! Hey! I think we may have a gig next month! I'll tell you about it on the way. I know Mike Z'll let you use his Fender Twin again."

"What's up with Carrie?" They were the kind of couple that didn't talk, but it seemed like it would have been irresistible for her to tell him I was a crackhead.

"She's down at Walmarts in Steelyard."

My gut went cold. I hadn't even missed my guitar, and the last time I jammed with these guys was when? I struggled for a minute to remember if there had been Christmas stuff up. Keith's smile was so eager, there was no way out of this.

We climbed the stairs to Mike Z's attic bedroom/Cheap Kiss practice spot. I was an imposter, but as rhythm guitarist, I just kept the amp turned low and got by. The guys mostly listened to themselves anyway. My bandmates set up. Keith ran through scales at full volume while the rest of us muddled through our masses of cables.

"Thought you quit on us Margot!" I don't know if I'd ever seen Mike Z anywhere but behind his giant kit with the double bass drums.

Cheap Kiss was a mixed metaphor of a band. Keith was the guitar guy, into classic rock stuff like Cream, veering into progressive. Cheap Kiss was his baby. But he wasn't a dick about it.

Mike Z was in tons of bands. Drummers are always in demand. He was into Rush and ACDC and a bunch of other shitty bands that I don't know anything about. Grotesque images of women were taped all over his bedroom: orange and brown Cleveland Browns tank tops stretched over balloon breasts floating above sharp arthropod-like torsos. Close to fifty, but he still lived "at home". Drummers have the advantage, for sure. He was always on Keith about getting us paying gigs, and about how Cheap Kiss could be a moneymaker, etc., but I liked him. He was gregarious and fun to party with.

Mallory was the bass player. He was into cool melodic stuff like Television, Pere Ubu and Joy Division, along with lots of more obscure bands from the late seventies and early eighties. He wore black button-down shirts and kept pretty quiet. I'd think he was kind of sexy, except he clearly felt superior and could be quite a prick. Mallory was the master connoisseur who's insecure because can't write his own stuff. And, he was stuck in 1982.

I had the opposite problem. I had been generating material,

improvising for so long, *all* I knew how to do was expand, cut, disrupt and elaborate. It was stressful to try to contain the sound and replicate and play *with* and not *against*. And what was I doing here? At least I didn't feel superior to these guys like Mallory did. I would have when I was a teenager, for sure. My first love was Nirvana, then punk, then no wave, experimental and noise. Derivative cover bands were not my thing. But now that I'd been playing abstract guitar for almost twenty years, playing these other songs, unlocking their structure, fascinated me. It all seemed so weird. Last summer it had seemed like a great way to stretch and learn.

Now the honeymoon phase was over and playing with these guys only made me feel clumsy and incompetent. And frustrated because they didn't know my world, they didn't know that I could play guitar in another way, that I could get it to do what I wanted. They thought I was a hack.

That day, sick with endless withdrawal, I felt more stressed about *practicing* with these guys than I used to get about playing out.

Keith handed me his chromatic tuner. The needle was going crazy. I couldn't figure it out. Mike Z pummeled his drums—what, did he have to tune them, too? It put me on edge, and the needle moved a little with his high-hat.

Keith said with a helpful smile, "It's B-E-A-D-G-B."

"I *know*." Jesus. "That's not the problem."

Mallory leaned over, "You have it plugged into the wrong input. Margot."

Shit. I nodded a little thanks to him, then I was the only one not ready to go. My guitar felt cold, poor thing, stuck here with Mike Z's sports and porn. My fingers were numb and shaking, cold. I felt big and clunky, nervous that my huge feet would trip on a cord and jerk something important out of its hole.

I got my tuner plugged into the right place and started tuning, discouraged by the cold anxiety spreading across my chest. We were all on top of each other in the attic. The lights were too bright. It was weird that these guys didn't drink or smoke weed while they jammed. Well Mike Z had a forty on the floor by his seat, but that was all him.

"No wonder that Fender knock-off won't stay in tune," Mallory looked at the other guys and gestured to me, "she's got it stringed wrong."

Keith came over, "I can fix that for you, Margot, see, the E and the A are reversed, and also I think you have two G strings back-to-back." My eyes drifted to a yellow thong wedged in a skinny pink ass beyond Keith's head.

We were all within two feet of each other. It was hard to breath. "No, I know," I let out a laugh. "You guys, need to know that I know, see, the kind of music I usually play, I switch up the strings, pull it out of tune, fuck with the tuning *while* I play, sometimes pull a string out, or the middle two and just do a show with the two on each end. So, I just haven't gotten around to changing out my strings to the normal way. But yeah, it is hard to tune and keep in tune with the weird strings."

Mallory had turned away, stopped listening. Muttered something dark about noise rock cop out? Fuck him.

Keith beamed at me like I'd just handed him a cartoon drawing for his fridge. "Wow, Margot, that's really neat! But hey, did you know it's good to change up all your strings like once a month or so? I'll hook you up with my dude, he'll set up your Tele, your action's a little high. You won't believe the way she'll play once we get her set up!"

I didn't tell him that I liked the action high so I could pull on the strings or emphasize a sharp attack. The last time I'd played out was over a year ago, my amp had failed, and I'd fucked up. I hadn't been out in so long, my old friends probably didn't even remember me anymore. Well, Lucy did.

"Well, guys let's get going. We got to get these sets tight." There was an edge to Mike Z's voice. "No one will pay to hear art rock. That's why they call it '*self*-in-dul-gent'." He over-emphasized each syllable, making his Cleveland accent even more pronounced. "People want to see musicians who actually know how to play and can tune their instruments."

I felt frozen, too sober to stick up for myself. Mallory was turned away playing quietly to himself.

Keith said, "Hey, lay off man, it's cool that she at least was into something different. Different isn't always bad you know."

Mallory turned around and said in a high nasal voice, "You kids call that *music*? Sounds like *noise* to me!" He turned and winked at me.

Mike Z shook his head, clearly a little pissed. He counted off and we went into "Satisfaction". I scrambled to get my volume up and jump in.

I felt like shit as I heard my tone clash. I turned down a little bit in shame. I couldn't wait for this to be over. I've played that song so many times, but my fingers had become slipping stubs. We went into David Bowie's "Rebel Rebel", one of my favorite songs of our set, and my chest caught. I pinched my focus on counting repetitions, peeked over at Keith singing. His voice was kind of weak. He held back too much.

We went through a forty-five-minute set full of horrible corporate songs from the eighties and nineties, hair metal and grunge-lite mush. What would my brother and Lucy think if they could see this?

I drew the line at Creed. Mike Z had put that one out there at an earlier practice. Luckily Mallory and Keith were as disgusted as I was. And luckily no Limp Bizkit. But three bands that made my top-ten hate list were in the mix: Nickelback, Meatloaf and Mellencamp.

At first, I was fascinated by playing the songs I loathed. It had the thrill of postmodern deconstruction. Why and how do I loathe?

And how strange to find certain interesting turns, useful messages embedded in these radio torture devices that had antagonized me in my hairdressing days?

And Cheap Kiss definitely improved these songs. Keith's voice could have been stronger, but it was straight-ahead and sweet. His vocals weren't affected and corny like the original butt-rock singers. Our guitars were bright.

Now, I just wanted it to be over. The practice wore on me. My nerves were shot. The attic was a freezer. I tried not to think about crack, but more and more each time I closed my eyes to find my place, I saw my pipe and Clarence waiting for me at home. Adrenaline pumped my heart at the thought of going home to fix, and that's what kept me going.

Not having any beer made things way more painful. Why hadn't I asked Keith to stop at the corner store on the way? Next time. But no next time, are you fucking kidding me? I've got to quit the band. I'll email them.

The occasional Animals, Blondie, Nirvana or even Led Zeppelin song picked up my mood. There were even moments of ecstasy as we swung together. (Although Keith was a little hard to take as Kurt Cobain.) Once I suggested some Motown songs, and they looked at me like I was crazy.

I panicked when Mike Z called out "'How You Remind Me.'" I knew the other songs in our set pretty well, but not this Nickelback shit. I had a cheat sheet somewhere in my room.

There was a kind of D, and maybe a kind of C. I turned way down, stayed with the rhythm. This was one of the few that Mike Z sang with his drawn out commercial rawk drawl. You can't turn down a drummer when they want to sing a song. I literally gagged, and knew I'd have to drink some water after this one.

Mike Z slung sweat and canned emotion. When we slid into the banal question at the end of the chorus, my hands betrayed me. Sour chords elicited disapproving headshakes and glances from Mallory, of course. Mike Z was too into his own shit to notice. He sang and drummed with his eyes closed. When we finished, I was just clawing at my guitar.

Finally, it was over.

I pushed past them and ran down to the little bathroom off the side of the stairs. I washed my hands under the hottest water I could, and then I gobbled cold water from my hands. I was close to vomiting.

The attic was transformed. Hot. Sweaty. Relief made me high. I hugged them, made plans I wouldn't keep to jam with them next time. I remembered my guitar.

By the time Keith dropped me off, I had one foot out the door. He hugged me a little too long. I looked into his eyes for a sad moment and said, "Tell Carrie I said 'hi'. See you guys tomorrow at the Villa."

After getting high I felt itchy. I played my guitar a bit, tearing it out of the ugly orange and yellow standard tuning. I had to get out. The night was long. All the nights were long. I took the train to 65th and Lorain. It's true, I was broke, but I had five bucks. I walked to the Remarkable Thrift store on Lorain. I hadn't been there in years. Maybe my five bucks could get me some kind of totem. Some talisman to hold. Get me through till payday on Friday when Liz would help me get off this ride.

I got there ten minutes till close but went in anyway. I didn't want to be *that guy*, but I couldn't stand the thought of turning around and going home, of the day ending without some precious object or clue. I ran my hand along the dresses, orange red with little eighties polka dots, heavy navy blue, bletch bletch bletch. I saw an itchy looking wool coat. It reminded me of my grandmother, so I wanted to try it on.

"There's something in the sleeve." I felt cotton and then a stink rose up out of the sleeve-hole so *profound* that I rejected the air in front of my face and dropped the coat to the ground. Some grey socks and men's underwear tumbled out of the sleeve. I shook my hand. What the fuck.

Then Wendy walked up to me. Still in the red do-rag I'd seen her in before, but also wearing an employee apron. Was I hallucinating? Her face was pretty and strong. Like a comic book heroine. "Hey I remember you! From the other day."

"Yeah, hi! Yeah. I'm Margot." I took hold of a piece of my hair and spun it around my finger like a dork.

Wendy put a hand on her hip. "You've stumbled onto our dark secret here at Remarkable, Margot. The homeless come in and steal shit, which is fine with me. But then they leave their old clothes here, sneak them up into our other clothes. The socks are the worst, worse than the undies even."

The sink circled us. She picked up the coat and used it to sweep up the underthings. "Well, this coat has to go now. Hey, you want to go to a party Thursday night? I'll give you the address. I get off at nine."

"I just saw Simon. Yeah. Give me the address."

Instead of asking for my number and texting me, she pulled a paper tag off a dress and wrote on it with her mouth open. "It's just some partiers trying to jump-start spring, but it's something to do. You and Simon, tight then?" She looked up with her eyes. Startling blue but diffused, like a harsh April sky gone flat with cloud.

"No—so… He's not real cool with me right now, so you know."

"I hang out with who I want. All the better if he's not still trying to get with you." She smiled wide again and handed me the tag. I took it and smiled in return.

I walked home. The snow was new again with sparkles in it. It seemed as if the last of daylight lingered in violet, but it was just city light in the clouds. Pink Cleveland winter sky. But I felt the days lengthening. I was getting used to this neighborhood. It was quiet in the winter. It went bright when the Moon poked out of a rare hole in the pink cover.

I stepped into our shared bathroom to look out the window and saw the clouds had cleared and the Moon stood alone against the black sky. I looked out into the patch of yard. The snow was blue under the Moon. I whispered into the night, thinking of playing again. *Comes it breathing breathing night—don't fear the night—coming eating all the light—lighteenth biting just under the bones of it—if it was let loose from he from she—it its eyes were open—open me.*

Alicia stepped into hall behind me. "What's up crackhead. You okay, Margot?"

"No, thanks, I'm good."

She walked over to me and looked out the window. She put her hand on her swollen stomach. My song continued in my mind. *Mother makes me—the unveiling manifestation of continuing continuous light—the thing—not from but here and Now, Shakti boom beast make on the make come monster of continuous night. Watts—Allen Watts Mike Watt corridor—who put the net on Creature, first little bits, then All?*

"What?" My mind was like an attic filled with bats whipping around, doing their thing.

"I said they never going to catch that guy who killed Joe over at Alexandria's market. Never."

"Yeah. Oh God. Joe." I put my hand on the glass and closed my eyes. "Alicia, some guy in the garage said he saw an owl's nest in the oak tree out back... you ever hear any owls or anything in the night?"

"Naw. Just chicken hawks."

"Oh, that's the same thing as red-tailed hawks, right?"

"I don't know." She turned to go back into her room.

Sickness, fear and joy all bundled up in a tight balloon in my belly. I whispered, "Wait—Alicia, if you ever need any help or anything, I'm here."

She smiled but looked sad, like I was no help at all. "Thanks, Margot. And likewise."

I opened my eyes. I was sweating in the radiator heat alone, the window steamed up. *Io Pan. Who caught the net in the world? Those lines are lies and not the time on its back like a laughing upturned crawler. The paint changes yellow fast house paint yellow like the light in there, gloss—Artificial Tears—come who who face is green and moving in the paint change bird beating change the green face moves inside the grid is burned back.*

The bathroom was always hot, and our rooms were always cold.

It was only nine but felt like the middle of night. I entered my room and found the yellow painting whose ghost had become the song in my head. Glossy house paint on black abandoned stereo-stand wood. I couldn't hang any of my paintings, at least I didn't know how, so few were on canvas. I painted on wood paneling. Black boards from stereo stands. Et Cetera. This song in my head. *Come and look at the mighty messy stars—the underside of the lip of the monster Creature. Sharlee off the net come back off the facegod.* I'd made the yellow painting after I had a natural initiation on March 3, 2000. In the Giant Eagle on Clifton, now closed. My consciousness was split, the air was more real. The aisles made me dizzy. I stopped in front of the product: *Artificial Tears for Sale.* To see the tears again at Liz's house—were they really there?

The painting was harsh black lines on grocery yellow—in dreams I was murdered in a grocery store in a past life. *pieceholes. Io Pan. Pan.* I hunted down a scrap of paper and jotted down notes for the song jumping around my head. All I'd eaten were a couple Saltines. But I felt like I'd swallowed the Moon and would never eat again.

I was feeling good for the first time since summer: why was I so excited about seeing Wendy again at the party?

Then, I saw Clarence lying on his side.

He didn't look up at me, he didn't come chirp. I picked him up. He meowed low as if he were in pain. He felt lighter than he used to. The black points on his ears sagged. Panic. I had to get him to the vet, but, I had no money, nothing.

He hadn't eaten his cheap dry food. I put some warm water on it, to make it more savory, but he just crawled under the little bookcase and hid. *Just a few more days, hang on my friend, just a few more days I get paid, and I can get you to the vet.*

8

Moon

Thursday I was demoted for being late to work. I'd clocked in a couple minutes late a couple times over the last year, and so Monday was the third strike. I was sent to nursing.

At least there was no word about the results from the drug test. This must be good news like when you don't hear back from Planned Parenthood after a pap smear. No news is good news.

It was March second, but I wasn't too worried about my late rent, because I was getting paid tomorrow. I would take Clarence to the vet tomorrow. I had enough rock to keep me going until meeting with Liz after that. Keeping things going till then.

The independent living side had clear well-ventilated air, ornamental flowers and Christmas music at Christmastime. The walls were lavender, the residents were private-pay and fully dressed. The work was more challenging in independent living. The folks had knick-knacks and paid attention to detail and had carpet to vacuum, but they also had an atrium with real natural light. Independent living was the goal, this was where Carrie worked.

I'd been in assisted living, the purgatory between, heading towards independent living.

Now I was demoted to nursing home Hades. The nursing side stunk of medicines that smelled like burnt lampshades (sometimes like crack, even, for a second at least), bottoms wiped and deodorized, mucous breath and spit up milk. The split between sections was like in that Shirley Temple movie *The Little Princess,* how Temple had it made at the boarding school, but when word came that her rich father had died, they sent her to live as a child-maid with another orphan girl-servant in the dirty attic, and suddenly she had soot on her face and the rich girls made fun of her.

That's how it is when a resident moves from private-pay independent living or assisted living to Medicaid-pay nursing. People had to pay thousands each month, and assistance didn't come until they'd sold their houses and gone through that money. Then Medicaid kicked in, and they had to move to nursing, regardless of their health. Some nursing residents were very sick, others were quite healthy in some ways but some way dependent and just too broke to live in assisted living, so they had to move to this place that would make anyone sicker.

Rush Limbaugh blared through the narrow grey hallways. I remembered it from training. I'd started on this side. Returning was a low point for sure.

A woman with fine posture and round glasses sat in a wheelchair by the nurses' station with her hands folded and called out day after day in the strange upright faux-proper vocal style of old Hollywood: *well that would depend on him I guess, that would depend on him, well that would depend on him I guess that would depend on him. Well, that would depend on him I guess that would depend on him, mothuh.*

This is my 116ᵗʰ birthday, muthuh, this is my 116ᵗʰ birthday-ay.

An old man in a button-down shirts and no pants lunged forward and banged into his feeding tray used as a chair-restraint. Drooling over giant bottom teeth, teeth that seemed to keep growing up like tusks long after the mind stopped going. Sometimes the people in bed were partially naked, exposing breasts melting into stomachs, or the occasional glimpse of a penis on its side like the leftover ash of a fourth of July snake.

That'll be me someday, if I'm lucky enough to survive.

Obviously, the worst off were the ones still fully conscious, still aware, who just needed care and had no money.

Sharon paired me with Karen. She was "training" me this week. Grey soapwater and disinfectant spray. The directions on the spray were pretty severe: IT IS A FEDERAL VIOLATION TO USE THIS PRODUCT IN ANY WAY OTHER THAN INDICATED. It went on to describe specifically how to clean up organic waste and then spray with the disinfectant in a ventilated room, leave for ten minutes and then rinse thoroughly twice.

Karen took me into our first room of the morning. She sprayed the disinfectant in the middle of the room. The old woman watching the *Price is Right* coughed but was clearly used to this routine. Karen said to me, "Margie, you need to spray this whenever you enter a room and whenever you leave the room, right?" She was built like a bowling pin with lank hair parted in the middle. "That's the most important thing. Sharon says it needs to smell clean in here, right?" She constantly evoked Sharon, who I'd always liked okay, but after my demotion was starting to seem more like a typical slum-boss.

It was eight-fifteen. We had fifteen minutes before we needed to start on our next room. Karen wouldn't let me do anything in the first room but watch her. She sprayed the foaming bubbles on all surfaces. One nice thing over here in nursing, the surfaces were all flat, waterproof and easy to clean, and the residents had almost nothing in their rooms, even less than my Maries in assisted living, so it was easier really, although there were more encounters with "organic material".

At one point, I was wiping down an especially dusty television set. The old man shaped by his chair into a microwaved potato grunted and waved his hands whenever my hand blocked the screen for seconds.

"Mar-goat! Hey." It was Liz—calling me from the hallway.

But when I looked out, no one was there. I looked at the floor and it waved, as I retraced everything. Holding on. I had a Monster energy drink stowed under the cart. I drank it.

I asked Karen about the drug tests—how long it took to get results.

"Uh, I heard pretty quick, I guess. Unless there's a problem."

"What do you mean? Isn't like a pregnancy test or something? Yes or No?"

"I mean. I don't do drugs, right? But if it's positive, they have to look at it closer to make sure."

"I don't know. Okay." That sounded bogus to me.

On the assisted side, I was too slow but also somehow too sloppy, but over here, man, watching Karen wipe and wipe and wipe down the flat tray... Shit, I wanted to grab the rag. Wanted to scream in her face, *leavemealoneleavemealone!* Okay. It was still an hour and half till our first smoke break, lucky for me there was no smoking on the medical campus anymore, so it wasn't weird to dip out into the little patch of woods alone.

I couldn't keep my hands still. I couldn't wait. The more she wiped, the longer it was until break.

Back in the trees, I took a hit and closed my eyes. Behind my eyes, I saw early blue light, the hour that *is* March, just pre-dawn, when the black breaks into blue. And for the first time since summer, I touched a sustained desire to paint that had strengthened through the night and morning.

"Hey. Whatchu doing Margot!"

I turned to see Carrie and Karen walking up, Carrie taking pictures of me with her cell phone. Me holding my gear in a daze of satisfied brain chemistry.

Karen waddling and panting, looking back and forth from Carrie to me.

"I thought so. Like I said, Liz ain't good company. She ain't good people."

"Carrie. It's not what you think." The words came out like they do on tv.

"Well, I think it might be worth it to you for me to keep these pictures from Sharon.

Sharon. I didn't want her to see this, to see my ugly face contorted in desperation over a crack pipe by these naked trees.

"I don't have any money, Carrie. Blackmailing me is worthless." My lips were numb.

"Duh, payday's tomorrow. You know how to get money for crack, crack-ho, I don't want much. Maybe 200?"

"That's more than half my check, more than a whole week's pay!"

"No shit, Sherlock. Less crack money. Not my problem."

They turned to head back.

"Carrie, please don't tell Sharon. Please, I need to keep this." Panic made my voice awful.

She stopped, gripping Karen's arm to stop her, too.

Carrie looked back. "Why don't you have some crackbabies, scum, so you can get on welfare. It's white people like you that turned this city into shit. It's one thing to expect it from blacks. They can't help it. Lazy hippy white trash like you killed the working class in this town. No wonder all the jobs went to Mexico, North Korea, I-ran, whatever. So now my husband is pushing trash around while you smoke crack in the woods like a..."

I held up my hand. "Stop! Fuck off." I laughed. "I'm not taking shit from a dumb, racist grotesque such as yourself. Fuck the fuck off. Your face is freaking me out."

"Stupid Bitch." She shook her head at me and walked off.

My laughter became dry, hurt my throat, my eyes teared up.

Before following Carrie, stooge Karen said, "Well Margie, I guess I'll see you back in 107 after break, right?"

My laughter was fading into stomach cramps. I nodded and shook my head at the same time. She left. I had to get out of there. I texted Sharon that my cold had turned into the flu, that I'd vomited, had a fever, had to leave.

I left.

That night, I ended up in front of a west side double. The sky was falling dark, but the cold air smelled like the possibility of spring. I knew the near-full Moon had risen, even if the clouds obscured its light.

My throat felt scratchy. I was tired, maybe sick. Maybe a cold would help, maybe it would slow things down. I didn't want to be sober.

I thought of my friends, how I'd fucked up with my friends. My show-friends. I'd loved them. It had once been so easy. I felt shy about going into this party of strangers alone.

Inside was all blue and green, light bulbs of blue and green. Heavy reggae bled. I felt itchy right away, but I was going to try to not smoke tonight. I was going to try to drink my itch away. I had two rocks left at home. (Meeting Liz tomorrow. The future. Okay okay. The Spider Moon Festival. The future. Okay.) I'd bought a six-pack of Black Label with the five bucks I didn't spend at Remarkable the other day. I stashed a couple of cans into my deep coat pockets, opened a third and carried the lopsided three left in the pack to stow in the fridge.

Some talisman.

I wasn't often at parties where I didn't know anyone at all. There were a lot of people from the neighborhood, mostly white and Puerto Rican, couple black people, people who all knew each other, but didn't seem to look at me too strangely. Two curly-haired children, a tiny boy in a red sweater and a girl of maybe five in pajama bottoms, tore through the house from the back and tumbled behind the couch. Before I spoke to a soul, I'd drained my beer, felt okay and opened my second, wishing I'd had some liquor. I slipped into a group of people standing by the front door, some on the porch smoking, some just inside.

"Why you always say that shit, 'like stone soup'? You beat that shit to death, girl, what the fuck does that mean anyway?" said a man to his woman friend. He was a middle-aged black guy with long sideburns and an electric blue t-shirt stretched over a tight round belly, and she was a fat middle-aged white woman leaning into the room but holding her smoking hand outside. Her eyes were closed behind large glasses, closed with the joy of the night and of being stoned, her hair was white at the part and faded rusty red the rest of the way down.

"You know, like it starts off one thing and ends up another, like the story," she said with her permanent grin.

"Oh right, that story where that guy tricked the farmer into making him some soup," said a skinny young black woman coming in from the porch, her hair pinned all over in a little spiral set.

"Fools," said the man.

"No, that's not right, it was no *trick*, hun, I mean, he was like the magical *Trickster teaching* the farmer how to make a good soup. It's about sneaking in some... transformation, right? Well, also it's about community. Everyone adds their special thing. It starts off everybody's pissed off, and there's this guy with a stone asking for water, and it ends up with this rich soup and everybody happy," said the stoned white woman.

"I know this story," I said.

The young woman with the pinned hair pushed past me and into the house, bringing in a clammy chill. The man asked who I was. I told him Wendy had invited me, although I hadn't seen her here yet, and he said, "Fuck that bitch."

"Why? I mean, I don't really know her, who is she?"

"She's okay, come on, she's a good girl," said the white woman.

"She ain't a good girl," said the man, "Stone-cold bitch is a drug-pusher."

"Well, I don't know about that. Maybe she is, maybe she isn't, but she's always been nice to me," said the woman.

"Is that all you care about? I bet she *has* always been nice to you," said the man. Then he started talking to me, and he was more than a bit pissed. He put his hand on the door, so people had to push past him to come in and out to smoke. "That Wendy, she don't know shit, I want to ask her, *you* bring that shit in here, and you want to talk about 'partying'? *You* weren't around in the eighties when that shit hit our parents, my folks, they were partiers, okay, so my mama liked Quaaludes, my dad liked whisky and weed, they both liked a little coke, but it was the seventies, you know? They worked hard, we lived down on Kinsman, you know? They worked hard, my dad was a mechanic, my mom was an operator for AT&T. They were working-class people, same as any west side folks, okay? Then it was the eighties." He proceeded to tell me the story that served to stimulate my desire to smoke the story away. That people in the eighties didn't know shit from *shinola* when crack hit them, they weren't looking to be *villains*, ho's, gangsters, they weren't looking for HIV/AIDS, skin and bones, life without parole, they were just looking to party. "Then *you* come along," he pointed at me. His girlfriend pulled his arm back.

"Wendy, you mean. Not me." Some people were staring, and of

course, I was starting to twitch. "Not me."

"Right, Wendy, that *anachronistic* drug-running dyke comes back, bringing it all back."

"Well, Baby, to be fair, it's not like it ever really left." A nervous laugh from his lady-friend. "And come on, don't say "dyke", it's not the gay part you have trouble with."

"I know. I don't care who she fucks, I just want her out of this neighborhood."

The woman whispered loudly through her dry laugh, "You know what Tony called her? 'Dead-Eyed Debbie Harry'! Ha, that's good, right? That's about right."

He laughed a little. "'Dead-Eyed Debbie Harry.' Yeah, that's funny."

"Like I said, I don't really know her." I turned away. Okay. I had to get the fuck out of there.

I turned and saw Johnny Maker watching me from across the room. I went to him. He looked good in a long fake-leather jacket spray-painted black. "Hey Johnny, how are you, nice to see a familiar face."

He bent down to meet my open arms. "Hey Margot."

"I know you don't like parties." I thought maybe he and I could go somewhere and talk. Maybe we could be friends. I'd liked him from the start.

"Yeah, well, my cousin talked me into it."

"Oh, Simon? He isn't coming, is he?"

"Naw, Simon's sister. She said it's bad luck not to go out before the equinox. She's kind of crazy, but I like her." He was drinking a dark tea out of a tall jar. It smelled like blackberries and medicine.

"That's cool. So, what are you into, Johnny?"

He didn't make eye contact, looked at the couch instead of me. "I like comics, as you know, I do some art that's, inspired by the comics. I think I'm going to head out."

"Wait, okay, but can we hang out some time? I paint, and I've been out of it, but I really want to get back in on it, and maybe we could throw around some ideas or something."

He swallowed and looked at the couch again, shifting around his pocket for a piece of paper, but I pulled out my flip phone, and let him key it in. he pulled me in for a quick hug and a kiss on the forehead, and looked like he was aiming for the door quick. The sensation of the kiss lingered and tingled.

I took it he was out, but then he turned and walked back. "Listen, Margot. Simon was into you, and so, I know you guys didn't end up together, but I've got to tell you... I love him. But, his heart, it's hard to read. He's always had something good, but he's also always had a temper, and a hunger, and I'm just saying, since you don't want to hang out with him, you might want to keep your distance."

"Okay, thanks. Yeah, I know what you mean."

"But if you need me, call. It's okay." He looked at me for a minute, then looked away and then he was gone.

I walked around the party for a while, wondering if Wendy would show. A woman carried the little girl to the back, and she came running back out a minute later pulling a shirt over her head—it was pale blue with white snow fairies on it. The boy came and wacked her on the leg, and they thundered off into the kitchen.

I thought about Johnny and his art. I hoped we could be friends. I started to feel nice and loose, talking a little with booze-warmed people as the music got hotter and louder. It was a typical west side party in a typical west side house: a double with a front door opening into a living room that opened into a dining room and then a kitchen with bedrooms to the side, but there were no hallways, each room just opened into other rooms.

I came back into the living room and started talking to the first people I'd seen, the angry man was friendly to me now, his woman friend dozing on the couch with a faint smile. We were talking about how dirty the beach was, and I wanted to ask him about if he was into local music as a kid, and...

Then Wendy walked into the room. I put my head down. The air split around her. She sucked in as if it was hers alone to breathe.

"Hey, what's up, girl?" She came in and hugged me like we were tight. I realized she must not know many people here. I realized this was all business for her. I realized she probably had some crack. The man walked out onto the porch, shaking his head. I followed Wendy as she made her rounds, laughing fast and loud and saying people's names at them, and then into bedroom off the kitchen.

She laid the shit out. There was a mean overhead light and just a mattress on the floor with a green comforter thrown over it and a teak dresser with various baby powder covered nick-knacks. The skinny woman with the tight-set hair I'd seen earlier was with us.

"Cher here?" Wendy said to the other woman.

"No."

"Shit. Okay, here you go, Margot, okay, and thank you, I'll tell Simon you said hello and all that." The woman gave her a twenty and she palmed it, but just glanced at me. I'd spent my last five bucks on the beer. I was lucky the skinny woman didn't notice, didn't care that I wasn't charged. But I wondered what that meant.

Me and the other woman, I forgot her name, we got high. Wendy didn't, "never touches the stuff", naturally, but she stayed in the room to bullshit. I gave her a beer. The other woman went to the window and looked out. Her eyes were pins. *Shit, my eyes must be pins, too, shit, when I go out there everybody will know I just got high, with this woman they hate, shit I've got to slip out of here somehow and get home.*

Wendy put her hand on my arm. "Thanks for the beer. This is my girlfriend's sister's place. Have you seen my girlfriend, Cher, around here? She's a thick dark-skinned black girl with purple hair, about this tall?"

"I don't know. No."

"Shit. I think she's pissed at me again. So what's up with you Margot? I heard you played guitar? What, some heavy doom shit or hardcore shit or what?"

"I don't play much now, mostly just smoke crack. Ha. Well, yeah, I played noise guitar." I thought of the piss test at work. I'd drank vinegar but hadn't really thought it would work, but it must have because I hadn't heard anything. Sharon had just texted back "okay b safe" after I left.

"Noise guitar, what's that?"

"Uh, you know."

"No I don't know." She smiled, amused and bemused, crossing her arms. Her face was elegant and sleazy, open and closed. Beautiful. She blew a piece of her white-blond hair from her mouth and her eyes were on me, cut into me, she had to see me seeing her.

"It's, my band, was like, abstracted punk, like abstract expressionist music, that's what it is. Was. I did solo stuff, too, especially the last few years. I haven't been out in a while, I was out a lot before my husband left, but then, a while back, I just got sick of going to shows, I was sick of all the sour beer, and then yeah, I figured out that I liked crack more." I smiled.

"Well, you should play, I'd love to hear you play sometime." Her pale blue eyes moved quickly over me, her jaw worked. Her arms, always bare, showed muscles that moved like water. I was revolted by the potential for violence but attracted to the power.

"I don't play shows anymore, but I still play in my room…" What the fuck was I saying. "I was roped into a cover band, but I'm quitting."

"Okay, okay. Simon says you are a sweet girl, Margot." She rubbed my arm and I felt pretty turned on.

"No. Simon's pissed because I don't want to date him."

"Okay. Okay." Her hooded eyes drooped slightly on the outside edges. I just wanted to look at her, to touch her. She burned in this room, her skin pale gold, her hair starch white.

I put my hand out to touch her arm. "Aren't you cold?"

Then the little woman in the room said OH SHIT and pushed past us. Sudden shots from the backyard. We dropped to the floor. Broken glass as the window shattered, the mirror shattered. My heart was an awful machine. When I opened my eyes, Wendy was gone, and the light was still on. I heard someone crying. I couldn't unclench my hands. I felt like I did once when I had a panic attack from this shit and ended up at Lakewood Hospital thinking I'd had a stroke. I rolled over on to my back and stretched my arms out from side to side and looked into the overhead light. I counted my breathing, and eventually the counting slowed, and I could move my hands again.

Cognitively, I'd registered an echo, that there had been shots in the front, after the shots fired into this room, but I didn't remember hearing them. No one came into this room. I was alone. The music stopped, nothing but the sound of crying.

I had to walk home. The skinny woman cried in the kitchen, but she didn't look hit. I stepped past her into the body of the apartment. Police lights washed over the dark living room, someone was moaning. I peeked for Wendy, but she'd vanished.

The children huddled under a bureau in the dining room. I didn't know what to do. I wanted to split out the back. I knelt down, "Kids, come on, let's get out of here." They looked at me for just a minute, then scrambled out, scared of the police who were now pounding on the front door.

The skinny woman got up when she saw us in the kitchen, and we all ducked out the back. I don't think she was their mother, but she knew them, and they followed her, all holding hands, across the yard and alley into another yard.

I took the alley to the next street and then picked up speed taking streets catty-corner to get back to Madison.

I ran. How many blocks? Fourteen? Seventeen? The air cut my throat, heart and lungs.

At least there was the Moon, with me the whole time, nearly full, bopping along the tops of houses.

Knees shaking, I passed Alicia in the hallway. She touched my arm, "I heard your cat crying. You've got to keep him quiet. What with the fumes I think this headache's going to kill me."

"He's sick. I can't get a credit card or anything, I can't take him to any vet on credit. But I get paid tomorrow."

"That sucks. I hope he's okay."

I glanced at her belly.

She raised her eyebrows at me.

"I'm sorry."

"No, Margot, it's okay. I know, it's getting ridiculous. You can touch it." She was a small woman and at nearly nine months pregnant each breath was a strain. I put my hand on her belly, and then I put my cheek there, my ear, like I was listening to a shell.

Alicia kind of petted my head a little bit. "You are a weird one, Margot."

I squeezed my eyes closed and felt the lump in my throat threaten to suffocate me. I stood up. The Moon watched from the bathroom window.

Alicia said, "I'm going to Aldi's tomorrow. You need anything?"

I touched her hand, and she seemed okay with it, so I gave her a hug. "No, but thanks for asking."

I smoked. My guitar was numb. How long before I sold it for a rock, for twenty bucks? I laughed in the cold room.

I could still feel the sound of the gunshots. The children. And Wendy gone. Her voice. Okay, okay. I could taste her words in my mouth.

I thought of my father, who'd bought me not that guitar, but my first one at age fifteen. The house we'd lived in, now other people lived in. Where he is, is two hours earlier than now. I wanted to cry, so I could feel good. Something had been ripped out of my body. It was another Margot who ripped it out of me.

Clarence was burning up. His eyes were glossy. I held him. He felt like a warm sack. Oh no, I said, *not you, please, anybody but you.* I softly pressed his limp black paw between my thumb and index finger. *Just wait till tomorrow, I get paid tomorrow.* He breathed. He looked up at me with black and gold eyes.

9

Chinnamasta

I worked because I knew if I called off, I would be fired. I worked because I needed to get my paycheck, and they are passed out at the end of the day.

Of course they didn't offer direct deposit, and I didn't have a bank account anyway. I had to cash the shit at the grocery store. *How late is the vet open. How will Carrie want me to pay her. When can I get to Liz.* These words ran together in my ears as I showered.

I didn't want to leave Clarence. I scooped him up in my arms and held his forehead to my lips. He smelled like him, but he was so light. I took a chance and asked Alicia to look in on him. I left my room unlocked. She said pregnant women couldn't change cat boxes. I told her I just wanted to make sure he stayed alive. To make sure he drank water.

The day began with sun breaking into the cold, bringing the feeling of earliest spring. I did not see a crocus in my neighborhood, but it was possible that one was breaking out somewhere.

I thought maybe Liz could drive me to a rehab place, not the hospital downtown. I'd heard that Amy Winehouse song at the parties last summer, and it had stayed in my head, but I wanted to go, I wanted rehab so bad. But first, I'd need a vet, my check. I kept reminding myself of each thing, flinching as if I'd dropped one.

I thought of Lucy and playing the Spider Moon Fest. Working a job without going through withdrawal, maybe even getting out of housekeeping and working with Liz at the spa. I would be free. The idea, if not the feeling, of freedom kept me going through the rooms, the motions, like a switch had been turned on. But I had to keep my mind simple. When a hopeful image rose up, I had to blink it away, for fear that I'd call out, that I would cry, make a misstep, and lose everything.

I could not think of Clarence.

I had to follow the sequence.

Karen wasn't there for me to shadow, for whatever reason. That was a relief. I had the list of my new rooms. The novelty, physicality and homogeny of the job soothed me.

I didn't go to the break room, or anywhere for any breaks. I didn't want to see Carrie, or Keith or anyone. I was done early. I killed time until my shift was over so I could get my check. Then I left.

I felt almost happy because I knew I would be getting high soon. And then I could think. Get high, cash check, get to emergency vet? My body was assaulted by wind, my face cut with sharp snow. A blizzard had sprouted while I was in the dark halls and rooms of Autumn Villa.

I headed toward the rapid station across from the West Side Market. Someone grabbed my shoulder. I wrenched out, turned, suddenly flashing with hot anger.

Carrie. In her puffy brown and orange winter coat, sucking on a cigarette, the smoke torn off by the wind.

"Hey, it's too cold for shit. Can you lay the fuck off me?"

"I'm showing the pictures to Sharon."

"Monday morning. Two hundred."

"Tonight. Two-*forty*."

"Man, Carrie. You talk about housekeeping like you have some work ethic. Fuck you—*tell* Sharon. I'm not giving you the money I earn cleaning pubic hair off toilets." I turned into the wind. The sky was already getting dark. The cold. I was done with it. The rapid station looked like a jolly red erector set against the dirty white everything else. I marched to it. Expecting to feel her at my back again.

But from half a block back I heard her call something like, *I will tell Sharon—it don't take much.*

I walked to Lizabeth's from my rapid stop, which took twice as long with snow up to my ass and flying in my face. I was a jerk in pink scrubs soaked with snow and sweat. I had to get high then get Clarence to the emergency vet. I hoped I had money for a taxi. I wished I had a credit card, no way I could get one because I owed the hospital money from one time I stepped on a rusty nail on the beach, and they charged me $1100 for a band aid and a tetanus shot.

There was no hiding how sick I was for crack. I babbled to her not knowing what I was saying. She listened, but all I heard myself say was, "...sorry sorry sorry sorry sorry...".

I smoked. My awareness returned. I sat down on the couch.

"Well," she said, wearing wire-rimmed glasses I'd never noticed before down at the end of her nose, "are you ready to work for me? I don't think those teeny tiny bi-weekly paychecks are going to cut it for you anymore, Margot." Her lemon yellow hair had grown out and been cut off, leaving naturally white hair standing up all over her head.

"Yes, yes, yes, anything, for fuck's, sake, I can't feel like I did today again. I was out of my fucking mind." I felt so relieved, what an idiot.

"Well, don't worry, Old Liz won't sell your ass like Simon would."

"Ah." I just waved my hands at her. I was starving suddenly. The room seemed brighter than usual. "Don't want to talk about him, but look, what we talked about the other day, I need to get off this shit soon, can you help me? What about the spa, do you still want to do the spa?"

"Absolutely. Yes. But thinking of the financials of the situation, I think we need to raise more capital. A few more months, and we can go legit. For now, you work for me. I just need an assistant, look-it, and yes, first thing we'll get you off that shit." Liz smiled. "I see some blemishes on your chin..."

"All right. I get it." I sat back. Whatever.

"Anyway." She smiled and sat back. Her hands folded across her gut like she'd just had a good meal. God damn if I didn't want more rock already! She went on, "I just need someone solid to make deliveries, maybe. You know I need more of a buffer—I don't want any more cell phone bullshit. With the economy in the shit-dump, demand for crack is up, to be honest, but, like I said, I'm sick of all that shit."

"So, you want to wait on, the spa." I wanted to ask if she'd heard about what happened last night at the party, had it been Sig's guys? I was afraid to tell her who I'd been hanging out with. I knew it couldn't be Liz's family who'd shot the house up. Whoever did it must have known kids lived there.

"Liz, if you want to keep selling, maybe, I could talk with Wendy..."

She waved away my words. "Bah, forget it. Margot, you know my younger brothers, Billy and Jeff."

"Sure."

"They're a couple of assholes, nice boys, but idiots. But I had a daughter. Oh, she was so good. She was my girl. She had cystic fibrosis. Died when she was twenty-eight. It's been going on twenty years now. She was the smart one, of all us Vickers, she had heart. Her heart was her strength, you know," she placed her hand on her heart, "but in this world, it was also her weakness. I got her out of Cleveland as fast as could be. Got her to school down in Athens. She majored in biology, but when it was time for her to look into graduate programs for marine biology, she was sick, you know, going through a rough patch. We knew, you know, but they'd first said she wouldn't see seventeen, so when she did, we hoped..." She shrugged.

"Liz, I'm sorry."

"Well, Margot. I see your face, the way it changes color so easily, the way you wear your heart on your shoulder. Sleeve. Trying to be so tough is what's got you all beat up, honey. Your heart reminds me of her heart." Her voice had gotten wavery, her eyes watery. My stomach jumped.

I thought of Carrie telling Sharon, and not being able to go back to Autumn Villa again and my stomach went cold. I wanted to stay with Liz.

I looked down at my hands: my right hand gripped my left hand. "Liz, I got to go soon. My cat's sick. I was wondering, about rehab, if you could help me figure..."

"Oh, sure, sure, honey, I'll make some phone..." She was cut off by a knock at the door.

Before she even began her battle to get out of the chair, I was up and heading toward the door.

"Margot! Don't get the door, Margot." She stood up after me and tripped over a pile of magazines. As I opened the door I turned and saw her on her knees.

It was Wendy. "Hey, come on in, you here to talk to Liz about..."

"Hey girl," she looked me up and down, reminding me of Billy, "good to see you last night. Why you come here for that nasty Vickers sleet, when you know I'll take care of you?" She shoved past me and was up in front of Liz in one motion. Liz struggling to her feet. I stood behind Wendy.

Liz said, "Margot? You with Wendy?"

Wendy pulled something wrapped in a green bandanna from under her jacket and shot Liz in the stomach.

Red billowed out across the pale fabric of her housecoat.

I stepped back. Wendy dropped the green bandanna and the gun on the floor and grabbed my arm. The gun was small and black with a long nozzle.

Liz looked at me with wolf eyes and blood came to her mouth. Her hands over her stomach were covered quickly in blood. And blood came out of her mouth. And Liz looked at me with wolf eyes.

I moved toward her and Wendy pulled me in and put a blade to my throat.

Things went grey and after she took the blade away, I could still feel the metal pressed into my skin. She took my hand, and I went like a child.

I don't remember getting to Simon's, but there we were. Wendy must have sat me down on the couch. It was a party. A low-down winter party. Windows closed in on months of smoked cigarettes, weed and crack. People drinking too much to drive in a blizzard. Last summer's loud music bumping menace over violent Japanese porn. I couldn't look. There was a dude passed out next to me and some dudes joking in the dining room and a couple fighting under the music in front of me. I went to the kitchen. Simon and Wendy were talking. Her hands were shaking.

"Margot, what's up?" He came up to me.

"It was loud." I said to Wendy. Simon looked at her.

"I used a silencer. But, she doesn't know shit." She pointed at me.

"The oxygen machine," I said to her. I looked at Simon and said it again. Wendy shook her head. "You killed her," I said.

"Yeah, and you're a lucky bitch, Margot. You were *this* close? *This* fucking close," said Wendy, she was shaking more now, her voice, too. She lit a cigarette and looked away.

Simon put his arms around me and I went numb.

"We have to call the police. Why didn't the oxygen machine explode? You killed her." My teeth were chattering.

Simon swayed me, shaking his head. "No baby, that's crazy. Just forget it. I know it's fucked up, but she knew what she was doing and she had it coming, you'll see."

I couldn't see shit.

"Simon, do you have any rock?"

"Ah, Margot." He hugged me tightly. My eyes sunk into the Mediterranean blue tile he must have added around the stove and above the sink. The contrast of the elegant tile and the generic hard lighting and eggshell walls made me dizzy.

"Simon—she was getting out, of selling." I cried, and with shame I knew it was more for crack than the old woman. My elbows felt like they were going to snap. Wendy lit another cigarette.

Simon was a hair shorter than me, but he rocked me a little. "Hush, baby, she lied. I'll take care of you, come on, let me draw you a bath and then you just get in and I'll get you some rock and then a back rub, okay, it's been a rough ride, I know. C'mon, Margot, it was *Vickers* shot up that party last night. You must know that."

I was sobbing like a two-year-old. It was disgusting. I knew he was pacifying me, and I let him.

He gave me some pills to calm down. I was alone. Naked in the tub, fixed and feeling my head again, I wondered if they were thinking of killing me. I didn't think they would, but they might. They could. I was, after all, a naked crack addict who'd just witnessed a murder and sobbed like a coward. I was a liability. I'd almost rather they kill me than use me for anything.

Then—I felt happy, happy because I didn't care what happened to me. It was like *trataka* meditation: the candle doesn't waver, the tree stays planted, they could kill me, use me, or leave me alone. I didn't care finally. I stopped shaking in the hot water and went still. I closed my eyes and exhaled.

In the quiet, I could hear Wendy's voice from the other room. She was one of those people who couldn't really whisper. Not Simon. His voice was too low to understand.

didn't think you'd want me too—one of your girlfriends or some sh—
yeah—I am not new at this—you—actin like some killa'
don't care—use for
Her words trailed off.

I woke up to Simon fucking me. I kept my eyes closed. We were in his bed.

During, I opened my eyes. His face looked like he was working an assembly line. Eyes looking into nothing, sweat beads, mouth hanging open a little.

I reached my right hand up, to touch his face, but he jerked his left hand up and slapped mine down, holding it back. I closed my eyes and went still again. He let his head fall over my shoulder while he finished.

I kept my eyes closed when he rolled off. I saw Liz lurch when the bullet hit her. I kept my body still. I pretended sleep for hours, until I did fall back into the dead sleep just before dawn.

119

I woke late in the morning. A dream lingered, a vision: a woman with crimson skin, clothed only in long chains of seashells. Her head cut off, her head in her hands, her face sublime. She is perched on a lotus of two lovers intertwined infinitely. From her open neck spurt two rivers of blood, each feeding a daughter on either side of her. I shook the image, but it stuck for a long fading frame, before vanishing into the darkness behind my eyes.

My clothes lay folded on the floor—I scrambled off the bed and sat naked on the beige carpet, finding my scrub pockets and feeling for my stuff. The wallet and keys were gone, but the phone was there—I'd wrapped it in a plastic grocery bag to protect it from the snow, maybe they just thought it was some trash, leftover lunch, thinking I'd carry trash around in my scrubs. Fuck.

I flipped open the phone. Shit, I'd meant to sneak off last night and text, someone, I don't know who, to call 911 about Liz, just in case she was still alive, but after the bath and the pills and the drink, I'd fallen deep into sleep. I didn't remember getting from the tub to the bed even. Liz's eyes came to me and the blood at her lips.

Shit. Work had called twice. I thought she was off on weekends. I called Sharon.

"Margot, I'm sorry honey, but there's no way around it."

"Sharon, I didn't listen to the messages, I just called you back." I smelled bacon.

She was quiet for a minute. "The results came just after you'd left yesterday. Margot, your urine tested positive for cocaine. That's automatic dismissal. I had them run the test twice. I was going to try to fight for you, if it was just weed or something, but there's really nothing I can do..."

"I love my job," I croaked and hung up the phone, realizing both how pathetic and how true that was. My head rang with withdrawal, but for once the wall rose up inside me, and I did not want to smoke.

My eyes watered, my mouth went dry, but the thought of the taste of crack made my stomach roll. (June will be here someday, the solstice, the Spider Moon Fest, and the blood at Liz's lips, and the wolf in her eyes) Clarence—I had to get to Clarence. I wished Alicia had a phone. I had to get the fuck out of here.

Clarence. The last of the shock and sedation wore off and I knew Simon wasn't going to let me leave. I had to get to Clarence.

I texted Keith. I could think of no one else. COME GET ME NOW THIS IS AN EMERGENCY. I didn't know Simon's address. I sent the text. I started another text with the nearest intersection. My body locked with fear and rage and withdrawal. I tried to send the text, but my shit phone said it was out of service range.

Simon was playing Bob Marley. "Redemption Song." I pressed send again. Nothing.

Simon opened the door smiling. "How are you sugar? Time for you to get out here."

I walked into the kitchen. Naked. With my cell phone in my hand. He raised his eyebrows and shook his head. "Dang girl, you walking like a straight-up Haitian zombie. Didn't take your ass long to go full blown crackhead." He was talking about me not to me.

He grabbed a sheet from the hall closet, and I wrapped it around myself. He turned around and held me by the shoulders. "Margot. When I met you, I thought you were so cool. But you're just a tourist, and now you're stuck. Here's the situation. You need crack. We need you to be quiet about last night. You need us to feel *good* about you keeping quiet about last night, right? You understand?" I nodded. I hit send.

"Is This Love?" played, bubbling through the apartment on a cloud of strawberry smoke streaming from an oversized incense stick. Even the drawn blinds couldn't keep the sun from slashing into the rooms.

"Okay, that's a good girl." He hugged me, "So, we need to establish a solid relationship and understanding." He hugged me tightly, but only with his upper body.

Bob Marley sang, wondering on love.

Simon went on, "So we will make sure you have all the product you need, and we will make sure that no harm comes to you for what you *think* you saw last night, and in return, you will forget what you saw last night. And you'll do a little work for us. Okay?"

I nodded.

"Or I will kill you. Myself. I will kill you. Do you understand?"

"Yes."

"Good, now let me introduce you to a friend of mine. Maybe you guys can hang out for a little while, and then I'll get you good and fixed up, okay?"

I followed him into the living room. I wore sheet wrapped around me like a towel. I looked at my phone. My second message still had not gone through. Keith had texted me WHERE? I pressed send again, and it worked. I hid my hand with the phone under the sheet. Simon looked back, and I smiled a genuine smile.

I felt faint, but rage crept up around my ankles, burning out the fear in its path. Rage climbed up my thighs like fire.

A fat white guy with wiry grey hair growing halfway down his forehead leaned back in the recliner. He raised his eyebrows in surprise. "Well, okay, Simon!"

Bob Marley filled the room with throbbing domestic love.

Simon smiled. "Margot, this is my associate, Mister Smith. He wants to spend some time with you on this lovely morning."

I looked away from the boner in Smith's brown slacks. I looked at the door. I looked at Simon. He looked at me. "Simon."

"I called the man over for a freebie, see how you do. Go on, girl, get down there." He shoved me hard as Smith unzipped his fly.

The fire reached my chest and even though my eyes weren't steady, and even though I could have run for the door, I lunged at Simon. The sheet fell. He looked surprised. We both went down, hit the floor, half in the living room, half in the kitchen, his head sliding into linoleum. I spread out on top of him, and the fire reached my hands, my face, my hair. "YYYAAAAAAAAAAAAA" I was stronger than Simon.

I straddled him and pulled him up by the shoulders once and then slammed him back down onto the hard floor. I heard his head hit. I could have done more, but I jumped up, and was out the door and into the snow before he even got up. He wouldn't follow me. I was not something good for him to be seen with on the street that day. Not in his quiet Cleveland cop neighborhood.

Simon's door hung open. Bob Marley sang about the dream of shelter, the dream of sharing a bed.

My naked feet burned holes in the snow.

10

Blind Violets Rise Up

I chased a tiger in the snow under a full Moon that flickered and darted from side to side like a stage light. The tiger wasn't a tiger but a smaller, wheat-colored beast. Ohio. The trees were black cut into silent white snow. The air cut my throat with cold, but I swallowed it. I knew the lake was to the left somewhere, and we ran. East. I knew somewhere in the blue light there was a clearing, and in the center would be a silver maple tree in full leaf, within a circle of oaks just above Lake Erie, under the Moon, and then the Moon would be still, and we ran. And then I *became* the puma. Killer Queen. I could run without breaking the snow.

I jerked awake into a room I'd never seen before. I felt bruisy from shaking. It was dark. I was on a couch in a living room. I looked into a dining room with a dead overhead light on, and it looked like one of those houses where the dining room leads to the kitchen on the left. French doors opening to a deck. I grew up in a house like this. There were stairs on the other side of the living room. Lots of houses like this on the west side of Cleveland, and in Canton, too.

Was I in Canton? Was I in my childhood house still, my whole adult life a fever dream? My foot jerked. I remembered running in the snow, and I remembered getting into a car. Terror. That's all I remembered. I heard someone in the kitchen. Terror. Jackals sniffing and biting at the backs of my arms. Tattered dark grey jackals in my dreams. Why can't I *remember*. Pieces of meat had been chewed out of my brain. I tried to breathe, but I was shaking hard. My teeth were shaking. *Keith.* I whispered. Keith is my friend. He was here. Because I remembered something else, feeling better, I remembered him putting water to my mouth, a low light in this room, the tv on, no not him. White hair. And an orange plastic cup, drinking water and then back to sleep. It must be Liz, she must be alive.

Heat tickling awful up my back, my feet twitched, and I went fetal again, turned and faced the back of the couch and pressed my eyes closed my jaw clench clench clench. I whispered inwardly, *come to me.*

I fell back into the dark. I remembered a terrible thing.

"No, no no, not him, no he's dead, no, oh, momma momma."

I rolled over on my side, soaking wet, a soaking bed. I saw cracked flashes when I closed my eyes. My mouth opened in my pillow, dry sorrow, no end to the dry scream. I had no body, no guts, just head pressed face into the pillow. I gripped with all my hate fighting into it. I felt horny and I lifted my ass into the air writhing. "Why won't you touch me? I need it." My mouth was glued from crying, my words were on a hinge. "Won't you touch me touch me, be mine," almost pleasure, the awfulness and someone was there and did touch me. The touch was a strong hand pushing my lower back down, and all the awful almost-pleasure fell into hate shakes. My legs jerked.

My feet ached and I remembered, again, running barefoot and naked in the snow, in the morning, I remembered no one was out, but all I could feel was my feet, I saw only an old man in a window, watching me, I remember seeing the grey car in the snow and pulling at the locked door and I didn't even feel naked, I felt a wind, I felt my feet moving, but in the car it was warm and I felt naked but clean like a baby, and that's all I remembered until the dreams.

I tasted spinach pressings limp and rotten veined. I wasn't green at all but fading white like a strawberry farmed in a winter warehouse in Cleveland. That's what I am.

Another day or season, and I woke on a bed alone. Suddenly I was breathing. Suddenly I saw *Clarence* round and glowing black softness, golden yellow Moon eyes, pressing his forehead lightly into my face, dusty purr box.

Someone sat on the bed looking out the window. The light coming through the window was so bright—I only saw the outline of the person.

Clarence! You're alive! And his fever was gone. He felt strong. I pulled my face into his body. I pulled him to me under the covers.

"Who." Breathing felt good, like water to thirst. I was wearing some kind of long blue t-shirt. I wanted the feel of a hand between my thighs. I moved my thighs together. I hadn't felt them in years. Deep in my guts I felt purple, *ohh*cramps. I gripped the bedspread.

The person turned at my voice. It was a woman.

I backed out of bed and fell to the floor, my legs numb. It was *her*. Wendy.

I was sprawled on my back like a crab.

She put her hands up. "Sh… listen."

I pulled myself up and stumbled on shaking legs to the door. It was locked. I moaned.

She came up behind me, put her hands on my shoulder.

I jerked. "Let me out, why, where's Liz."

"I know... look—you're detoxing, okay, I've been giving you roofies and shit to help you sleep it off." She wore no bandana now. Her hair's texture was crunchy, and starched strands lifted from her scalp. Even her eyebrows were bleached. She was older than I'd thought at first. And tired.

"No. Did Keith come?"

"Keith never came for you. I did. You need to trust me now. If you leave this room. You're dead. That is something you can trust. Take these pills."

My hair felt wet with sweat. My guts cramped. My vision was greying as if I would faint.

I looked past her at Clarence, not purring now but watching us closely from the bed.

"Yeah, I took him to the vet. He was dying from a kidney infection. I give him medicine. Trust me. And you'll get through this."

I took the pills. I swallowed them. She left the room. I leaned up against the door, wanting to cry, but I couldn't. There was another door in this bedroom that opened on a bathroom. I went in and urinated. My mouth tasted like iron. Clarence came in and watched me. There was a clean cat box under the sink. I felt pressure in my lower guts but couldn't shit.

I didn't realize I was shaking so hard until the shaking started to pass. I saw the room, the window, but I was too tired to think about it, so I went back to bed, had to sleep, even though it seemed like it was a bright morning.

I was on land, no water at all, and Simon and my mother were walking in the desert. They were a mile or five off, but I could see them, their hands brushing, my mother in a white terry-cloth robe and huge hat. Do they know there's rattlesnakes in the desert? This desert's dirty with life, not like the Sahara, not like Mars, but rusty with dry life, sideways roots, repeating brush piles. I heard a crackling sound, and it was crack rock burning, but I looked around me and then I realized it was a rattle, a rattlesnake.

I wanted my mother, I wanted to save them from the desert, what do they know about the desert, but I couldn't get off the road and into the desert, because I knew, even if I couldn't see them, that the snakes were just under foot.

In a dark cool motel room with a stout young woman wearing nothing but a Dead Kennedys shirt standing in front of the window. I looked away from her. She'd left a carton of Kools on the table. Maybe we were just north of the desert in Flagstaff, in a motel on Route 66. I asked her about it but couldn't hear myself. I sat down at the cheap table. But the chair was a blue wooden child's chair. It was hard for me to balance on it, now, I was too big. A man's hands underneath the table planted on each of my knees. I stood before he could open me up.

I peeled open the cigarettes and took one into my mouth and fired it up. It tasted like crack. Is this crack? I asked her. Did you trick me? She was by the closed window, the curtains made it dark. Her back was to me, and she was saying something into the heavy smoke-soaked fabric. *I can't believe I'm smoking.* My throat burned. I think it always burned now. Shit, I've fucked up this time for good. I looked at the cigarette, grey smoke like a line to the ceiling and it tasted like paint. *Did you trick me?* I looked at her. Her bottom was sticking out a little under her shirt. Her teased hairdo was flat black in the back from sleeping. *Is all you can do is sleep, lady, or what? All you've done this trip is sleep, anyway.* I expected her to shrug, but she was still. She made

128

words I understood for just a minute and then forgot, as when ghosts speak from the ceiling to children below. The Jackal breathing.

I had to get into the bathroom. The light was real, and I woke up. I looked into my face in the mirror as the florescence fluttered up to full blue force and my face was awake but dead flat and pasty white. Blue and red and white and pocked. My hair was dyed bad red-orange, and it was coming out a little. I touched it and it stuck to my palms. I was awake, who woke me up?

My hands on the counter, black nails, my hands were young again. There was blue tub of Noxema. I could smell, and I opened it up and scooped out white opalescent paste with short black nails, this is YOUTH, I thought. I put it up to my nose and smelled it, cream, menthol, eucalyptus. But my face was still old and awake. My dry eyes confirmed it. Crack and Kools made the sadness stick on my face. Then my hands were old again, older than anything else. The scent of Scrubbing Bubbles sprayed on urine. My hands the oldest objects, used-up hands glossy and scaly lined, bulging and aching.

I was wearing the woman's shirt then, and I tried to cover my red bush with the bottom of it, I knew someone was in the other room, but I didn't know who.

I didn't bring any underwear. And my young breasts were still budding, their sides swollen sore. I had to sit down on the side of the square tub and hold them, heavy in my hands like puppies, what would I do without a bra on this trip? They were too big and my nipples burned against the inside of the shirt and filled me with angry rage, low and cool.

Wendy called, *Margot, Margot.* Oh, it was her hoarse voice all right. She must be on the other side of the small black window. I hoped she couldn't see me in the tub, my bare bottom, my sore YOUTH, my tired old face, holding up my face for living would have to wait until I got out of this motel room, I needed sleep, but that's all we do here,

129

how can it be?

I hated how the woman in the room could sleep standing up with her eyes open. *Margot, Margot.* Wendy was singing to me. *I don't have any underpants on this trip Wendy, and I don't want you to see my red bush, but it is redder than my dull gold hair.* My dry feet on the 1950's pink tile confirmed my waking state. I needed to go get the sheet off the bed and wrap it around my crotch like a diaper, so I could let people in.

I walked back into the bedroom. The woman was curled on her side in the bed under the covers. I had to leave her. *I can't help it—the Jackal's been at my back my whole life—I can't help it—he's the one with the beetle in his hand, the heart in his hand—the Jackal's breath is on my heels—I have to go—I have to run.* The Kools were gone. Shit. We need more.

The woman looked at me and said without moving her mouth: "You shot Liz. You were the gun who put the blood in her mouth."

She shook her head at me in disgust and lay back down. A movie played on the wall behind her all black and red. It was me riding a man, a stranger, and Liz watching, with her hand at her mouth and the blood coming to lips. The movie played on a short loop as I struggled to open the door.

I backed out of the room, the woman's face dead as a closed door. I could feel my adrenal bulbs balking at her.

I ran OUT into a field of grass under sunlight so far and green in an afternoon so long, I wondered with an awful lilt if this was the afterlife already after all. I walked for hours coming up on nothing. I knew if I stopped and lay down on my back like I wanted to, I would feel that pain again like the eardrum rupturing deep inside me.

If there were any shadows on the grass, I couldn't see them, just long shades of golden sounding green. I saw a man in black standing far out by an oak tree, the only tree in this field. Flowers bloomed up, and the field transformed into a meadow with wildflowers, and it felt good to see the man. I knew I loved him. I knew he was my friend. I ran up to him, but as he turned, I felt ashamed. He slipped into the oak and was gone, and I kept running.

My hands gripped and I knew what they were longing for. My hands were gripping for a guitar. My hands gripped for my guitar, but I just cried into them. There was so much water coming out. I looked at my hands and they were so wet. I knew they would fry if they touched an electric guitar. I could see it. A good way to die.

Now the water coming out of my eyes was teal, and I pulled it out with my fingers and painted the good way to die on my thigh. I was late for the procedure. The black and white guitar and the wet hands and all white all made in teal. It must be because I was painting on skin.

I waited for the painting to dry, and I walked on.

The grass thinned out to dry patches in concrete, and I was coming up on a great sudden city, sideways from Cleveland, a city facing Cleveland, facing east. I'd followed the sun west, so this long day took me here, but I didn't understand, but I tried for a long time to figure out how I'd gone west from Arizona and ended up in Chicago. I must've never been in the desert after all. I came up to the Lincoln Inn, I was off 66, if I'd ever been on it at all, and now I was on the Lincoln highway. The Lincoln Inn.

Swallow pennies. Tuscarawas Avenue cuts Canton in half, the first ever trans-American highway, all the way and it is the Lincoln Highway, to Chicago, flat brown wooden Lincolns and Inns all the way, my mother found a shiny penny in Noam's diaper.

I choked on the heart in my throat and didn't want to go into the Lincoln Inn again. It was cold and the rain came down raging and blind burning again. My friend called me from a window high up. Margot. He called with Mark's lazy voice! How could he want me in there again? This wasn't Flagstaff, this wasn't 66, this was broken 66, cold Chicago, empty pool, no sky, just guard hairs hard and scarred.

Lincoln Inn, the lobby A PROSTITUTION FREE ZONE NO KIDS PETS OKAY Lizabeth behind the counter. I was relieved to see her, but then I saw the line of blood on her chin. She started to say something but turned away, it was too late. Everyone has gone away.

Then I was in my motel room, light bulbs stolen, mirror climbing up the wall and onto the ceiling, a flat mirror with black lines in it, the stuffed chair tilted, staph bacteria dry humping on the stiff couch, water doesn't stop running, thin hard sheets, rattling outside, broken locks and a smell, the bed, and even the inside of the desk drawer all tagged up, not one, but two bibles in there. Hard lights.

I did not look up at the mirror on the ceiling. I closed my eyes. I left someone back in Phoenix, not Phoenix even, but north in the desert between the city and the reservation. Near Sedona? Nothing. Without water. *Margot.* Wendy's face turned balding ghost in the window. I stepped back and almost fell into the street. What was she doing in that window, why was she in this room? No one would look at me. I fell back again

and smelled the ocean, but this was Chicago. That man in black from the prairie was in the bathroom. I put my hands on the golden-brown particle wood door and I put my left ear to the door. I heard the water spinning. I said his name, but after it left my mouth, I forgot it. I tried the door again.

Then I was in the bathroom, but the man was behind the curtain with the water running—oh oh I needed him, and I pulled the curtain, and his back was to me all in black, black sweater black jeans and his silvery brown hair was pushed back, his arms crossed. I touched his arm, tugged but he was hard and wouldn't turn around. He stood in wet cotton. The smell: leaves and sand, but the man in black didn't know me, the floor was wet, I stepped back but I didn't want to, he turns and I see his face, his eyes for one blue flash and

I fell back again

I was in Bela Buda. My favorite place! How could I have forgotten? I was behind the bar with Henry. I was playing a show that night. There were paintings on the walls like the one on my thigh of the good way to die. Henry, my old friend Henry—he asked me about my guitar, and he gave me a tall amber beer, and I wanted to drink it but when I tried it just tasted like sweaty ham.

Then I was on the other side of the bar. I put the glass to my mouth, but it was just my awful sweaty hand. I sucked on it anyway because I needed drunk. I felt like it was the ocean. A painting was of the ocean, but it looked like a mouth.

I laughed and pointed to the painting. I looked at my hand and saw that it was in the painting, and it felt like bathwater like I wanted it to. I slipped my arm into the humid painting.

And jarred up in bed. Human painting. Soaking wet, all my covers pulled off of me. "I smell the ocean."

Wendy turned around and put her hand on my back. She was tired as hell, I could feel it, and high up above me. I couldn't see her face. I put my hands on her blue cotton back and slid them down. I shut my face and clenched up.

"Hey kid, how are you feeling? I've got some soup, or some ice water, or bread. Saltines." She turned and looked at me.

I sat up fast and spinning. I held the mattress down with both hands, but I was sinking. Wendy. I backed up panting.

"What's happening? How long have we been doing this?"

"Here, you need to drink. Your lips look like raisins."

"What. Okay." Wendy had poisoned me. I drank and drank the

ice water from a giant plastic white Geauga Lake glass that I didn't recognize. I swallowed with both hands. I swallowed the Cuyahoga. I wanted to put the ice in my mouth, but it was too sharp with cold, I was afraid it would cut my lips and burn my teeth.

I set it down on the floor, and, spinning up into straight clear vision, I looked at Wendy. She looked at me.

"How long has this been going on?"

"Three days, well, two and a half."

"Wow, no, it's been months. I don't even remember. I don't remember what happened before… The deer walked into the street. The snow." My feet felt burnt, and I remembered the snow. Oh, shit I forgot to go to work! "Shit—I was fired!" I was spinning like a hangover but worse, I was spinning so I could hardly see.

"Don't worry, you're coming to work with me. Straight work. I'll explain later, just relax."

I sat up, backed up. She was a killer. I needed to think. And breathe.

"Wendy. Are you holding? I need to wake up."

"Down to Nyquil, kid, sorry. No more roofies. I only have so many doctor friends."

"You know what I mean. Wendy."

"You are off that shit, Margot. Thank me later."

She came back with a shot of Nyquil.

"Fuck. I don't want that shit. Do you have a cigarette? You killed Liz. Where are we."

"My place. You're safe. Your cat, remember? She had a kidney infection, but the vet gave her some shots of antibiotic, but she'll be fine. Actually—she needs to get these fluid shots a couple times a week. I did it once. I'll show you later. Maybe tomorrow."

I shuddered remembering the feel of cracking Simon's head into the linoleum. *He'll want to kill me.*

I stood up quickly and things went a bit grey. "Well, I'd better get back to my place."

"No, you can't go back there. Nonnegotiable. But listen. You made it easy for me."

Wendy told me Simon had called her to come and haul my ass back. She found me running naked in the snow a mile away from his apartment. I hopped in her car and she took me to her place and told Simon she couldn't find me. He gave her the address to my room.

"Why don't I remember getting in your car? And how the fuck did he remember where I lived?"

She gave me a look.

"You made it easy for me to rescue you, girl." She stroked my thigh. "Your place was unlocked. That pregnant girl said you'd left a cat on death's door. While you were sedated, washing that crack cocaine out of your blood, I brought your shit here. This is your room. Got Blackie fixed up." She patted Clarence's head, but he backed his head back and looked at her with furrowed brow.

The sun shined through her clear blond hair making a halo. I said, "Clarence. He's a boy. Why did you do all that, why did you save me?"

"Here's the thing. You can't go back to your room. I told him you were there, and that I took care of you. I told Simon I *did* you, so, you can't go anywhere. We'll dye your hair black. We'll call you Alice. You will wait a month to go out, and then wear sunglasses. I told Simon I am done. After killing two people, I am done. You'll work for me painting houses. But you got to *lay low.* And all cats are girls."

"I have family."

"Yeah, your brother called."

"What? Noam called?"

"I know. Just lay back, I'll get you some soup."

I tried to stand up, but the grey hit me and I fell back down. "Oh, god, I must smell bad."

"I mean, who cares. You're okay."

"I'll get in the tub I think. But, what about the Lincoln Inn, do you know what I mean? You ever been to the Lincoln Inn in Chicago?" I was slipping back into a dream, but a waking dream.

"Yeah. I've been there."

"Arizona. No wonder your brother didn't come out."

It was three hours later after soup and a long shower and white pomegranate tea. I couldn't believe how clearheaded I felt, for the first time in forever. Waking up. Wearing a cushy blue robe that smelled like rosewater. The room was like a kid's room from a generation ago. Small desk with simple lamp. Deep plush dark blue carpet. Pale blue walls with rainbows. A window with blue shades drawn. I sat down on the floor. The carpet was so soft and clean—I hadn't felt carpet in ages.

(except for the monster green carpet in the old man's apartment—no.)

Clarence curled up against my leg. I petted him as Wendy straddled the small wooden desk chair.

"What did my brother...?"

"I said, 'get your ass over here—your sister's on crack.' I hadn't figured out this plan yet, so, but then I smashed the phone with a hammer and threw it into the street."

"Ah. He hasn't even been here in so long. He doesn't know where I live. We just email sometimes. They ask me to come out there for Christmas and shit, but I don't have money to fly all the way out there. They've got hummingbirds there. Oh, Jesus."

She put her hand on my arm. She smelled like sandalwood and weed but her eyes were bright. I jerked back. I asked her what the hell was going on.

"Sit back down on the bed, Margot, relax..."

"I can't relax. Simon wants me dead and you work for him."

I felt like I should run, but I also felt held by her gaze. I hadn't forgotten the knife she'd held to my throat after killing Liz. Wendy sighed and sat hard on the bed. It bounced like it was broken. She put her hand to her mouth like she wanted a cigarette and looked away, and then looked back at me. I was worried about Clarence. I was worried she'd hurt him. Maybe she fixed us just to hurt us. She looked down at me. I got up and sat on the bed by her, so I would be between her and Clarence.

"Look. I'd never done what I did to that woman to anyone else before. I'm not a killer by nature, Margot. I was fronting, okay? Before I worked for Simon, I was a *community activist*, for fuck's sake. He wanted me to do you, but he's no baller really, I mean, in a way he is, but, he's new to the heavy shit. It's like, we're all new to this shit."

I looked around the room at the crates of my things. I saw the neat bowls under the window for Clarence: water, hard food, and canned food. My hair smelled like someone else's soap.

Wendy told me she needed to be honest, so I'd trust her. She said after she brought me here and sedated me (and what else that I don't remember? Bound me? Gagged me?), but before she went to get my stuff, that she was planning on killing me, she just wanted to make sure it was all controlled and clean. She wasn't trying to get sloppy and do hard time. She drove out to the parking lot at Walgreen's and just sat there, looking at the shoveled-up mounds of snow. She was nervous, and then hungry, and then tired, and soon it was almost eight, and it was dark and cold, and she needed something to eat, so she took off for a break at Burger King, the same one where I'd met Simon and Johnny just a couple weeks ago.

"It stunk like beef hearts and moldy rags. It was as cold in there as it was outside. My feet were wet, there were puddles on the shitty brown tiles. I sat there eating cold fries that felt like fiberglass in my mouth. There was pictures of Marilyn Monroe, cheap ones, and James Dean all faded blue like they'd been there since the eighties. And you know that one picture with the diner and the lonely people, except it's Elvis and Marilyn Monroe and James Dean again."

I got up and closed the door. I was afraid of Clarence getting out. I didn't want to lose him in her house. I needed all my stuff right here, so I could get it out soon. "Yeah, the kitschy take on *Nighthawks*."

"That's when your brother called. I couldn't do it." She looked up at me. Her eyes were hard to look into. They were steady but too pale blue to know if she was lying or not.

I felt sick. Really like I might shit myself. "Stop lying to me. I know Simon won't let you get away with it, though, so you have to, so what the fuck is going on."

She stood up and got close to me. She put her hands on either side of my arms and looked me in the eye. Then she leaned in and whispered in my ear. "I'm only going to say this once more. I told him you were dead. I told him I dumped you in the river, that I sawed your head off and one leg and dumped you in three parts into the river, down by LTV Steel." Her lips brushed my ear.

I shook. The lie felt true.

She stood back up, looked down at me, then crouched down and put her mouth to my ear again. "You have to stay here in this room—you can't go back to your room. You can't. I'm gonna dye your hair black. I told Simon I was *out*. He let me go, he knows I've got nothing to gain by crossing him."

She licked my ear. I jumped a little, and she pulled me even closer. "I paint houses, that's what I did for money before. I've got a van. You come work with me. You clean, I'll paint. We'll be clean, from hard stuff I mean, it'll be good. You're good Margot. You're Alice now." She reached under my robe and put her hand on my hip. I felt heat, but it was crazy. I pushed back.

138

"No Wendy." Fuck it, I held *her* at arms' length. She wasn't lying, she wasn't crazy, at least as best I could tell. I was weak, but I knew my life depended on my looking into her right. But maybe she was a sociopath. Maybe I couldn't look in. I couldn't get to Arizona. I didn't have a penny. Not even my uncashed paycheck in the wallet Simon had swiped from my scrubs. And—somehow underneath it all I felt a strange desire, I wanted Wendy to touch me again. I hadn't been touched sober in years.

I managed to say, "Motherfucker lives on this side of town. Are you crazy? Are you setting me up? Just kill me if that's what you're going to do, but don't do this. He'll see me. Or you'll slip and call me Margot at the grocery store, and one of his dudes will hear it and tell him—what the fuck?"

She pulled away and turned around, flashing me her wide grin. "Fuck, Margot, he won't kill you, he *likes* you. He was scared shitless after Liz, he'd never done anything like that before, either. He'll laugh, you know, if he finds out. In time. In time, he'll laugh."

"Laugh? If that was his first kill, then he's even more dangerous because he's scared and because he's crossed a line. Jesus. I've got to get out of here. Plus—I hit him, I *embarrassed* him in front of another man. I've got to get out of Ohio."

"No look. I'll dye your hair black, I'll call you Alice, I'm sorry I touched you, I've got a girlfriend. Look, just let me get you something to drink."

"I want a phone." I could stay with *whom*. I had no friends left to stay with.

"No. Sorry."

"Wendy, Jesus, he's going to be following this, right? No body will turn up. *Alice*?

"Yeah, Alice. Let me get you a drink." She hopped up and I lay back.

I wanted to be Ebenezer Scrooge waiting for the Ghost of Christmas

Past after his visit from Jacob Marley. I yearned for initiation. I yearned for ordeals, and to be cleansed from all this. Clarence hopped up on the bed. My heart beat hard. I had my brother's number only in my cell phone, and he only had my cell phone number. I thought of him, Noam, his dark red hair like cedar, and my throat got tight, and then big sudden tears. I hadn't been able to cry in so long. Clarence purred and butted his head into my hip that Wendy had just touched, and I felt sick for all tender things.

She came in backwards with a drink in each hand. She handed me one. I sniffed and wiped at my face, obviously red and awful. The drink was whisky in a wine glass smelling strong. I could email my parents. I've never in all these years asked them for money or anything.

"Don't cry, sugar, listen, I just couldn't kill you, but I can't let you go cause then he'd know, okay? Look, the other thing in our favor is today he left for Chicago for a couple weeks. He's small time, baby, he's just got some dealers selling when he's gone, but I was his only enforcer, and I'm out, when he comes back, he won't care about us, he'll be busy with his new Chicago contacts and getting someone to replace me, and avoiding the heat from Liz's family, for sure. Not to mention Sig. See, he's got bigger worries, okay? Liz's brothers and cousins, she was well connected. Vickers are an old west side family. I know that's part of why he's going to Chicago for a couple *weeks* instead of a couple days."

The drink hit me hard. I was a fucking idiot. But I figured I was so tired, and the glass was so full. (And I needed to get something off in my brain.)

"Wendy, how do I know I can trust you? How do I know you're not just holding me until he gets back so he can do it himself? I hit him, I embarrassed him. How can I trust you?

Her eyes were soft now. "Honey. Look at my cell phone. You've been here three days. He would have done you by now. If that was the case. Look, you'll be with me every day. Okay, so I could kill you tonight in your sleep, even though I didn't the other nights, but I won't. And then after that, you'll see. I'm good, too. Like you. We're good."

"Good. You and I are *good* people, you mean. We are good." The word didn't seem real. It sounded like *bread* or *hood*.

"Oh, also before I killed your phone, Keith? Texted, said he was sorry he was tied up and… something about Kiss, or Easy Kiss or something? Is that some coded Liz shit or something? She was so old school."

"Oh, oh, that's just something else. Never mind that, not a problem."

She took my empty glass from my hand. I felt pink in the cheeks. She laid me back. "Well. Anyways. Even Simon ain't all bad. We go back a long way. He knows he's fucking up. Hubris, murder. My guess is by summer he'll probably be back down with his aunt in Atlanta if Liz's brothers don't get to him first." She put her hand in between my legs. I closed my eyes. "Don't worry about us, though. Liz's boys have no way to know we were involved," she whispered in my ear as she moved deeper inside me. It felt so good, tears came to my eyes.

"I wasn't involved." I whispered.

"No, you were involved." She put her other hand on my mouth, my robe opened, and she and kissed my exposed breast. I opened my eyes for a second and saw my self-portrait by the closed door. I decided to trust her. I listened to her breathing.

11

April Fool

March was one long, lavender night. Wendy dyed my hair. I'd let my license go, so I couldn't get the good stuff anymore. The color was a shiny blue-black that looked stupid with my reddish-brown eyebrows, but it faded to a muddy brown soon enough. I ironed it straight, and I did look different. She brought me gross green hipster sunglasses for when I could go out again, and I let her get used to calling me Alice. She brought me new clothes from Remarkable Thrift where she still worked on Thursdays, dresses with flowers and things on them and blue sneakers. All my old clothes were black, and I used to wear boots. She guessed pretty well about what clothes would fit my body, on the safe side she often guessed big, and we just figured on using safety pins to make things fit better.

Wendy's house was in Lakewood, a small but dense inner-ring suburb on the western border of Cleveland, adjacent to my old neighborhoods on the west side.

March was a lifetime in a minute, another birthday passed. Now I was thirty-four. Clinton won the Ohio primary. I paced the room. I filled a notebook with *aum* symbols. I did sun salutations. I woke up twice with my hands clenched on my guitar, noise fuzzing in my ears, but in waking the sound and tool dissolved. I asked Wendy about my guitar, but she said she found no guitar in my room. It must have walked off. For the first time in twenty years, I had no guitar. I felt like I was missing my liver. I didn't paint because of the carpet.

Wendy cooked for me. I really wasn't into eggs or dairy, but she made eggs for me every night, and I didn't complain. She brought meals up to me, and I was so hungry and ate so much. Soup, fruit, eggs, bread. The yolky eggs came from hens in a city garden. She kept my room locked.

I've always choked at the idea of being locked in a room. Once, my mother put me in a cardboard box to amuse baby Noam, and I was in on it, too, smiling with anticipation, but as soon as she pressed the lid down, my throat went thick and I kicked. I hate being closed in, trapped.

Being locked in the powder blue room should have been the worst thing, but it was not, it was something else. I felt more that the world was locked away from me. For the first time in my life, I didn't have to worry about money. I didn't have to worry about getting to the train on time or getting crack or checking my email or listening to NPR or getting rated at MetroHealth or filing taxes. I didn't have to deal with people at all.

The blue room was the safest place I had ever lived. Safer than my room above the car shop, much safer than the apartment I shared with my ex-husband who hit my hands and legs. I'd had good years before that, living with my brother, then on my own, but there were always people in the street trying to get my name or my number or money I didn't have, always bosses watching for me to slip up, guys trying to crash.

The house I grew up in was full of love and books and laughs, but it was also full of quickly changing tempers, confusing moods and

143

long periods of silence. The streets outside my childhood home were crowded with strange men saying things that made me feel ashamed and not safe. My childhood was spent in menacing factory schools. Teachers who hated children. Bathroom stalls with no doors and kids pouring glue in my pockets and gum in my hair and even worse when they messed with my little brother...and these eight years of a president who hates gay people, dumbed down schools, abandoned climate and health care... flooded New Orleans and oil wars, years of performing and not performing, and drunk like bombs in the head and missed time and strange dick...all that was gone.

The room was sky blue and the rainbows on the walls did not move.

Wendy came into my room at night, I'm not sure how many times, but always when I was sleeping. We'd have sex and then sleep a little more, but in the morning, she would be gone, and we never talked about it. I tried to take her hand sometimes, in the daytime, and sometimes she held my hand, too, and more often she pulled hers away. But she was the one who came to me in the night.

She did have a girlfriend: Cher. Who was at first, the only one who knew I was there, or a version of why I was there. Wendy told her I was a friend recovering from drugs and hiding out from my old drug friends. True enough.

Mostly I was alone. My throat burned for a week after coming off, and I was sick from not being able to shit for three days, but after all that I felt good. Physically.

When Wendy came to me in the night, it was as if we were free from words and names, and with her, I came easily and got her off easily, and loved her quickly. But I was glad for Cher, because it would have been too much in the daytime, and I didn't want the future to close in. Though I never thought of leaving.

It still took a few weeks to concentrate enough for reading. I had to start with a box of Archie comics she'd brought from my room. All

I could write was *aum*. I couldn't cry yet either, just eat, pace, sleep for fifteen hours at a time. And write *aum*.

While I was locked away in the child's room, Wendy was getting her painting business up and running again. By April, she was ready to let me out of the house. We were ready to work.

Each dawn came earlier. And with them, my soul woke before my skin, my eyes. I woke into a city, but a city locked into its trees, its birds. A waking into birds and trees that I'd known my whole life in Northeast Ohio. Birds screaming in the opening spring, the waking buds, the baby leaves. The birds whose voices I knew intimately, wordlessly, a knowing beyond recognition, a body knowing, whose bodies I knew, too, but I could not match the voices to the bodies. How wonderful it would be to see a body quiver with the singular call and think, *oh that's you—that's your call*. We all were covered with the same highway soot.

On April first, Wendy unlocked my door. I hadn't been downstairs since the first day. The house was still. Full of dark wood. It felt like kids had grown up here, and then the whole family left. Wendy felt small in here. It wasn't a big house, but I was used to apartments and single rooms, the blue room.

I followed her down the stairs into still air. She turned back and smiled at me, "Excited for your first outing, Alice?"

I smiled. What was I supposed to feel.

Out on the porch it was bright. I shielded my eyes.

"Put on your glasses."

I did. "But they're not sunglasses."

There was an old bike painted flat black on the porch. It had a

145

handmade sign on the back: *Share the Road or Die.*And a sticker: *MEDICARE FOR ALL.*

"You like that?"

"Yeah."

"Traded it from an old black guy for a rock. I made those signs, though." She trotted down the stairs and I followed her.

The air felt weird around me. Big. I squinted behind my glasses. Alice's glasses. We walked up to the corner store, a gas station called Fuel-Up, just on the Cleveland side of the southern Lakewood/Cleveland border. It was a busy place, but the pumps were older than me. Inside, the smell of commercial air slapped me in the face. All the things, and the shitty music and radio commercials. I stayed close by Wendy.

She picked up a six-pack of Saint Pauli Girl and told me once again about our first job tomorrow. The sight of the blue package filled me with a crushing desire for crack. I looked away, breathed, shifted my desire toward the beer.

While she was in line, I ventured to the racks and looked for sunglasses, but there was just a bunch of weird shit instead: sleazy strawberry incense supposedly designed by "a top tattoo artist" but covered in cliché images of hearts and arrows, purses made from Pittsburg Steelers sweatshirts, do-rags with little brown brass knuckles on them, and faux-rustic jars of scented candles, one scent: *Smell My Nuts* tm.

I didn't have any money anyway. I'd have to wait to get sunglasses. Outside I asked Wendy what's up with the place, it was crawling with cops and there was a banner announcing the chance to win a Camaro. "...It's like this place is designed by a cynical East Coast corporate computer program. They think this is Ohio, right, Nascar country, and they can't even get it right that the Pittsburg Steelers are the wrong team, the enemy team. This is Cleveland for fuck's sake."

"Ha! Yeah, for real."

"It's just weird." I was used to minimalist convenience stores with bullet-proof glass and wire between attendant and customer.

"Look, here's the ground rules: your room will remain unlocked, so long as you *become* Alice, and keep your head down. Stick with me. This is to keep us both safe. I know you don't have people anyway, but don't think about looking up old friends or whatnot. Just stick by me, and the door will remain unlocked."

I said okay, she said *understand* and she meant it, and I said okay again. She watched me hard, her hooded blue eyes paler in this light. I knew she was a little crazy. But I liked having this re-set. I felt lucky to have someone conspiring to make all the fucked-up things that happened before disappear. During the month-long transition, she had become the only person in my world. In this strange and powerful way, I loved her.

I sat on the couch by the window. She cracked open a beer and handed it to me without looking and went to bang around the kitchen. The front door was open. The ninety-year-old house had the same floor plan, the same dark wood and French doors as my childhood home, the first house of memory.

The way the light came in. The April air, this first warm air full of life that brings other times right up to your face. Thirty years ago, late night parties, blue lightbulbs. Enchiladas. Daddy in black, Momma in red, Noam sleeping. I could stay up.

And later, just seventeen, within my last eighteen months in the house, just a few scattered years before my folks would leave forever. And after that, in quick succession: the apple tree cut down, and the pine trees cut down. And the little playhouse for us that my father made torn down, but then, maybe it was rotten, I don't know.

But that year held steady, shifting into focus. A new seventeen in another April right here, right now:

My mother (like a river, runs forever round curves to places unseen) over there at a black metal desk working a fat tan computer. Her hair: long, thick and red, but straighter than mine, strong hair, not crazy like mine, gently faded, but never dyed, just sparks from a sprinkling of white hairs.

"Shit Walter." She hits the side of the computer. The green letters on black background stare back at her silently.

"I know, baby-shakes, take a break?" My father, black curly hair, slouching over six feet.

She pushes back, "Yeah." Stands up. "The fuck. Drafting, by hand. I don't even want to do this if it's not by hand."

I watch like a ghost.

She walks over to the front door, opens it like the one at Wendy's is open. Pulls a silver cigarette case out of her pocket and slides out a joint. Turns away from the open door. Passes it to my dad, he shakes his head.

The street outside is always busy, fine black dust from the exhaust covers our things. Fat maple leaves offer some protection through the summer. But it is spring, and the trees are just budding.

"Margot," She waves the smoke away with her hand, "if you don't go to college, you'll live an idiot's life." She turns away, sucks hard on the joint.

"Come on Julie, not everybody has to go to college." My dad opens two Heinekens and hands one to her, drinks one, himself. He lights some Nag Champa incense perched in a holder on the glass coffee table, waves for her to get away from the open door.

"My grades are shit and we don't have any money, so how the fuck do you expect me to go to college?"

"Figure it out! Look-it," she points her index finger at me, "You want to just be jerked around for the rest of your life? People will jerk you around if you don't dig deep, Mog, you must dig deep. No compromises, no way."

"Julie, lay off." My dad waves at the window, like the one here at Wendy's house, he waves at what it is: the first beautiful day of spring. "Let's go to the park or something."

My mother puts her hands up. "Margot. You've got to do what you love. No one will ensure of that but you." She crosses the room and tears up the steps. She is a storm. More perfect than me, in bones, in passion.

"Honey," my father rubs my arm, "there's more important things." He smiles, but his face goes dark. "Doing what you love is overrated, it's Hollywood bullshit. Family is more important. Contributing to society is more important. Maybe wait a few years, go to Stark Tech and get an occupational therapy license. Use your mind to help people." He is underemployed as an assistant manager of an OfficeMax. He has an MFA in jazz guitar from Purchase College at SUNY. "You can stay here as long as you want."

Two years before, drunk, crying, he threw his guitar, amps, keyboard, down into the basement. They lay unmoved beneath us as we speak.

"You're right, Dad, I know."

Then I walk to the cemetery with a friend and get high. When I look ahead, I can't see anything.

After a few days of working a painting gig with Wendy, and a run to the grocery store, I felt free. I felt maybe Simon *would* forget about me and I could move about the world freely. I had spring fever, and I wanted to stay with Wendy, but I wanted to leave, too.

I had to get out of Wendy's house on my own sometime soon. I felt the itch and creep of metamorphosis. I found myself crawling under her dining room table. Lying flat on my back staring up at the dull wooden underside. My eyes were prickly. After a month of dry eyes, I felt a torrent coming. Things were coming back too fast and all at once. "Wendy, can I walk up to the library, to email my brother? Let him know I'm okay?"

She walked up and stood over me, smiling down at our feet as she gently touched her toes to my toes. "Okay. Since he and Simon are half a country apart, but *just your brother.* But no one else, no *myspacing,* no *facebooking,* no motherfucking *tweetering,* no nothing. And be back in an hour. Know this: I got eyes at that branch."

It felt GOOD to be walking around a neighborhood again. The little Lakewood library was right around the corner. My body in motion cleared the smoke out of my head but left the mirrors.

Hey Brother,

How are you? How's Marcia? I lost my phone. I'll let you know when I get a new one. I know my friend told you about my troubles, but please don't worry, it wasn't long, I;m totally clean now and don't want anything but booze and coffee and tea. I miss you – how's music out there? I've been out of it for a while, but I think it's still a really good scene here. Maybe you can come out for the Spider Moon Fest? I would love to see you! How's mom and dad? I'm staying with my friend and just a bit ago I lay on my back under her dining room table, it's old like the one we had growing up, and I just looked under there at the wood and the little shelves and things and remembered how we used to play with our guys, Peter Venkman, She-ra, etc and it was like Wayne Manor in our eyes. Remember when there was the wedding under the Christmas tree and then when the guys ventured out in the alley in the spring? The puddles in the potholes were ponds and lakes. No shit – remember the first time you got high? When I got you high when you were 14 and I was 17 and I still picture you a foot shorter than me in your Greek fisherman's cap, even though you're taller than me now by a bit because I never vever get to see you.. But remember and I think of you high for the first time and I'm going on and on about how now that I can drive, we should get out our guys and take them to the woods to play! I felt so bad that I was blabbering on and on to you but I just couldn't stop talking I was so high and it was so weird. Lol I felt so bad when I'd wanted to stop playing guys, and it's funny cause it was just when I was 13 or 14, but you were younger and wanted to keep playing but I was into Nirvana and makeup and I wanted to play still, too, but I thought I had to stop, then just a few years later it was too late – but at least we could still jam and get high together! Your feet looked like little monkey feet - at least in my mind's memory. Sonic youth – the Misfits – working at Rally's and Pizza Hump when you first moved up here with me to Cleveland? Big Black, Glenn Branca, us playingin dark warehouses, shitty green bars – oh fuck, I'm crying at the library cause I miss you so much – that's what junkies do when they dry up – they get all cornball, do you call crackheads junkies or what? Remember that Burroughs book JUNKY? And then he wrote QUEER. They were so good – but he kept them secret. He was more ashamed of being gay than an addict – but remember Queer was after he got off drugs – and he just wanted someone to lie in bed with. Remember basketball diaries? Have you heard about that drug jencom? It's people getting high off human turds, seriously the residual methane or something. I'll stick to the tequila and red zinger tea, thanks.

I love you Noam. Maybe It's time for me to figure out how to move out there.

I thought you had fun when you lived here, cause I had my most fun when you were here, but Iknow you hated Cleveland. Maybe you're right.

I love you,

Let me know how you are,

Sister, Margot Jones

I wrote fast without looking and pressed *send*.

Both Lakewood libraries smelled like Band-Aids instead of books. I looked for on old lover online, but he wasn't there. Georgie's friend request lingered, and I ignored it. I looked for the event for Spider Moon Fest, but it wasn't up yet. I looked up Lucy's Facebook page. I wasn't surprised to find her very active on Facebook. Wendy told me not to "tweeter", whatever the fuck that is. I cyber-stalked other acquaintances, old friends, some I'd forgotten about. Unsatisfied, someone was missing.

"Alice, what are you doing?"

At first, I first I didn't get it, but the woman was standing behind me, so I turned around. "Cher?"

"Wendy said you'd be coming up here. I work here. So. She said since you're in recovery, you're not supposed to be haunting around any of your old drug friends. She said you were to email your brother and that's it."

"Well, that makes sense." Under Wendy's thumb. My chest went tight.

"Come on girl."

She waited while I got my things and we stepped outside. She lit up a cigarette. She wore tiny purple rimless sunglasses that matched her hair. I needed sunglasses. And a phone. There was an awkward moment of silence. I didn't know how many secrets Wendy had from Cher, but I knew the big one.

She said, "You seem like a nice person, Margot. I know shit's not easy. You'll be delicate for a long time, I imagine. But Wendy's helped other people get clean, you're in a good place."

Did she know Wendy was selling crack just six weeks ago? "So, are you a librarian?"

"Yes, and look, I do like you, Margot. But I know how Wendy is. And I want you to know that if you fuck around with her, I'm going to get you. She says you're straight, but I know how it is. With Wendy."

"Oh, no. Wendy loves you."

"I know." She butted out her cigarette. "Nice day."

"Okay, yeah. Well, see you later."

Breathing in the spongy-moss air invited spirits in through my nostrils, into my guts. Woke up some monsters inside me, too. When I'd been in the powder blue room, locked up and safe, with Clarence, I could push things away to think about later. Mostly Liz. I thought *later. Now survive. Now heal.* I closed my eyes and felt the fabric of the blanket. I ate warm soup and listened to the hum of electricity.

But now, walking home. Home. And the air still had a bite. All the houses stared at me. Black windows. I could have pushed Wendy back out into the hallway at Liz's place. I could have said she wasn't home. I could have talked her down. I should have known, but, no, I let her in. I was the one who let her in.

That night when Wendy came to my bed, I was in deepest, blackest sleep, dreaming of a wall in a basement with flowers growing out between the cracks and ivy coming in through the windows and the elevator was broken, squashed, and so I waited as each bare bulb burned out. And of course, there were jackals in the shadows.

I felt her slide under the sheets and was already aroused, as I had become conditioned to this dreamy night pleasure, anonymous and easy, attached to nothing. But as she slid her hand between my legs and pulled my hand to her breast, I woke up, more than usual, too much. I asked her why she was doing this with me when she had a girlfriend.

She froze. Exhaled and rolled over on her back. I felt afraid and stupid for feeling afraid. Stupid for making it stop. After a long minute, she said in a hoarse voice, "You know, I wanted to get with Cher for a long time. I met her there, at the library. And I knew some of her cousins, who were bad. Cher has a bachelor's in women's studies and a master's in library science. I liked her. She wouldn't talk to me. She knew I was bad. It took me a long time to prove myself, and then I was still bad, really. But now, I'm good, and things with me and her are good. But there's you."

My eyes felt sticky. Sudden weight settled on my chest: we'd had our last time and I hadn't known it, and I wanted it. I could smell her chest, her skin like paste and sandalwood.

"Margot. You hear what I said? I said I liked her, I said I wanted to get with her. From the *start.* But you—from the minute I first saw you at that old lady's place, I wanted to *inhale* you. Lie on top of you and smother you. Eat your fingers. Stick your toes inside me. I didn't know you, let alone like you, but I wanted your eyes, I wanted to see your eyes again." She didn't touch me.

"Well, I guess you better choose. I don't really care about monogamy, if you're with both of us, but Cher cares."

"Man, fuck this." She tore out of bed with such force I felt hit. She tried to slam the door, but resistance from the carpet stifled the sound. *She moves like my Mother.* I lay there awake all night, hoping she would come back, knowing we had a big job in the morning, and knowing I needed to sleep, but each time I thought I was asleep, I realized I was not. Naught.

12

Woodgroan

I stayed off crack through April. I stuck by Wendy, and we worked in the day. We didn't talk about that night, but she didn't come into my room and Cher started coming over all the time, so I knew she'd made her choice. I missed her body so much it was unbearable sometimes, but I felt free, too. Free in my heart at least. I still couldn't really walk away while she was protecting me.

Wendy helped with Clarence, too. Twice a week I held him and pinched the skin on his back between his shoulder blades, while Wendy stuck the large needle into that soft wedge of flesh, and we felt the saline solution enter his body. Afterward he sometimes had a weird fluid lump, but he had gained back his weight and was pouncing flies. Wendy scooped him up as I did and held him like a baby, rubbing noses with him and calling him her fat man.

I'd been doing yoga since I was a teenager. I had my first lessons at my neighborhood occult shop in Canton, with an eclectic witch named Astarte Raw. Since then, I practiced not at studios, but alone, from books. Mostly books from the Bihar school, Satyananda style, but also from other books I'd picked up at outlet stores or library sales. My practice was eclectic and patchy, weaving bits of tantra and earth magick ritual. I'd taken some hatha classes through the rec center, but I couldn't afford studio classes. It seemed like they all taught Vinyasa now, which I understood to be flows of sun salutations and warrior poses. I practiced alone. If I'd allowed more stillness into my practice, and practiced more steadily, maybe I'd never gotten on crack in the first place, or stayed with Georgie so long.

I aimed to do better now. I had a desire to know the truth.

Every morning since the fifth day after I got off crack, I'd practiced this ninety-minute *Sadhana*:

I get out of bed and slip naked into the little yellow bathroom attached to my room, brush my teeth, drink a glass of cold tap water, shower, slip back into my room and pull out the raggedy old black yoga mat I'd been using for twelve years.

I strut around counterclockwise and say *'ch 'ch ch* to get the bad out, to push the plaque out of me, out of the blue room, so it can flicker back up into the All and burn out.

Then I face east with my hands open and sing, *ieieieieieiei* and visualize the sun peeking over purple mountains, birds singing and trees budding.

Next, I face south and throw my hands up to a big blood orange sun high in the sky over fat magenta lilies, heavy hanging fruit, lions, and fires where all the old stories were told, and I sing, *ahahahhahhhah.*

I turn west and meet the ocean rising up, up continuously, a wall of peaks and salt, filled with octopuses and flapping fishes, ravens and nameless birds with rainbow plumes flying over and the sun melting like red and gold orgasm into the sea, setting with golden leaves, red leaves, falling on the beach, and I moan with my hands down in peace, *ohhhohhhohhhohh,* and the horses run by.

Finally, I face north and close my eyes. Full Moon over black ocean at midnight. Snow. The silent dark earth both cool and warm beneath my feet, and the silent starry sky above, endless and present. Owls in the black trees. (The wheat-colored tiger I'd chased and become, was not a tiger but an eastern puma, I learned in this place.) And I say, *AAAAAUUUUUMMMMMN.*

There is a silver circle in the blue room. I stand in the middle and invoke the great dancing mother, sometimes loudly and sometimes quietly. I build a fire inside my core and hold my hands a certain way like a purple flower, and the *small rain down can rain: Grace.*

Then I do the postures and breath work: nine sun salutations, swimming in air, continuous and moving blooms up the *chakras* from *Shakti* through *Shiva* and back, followed by a series of *kriyas, vinyasas, asanas, mantras* and finally meditation. At the end, I put both hands on the ground, and whisper a praying spell of love and peace and freedom for all and the silver circle opens but does not break.

Wendy got me clean, but yoga was keeping me clean.

I walked the neighborhood when I could, to the library, when Wendy went out for groceries or whatever, because I didn't want to fight her about it. My old hangout, Bela Buda, was next to the library. I stayed away from its face—I didn't want to be seen.

I started walking farther, all over Lakewood, which was a rectangular grid on the cliffs of Lake Erie, very densely populated but only about three miles long at its widest, so I got to know the city on foot.

Lakewood bordered Cleveland on both the east and south, the Rocky River to the west and the lake on the north. Lakewood was mostly built in the 1910's and 1920's and is just the other side of west 117th from the Cleveland neighborhoods I'd lived in. I was aware of being in a much smaller container than Cleveland and everything seemed close. Lakewood was fairly cheap and pretty safe. It was

LGBTQ-friendly with big old houses sporting rainbow flags, which was brave since Bush had stoked the homophobes into a fury for eight long years. It was home to activists and artists, and almost ten percent of the city's population were recent immigrants, mostly from Africa, Southeast Asia and the Middle East, and though the city had been known for some overtly racist incidents in the recent past, more black people were moving in and everybody seemed to be getting along pretty well.

I noticed watching the high school kids walk home that cliques didn't really seem to be segregated like when I was a kid in Canton. There was a much higher black population in Canton than Lakewood, but while my early nineties underground music crew were mostly white, almost all the black kids were into R&B. Maybe the jocks were more integrated, but my high school was so big, the football crew weren't even on my radar. Now I was seeing black and white and Middle Eastern kids walking together united by long emo bangs and pastel t-shirts, and I liked it. I wasn't sure if it was because the culture was changing or because Lakewood was more middle class than where I grew up.

Wendy had told me that as recently as the '80s and '90s the Lakewood police had a code: NIL—which meant a black person was in the area, and they would be followed until they left the city. Years ago, working at the pizza place in Lakewood, I heard an asshole talking about "N—- taking over the 'Wood.'" Probably many progressive white people in Lakewood had no idea about this stuff, didn't have to.

Just the other side of 117th from harsh Cleveland streets, Lakewood seemed bouncy and healthy. I'd hung out in Lakewood plenty but didn't really notice the difference until living there. I saw more clearly now how Cleveland had been abandoned. I couldn't think of a single Cleveland neighborhood that was safe and not beat to shit, except for one lakefront millionaire enclave that kept the city at a distance with a highway border. Even the pretty, hip neighborhoods were food deserts with gun violence.

I didn't think often about children, but I knew there were children in all those neighborhoods. I knew that the city was built by immigrants and later made strong by black people who'd moved up from the south after the world wars, and that capitalists had made money on their labor and then let them sink. I heard we were now in a surprise (!) recession and a housing crisis, and I had to laugh. That's all I'd seen in Northeast Ohio my whole life.

Here in Lakewood the libraries were bright and cheerful, and the main one even had beautiful murals and large windows. They didn't have metal detectors. There were parks and playgrounds all over the place, every few blocks it seemed. I wondered how long I'd be able to afford to live in Lakewood before the rich people started buying up all these newly cheap houses.

The whole west side of Cleveland, from the Cuyahoga River downtown to the Rocky River on Lakewood's western border, was built up between 1890 and 1930, pretty much. There were ridges left from earlier eras when the shore of the lake was farther south, before it receded to where it is today. Those ridges became Indigenous roads, and then when white people pushed into Indigenous land, they used the same roads and connected them to their encroaching transportation web. One of those roads was Detroit Avenue, which ran a mile south of the lake through the middle of Lakewood, east to west.

I imagined when Cleveland only existed on the east side of the Cuyahoga with Ohio City on the west, beyond that dense forest, and this Native American road we call Detroit carved a path through the trees. About two hundred years ago, Cleveland and Ohio City battled for territory, and even fired cannons over the Cuyahoga River. Cleveland won, absorbing Ohio City and pushing west. My understanding is that no Indigenous people lived in what we call Lakewood, but it was their territory and Detroit Avenue was their road and they had a burial mound at the mouth of the Rocky River.

First a few settlers built humble cabins on Detroit, then wealthy people built larger houses, their land extending to the lake. They grew fruit orchards and hired families, mostly children, to work them. I borrowed dusty, dogeared books with black and white photos and tried to piece together the history of the land. Some rich Clevelanders built vacation homes on the lake near the Rocky River, and Lakewood became a nineteenth century resort destination known for its fruit farms.

There were hints that some of the fruit-farming founders, such as James Nicholson and Dr. Jared Kirtland Potter were kind of cool, maybe even transcendentalists. They were abolitionists and naturalists and the first church founded in Lakewood was a mystical Swedenborgian church built by James Nicholson on the corner of Andrews and Detroit, across from where the Masonic Temple is now. Pictures of Potter reveal a Walt Whitman vibe, and some of the streets are named Emerson and Thoreau.

The founders' homes on Detroit were torn down in the 1940s and '50s, all but the Nicholson house, and turned into grocery stores and gas stations filling in what would become Lakewood's downtown.

South of Detroit stayed wild a bit longer. Just a hundred years ago, no one lived where Wendy and I lived, there was no house, only trees, and as far as I could tell, there had only ever been forest in this place before that. But who knows?

Lakewood's cliffs were eroding. The lakefront park used tetrapods to maintain the shore, but the rest of the lakefront was privately owned, and it was plain to see hunks of backyards had fallen into the water. There was only one beach in Lakewood, and that was down by the mouth of the Rocky River. Early on, the rich folks with the resort homes founded a secretive country club there and to this day don't let outsiders in. They paved over the Indigenous burial mound in the river so there'd be parking for their yacht club.

The National Carbon Company arrived in the 1890s. They took over the southeast corner of Lakewood, which bordered an industrial Cleveland neighborhood. Lakewood developed as a "streetcar suburb." In the pre-car era people could commute as streetcars ran up and down the main east-west streets of the city. Birdtown was the neighborhood built for the workers of National Carbon, and it was one of the oldest neighborhoods. It was like its own tiny town with bars and churches wedged between houses on streets named *Lark, Quail, Robin, Dowd, Magee*. A historic marker graced Birdtown, but crime and poverty were a little higher there than the rest of the city, so Lakewood old-timers still looked down on the neighborhood. Which was laughable since everyone was packed so close together in this tiny town.

We lived in the Madison Park neighborhood, just west of Birdtown.

Lakewood's structure reflected the fragile, unprecedented rise of the so-called "middle class", the resilience of the buildings making that middle class seem more solid than it ever actually had been. Clifton Park, the rich neighborhood that wrapped around the country club and beach, was on the opposite corner of Lakewood as Birdtown, and was separated from the rest of the Lakewood grid by winding roads. Between 1900 and 1930 the whole city filled in between rich Clifton Park and working class Birdtown on narrower and narrower streets.

The city was filled with doubles. Doubles are up and down duplexes with porches, and Lakewood had miles of them. I read doubles were an innovation during the Progressive Era when activists worked to get working people out of tenements and into homes with yards to benefit the lives of the workers, especially the children. I can't imagine an era when so much was invested in low-income housing. It was the seed of what would grow into the decades when working class people had real power, when unions were strong in Cleveland and its inner-ring suburbs. The decay of these homes reflects the decay of that power.

They don't build new affordable housing anymore, and upkeep is not supported. Many of these doubles still have exposed lead and asbestos problems. Some are kept up well, some aren't. The streetcars are long gone.

Most of our work was in two slightly older west side Cleveland neighborhoods, Ohio City and Gordon Square. These gentrifying neighborhoods were packed with old Victorian homes, painted in purples and oranges, some cut up into apartments, but lumped in with poor Clevelanders with no work and rising rents. Edgewater Beach and Whisky Island bordered to the north, the brutal Cudell neighborhood just before Lakewood to the west and on the east, the west bank of the flats on the Cuyahoga.

All of it was Simon's territory.

In recent years, expensive cookie-cutter condos squeezed into the available space close to the lake. The neighborhoods get violent fast south of the tracks just a half-mile down from the lake, my old room being in a bad one. Gordon Square, both hipper and rougher than Lakewood, was the district between the cocaine condos and my old crack room. Its heart was Detroit and west 65th, thick with record stores and bookshops, boutiques, chic bars and restaurants, a restored movie theater, and galleries.

We spent a chunk of the spring in a house on Franklin Avenue facing the Franklin Castle. We got chills as our eyes caught the boarded-up black windows of the deranged Queen Anne structure. The Franklin Castle was built in 1881 by Hannes Tiedemann for his large family.

By the First World War, all the Tiedemanns were dead. No one quite knows how many rooms were in the Franklin Castle, and there were rumors of murdered children, maybe his wife went mad, maybe a housekeeper committed suicide... lots of stories, most of them loosely hung on some known fact.

German social clubs owned the place throughout the mid-twentieth century. The Germans were maybe Nazis, they say. In the 1970s a family lived with the ghosts—they performed an exorcism that didn't take. Over the last thirty years, it's stood empty. People have put millions into the Castle before abandoning it. It's *almost* been a restaurant, bed-and-breakfast, nightclub, and more, but fires, taxes and other things kept anything from working out.

A woman bought the Castle in the late nineties with plans to turn it into a bed-and-breakfast. But some shit went down, and she went to Canada, leaving the caretaker she'd inherited with the place to claim that it was his own, and that he was starting an exclusive club. He put up bogus web pages. Meanwhile, the Castle sank into disrepair. Dark rumors slithered around of porn being shot within the ruins.

The Castle faced us as we worked.

The house we worked in was cheery enough. No ghosts so far.

The money was better than I was used to, and Wendy wouldn't take rent from me. I got a phone. She gave me Adderall at work, and Stoli Vanilla on ice when we got home. Our friendship deepened. I got as used to her being around as anyone I'd ever been close to.

She said she kept away from Simon and his people, but she kept her ear on the situation by talking on the phone with Tasha, fresh out of the joint and back in touch with Simon, though she was living clean now. Tasha told Wendy that Liz's brothers, what was left of the Vickers family, were going after a whole other crew for what happened, some Puerto Rican guys. Vickers shot some guy, but they only got him in the thigh, and then the Puerto Ricans killed one of the Vickers's young dealers, not even knowing why they were attacked in the first place.

I'd taken anthropology at Cuyahoga Community College when I was in my twenties. I did some independent research hours studying the Dani. According to what I read, and the 1960s films I watched in the school's library, The Dani people of Papua, New Guinea have lived for millennia in an unusually peaceful, safe and healthy environment, uniquely free from predators and snakes and disease, and rich with sweet potatoes, bananas and pigs. They had ritual pig feasts, dances and elaborate funeral rites. They had adapted so successfully and lived in such a relatively benevolent environment that they've been able to maintain their culture for millennia. But they still had that existential human itch to dash utopia, so they practiced the ritual of endemic warfare.

Long ago, they chose to identify not with the immortal snake, but rather with birds who, like us, die. Their war was a game played to injure, insult or very occasionally kill someone from the other tribe, rather than for land or to vanquish the enemy. They needed the enemy. The war was always to avenge the last killed, so they take turns occasionally killing young men. All women close to men who died in battle had a finger segment chopped off to memorialize their grief.

Maybe war itself started the same way all over, or maybe that's overly simplistic bullshit. Maybe the battles are a way to focus a community, to keep the human population at a sustainable level. Cultures like the Dani last longer than cultures like ours. I wish they didn't have to fight. Their wars are at least better than our wars, because each time one precious life is lost, the whole village moans and cries for days in mourning. The segments of women's fingers are burned, and the ashes are offered to the ghost. They know fingers and hands are connected to each other and the universe. The loss of each man, and each woman's finger are felt in the whole group.

Here and now, we were at war in Iraq and Afghanistan. For no better reason than the Dani, truly for worse reasons, to increase the wealth of a few people. More people died. And not only brave young warriors who chose to fight were dying, but also young children, old women, anyone in the way. And the young men and women who signed up to fight often did so because they couldn't find any other way to live in America.

Unlike the Dani, we didn't face or feel the dead. The dead were far away and veiled behind screens of reality television and commercials for fried meat, toilet cleaner and sugar-rolled bread stuffed with cheese.

Recently, finger cutting has been banned, but in many ways, the Dani are living as they have always lived. Here on the west side, the situation had developed into a senseless back and forth of retaliation acts. Or really, a back and forth in order to make sense. A rhythm.

"How is Tasha is, is she…" I sat on the tub, as Wendy worked the walls. Hanging out with Tasha last summer felt like years ago. I still felt bad she went down for trying to steal clothes for me.

"Get this," Wendy blinded her eyes and stepped back from the primer for a minute, "Liz's brothers, the Vickers crew, have *united* with Simon, even!"

"What…" I nearly fell into the tub.

"Oh *yeah*, Billy and Jeff are dim bulbs, man. Else they just see what they want to see. It's not like they haven't benefited in a way, right?"

"Jesus."

"Dude," she got in close and quiet, "they did *Sig*." Wendy stepped back, nodding and smiling wide.

"Are you serious? No." I remembered the old man ceremonially

165

passing the crack pipe way back that first day I smoked.

Wendy was laughing, amazed, relieved we were off the radar. But to think of Liz's brothers unknowingly aligned with her killer, and Sig, so well respected, killed. Innocents shot. Tasha wrapped up in it somehow. I felt sick. "But, they all seemed to love Sig. They *venerated* him."

"No honor among these thieves. He was in the way. They tried to get him to move on down to Florida, but the old man was holding onto some critical links in the chain. I know, it's fucked, but that makes it all the better for us to be out of it, right?"

"We slipped into a different future."

"The best part is, now don't worry, Tasha doesn't know shit, she thinks you're dead, too, but the best part is, she said Simon said he felt *bad* about how things ended up with you, isn't that great? He feels *guilty*, not pissed, not justified."

"In ordering my death."

"Right."

"Uh, okay. You didn't hear anything about a spa, did you?"

She turned from the liquid wall, "Wha-no. You on some other frequency, Alice?"

I smiled. I felt like a maniac. It seemed like Liz had been dead years, also, like she was dying over and over again.

"Wendy, do you know Johnny Maker? Have you seen him since all this?"

"Johnny doesn't have anything to do with this shit. How the fuck to you know Johnny?"

I left the bathroom and walked over to the window in the hallway. I looked out at the painted flat black windows of the Franklin Castle. I could see Johnny walking out the door that day at the party. What if I'd followed him. What if I'd gone clean on my own, never gone back to Liz's apartment. What if I never even drank again, just walked away from this house, down Franklin Avenue into the what. Wendy called me by my fake name. I wondered what Johnny was doing, if he knew about Sig and the rest of it. Where was Johnny Maker? I pressed my hands into the sill and my nose into the glass. Was he lying on his back in a bed somewhere blocks away in a small apartment, looking up at the cracks in the ceiling? Thinking maybe, he could turn into a shadow and slip inside them and away into another dimension—maybe into the trench at the bottom of the ocean, witness to the volcanoes and worms in motion there right now.

13

Am I the Sender or Am I the Receiver?

In May, Wendy started in at some community garden she'd been involved with before her criminal life, and I went with her. It wasn't yet the May I hungered for. The sky lingered low, cold, clammy and opaque grey. I shivered in cold sweat as Wendy, Cher and I overturned the hard earth.

"Margot?" I knew that voice—Henry! I turned to see my old friend approaching us. The young-looking forty-year-old with a crooked smile and sandy hair ran up to me and we hugged.

Wendy jerked her head up, her red bandana falling to the ground. She'd had me to herself for two months now, and I hadn't heard my true name since detox weekend. Cher looked up too. Wendy jogged over to us.

Henry asked where I'd been, and I told him I guess I'd been keeping to myself since the divorce.

"Oh, yeah, I'd heard you left Georgie, but why'd you leave us?"

Us. It felt good to see his face. They all came back. My music friends, my best friends. The hot sweaty shows in Bela Buda and Scum. Drinking beer in the dark. On Wednesdays, on Fridays, for years. Henry was one of my closest friends, and it was as if I'd forgotten.

I started to shake. Why hadn't I gone *to* them instead of *away* from them? There was no way to undo all the bad things I'd done.

"*Oh* Henry, I don't know, I was depressed, he left me, and I just wanted to be alone I guess, I couldn't play, I guess."

"Margot, you could have come by just to *be*, you wouldn't have had to perform. But. I'm sorry, I should have called you, too." He pulled out his phone.

"Well, I don't have that phone anymore."

"Who's this." Wendy kept her eyes on me but jerked her hand toward Henry.

I introduced them. Henry explained he had a plot in the garden here, too. It was practically in Bela Buda's back yard, he worked there and lived in an apartment above. All of it, the library, our house, were all so close together.

"Why do you keep calling her Margot?" said Cher.

Henry smiled, shook his head and looked at me, bemused. I looked at Wendy.

"Her name," Wendy put her hands on her hips and looked past Henry, "Is Margot Alice. Life changes, et cetera. Now she goes by Alice."

"Well, *Alice*, can I get your new number?"

"No," said Wendy, and we all looked at her. "Go on Alice, that compost won't spread itself." She jerked me by my arm and swatted my ass. My face flushed, quick hot tears jumped to my eyes. I turned toward the garden. I couldn't look at Henry. A brown rabbit slipped through a hole in the fence near a man and boy working their plot. The man looked at me with an overly tender expression, a bullshit expression. Then he looked away.

"Hey, what the fuck was that?" said Henry.

Cher put her arm around my shoulder and walked me toward the garden.

Wendy said, "Just shut it and leave it, Mister Hipster. I'm this bitch's sponsor. Go on, get out, she'd have called you if she wanted to see you, right?"

Henry's voice, receding, angry: "Wednesday nights at Bela, Margot, you know where you've got friends."

In the garden Cher turned on Wendy. "What the fuck is that! You've got this girl under motherfucking lock and key!"

We stood on hard dirt. Wendy slung some shit about how she was keeping me away from my old drug friends, new life, etc.

"I'm not buying it, Wendy, I think you've got something freaky going on."

My stomach lurched with humiliation. "Cher, really, I appreciate your concern, but Wendy's right, I told her to keep me from the people I used to party with."

"*Bullshit* that boy's a crackhead. Bull*shit* on that shit. Probably doesn't party as much as the two of you do now—which by the way, is a pretty fucked up way to help someone get and stay 'clean'. He's a craft beer and fancy weed dude, easy to see. Plus, he hasn't seen you since before. I can *tell* he doesn't know she was on crack."

"You better mind your own, Cher." Wendy came up to her.

"I *am* minding my own." She pushed Wendy's hand off her arm and turned on me, "You fuck her?"

"What?"

"I said, do you fuck her? You fucking my girlfriend?" I saw the dried tear on Cher's left cheek. I'd never noticed it until Wendy told me, defensively, that Cher often had a dried salty tear on her left cheek. It was because she had to use drops for a sticky cornea, so it didn't stick to her eyelid and get torn. She'd had to use them four times a day for years, so she was careless about wiping it as it drizzled down her cheek, and so the tear lingered and dried. I saw the dry tear bare in the pale sunlight and looked away.

Wendy stepped between us. "Come on, Crazy, cool off, you know I don't go for white bitches."

The tender-faced man gestured to his son and they started putting their tools back in the community bin.

Cher pulled her hand as if to backhand Wendy, but then started laughing from deep in her belly. "What's that you say?"

"You heard me. I-don't-fuck-white-bitches." She pushed her insolent face out half-smiling at Cher. I stepped back. To the mulch pile, working the shovel with shaking hands.

"Oh, you are so hard, Wendy, you *are* a white bitch." Cher crossed her arms and tried to keep a straight face.

Wendy stepped up to Cher, whispered in her ear, touched her hip with a long finger, trailing up her body to her neck.

Cher doubled over laughing, and Wendy laughed too, looking at me, put her finger to her lips and winked. Something like jealousy and resentment and shame quivered up from my guts.

Cher laughed. She straightened up and put her arms around Wendy. "Wow, girl. You are a weird one."

A wind picked up across the brown patches of gardens, a wind with some heat in it. I opened and closed my hands to get my joints moving.

In the morning I woke short on sleep. An old feeling clung to me like a rash and kept me turning in my bed, but I couldn't shake it. I was angry. And no matter how I twisted my body, I couldn't cool it, couldn't contain it.

I didn't even want coffee because I felt like I had pepper in my skin. But I took a cup because we had to work. Wendy sat at the kitchen table reading an old anarchist zine that stunk like mildew.

I had to talk to her, but I didn't want to because I didn't want to lose control of my words. "Wendy. Yesterday in the garden."

"Yeah. Uh—hm." She didn't look up, but she was alert, and I knew she was listening closely. "What."

"You treated me like a dog. I don't know why I just took it, but I don't want it to happen again. And I don't know why you are... I guess I understand why Cher freaked out because I don't know why you are *keeping* me like this, treating me like this, and you don't even want to, be with me."

Now Wendy set the zine down and pressed it with her hands. She looked up, her cool eyes on me. "Is that what *being with someone* means to you? Keeping them? Treating them like a dog?"

"It's time for me to move on."

She came out of her chair with a start like a bird leaving a tree and with all the disaster of feathers and wings and dinosaur gullets and things she was on me, not touching but close, up in my face like an aggressor, but just breathing, looking me over. She put her hand up to touch me, then put it down. "You can't go."

I almost pushed her away, but I knew her, I knew her body, and I knew she was tensed and would fight. "Oh yes. I appreciate everything you have done for me, but I *can* go. I am the one who survived my life, Simon, my addiction, my divorce, and other things." The vision of Wendy before me faded into pixelated grey rage. "Getting *raped* by some lazy arrogant boy! *You* did not survive *for* me. I survived and I will survive. I can work. I can make my own money. I can make my own meaning. I have art. I have music. I can find my own way. I've been born more times before, I don't need you."

"Fair enough. It's true. True."

"I don't need you."

"True. But. I can only protect you from Simon if you stay with me."

"It's a threat. I can protect myself if you don't tell him."

"No." She bit her lower lip and turned away. "No, I mean, I *could* tell him. Maybe I'm desperate to keep you here. I am the one who needs you." I could not see her eyes. But her hands fiddled with the front of her overalls, and suddenly, I was flooded with sick compassion for her. Maybe she was trying to manipulate me, or maybe she was being sincere about needing me, but in a flash, I saw they were the same thing.

"Wendy. You have Cher. I can't stay here forever."

"Yeah, I love Cher. But I just feel *good* when you're close to me. That's the only way I can explain it."

"How can I feel good being close to you if you treat me like shit and threaten to sic Simon on me if I leave?"

Still turned away, she put her hands to her face. "I'm sorry—when I get scared, I get mad. Please stay. I'll be good to you. I won't let anything bad happen to you."

"Okay, well, I will stay a month or two then, because really, I need to get my head together, and get some money together. Okay, Wendy? But come summer, I'll probably head out to New York or Philly for a while, stay with some friends out there or something."

She turned and looked at me, looked over my face, I could feel her eyes moving over me. "You can stay as long at you want." She smiled. "You're a great partner, Alice."

I didn't like that she called me Alice, but I liked that she called me partner. I liked her, most of the time. I felt good being close to her, too. But sometimes it felt like shit.

The days grew longer, and I remembered myself. Something was brewing in the twilight. I needed to get to a show. Sudden desperation hit me like thirst, blinded me: what had I been missing out on? What was going on? My pulse was thick, and I felt beautiful. I needed to be in a dark venue with a drink, I needed to see what people were playing. I needed to play, too, I needed the stage that was just a part of a floor, but also a sacred (safe) space.

I heard back from Noam. He and his girlfriend were going to have a baby! He said I should call the folks, that they were doing better with money, maybe even they could fly me out there. I wanted it, but the thought of them paying flooded me with guilt. My mother's voice in my ear—I would be, too ashamed to tell her my life. I said maybe, in a few months. I couldn't see it.

We went to work. The smell of the warming earth and the wind off the lake and the trees green again made my heart ache. I had spring fever in my head and when we got to the job, I lingered in front of the Franklin Castle. Children died there. On the other side of the year, the Castle thrilled with *Duende*. In that distant season of Autumn to live fully is to do the Argentinian Tango with Death by the glow of burning candles dancing in grinning pumpkins, kicking through the decomposing leaves releasing particles of transmutation into the smoky crisp air. In October the Castle is a metaphor made from earth and stone, a tall black Victorian death-poem. A mechanical Valentine.

But now, in May, with the robins nesting and the fat smell of lilac in the air, the Castle projected a sweet sickness, broke my heart, reminded me of the slippery transient nature of being. The Castle suffered on a cross. I stumbled.

14

Angelo

"W here ya goin?" Wendy sat on the couch, absorbed in an issue of *Adbusters*. The cover showed a woman looking at her face in the mirror and read: *Reversing the Catastrophe of F-i-x-e-d Meaning.*

"I'm going to Bela Buda."

"No." Her eyes stayed on the pages.

I stood over her. "I need this." I wore heavy black eyeliner and red lipstick. I didn't fuck with foundation anymore, just let my freckles be. I wore so much eyeliner that shadow and mascara seemed redundant. Lots of lavender and patchouli oil. I had one foot out the door.

She looked up at me. Then she stood up and put her arms around me. I never realized she was so tall. She'd only ever held me in bed. She smelled like sand. Her neck was bare. "Alice," her lips buzzed my hair, "precious one. Shining, brilliant one. You could get hurt out there." She pushed back and laughed it off, dry long laughs.

I tried to laugh back but it came out a hiss. "You give me a new name, but I have a long history in this town." I told her not to worry, I just needed that one place I could go to, on my own. I told her it was not the kind of place anyone related to the situation would be, and I

175

was in my disguise, dark ironed hair and flowers, not red frizzy hair and black, so, even if they saw me on the street, they wouldn't know me.

"Not even midnight. Be home by eleven."

"Okay."

"No look..." She gripped my jaw and what was it in her eyes? Fear or desire? I could only see in so far. She softened up a bit and ran her hand on my skin. "It's not just Simon, remember, Vickers are out there, too. Those boys come out when the weather gets nice. It could mean all fuck else if you don't follow house rules. Eleven."

"Yeah. Eleven." I thought, maybe I should just stay in, but my feet pulled me out the door.

My legs moved me through the neighborhood. On this eternally new kind of day, the sky fat and wide as it can be within its border of black oaks and maples, the warming earth released the scent of earth rising. The sunset stretching deeper into the day. And this new night, just violet and periwinkle slipping into deepest blue. The air...*going to the show air*... the electricity of the air. Twenty years of anticipatory nights flooded back to me. *Going to shows.* A flash from ten years before, flying down the highway to a show on the east side, meeting up with a guy I'd just started seeing, but driving my own car there, late summer, David Bowie on the tape, "Star Man", and then Wire on the flip side. "The 15th." Gliding crimson lipstick on in the rear-view mirror. A night to ride the sky.

Moving through the early night, I felt sure and awake. Wow—life is still happening. But coming up on Bela Buda, seeing people I knew from another life standing out front smoking, I faltered. I felt as self-conscious as an eighth grader. Quivering. The neon floated gently into the soft grey street.

It was a funny feeling: with this straight dark hair and terrible green glasses, there *were* people out front who didn't recognize me. It had been a long time. People come and go. Sometimes peripheral people move to the center and vice versa. *This guy*, with the long ashen face, whose eyes caught on me for a sec, then moved back to his companion, *that guy*, tall with tight curly hair, who did the same. Faces I'd known, names I'd forgotten.

I stepped into Bela Buda and swallowed my heart. The smell of coffee and beer and spice. Inside, it was as if I had been gone a month rather than a year and a half. Long enough to feel there had been a fold in the relationship, but still so close, so present. The months and years I'd spent in this dinky little venue, conversations in the black pleather booths, afterhours with Henry and Rocky behind the bar, looking up into the pressed tin ceiling during a rumbling noise set, feeling the set in my neck. The people were still here. They had not been suspended in glass the last year and a half. A dorky younger guy nodded at me, his hair was long and shaggy now, a woman with a half-shaved head I kind of knew checked me out, trying to place me.

There were people I'd hoped would be here who weren't, and other people I didn't know who seemed like regulars. No one was set up yet. There were maybe a dozen people there, really, but the venue was so small, and I was so raw that their presence overwhelmed me. I headed toward the safety of Henry behind the bar.

At once, two people said, *Margot—is that you?* Then looked at each other and laughed.

Nicolas and Paloma! They took turns hugging me. Nicolas was an industrial noise musician from Painesville—a small gothic factory town way far out, past the eastern suburbs—he had long gold hair in a rope with ties all the way down. Paloma was a tape manipulator with two grown daughters. She was beautiful with long raven hair and sharp eyes. They took a tent with them, so they could stop anywhere

177

they wanted to. They smiled easily.

Nicolas kept looking at me with his mouth open. "Dude, where have you been? What happened to you?"

I took off the glasses. "Man, it's good to see your face! I just had to drop out for a while, you know?"

"Yeah. Yeah. I hear you."

I felt lightheaded and needed a drink as Nicolas was in my face full of stories and schemes and jokes, and Paloma laughed. She took Nicolas's arm. "Dude, give her a minute!"

We went up to the bar, and Henry was there. He gestured to me, and I slipped behind the bar, back home like no time had passed.

How many hours I'd spent drinking behind this bar with Henry! And drunkenly working the cash register and taps and espresso machine while he went to talk to some new girl. I'd argue with Georgie about going out, but I made it out every Wednesday, and behind Henry's bar at Bela Buda was the safe spot. In this way, I was close to people. In this room. With darkness, alcohol, loud noise between me and other people. The bar between me and other people. Or I'd stand in the corner between the bathrooms and the stage where I could see the whole room. And then go home to Georgie, who would be there smoking cigarettes in bed, kicking at me to *stay on my side of the bed.*

"What's up with that woman?" Henry said to me.

"Who?" I'd drank a can of Pabst fast and was on my second.

"From the garden—what the fuck is her problem?"

I put my hands up, shrugged, and looked around. "Henry, these paintings are...wow!"

Bela Buda looked great. Henry explained that a guy we knew had gone into the woods for a year and came back with these, the biggest, baddest paintings I'd ever seen up in the little place.

Bela Buda was a coffee shop, but they also sold beer, art and noise.

After hours Henry locked the door, and the party went on in the dark. Art rotated monthly. Now, broad rough paintings covered the walls from floor to ceiling. It was like my dream. Vivid deep blue and magenta.

Henry told me our friend had nailed into the walls, and the owners were pissed. The paintings filled the space: burnt gold, phthalo blue, all flowing from ephemeral mist into the sharpness of evil faces splashed in strange light. The fauvist style paintings transmuted Bela Buda into a cave inhabited by breathing spirits in passages lit with low green fire. Our friend had pasted poetry written when he lived in a bus on a small farm in West Virginia. The scraps of verse were pressed alongside thanksgiving turkeys from his childhood dreamscape. Pictures of his mother and father and sister were carved in with dark paint, the mother's eyes lit with joy at the newborn him, but her upper lip and nose cut off (Liz's face flashed, with the blood at her mouth) But there were lighter spirits, too. Fairies crouched in corners. Rosy cheeked boys.

More people came up to the bar and looked surprised to see me, and they said sweet things to me, and some reached across to hug me. The green glasses sat on the cooler. I grabbed another Pabst as Henry sold them drafts.

"No, Margot. What's the deal. Why was that woman treating you like her indentured servant?"

"She was just fucking around, she has a weird sense of humor. I'm sorry she was rude to you, Henry. Plague Mother!" One of my favorites was setting up, an old friend, harsh noiser, power electronics. My heart leapt. What could I say to Henry about Wendy? What was there to say. I didn't have a cover for this end.

"Right. Well, if you want to talk about it. Here I am."

"I'm glad."

Lucy walked in, slash of chestnut-black hair slicing at her jawline,

179

laughing. Lucy looked great, even better than the day when she'd told me about Spider Moon Fest.

A man stood by her. The striking man I'd seen at Autumn Villa. Henry turned to me, crossed his arms. "It's fucked up. But I'm glad you're here. But what's up with her calling you Alice?"

My eyes caught on Lucy's man. His face was set. He carried himself with noble posture. His eyes flickered around the room, agitating me. He'd held the door for Lucy, and now he pulled out a chair for her.

His hair was shaved up one side and hung to his neck in dark cool waves on the other side. He wore an electric blue feather earring. He'd worn glasses, I remembered, when I'd seen him before, but tonight his face was bare. He was in black, but for the earring and shirt, both sudden blue. Our eyes met for three beats: I almost remembered something, but then Lucy spied me and pulled him across the room and back behind the bar.

Henry played Skin Graft's "Dystrophy" while Plague Mother finished setting up. It felt good to hear the popping dark menace. It hit me good like the beer. (I was glad I'd swallowed a couple of Cher's Vicodin before leaping back into this.)

Lucy's bangs were short and her face long. Her mouth was set hard in a grim smile as she squeezed behind the bar after me with open arms. Lucy had a realtor vibe. She squeezed me, but then we were clearly in Henry's way, so I pulled her out the side door. The Moon was big and sweet in the sky. Lucy held me at arm's length and smiled sideways at me. Her serious man stood just behind her watching us from under leggy lashes.

"So?" She asked me.

"Yeah?"

"ARE-you-going-to-play-the-Spider Moon Fest? I've been hoping you'd come back? I've been waiting to hear from you? You look great by the way. What's up with the hair? I like the short flowy dress, *tasty*."

I felt shy. "Thanks. I've been working a lot, doing yoga. Herbal teas. Like I said before, I will play. But, I need to get my hands on another guitar. I should be able to. By the end of June." I danced from foot to foot.

She jumped and clasped her hands to her heart. The way she looked at me with some pity, I wondered what all she knew. Maybe she felt superior because my husband had left, maybe Henry had told her I was Wendy's dog—why was I thinking that way? "Margot honey, it's so good to see you, you were looking a little, tired, when I ran into you before, and then you ditched me that night—I was worried! Are you still working as a maid at Autumn Villa?"

The man stepped up. She hadn't introduced him. "Are you...Margot Jones?" He held out his hand. His eyes were oceans, the same living blue-green.

"I am." I shook his hand.

"Angelo Qamar." His stiff expression broke into a quick smile that lingered as he held onto my hand, and I smiled too. "I saw you before, I saw you play years ago at Mahall's 20 Lanes just before OIF VII. You were phenomenal. When I was in Iraq, I looked you up on Myspace. I hit you up, but you didn't write back. I'm eager to book a bunch of shows this year. I just got back to Cleveland last fall. I was wondering if I'd see you around, Lucy said she knew you." He nodded as he spoke rapid-fire.

He'd seen me and remembered me! Wailing and drooling on the floor no doubt. "What's *ohaief*..."

Lucy was all business. She took Angelo's arm. "The war. Operation Iraqi Freedom. '07."

He smiled and ran his fingers through the longer half of his hair, "I got sick of that military cut. It grows fast." He looked down, shy.

Noise rumbled up, and we ran back inside.

From the corner of my eye, the door opened, and a blonde walked in. Fear leapt, but no, it wasn't Wendy. Relief. I felt guilty, but man, what pleasure in having a few hours away from her. We'd gotten tight, but, away from her I realized that being around her—being Alice—kept me in a constant low-level alert mode. I felt free back at Bela again.

Mona Cost opened her band Red Liver's set with a short solo set. She gripped a black suitcase. The sounds were brutal and satisfying, roaring boils with high-end shrieks and gurgles. She put a contact mic in her mouth and leaned into the case. OOHHHHH NNOOOOO. She stomped a foot. Her black hair hung almost to the floor. Behind her on the wall was a painting of a blue door.

Rocky, my friend who worked the bar with Henry sometimes, popped out of the bathroom and jumped onto her own suitcase to join Mona. I was so happy to see the little sprite! I thought Red Liver was a three-piece with Mona's husband on shit-guitar, but I saw him sulking in a corner, not playing tonight for some reason. I looked around and saw other friends: tall shaggy Murder and his best friend Juniper the dandy sucking on a toothpick, sneering and nodding at the set.

They finished. We clapped and hollered, and they saw me and waved, and I realized to some people, maybe it didn't seem like I'd been gone so long. I grabbed another beer from the case and wrote it down on my tab. I felt good. I asked Henry quietly about Angelo.

"He's good. He's got a grindcore band, or cross-over maybe, thrash? But they're good, they've got a drummer with a double bass drum, but really, they've been turning everybody onto metal. Even Lucy!" He made the goat-horn sign and transacted with a customer.

"So, he and Lucy are into each other pretty hard?"

"They've been hanging out, I don't know. He's a solid dude. He's been booking shows, runs things nice and tight. He's lived all over, but he's from here, I think, originally. He loves noise, all harsh music,

182

he loves crossing things, very eclectic."

"Good. Yeah, we used to try to mash things up, you know, when Noam and I first moved here. I'm psyched to hear about Angelo's band. That's so cool. And these paintings are so cool, oh my god, they've got to stay here!"

"Yeah, he damaged the walls pretty bad, so they might have to. Hey, it's so good to have you around, M!" He put an arm around me and gave me a squeeze. "I have a welcome back present for you."

He gave me a little pack of wrinkled up mushrooms.

That night I woke in a terror to realize I'd left my fake glasses behind the bar. I jumped, but Clarence stayed put on my pillow like a snail. I petted him till my heartbeat slowed. Wendy didn't say anything to me the next day, didn't ask me about going out. Nothing.

I went back to Bela Buda the next Wednesday and found Angelo there alone. My flat-ironed hair was starting to kink in the warming, slightly humid air and my roots were coming in red. I was happy to see Orange Luna Temple playing. Drums, horn and guitar, but like nothing else, lots of quiet, whistly places, then rises and crashes, too. The days were longer and stronger and there was still violet light in the sky when I got to Bela. I got a drink from Rocky, and when I turned Angelo was there. He was wearing a wildly painted shirt, an amoeba or something.

"Margot."

"Yes. Angelo."

"I was wondering if you were interested in something."

"Yes. Yes?"

"Would you like to play a solo set in Elyria? My band is playing. If

183

not that's cool. That's cool. It's May 25th. At the Tick Tock Tavern. On Belleview."

Uh oh, didn't sound very noise-friendly. Elyria was a mysterious little town with a waterfall maybe a half-hour west of Cleveland. Elyria was suffering violence. Suffering with poverty and meth and street gangs. The kind of place experimental musicians usually got boos and beers tossed at them. "Oh yeah, I'd love too! I mean, I haven't played in a year and a half, it's the longest I've gone without playing ever, but I'd love to! Oh. I'd need to figure out a ride? I..."

"Oh yeah, yeah, sure, of course. Cool. Also, Lucy said you were a *pain*ter? Or an artist, yes-no? Would you want to work on a flier with me for the Spider Moon Fest?"

"Sure yeah! That would be cool." My face hurt with smiling.

We made plans to hang out at his place Sunday night. He lived in a house just a couple blocks up from me and Wendy, up on Wascana. He got us a couple of beers. It had been a long time since a good-looking man had bought me a beer. When I was a single kid, the guys were all too broke. More like twelve pack cans in a parking lot that I'd bought with tips.

He said, "So, have you talked to Lucy? Dude, I don't know what I did, I fucked up. I don't know, she won't talk to me. I messaged her on Facebook, and she responded, but then when I asked her about coming out tonight, she didn't answer. I was hoping she'd be here." He looked at the door.

"I don't know, I wouldn't worry, I mean, I'm sure she's crazy about you. Lucy is kind of mysterious. I've known her almost ten years, and I still don't know much about her personal life."

Angelo was fine and strange. I could feel energy and enthusiasm coming off him like heat. Lucy was crazy to blow this dude off. I felt close to him right away, he was that kind of person, and the way he talked about his friends and Lucy, with love and respect, I felt I could

184

trust him. His heart was right there in his voice.

The feeling made me see things I wanted to paint, webs of lines and color: insect wings wrapped over the thick yellow of a setting sun, windows with melting glass and unnamed animals looking in. Moons and starry trees. Our talking made me laugh more than I had since before my brother left Cleveland. And this talking with Angelo made me want to jam. We talked about Lucy, her nature. He told me the history, in detail, of their brief relationship. But I heard future collaborations of blood-rhythm and atonality. I heard the Summer Nights ahead, the Shows!

He brought us more beers and handed me one, and when that was gone, we were sharing his, and I felt shimmers every time our bare forearms touched. My arms had been covered for the longest winter of my life.

"So your last name, what is it again?" I said.

"Qamar."

"Is it Arabic?"

"Maltese. My great-grandfather moved here after World War I. He'd been in the Italian army. He helped build Tower City in the twenties. FDR put him into an internment camp. Because he was a fascist. But still. But that's good, on your part, Maltese *is* a Semitic language." He cocked his head and looked at the stage, which wasn't a stage but just the part of the room where the musicians stood. "Oh dude look at *thaaat*, hell yeah." He nodded at the dude setting up his sampler for the next set. "I've got to get one of those."

He looked at me. "I've lived more of my life in Asia than in Cleveland. That's why I joined the army when I finally came back. To re-assimilate. That's how the indigenous people in Malaysia assimilate."

I asked him why. Were his parents teachers or in the military?

"Missionaries. Cultists. They are dead to me."

His mouth shut, his eyes on the painting of the blue door. I wanted

185

to bring back his smile. "Have you ever heard of *jenkem?*"

"Oh yeah, sure, in Malaysia dudes would put a coconut shell over cow shit and get fucked up. " He took the beer from my hand, drank, and passed it back.

I laughed. He stayed stoic and watched the duo play. I swayed a little to the abstract rage. The next time we shared the bottle, our fingers lingered, touching for two sweet seconds.

After the set we cheered. "Well, I don't think *I* could get off on methane gas. I'm very sensitive to bad smells, I love real jasmine and thyme." The lights came up and Henry put on *The Wu Tang Clan*. I didn't tell Angelo that since getting off crack, I'd become more sensitive than ever to smells and everything else. My heart was a rat with white blind eyes. Stroking it into something else. Stoking it into a new animal with fire in her eyes.

He said, "I've always liked things that smelled nice. When I was ten, I went around picking flowers and collecting them in a jar because I wanted to make my own potpourri."

"Really?"

"But it just turned into green mush." His blue eyes flickered and I felt touched.

"Oh no, really? Aw." I was smiling so hard that I could feel my lips twitching, but I couldn't stop. Our faces were very close.

"Really, really." He nodded and took the empty bottle from my loose hand and walked up to the bar for more.

Angelo and I were fast friends.

Me, Angelo, Rocky and Henry bullshitted ourselves into afterhours. The two guys passed around a bowl as Rocky and I drank the inventory. I felt bright and tall.

I was telling them about *The Last Hours of Ancient Sunlight* by Thom

Hartman with the fever of a convert. And we talked about shows.

A knock at the door.

Police or ?

Henry looked up like an animal.

It was Wendy in a raincoat, her fried-white hair flying around like Debbie Harry's. (I remembered what they guy at that party called her, then: dead-eyed Debbie Harry.)

Henry would have rather it been the police. He looked at me, she banged, he crossed the room to let her in.

She tore past him into me. "IT'S PAST THREE WE HAVE TO WORK TOMORROW YOU WANT ME THINKING SOMETHING HAPPENED TO YOU." She said it fast and loud and gripped my arm.

"Remember that spring-time air smell that makes you so crazy is not the smell of growing things, but the stink of decomposition." She spat the words at my drunk, stunned face.

I knew what she was afraid of, but the others didn't, and I couldn't tell them.

"I have to go, guys, sorry, I'll see *you* Sunday, I'll see *you* Wednesday… " My smile had an ill fit as she pulled me out of Bela Buda. They watched me leave in shock dulled by alcohol and weed.

15

Poison Arrow

Each bump in Wendy's truck kicked in the hangover threats gnawing in my gut. I wished I was pissed, but I was just scared. Waves of nausea registered as fear inside me. I'd had a dream in the night that stuck. Now we were on our way to a short job near Liz's old place. I finally had sunglasses again. Suddenly, it was near a hundred degrees and muggy as fuck. The very air pulling on my hangover.

One nice thing: we'd stopped at the library on the way to check our email and I'd looked up Qamar, Angelo's last name. It means *Moon*.

She pulled at my hair. "What's this? It's growing in. You need to cover this shit."

I yanked my head back, the aches clanging with the layers of my brain. "You're worse than my ex-husband. Why did you have to talk to me like that last night?"

Wendy's sunglasses were mirrored, opaque. She wore a stained and faded blue ball cap with her ponytail sticking out the back. She frowned as she lit a cigarette. My stomach lurched at the burnt hair smell of the Camel knock-off.

I'd dreamed of a bear, musky dog-bear breath on the back of my neck, a bear tearing me to pieces, in Liz's apartment.

"When you start smoking, Wendy? Fuck. I know I was late, but man, you're not keeping us with a low profile when you come in on folks like you did at Bela Buda last night."

"You need to color that Ronald MacDonald hair, Alice. Shit's too loud."

"You look like a fucking cop in those glasses."

"Here's the deal. When you're with those overgrown kids at that hipster café, you've got a special cover. You tell them, I'm your girlfriend, very obsessive and possessive. You tell them, no, you can't date them."

"Wha— Cher's your girlfriend. Wendy, you're making things too complicated, okay? I just want to go out a couple times a week. I can't date anyone anyway until I get my shit together. I'll keep my head down."

"Well, you can go out only if you say, I'm your girl, and so you have to come back to me at night and that's why."

"Okay. Sure. But you'll keep Cher off me if any of these wires get screwed up, right? Covers and covers?"

"Don't worry about it." She actually looked pretty cool in her mirrored sunglasses

"Wendy—what about the cops?"

"What."

"Are they investigating, about Liz?"

"Ha! No. No more than they are investigating about that kid who got hit at the house party. CPD could not give less of a fuck."

I closed my eyes and breathed, trying to cool out my body.

"Margot, right over there, in the parking lot of that rec center? Police recently shot a twelve-year-old boy with a toy gun. Black children all over getting shot."

I looked out the window as we passed low rows of ratty brick apartments, the black house that was a mosque, the 216 Bike Shop, the hexagonal chapel with dark city glass leaning over a parking deck, and then we crossed the tracks and drew closer to the lake.

It was good to have a break from our regular house across from the Franklin Castle. There wasn't much for me to do, Wendy was just painting one simple wall a soft pink-beige. I handed her rollers, rags, etc. My fears and pains were slipping away as I stretched and let the pain pills and caffeine kick in. I was excited about nursing my hangover. "Hey, will we have enough bread to get some bread? I mean, want to go out for Mexican or get some pizza or something? Or Thai? Yeah, that little place on Madison. I love that place. Thai Kitchen."

She stepped down from the ladder, shrugged and pulled out another cigarette.

"You asked when I started smoking? Well, smoking *again*, rather, it's not something you pick up at this age, right?"

I nodded.

She turned to the door and then looked back at me, came over and embraced me. I let myself go soft in her arms. I wanted her to touch me. She put her mouth to my ear. "Last night I ran into Tasha. She said Liz's brothers won't let this shit die down. The Vickers aren't as happy about joining up with Simon as he is about joining up with them. Well, especially Billy. Billy's been acting crazy, not convinced the guy Simon pointed to was the one who did Liz. I think you and me might need to leave town after all."

She stepped back and looked at my mouth. She put her finger there when I started to say—

"You're lucky I let you out at all. If Simon or the Vickers see you alive, they'll know something weird is going on. I'll dye your hair

190

black again, and you tell those boys you're spoken for."

"Stop. I want to go to Liz's place, I want to go back."

"What the actual fuck?" Wendy pressed the AC button even though it was broken.

"I had a dream, it was so real, it was there."

Wendy drove past Liz's building and didn't slow, didn't look. "You need to erase her and that building and all of it from your mind. Delete."

"Some people believe in a man in the sky, and some people believe that dreams are just brain-roof clatter," my throat swelled too easily these days, "I don't believe either of those things, I believe in dreams. Yoga says everything is real. Everything is alive."

"Pizza. Nap. That's what you need, Alice."

"No, I need to go there, I need to see, I feel like there's something there I'm forgetting."

"Dreams are bullshit, there is no 'underlying matrix of reality', like you go on about. It's just what you do, it's how you do people. Or nothing, maybe it's just nothing. When the light goes out, it's all over."

But the scent of the bear at the back of my neck lingered, and I knew I'd slip out and go back. When I could. The choice wasn't a choice but a bear claw lodged in my intestine.

Friday, I went back. We had no work that day, and Cher and Wendy stayed in bed late. Wendy came out to make some toast and tea, and told me they were working on their relationship, so I shouldn't expect to be seeing them. I told her I was going to take the long walk down to the beach and then catch the bus home later, if it got too late. I don't know if I was lying or telling the truth because the beach would have been a better place to go. But I walked right to Liz's instead. I had to go in.

I'd last spent time in that building at night, in the dark months of November, January, early March. Now everything seemed nicer. The bare oaks were suddenly fat with healthy green light. Spider webs glossed the surface of flat-topped bushes. Even the hallway smelled better, old wood, wood cleaner and coffee. The strange red wallpapered walls of the hallway seemed vintage and chic. People were at work. The building had the classier silence of the space between grandfather clock ticks. I remembered how good it seemed when Georgie and I first moved there, so much safer than my earlier Cleveland apartments with ceilings crumbling down and bathtubs that wouldn't drain and windows vulnerable to neighborhood thieves.

I'd forgotten how happy we were when we moved there that spring—it was a brief honeymoon respite from the violence of our marriage that came back stinking and heavy soon enough. Returning to the building to buy crack from Liz had wiped so many things away that were coming at me fast. And returning again to visit the ghost of Liz...

I'd had two more dreams of the apartment. One with a mural or projection of Liz on the western wall, and in the corner, a tiny door. The other was forgotten except for a voice lingering in my ear, something about an eclipse or ellipse, coming with a deep knowing that I had to revisit this place.

I didn't know if her place would be empty, or rented by new people or what. I don't know how I thought I'd get in.

I walked up to that door. It occurred in a flash that I'd dreamt this before, but I couldn't say how long ago.

My heart pounding at her door, like before but different. Heavy—as if I had done this to her. I was the killer.

The door opened. Mark looked at me.

I said, "ah'!"

He hopped back.

I jumped back too, my arm brushing the door of the old man's apartment. I recoiled with a shiver.

"You're dead." Mark pointed his index finger at me.

Standing between the old man's closed door and Mark, I looked at the floor, dizzy.

"I'm Alice."

"You were dead." He turned his head and smiled.

"I'm not who you think I am."

The apartment had an awkward entrance, like a *feng shui* poison arrow where the hallways connected at the peak of the teeny kitchen. I pushed past him into the hallway that led to the living room, as if moving through him were escaping him somehow.

I felt bad for just a pulse because he still looked off from his beating months back. A chunk of scalp bared stitches. He should have shaved the whole thing. And his mouth seemed different, like something bad had happened to teeth.

"Well, okay, Margot, I guess you're a survivor, too. I get it. Alice."

I walked around in a calm rage. Most of her shit was still all over the place. Magazines, paper plates, yellow cans of wood dusting polish with dirty rags on top. I've ruined everything just for this. (Angelo's deep lake eyes rose in my mind and my throat locked.) Stepping into the ruins.

All the windows were open. The air smelled like lilac, and the birds talked, and the squirrels barked. I thought of a small neighborhood library from my childhood. How different this space is after death and in the daytime. Her chair was gone, leaving a square of lighter floor in its place.

He saw me looking at the hole in the mess.

"What are you doing here?" I said.

"Evidence. They took the chair to evidence."

"Doesn't the landlord care you're here?"

"She was the landlord. This was her building."

"Right. What?" When I'd lived there the place was run by a management company. I had no idea Liz owned the building the whole time.

"The legal stuff is happening, but it'll go to my dad." He lit a cigarette with a match, making a flourish of blowing out the match and sucking deep. He had a bandage on his hand, from some more recent altercation? He shook his long cuff to hide it when he saw me looking. "Why are you here? I'm not holding. Obviously, that part of the operation has been relocated."

"I quit. I was just wondering." I sat down on the couch, surprised to feel my knees shaking, my hands shaking, my stomach shaking.

"And obviously…" he half twirled around to grab a black plastic ashtray and return, flicking the cigarette. He'd popped his collar, trying to look cool all alone in this trash. "Obviously, I'm not working for my dad, I'm *nothing* after what happened in January." Flicked again, nearly knocking his cherry off.

"After what happened. Like it was an accident. And like it happened to *you*." I felt my eye twitch. I realized it hadn't twitched all spring. I put my fingers to that place, to still the tiny muscles.

"He's trying to get me to go to *college*. For fuck's sake. Meanwhile, it's my job to clean out this dump." The room was filling with foul blue cigarette smoke.

"Is your dad… and your mom, opening a spa? Right?"

He just looked at me.

The walls were so yellowed that there was a big white square there, too, where her chair had been. No mural. No tiny door. I started to cry. I leaned forward and stroked the backs of my own calves, smooth and cold like milk. The sun shined on my skin. I leaned into my own

194

lap, my skirt blue, purple and green.

I didn't try to stop as he watched me. Sobbing with angry snot and ugly red face. I didn't care. I lurched up and held my hands at him in frustration. "My vagina burned like you put poison ivy in it."

On my feet, my two fingers, index and middle, in the hollow at the base of his throat. Suddenly, I had him with his back against the wall.

When I'd had the abortion, no one told me it would hurt. The embryo had only been growing for three weeks. I told Georgie I was ovulating. He said he would pull out. I wanted to remind him, but he'd be mad if I said anything. I held my breath the whole time, because I didn't trust him, and he came inside. After, he said, "Don't worry, we'll get the morning-after pill." But the pill didn't work.

They said it would be like having my tooth drilled. Numb. That's what I chose instead of the twilight sleep. Because I wanted to have a clear head. I didn't want to be out of it when I left the clinic and had to face the old white guys yelling at me to check my belly button and remember my mother and that I'd stopped a heartbeat.

I saw the circle. It was a circle in the ultrasound. They make you get an ultrasound in Ohio. I knew Georgie would twist this Living One and me into old, tired dogs over the next few years if I let this happen. It was so early on. I thought of it as bringing on the menses before the quickening, like women used to do in old times.

They said it wouldn't hurt, and they said there would be someone whose job it was to hold my hand.

The room was full of people. I'd swallowed a Valium and something else. They'd moved us from room to room, some with no windows, like chambers in an initiatory tank. Who were all the people in this room. They *have* to counsel you, in Ohio, they have to show you a model of the embryo, to discourage you. I said I wanted the abortion pill, but she recommended I do it in the clinic, it's quicker. I was glad, for it was quick. But at the clinic it's less like witchcraft, the Crone of the waning Moon, the flow of blood. No, at the clinic it was a *procedure*.

The pain opened up and felt like what it might have been, a spark of spirit getting torn from the darkness of my core. The pain was worse than being burned, or hit, or an infection deep inside. No one held my hand. The pain opened me up, and I finally saw the god I wanted to see on the ceiling, like Venus with the Lion's face, hair in lines like waves, a mammal face, a face that was all faces, beyond the hanging thing, Pan, all Animus, all living things at once, and individually squirming there as well. The creator that was also creation: *Creature*.

I said to someone, *hold my hand*—they said someone would hold my hand.

After the pain came nausea, rising up to my head, grey blood pressure plunging. Later I would realize I'd had a vasovagal response, maybe it isn't painful for other women, I don't know. But that day, no one acknowledged my pain.

Someone helped me into a wheelchair, and then I was on a bed recovering alongside a dozen or more other women in beds.

A sharp British woman, well past menopause, asked us, there were so many of us, how many would like birth control pills. Blurry eyed, we watched her pace the room, *Raise your hand if you want pills, pills.* I didn't want birth control pills. I'd been on pills since I was fifteen until the year before. I'd fallen in love with my natural body. I'd come to learn that birth control pills had killed my libido and likely caused a dangerous depression in my teenage years. I wanted condoms. Georgie wouldn't use condoms. The woman said, *well I guess you all want to come back here, we'll be seeing you again.* I wanted to kill her—push her face into the wall—break it.

Georgie walked me to the car. A man lunged at me and said, *Well, your baby will be dead forever.*

I got in the car. I told Georgie to leave in the morning. He laughed. In the morning, I told him to leave. He said to go make him coffee. *Chop-chop.*

I played a show only once after that. It all fell apart. I didn't play out again. I slept on the couch. Georgie slept soundly in the bed. He finally did leave a few months later, of course. I was relieved but couldn't cry.

I was crying now with my fingers pressed into the boy's neck.

He was holding his hands up in surrender. He coughed out, "I know, what I did was wrong? Okay, like, if I hurt you, I apologize."

I pressed deeper and walked him harder into the wall. *Het. Het. Het.*

Georgie and I had stopped at the voodoo shop after the clinic. I wasn't used to things like Valium then, so I felt strangely good, and the sun was bright that day. I bought a little kit for purification called, "Nuit's Mojo Bag."

Mark stumbled over some empty shoeboxes or some shit. Receipts on the table. Red and white boxes of Saltines. Cat food with maggots wiggling around.

"Where's the cat," I said. I moved him up against the wall with my elbow at his throat. I felt his Adam's apple move.

He gagged.

"Here," I pressed my hand over his mouth and nose, "do you know, my head smells like cinnamon." I jerked his head back into the wall hard. "GET OUT." I let him go, but he locked eyes with me. "GET OUT."

"No. This is my place. You need to leave. You're acting crazy."

After the voodoo shop we stopped in a dark cold Mexican restaurant the size of a living room, I drank dark cinnamon tomato soup. I wore thick pads that filled fast.

I said to Mark, "My dad said that when I was a child, my head smelled like cinnamon. My ex-husband listened to Neil Young, I told him once that it reminded me of when we got together, out in Arizona. I asked him if he thought of me when he heard 'Cinnamon Girl', he said no."

Mark held up a hand at me, he coughed a little, pointing his finger, "You need to go. I'm done listening to this. I don't need to take this. If you don't go, I'm calling the police."

"Did you hang out here when you were a kid?" I picked up a whistle. "Was this your toy? I can see you, running around here, underfoot, blowing this thing at people." I sat down on a little wooden chair, tears coming again, but cleaner this time.

I didn't kill a baby—I knew the small circle of life would be released, re-absorbed—I knew the physical being was smaller than a poppy seed. I didn't feel sorry for myself, either. I felt sorrow for my uterus and my cervix, down in the dark ocean of my body, innocently and independently creating inside me, and then, undergoing that pain, physical, and their own private sorrow. Silent organs breathing.

He put his hands down. "Look—I was just trying to calm you down. You were so stressed *out* that day."

A pop song from my earliest childhood screaming in my ear through the end of that marriage and again now. Waking up with it transmitted straight to my brain. Not the fortunate ones.

Mark said, "I just rationalized it, I told myself you weren't really asleep."

Out of tears. "I'm out." I stood up and headed for the door. Not ashamed about my crying, but relieved.

"Wait—are you going to do something?"

I stopped at the door, turned and looked at him. "Don't you even care about who really killed your aunt?"

"What do you know about it—do you know something?"

"Nothing." I held up my hands. "We're done."

"Well, I'll give Simon your regards, *Alice*. Showing up here. Crazy, crazy bitch."

I was up in his face again. "You do what you want Mark, but I've got ghosts all over this town. Triggered. You breathe a word of this, and you'll be getting hit on all sides, you'll never know what's coming."

He smoothed his hair, breathing heavily, he forced his lazy grin. "So *saucy*. I'll keep it under my hat for now, just to see what happens. Just so you know, it's under my hat if I need it."

I made it to the corner, close to the bus stop before I threw up in the bushes.

16

Dog Tags

Wendy stayed at Cher's the rest of the weekend until Sunday afternoon when she came home with her hair cropped short. She stood in the doorway of my room. "I like your hair."

"You've always liked pretty butches, haven't you, Alice?"

I blushed and felt an awful rush. "You and Cher work everything out?"

She kept her eyes on me, looked into me.

I was listening to Leonard Cohen's "Hallelujah" and getting ready to go to Angelo's. I was thinking about him, about how much I liked him, and about how scared I was. The song gave me courage, turned me on.

"Where're you going?"

"I told you. That guy Angelo's. We're going to work on a flier together."

Wendy got up in my face. "I don't think that's a good idea at all, Alice. Why don't you just stay in with me. I got some beer."

I told her, "He's cool." I said, "Be cool. I'm going. You should come with me." I hoped she wouldn't. I'd missed her when she was gone, but just being with her five minutes and I was suffocating: Paint fumes, fumes from the Dinty Moore beef stew she ate every morning for breakfast with watery coffee. *Alice Alice Alice* to me all the fucking time.

"Every time you leave this house without me you are risking your life."

I said, "I'm sick of living like this. Maybe we should talk to Simon." I hadn't told her I saw Mark, that he could talk any time.

"We need more time. He'll still be angry."

I tossed my hands up.

"Look, he'll leave me alone most likely because he and I have history, but he'd be pissed, you knocked his head into the floor. And then he grieved you like a fool. He'll have to do something. Maybe he'll feed you to Liz's brothers, pin shit on you. Maybe he'll try to blackmail me into doing you, I mean, he knows what I did, he's got that over me."

She must have seen the chill in my eye, the desire to run, for she relented, gave me her blessing to go out. But her threats stuck in my gut.

Then she came up to me, and as the song swelled, she wrapped her arms around me. She whispered in my ear, "I'm sorry, you know I could never hurt you. Don't forget to tell that boy that I'm your girlfriend. I'll protect you. If it weren't for Cher, I'd get you to stay in with me tonight." She kissed my neck so faint and soft, I shivered. "I'll always protect you, though."

When we were together, though hardly anyone had ever turned me on so much, or got me off so easily, I feared she was just fronting with me. My heart ached, but I knew it.

I felt like walking the couple blocks up to Angelo's, but Wendy insisted on driving me in the paint truck. I acquiesced. The sun was almost down, but she made me wear shades.

"Should I wear a moustache, too?"

"You should. I'm gonna cut your hair short, too. Bleach that shit."

M.I.A.'s "Paper Planes" played on the radio and we cranked it.

She walked me to the door because she wanted to see him again. Get a better feel on if we could trust him. Whatever. He lived in a house a lot like ours, but it was a double, and he was on the bottom. I was nervous on the porch, and then chagrined when a woman answered. She had thin wheat-colored hair in a ponytail, no makeup, perfect rich tan. She was skinny and young-looking, but lines by her mouth made me think maybe she was my age or older.

"Yeah."

"I'm here to see Angelo."

She looked bored. She yelled his name and stepped back into the house, gestured for us to come in, and then disappeared into the back somewhere. Rich jasmine resin burned, and the smoke swirled out of a bowl on the floor. The house looked like a living collage with purple Christmas lights, green Christmas lights, gauzy magenta fabrics, punk rock and metal posters pasted to the walls. A skinny black cat traipsed out and dropped at my feet.

Angelo came out of the kitchen and rushed over to us. "That's Violet," he said and picked up the cat.

"Oh she's lovely, Angelo, she looks like Egyptian royalty. I love your place. Remember Wendy? We live just a couple blocks from here. She and I both paint, we love all these colors and lights!"

"Pleased," said Wendy and they shook hands. He placed Violet on the loveseat. I turned and saw red stained glass hanging in the window. Ivy grew everywhere. Wendy kept her eyes on him and didn't try to hide the fact.

"Did you put all this up, or, that other person you live with?" I didn't look at him but put my finger out to Violet who rubbed her tender narrow cheek against it and then unfolded instantly onto her back, nearly flopping onto the floor. She caught herself and flipped back up in a seated position and began to intently clean her right paw.

"Oh Melissa. No. I like colors. She's just staying her for a while. She has a room. She's a slob." He looked over his shoulder and waved his hand in front of his face and whispered loudly, "Her room *stanks!*"

Wendy stepped to the door. "Well, Alice, I'll let you kids go, call me if you need a ride, okay?"

Angelo looked at Wendy, then me. Wendy saw his confusion and pinched me hard on the back of my arm. Presumably for realizing I'd told him my true name.

"It's my nickname for her," she said with anger in her voice. Then she gave me a little spank and took off.

Angelo had a tarp over his dining room table. We drank Pabst from cans and worked for hours on the flier. Man, it's crazy how the hours can go during a project like that. We talked about music and told our music histories to each other.

I picked up bass after seeing Nirvana on Saturday Night Live in 1992. I got turned onto old punk, switched to guitar and vocals, and started writing my own stuff because learning covers or other guys' stuff was too hard and boring. I started jamming with Noam in the basement, then our punk went abstract as we discovered experimental and no wave music. We moved to Cleveland thinking we were punks, but the few punks we met were into retro stuff and thought abstraction was pretentious, yet we were way too gross, poor and uncredentialed for the art scene. As we understood it, at least. Then the noise scene exploded, and we found a home. Noam left. I stayed, played in a few bands, but mostly just solo. I told Angelo my guitar was stolen.

Into music from age four, Angelo stayed up late as a kid watching local access music video shows. He was rooted in the west side, 73rd and Denison. His early memories were made more vivid by the trauma of leaving with his missionary parents when he was six. They took him around the Middle East, Northern Africa and out to Malaysia. When he was twelve, he ran away from them, and bounced around houses of musicians. He was always into music and comics. He played in Malaysian hardcore punk bands. He worked beach clubs in cover bands and played original stuff in basement halls lit in dull florescence, to a hundred or more wiry Malay kids in black t-shirts, tumbling in the heat. He went to Italy with a girl for a while, and then finally came home, all the way home, to Cleveland when he was in his mid-twenties.

Bands were the common thread in his life. Angelo revealed himself to be a researcher and anthropologist by nature, a cataloger. During his two tours of Iraq, he combed social media and underground music sites for Cleveland bands to hook up with. He formed his band quickly between those two tours, and that's when he saw me play. Now he was back and ready to go. He was leaving the army. But I heard his dog tags tinkle as he moved, and I shivered. We were sitting close.

He cut out eyes. I tore from his *National Geographics*. I tore out seahorses and red-tailed hawks in flight and desert sands and many blue waters, and he cut out letters from circulators. I handed him a page with a hummingbird dipping into a red flower, and he cut the image out with care. Careful with the wings. Careful with the petals. I made strips of *living structures*: echinoderms, veins, mold, moss, tree roots, bones. He had glue sticks. I told him I'd bring over rubber cement next time. He made jokes about sniffing glue. I said what we really need is clear acrylic medium. I wondered where I could find that in Lakewood.

He told me researchers discovered that subjects on DMT, which occurs naturally in the brain, most commonly hallucinated the vivid experience of the classic alien grey abduction scenario.

We worked. The work felt holy, our hands moving gently over the cut paper.

The morning tantra-yoga work I'd done the last two months brought me more into my body. I was ovulating that night, and I felt it with a new sacred buoyancy. I was breathing through my heart, I was breathing through my sex, *middlesmertz* made my eyes wet. Each inhalation was charged with erotic potency, each exhalation played like a violin bow through my eggs. I wore clothes but felt naked. Dressed only in gauzy violet astral plasma.

Angelo. His profile, his eyes. I think I'd known him from before, back in the twenties, or maybe in pre-Christian times, or both. This knowing settled in like ripples on a lake.

We talked about the summer and gigs, and local bands that were good. I'd been here well over a decade, involved with the noise scene for much of the last decade, so I told him things, and he was one of those people who knew so much about wide swaths of music from all different sparkling and belchy genres, he told me things too. He played records: Sore Throat, Suicide, Frankie Goes to Hollywood.

He said he'd had a subscription to *National Geographic* since he'd been back from Iraq. He remembered his folks having stacks of them around the house when he was a kid, in Cleveland, before they joined the cult. I asked why he came back to Cleveland?

"I like Cleveland—I thought of Cleveland when I was gone. When I was a kid, I kept wondering when I'd be back in Cleveland. But, I've hardly lived somewhere longer than two years. I'm restless. I might leave again soon. Maybe Texas."

I told him I hadn't seen my parents in a long time, and I didn't really know why, beside the fact I couldn't afford to fly out to see them.

I told him how I stopped playing after my husband left. More beers and I told him about crack and coming off. (Omitting the nasty things I'd done, and the murder of Liz, the worst things.) Crack was not a word I'd let myself say out loud in some time.

He concentrated on the letters and eyeballs in front of him.

I put my hands down and looked at him. "Did you..."

He looked up. "Hmm? Yes, I heard you. It's cool. I smoked crack once. I was addicted to heavy drugs, at a point in my life, too."

I exhaled. I didn't realize till then how afraid I'd been, how I'd separated the two worlds in my mind. Mark's face at Liz's door rose up in my heart like a jackal.

Angelo put a hand on my hands and looked me in the eye. "It's strong of you to quit. Nobody did that but you."

"Thanks." I tried to not break this gaze.

"It's true. Remember it."

We went back to cutting, pasting. I opened some paints, indigo and violet.

I told him I needed a new guitar. Would get a cheap one before the gig. I found a photo spread of equatorial forests in Southeast Asia, and my breath stuck in my throat. All the green. He looked at the pictures quietly and then told me about *being there*. The Spider Moon Fest flier was looking amazing, and I said so.

He said, "It's a tribute to the collaboration of flora and fauna. Lucy will shit herself. She loves my fliers. And look," he pointed to a strange little cubby creature pawing its paw around the letter N, "a shout-out to Sloth."

He touched my hair. I was late in coloring it and the red was coming through. I'd been lazy about straightening it, and it was starting to kink. It must have looked curious.

"Margot, I have to tell you something. The Elyria show has been canceled."

I felt let down and relieved.

He said, "Fucking metal rednecks don't know what the fuck they're doing. Incompetents."

"Well, maybe…"

"Moved it to Scraps!" He smiled broadly.

"Scraps… oh!" He meant Scum. Angelo had nicknames for everything.

"Same line-up minus Reliance on Death plus Noumenon Device. So win-win." Then, he said he'd be back in a minute and came back with a knocked-around Fender Squire Telecaster.

"Here." He held it to me like an offering.

"What?"

"Here." He jerked it forward.

I took it from him. He told me to keep it. Then he sat back down and got back to cutting eyes. I said it was too much. But he said nothing, so I sat down and played it for a minute. It felt so good in my hands. I realized I'd been playing in my sleep, gripping nothing.

I played "Rebel, Rebel", and he sang under his breath while he worked, and it was great.

"Angelo. This guitar. And talking with you is so great." The beer gave me courage to take his hand, golden like the Moon is sometimes, and smooth, with a silver ring around his index finger. "I've been waiting for a friend like you for so long. Your heart is open." My past life, Georgie, Liz, Autumn Villa, it was all turning into shadows. I offered the memories like funny little phantoms that vanished into the ether. I prayed my phantoms wouldn't hurt him, that they'd be banished by the warmth of our friendship.

He smiled but looked down at the table. "I just can't believe we've only known each other a couple weeks. I feel like I've known you since I was a kid."

It was late, and I let myself look at his mouth, and it hit me like lightning down to my feet, and I thought I'd let myself look at his mouth again sometime. Then he asked me about Lucy.

I let go of his hand. "There's cats in this flier. No, I haven't talked to her since I saw her at Bela. I don't really talk to her like that." I wished I had some inside tip I could give him. Anything. There were tigers and black house cats like Violet and Clarence draped throughout the flier. It was almost together.

"It's a shout-out to cat-human collaboration." His voice deep and formal, even now.

I smiled.

"I don't know how I fucked up with her, I just wanted someone to hold at night, someone to take care of, she was hot, then cold. A *freak*, then freaked out. I hope you don't think I'm a pussy." He opened two more beers and put one in front of me.

"No. You can't control the subjective reality of other people."

"Next time I have to be more detached, I mean, who is she to me?"

"You tried to love her, and I admire your emotional courage. Just because shit wasn't right between you two doesn't mean you fucked up, or you should try to be coy or a douchebag or something. Who knows what's in her mind, her heart? I, find your enthusiasm intoxicating." I couldn't help myself. I smiled, shy, feeling heavy and light with lust.

"Really?"

"Yes."

Then he stood up and started clearing things. He turned on a harsh overhead light and all my flaws were exposed, my skin, my body.

I said, "Maybe Lucy's just been busy. Journalists, you know, work odd hours. Off and on."

"Well. We've had plans to go to that Murdered Man show on Tuesday, so, I'll see. I'll give it my best shot."

"Well, she should go for you, you should have someone at night, like you said."

"So, is your girlfriend coming to pick you up, or do you need a ride?"

"What—Wendy? Oh."

"Look… don't take this the wrong way, but she's a little controlling. Sometimes people see someone coming off heavy drugs, and they know they're vulnerable, and they take advantage."

"Wendy's been good to me. She saved my life."

"Well. You saved yourself, remember. Don't forget."

"Thank you, Angelo."

"Oh, okay." He was grinning again, holding me at arm's length. He'd slipped on the black-rimmed glasses that he'd worn the first time I saw him. "Well, the love between women is the greatest love of all. So, do you want a ride?"

"Uh, maybe, but I could walk, too."

We stood like that going back and forth. He said it was too dangerous, I said it was two blocks. We were drunk.

Then his roommate staggered out. "The fuck, Angelo, I told you never to turn on this overhead light! Ug, when is she leaving, I got to get up at five, huh?" She jerked a hand at us, tossing her limbs around like a movie queen.

I put out my hand. "Margot. Nice to meet you, I'm just leaving."

She shook it. "Melissa." Then she smiled one of those super quick smiles to show she didn't mean it and went back to her room.

I gathered up my stuff, and we shuffled out the door. I asked him what *is* the deal with Melissa.

"Oh her. She's my ex-wife. She's just in between boyfriends or jobs or something."

"Oh, so you guys…?" I made a hand signal that meant fucking.

"Ah, naw, she's more like a sister to me, we were married super young for just a minute when I first moved back here, we can't stand each other, but I feel protective of her."

We made it out to the front yard but lingered for a while. Still talking. Our talking built bricks around us. I put my hand on his forearm. A man walked past us, behind me on the sidewalk, and then I heard him stop.

Angelo said, "Margot, do you know about the Underwater Panther?"

"That you, girl?" Adrenaline slapped my heart. I turned.

"Billy? Hey Billy." Billy Vickers, even with his back to the streetlight I could see it was him, glowing red from recent sun, his mullet freshly cut.

"Oh my god, girl, oh my god." He leapt into the yard and picked me up and swung me around. "Margot! I heard you was dead, then I heard you was alive, and then I knew I had to find you! Come and get you! I'm at my dude's house, just on a beer run, and here you are! That Simon is such a bullshitter!"

"Yeah, we got into it, but, I'm clean now, this is my friend Angelo." Billy still had me held up and he started to kiss me on my neck. Angelo looked away. "Billy, man, put me down, okay?"

"Mark thought maybe you'd been a ghost!"

"Sometimes I wonder."

"Did you hear about Liz? Me and Jeff and Simon are going to find out who did her and we're going to tear them up, thought it was these one guys, but now we're not so sure. Man! Simon's going to be so happy when he hears you're okay? He said something bad happened to you. He seemed broken up about it, but it's hard to say. He's kind of fake, you know? I don't really trust him."

Jesus Christ. Angelo muttered something about crashing and going in for the night, but I turned and grabbed his forearm and looked him in the eye and he understood and stayed.

"Yeah, Billy, I was so sorry to hear about Liz, I always liked her so much, actually, that's what scared me into getting clean, I just didn't want to be around that stuff anymore. I've just been laying low."

"Aw, girl, you're so sweet, you break me up! Well, we are going to do what we got to do, you know, to make shit right. I'm glad you're not around that shit anymore, you look good, you look healthy. Hey, where you stay, now? Want to get out of here, or what?"

"Um, my friend and I are working on a project." My mouth went dry and my hands shook.

He asked about my number, I told him I didn't have a phone, took his number, told him I'd call him this weekend.

"You, better, sugar, you are so sweet, I'll be thinking of you till I see you again! 'mm!" He grabbed me and stuck his tongue in my mouth. Then he was off. Just beer or to cop? It was hard to tell with Billy. He never seemed like he was in withdrawal. Of course, he had a "nonaddictive personality." Angelo had walked back in the house.

Taking long strides, Billy was halfway down the block when he pumped his fists in the air and hollered, "Hot damn! Margot's alive!"

I ran back to Angelo's living room. Melissa was sitting in front of the tv, some reality bullshit turned up high. He was back at the table cutting out eyes. I had the awful oregano taste of Billy in my mouth, and I felt teary again. I couldn't believe the watery emotions of coming clean. Angelo looked pissy.

I went to him and touched his arm. It was hard. He didn't look up, I flinched for a second. I whispered, *Can I have another beer?* He nodded. I came back and gave him one, too and sat next to him.

"Who was *that* misanthrope? I thought Wendy was your girlfriend."

"She is. Look Angelo, I'm just a little scared of that guy, he's from the crack times, but I guess that's obvious." The truth was I was shaking all over. The truth was I'd known I was going to die the minute after I saw Liz get shot. I knew I would someday have to show people what

211

I did with men, people who wouldn't do those things. I knew I would be shamed and killed. I wanted crack bad. Again. Now. Billy's voice made me want it, let alone his mouth and his arms. I wanted to burn this white fear clear away with the all-consuming fire of freebased cocaine. How could I tell this to this lovely man? Angelo, Angelo. I just met him, but I've always known him. He's always been with me. I loved him. And my eyes watered up.

I jumped when Melissa yelled *motherfucker* at the tv.

Angelo looked at me and put his scissors down and hugged me. He called to her, "I thought you had to get up at five!"

"Whatever!"

When I saw Liz the person punctured, and I saw the blood come to her mouth so fast, the animal, and the wolf eyes that wanted to live, I knew I'd seen something outside of tv life in America. Noise and *tantra* were outside of tv life, sure, but Liz's death was beyond crack cocaine or sucking dick because some stranger asks you too, gagging, sore jaws, just because he asks you too, things outside of tv that you don't want anyone to know about. What I saw. It was her life coming out. I cried on Angelo, into his neck. I muted my cries, but he felt them. He smelled like leaves and sand. His dog tags moved and softly chimed.

17

Fools All Over

Wendy and I were back at work in the big attic bathroom under skylights in the old Victorian house on west 45th, across from the Franklin Castle. The sun was back, and we believed it would stay through October. The owners wanted us to paint Art Nouveau fairies on the walls once the pale pink base was down. And trees. I was psyched but intimidated. My painting style was more fauvist and wild, and Wendy said she only drew comic books.

"Comics! I want to see them." (I didn't tell about Mark and now Billy Vickers. I told myself they wouldn't tell and pushed the fear out my mind when it slithered up. Before it could strike.)

"Naw. Well, okay. There's this superhero, Cleo, and she lives in abandoned buildings in Cleveland and meets up with her friend The Spider down by the river in the flats. The Spider is an old fat lady who lives in a tent and drinks potato wine. There's also a red-tailed hawk, sea gulls, pigeons, those are the other characters."

"I love it! You'll do fine with the Art Nouveau, it's all lines." I felt jumpy. The show at Scum was in two days, and my stomach lurched at the thought of playing out again. And I had to tell Wendy about the

Vickers. I tried to stay cool. Was I more scared of her than of Simon?

"I mean, I haven't worked on it in a long time. It's something Johnny and I were doing together."

"Johnny Maker."

"Yeah. You're full of piss and vinegar today." She put a tape in the old black boom box we hauled from job to job. It had bloody red drops on it from our last job. *Pantera*. Oh brother, but I didn't say a word. I watched her pour more baby rose paint and gently work the roller though it. I tried to imagine her working on comics with Johnny.

"Wendy, how did you get started working for Simon, anyway, you're an activist with your own business, you're not an addict, what's the deal?" I got back to work on the other side of the wide room.

"Alice, I have to fully disclose something to you."

"Yeah?"

"Simon, is my brother. Actually."

"What. Wendy." I almost dropped my shit.

"I know, I should have told you." She turned and raised the roller to the wall.

"Wendy. What do you mean Simon is your brother."

"I know. I look white, but." She stepped down from her stepladder and came over to me.

"You look fucking Swedish! But that's not what concerns me, for fuck's sake."

"We have the same dad, different moms. Anyways, he's my baby brother, you know, he was born when I was thirteen. We didn't grow up under the same roof, but I babysat him, I was more like an aunt, you know? He moved out when he was just sixteen, but I'd been gone for years, hadn't seen him since he was nine or so..."

She told me she'd spent her twenties traveling around, not in college, but crashing at college co-ops on liberal arts campuses. She'd had a girlfriend at Oberlin when she was twenty-one, is how it started. She followed the girl to California, bummed around. Partied a lot, read a lot, worked here and there painting houses enough to get to the next town. When she came back to Cleveland at thirty-two, she had visions of transforming her old neighborhood. She settled down with her tender-hearted beagle named Lu. She hooked up with local activists and within a couple years, they had a community space going over in the Denison neighborhood.

She told me how she had a dream one night of a blue jay tangled in her hair and she woke up in a sweat and knew her brother was in trouble. She didn't speak to her dad at all, and hardly to her mother. But she called her mother, and the woman had no idea about Simon but still had the number for his mother. His mother said he came around sometimes, but she had no contact info.

"You said you don't believe in dreams."

"Well. It's not a *good* thing that I found him, is it?"

Wendy first heard about Myspace at a women's bar. It must have been brand new. She was like, "what the fuck is this nerd shit." She found Simon's Myspace page on the library computer. He was thrilled to hear from his long-lost sister. He didn't seem in trouble. Was working some telemarketing gig, taking night classes for coding. They started hanging out, she brought him to the community space storefront that she and her friends rented out on the southwest side.

They hosted meetings for Books-for-Prisoners, transition-movement groups determined to re-localize the economy and reduce power consumption in the face of peak oil, free yoga classes, the neighborhood kids would come in and do art. Wendy and her friends didn't have to worry about being in a high-crime neighborhood because they *became part* of the neighborhood. They had a garden in the back. Wendy lived there for a while, sleeping on the linoleum. Waking up to the pigeons cooing. She was in love with a woman who had served in Afghanistan and now protested against the wars and made poetry books by hand. She loved that her little brother hung out with the crew. They housed free jazz shows and independent book signings. Pro-choice escorts conducted trainings at the space. Simon was getting more involved. Simon brought Johnny Maker around and he and Wendy worked on a graphic novel for a while along with bright splashes of murals they created with the children.

"Johnny's your cousin."

"Yeah."

Wendy didn't know Simon sold crack for Sig. In the same neighborhood as the co-op.

The space thrived for eight months. Then the landlord kicked them out, saying he wanted to sell the place. Today the place still stands empty, the murals they'd painted with local kids still on the side of the building, but graffitied over with "fuck niggas get paid" and "kill the homeless." Wendy's lover moved to a reservation in New Mexico, the group of friends dispersed, still active, but decentralized in a way that was painful to Wendy. She said now some of them meet up every other Wednesday and read nursing textbooks and teach each other *reiki* and herbalism in order to take back medicine. They are survivors. Others cook dinners for the homeless every night at the Catholic Workers house. Then there's the garden. More, gardens around the city, all over the place.

But the loss of the space and the lover hit Wendy hard. She and Simon started hanging out more, drank Four Lokos most nights that winter. Johnny came by some. He tried to get Wendy to work on the graphic novel, but her heart wasn't in it. Wendy and Simon philosophized and rationalized. Fuck the landlord. Money is power. She told him about re-localizing economy in order to re-localize power. He told her about selling crack. At first she was pissed. But they talked and talked it into something else. It made people feel good. The war on drugs was a war on people. Crack had a stigma that coke didn't have. New studies showed that it wasn't as addictive as they thought. It empowered young men like Simon. It brought them money when they needed it. Simon was moving up and now had people selling under him.

Then Wendy's beagle Lu died. Lu had a cancer that Wendy had to just watch because she couldn't afford cancer treatments. She'd had to take out a payday loan to get her to the vet and get the diagnosis. She could afford purple hangovers from three dollar Four Lokos, but she and the dog were sleeping on Simon's couch. Lu was only three. Cancer from cheap dog food with cow brains in it maybe? Thousands of dollars to treat Lu's cancer, when Wendy had thirty-eight dollars at most at any given time? She worked at the thrift store, and made about thirty-eight dollars a day, she could only get a few days a week, even though her boss promised to get her on full-time. The hours were never regular: up and down, days, afternoons.

The brown dog got thin, but still liked to play. Still a kid-dog: her fur was soft and sweet-smelling. When the pain got bad, she cried, and they put cough syrup in her dog food. Wendy was too broke even to paint houses. She couldn't afford the paint: it was the independent contractor Catch-22.

She applied for credit cards but couldn't get them because she'd never had anything in her name. When it was time to pay the payday loan back for the initial visit, she had to go to Simon because she owed more than her paycheck. He said if she got another one, she'd be out on her ass.

She said, "Fine, I don't need you."

He said, "Don't go, just be smart."

Her old lover wrote to her from the reservation. She wrote about alcoholism, cancer, nuclear testing, rape.

Wendy held Lu at night and cried into her fur. Wendy shared her frozen dinners with the dog. Simon was making bigger money, not enough to help Lu, he said, not thousands, but eight hundred for a giant flat screen tv. Wendy waited for Simon to offer to help her get her business up, and he did pay for some vet visits. She said she knew he would help more if he could. He was her younger brother, after all, she said, she should be the one helping him.

Lu died on the brown couch, not in her sleep, but after vomiting blood and having seizures and panting out of her mind. Wendy was fed up. She was thirty-four years old. She couldn't save her dog. She was angry. So, she started selling crack for Simon, and when some poor old fool didn't pay, she hit him in his face. She could be scary. They called her White Lightening, they called her Thunderbird.

"So," she said, "that's how I know that Simon won't hurt me. He's my brother. I should have just told him about not killing you. That's not *him*. That's not *me*. It was all so sudden, that thing with Liz. I'll tell him eventually. You know."

"Wendy. Why didn't you tell *me*. I have to trust you with my life, and you lie, and call me by another name. What's, your last name? Even."

"O. Wendy O. and Simon X. Shit, girl. Much as I like you, you're never going to hear my true *first name*, let alone my true *surname*. Shit."

Wendy slapped the floor with her palm and jumped back up to work.

I wrapped my mind around her life. I went over to the windowsill and jumped at the face of the Franklin Castle. Disoriented: I didn't realize this window faced north. The Castle seemed so close with its flat black windows. I was grateful for the paint, otherwise, would a figure have looked back at me?

Mark popped into my head. The way I'd slipped around him. Lost control. Anything. The things I'd said.

"So, what's the long-term plan? How long do I have to stay Alice, then, forever? Alice Y? Do you want to stay in Cleveland, or are we going to hit the road, or what."

"Well, hey, what happens to the prescription when the doctor dies?" Wendy sounded cocky and muscular again. The door to her pain re-sealed.

"Okay. Right."

"My doc just died, that's where I been getting my Vicodin and Adderall. I met him at the plasma center when I was a kid. Come on, Alice, we got to get this second coat done, girl. You know how at the plasma place they ask you about your sexual history, what all you've done and stuff?"

"Yeah. Humiliating."

"Well, the doc who interviewed me was a pervert. I came out all dizzy and cold from the cold blood they pumped back into me, you know? I'm wanting a cigarette, but they said to wait a half hour, you know, I was nineteen. I'm thinking about having a cigarette anyway and this nasty old fuck practically pulls me into his van. Well, you know how weak young girls are. He probably just *asked* me too and I did what I was told, and I really needed a cigarette, and then he starts showing me pictures of mutilated genitals with huge red growths on them and told me that's what would happen to me if I kept sleeping around. I wasn't out yet, so I was sleeping with men. He was totally getting off on it, and I was scared and weak from being hooked up to the plasma machines, and I needed a cigarette so bad I couldn't *breathe.*

"Then, I mustered up just enough courage to back out the door. I ran. But later I was pissed. I showed up at his doorstep dressed in a white suit and flats. I told him I'd tell on him if he didn't give me a

219

prescription for Percocet. Ha! Poor old doc, I've been picking up pills from him on and off for all these years, when I've been in town, and now he's dead."

"Good Riddance. To bad rubbish."

"Yeah, but we've got to find a new pill hook-up. I know you like that blue up your nose when you're painting at home. And I like my vikes in the bathtub."

I'd been working on three new paintings of tigers and rivers.

"That's a long time to be eating pills, Wendy. Are you addicted to opiates? Cause most people would be."

"No, I don't have an addictive personality. Never have had. When I wanted to give up cigarettes a few years back, I just did. A little teeth grinding, that's all. The other day? I just smoked that one pack, and then I was over it again. I even shot dope a couple times in my life and didn't get hooked. Meth, too. Never smoked crack on the reg. But shit, I sure like those little pills. Up at work. Chill time at chill time. Some Vicodin and Chablis, yeah, girl, you know." She did a little dance with her knees.

"That's what Billy says, too. That he doesn't have an addictive personality."

"Sure, he and I partied some."

She was making me hungry for endorphin release by any means. "I'll ask around."

My phone buzzed and I pulled it out. Angelo and I had been texting constantly for days. It felt good to write back and forth with a friend. His texting self was so expressive, emotionally bare. He was obsessed with Lucy, but I didn't care, I indulged him every chance I got with advice about heart and courage, things I wanted to believe.

Wendy and I worked without talking for a while. When Pantera was over, I threw in a Skin Graft tape. She didn't say anything about it being "noise like AM static" like she did at first. We tolerated each other's music now. I just drew the line at Korn, and she drew the line at Massona. Fair enough.

The pink made me think of Arizona. I only went out there to visit my family that one time six years ago when I met Georgie. It seemed like a long time ago. They're happy now. My father was teaching piano, and my mother was finally satisfied with her work as an architect. They were hand to mouth in Ohio, but they were doing okay out there in Flagstaff. There's more money there, I hear. My mother designed their house up in those cool pines, the house the color of bark with long narrow windows all over the place. The house built up like a spiral. I felt sour when I thought of my mother and father, the sour feeling of forgetting to do something that can't be pinned down and may kill something if you don't do it. That's how I missed my family. We'd been tight as one person when I was a kid.

(They didn't call much when they had my number. I understand—maybe they felt rejected because I didn't move out there. I like to be close to water. I didn't know why I didn't move there, I didn't know why. My mother said the desert was like an ocean.)

I wondered if the housing crash would hurt them, I wondered if they drank. I wondered if they had dinner once a week with Noam and Marcia. It seemed like I hadn't thought of them for so long, till, that spring.

I heard the stars were best up there in Flagstaff, but I couldn't ever seem to find them on that only trip. Just the neon on the old hotels. And the snow-capped mountain. I'd never seen one before. So much still air. Air between everything. Driving, and the mountain is who knows how far away, but you can still see it. Unreal. And so quiet. Here walls of trees and buildings crowd up the horizon. But I like it here, being cradled by trees.

221

Here there's always traffic that sounds like waves, and birds, and cicadas or melting snow or the neighbor's laundry rolling, or lawn mower mowing, and the air smells like exhaust in the winter and asphalt in the summer, but out there in Arizona, there's nothing in the air but air. But I was only there for a couple weeks once, so I may be wrong.

We went to the Grand Canyon. All we could do was sit and look. My father told us about how his cousin had hiked down the mountain in sandals and lost both her big toenails by the time she got to the bottom. The pinks of the canyon changed, and we sat cross-legged in silence. Looking down, farther than I've seen before, down at the river that looked like a snake, wondering if it once splashing a few inches from where we sat, filling everything.

My parents stayed in Flagstaff because my mother hates the heat, while Noam and I rented an SUV and drove down to Sedona. It was lower and drier, and even pinker in the red rock mountains. We hiked and the sky was so blue and the quiet so thin, it was like we were on a stage set. We heard rattlesnakes in the red rocks but didn't see them. The air was perfect and empty. How did this air regenerate itself?

We went to *Arc O'Santi*. But the quiet was starting to bother me. Thick quiet. I'd heard of the commune there, the master architect who built a little utopia of sustainable houses where people could both live and work. The bells of *Arc O'Santi*. But the quiet bothered me. I worried about them running out of water after the collapse of civilization. The tour guide's words evaporated as soon as they came out of his mouth. The bells were beautiful like batwings. It was like a Dr. Seuss village. I bought a book by the famous architect, on animism versus animatism. I thought it might be about a new evolved mysticism, a cosmology organic like the buildings he designed. But no, it was anti-consciousness: a wild rendering of his ideas about the origins of evil being in the origins of the belief of spirit beyond material. *But the material is the spirit.*

But maybe I just didn't get it, I don't know.

We went to Jerome on the way back up, too, but before that we went down to Phoenix, checked out the noise scene, partied with some of his friends. Everything was flat. You could see so far. Noam and I were embarrassed by the SUV and talked like we had in the earlier years of the Bush administration about giant cars, cars like tanks. A future with gas-powered tanks sputtering in the streets.

We talked about the sequoia. The cacti that looked like people. I told Noam that I read they'd once been sea creatures but adapted and evolved by slowing down. They'd once had quick lives in the sea, cells regenerating fast like human reproductive tissue, but now lingered for hundreds of years. (Did they once breathe inside the Colorado river-ocean when it'd been all over this place?) That's why they were so old. They were protected, now. Hugged by little fences.

Now, I worked, painting the southern wall sunset pink. I could hear Wendy wrapping up, pulling up the tarp on her side of the room.

And now in the sweet now, in a pink room in May, Angelo texted. Wendy maybe regretted hooking me up with the no-contract phone. I couldn't stop smiling. He wrote [want to hang out saturday before the show?]

The show. I felt sick at the thought of playing again. Hanging out. He would see my face in the daytime. How could I even be with him without drinking?

Reading his words... I feel it down in my hips through my silky silver slip. I've swallowed molten metals—I feel heat hot metal in my digestive system, moving from my gut into my reproductive system. I touch my hair that frizzes softly today. I feel giddy for the first time in ten years. Where have those ten years gone? I try to ground myself in my age, the year, the president and how long he has been president. I'm amazed. I can't recall when I met Henry and Rocky or what hunting crack felt like. Now *billows out in front of me like the living crush of the twelve-year-old me seeing me at last. I'm crazed.*

Wendy said, "Hey, Alice—think we could get a house like this someday?"

"What would we do with it?"

"Dance hall or something? Maybe knock off the roof and make the attic a greenhouse or something?"

"We could make the front room a ritual space and the basement a venue."

Wendy smiled broadly at me. I felt like she was my daughter and mother. As if I'd made her, and she'd made me.

She scooped some blue cream out with a metal tool, a scrive or a scrowl or something, I always forget. I moved to the great tub where I'd let some scrubbing bubbles set and started in on them with a brush. She patted the stuff on uneven places in the wall. The window was open. It was a broad window with maple leaves and red robins. The air so sweet, lilac sweet, it made me crazy—*sweet and heady*—my phone buzzed another text.

Wendy said, "Is that guy texting you again? Look. You can't go getting yourself involved like that, okay? We've got to keep a low profile. You are getting goofy."

"He doesn't know anybody."

"Doesn't matter. You walk around the neighborhood all the time. Simon will see you, or one of the Vickers for sure, or Tasha maybe. There's fools all over. They come out when it gets hot."

I cringed away from her projecting eyes, thinking of Mark keeping me under his hat, and now Billy, Mark had at least told Billy, the very knowledge of my life a danger to it. "I really think we can have a house someday Wendy."

"That's a pile. We don't have credit, we don't even have names."

I held the thick brush under icy cold water in the basement utility sink. The end of the day. Wendy said, "Wow, Alice, you are daydreaming or what? Some crack flashback or what? You've been in your head all day."

I laughed and felt the pain of the cold water. I ran the bar of soap through the brush and worked out the pink acrylic paint. "I was thinking about our lives."

"Well, here's to your life honey." She pulled out something that looked like a black marker. It was metal and said, DEFIANCE: SECURITY THROUGH CHEMISTRY.

"What's this?"

"Pepper spray. Just in case."

"Oh." I almost dropped it but jumped and held it tighter as if it were a bomb, or I just realized I was on a ledge. "Shit, Wendy, what truck did this fall off of? It looks like it's from 1982." It had a little pocket clip to make it look like a pen. "How do I know if it works?"

"Well, someone brought a case into Remarkable's, but we can't sell that shit, so we split them up." She brushed her hand through my hair to my neck and gave me a shiver.

Then she pulled up her baggy shirt exposing the gun holstered into her jeans. "I got my Hellcat, baby, in case anyone comes at me, crosses me."

18

Ring of Fire

The heat came early and stayed. Angelo was a braced animal, his nerves set for the show.

We sat on his porch and drank Pabst tallboys. He offered me chips, but I was too nervous about the show to eat. I didn't know what to say. He didn't say anything, either, so I pulled out the can of pepper spray. "I need to test this. Wendy gave it to me, but it's old."

"Let me see that thing." He rolled up his bag of chips and stuffed it under his chair. The beer felt good. I would have been happy to stay on that porch the whole afternoon and the whole night.

I followed him into his driveway. He shook the spray.

I squeezed my hair. A fat black bird sat on a fat black wire. "We might get our first black president, or our first woman president. It's hard to believe. Too bad the democrats are owned by corporations, just like the republicans, but at least they're not evangelicals. The executive branch sucks."

Angelo squinted at the fine print on the pepper spray. "Yeah... Clinton's a hawk. She'd like to backdoor draft my ass to Iran. Politicians. Whatever."

"Their platforms are identical because they think they have to be.

Watered down shit like, same-sex civil unions, and that Mitt Romney, Republican, market-based healthcare plan. But, what if...I'm thinking, what if Obama comes into office and is able to, with a democratic house and senate, pass a single-payer plan? What if he can do a New Deal type thing based on a green economy? It could happen."

"That'd be tight. I never had insurance. Before the army, I mean. Not in this country."

"Me, neither. It could happen. It could."

He paced around a minute, looking at the pepper spray, looking at the ground. "How long you and Wendy been together, anyway?"

"Just since March." Loud packs of kids ran up and down his street.

"Just two months. You guys seem in pretty deep." He pulled the lid off.

"Well, you know, she helped me get off crack. Oh, do you know where to get any pills? Just Adderall and Vicodin, stuff like that."

We braced as he pointed the nozzle into the concrete. But just a little whimpering stream came out. He touched his finger to it and put it to his mouth. "Nao, nothing. This is ka-put. No spice."

I took it back and thanked him. He grabbed us two more cans, and I sat back in the wicker chair he said was mine when I was over.

"I don't know about pills. How'd you meet her, anyway." He looked past me into empty porches.

"Just, the old neighborhood, where I used to live. God. I wish I could just play right now and get it over with." I stretched my feet straight out and wiggled my toes in my sneakers.

"Would you want to, marry her, if it was legal?"

"Oh, man. No—I don't even know her real name. I don't think I'd want to get married again. I think I might be, leaving, when I get some money together. Head east, out to New York, Baltimore, maybe, or Philly, just head east for a while and get lost."

Angelo jumped up as he was getting a text. He wore tight black jeans and a blue Infectious Maggots shirt with a radiant golden man and the words, "Deep inside our grief factory, milk runs red."

"Oh, here's some bullshit. My guitarist says he has to work, can I pick him up, has to work till *nine,* what the fuck." His back was to me now, texting back. Anger came off him like heat. I sucked in the anger like fumes. My stomach went cold.

"Oh man, I can get things started, I can get a ride with Wendy, it's okay." I stood up behind him. But he stayed facing the street.

"Henry might know where to get pills. I'll ask some dudes at work, pizza shop dudes always know where to get pills."

His neck was tense, his fists tight by his side.

"Thanks. Wendy, wanted me to ask around."

He turned and took the outer edge of my hand, in kind of an awkward touch. "Thank you for helping me, dude. With the show."

"Oh, sure, it's nothing."

"Margot. I think you should go to New York."

"Yeah."

"Maybe I should, too."

"Cool, yeah."

"Margot—that blond dude with the mullet, the one who picked you up? I saw him, he walked past the house a few times, looks like he's looking for you."

Later, saying good-bye until the show, he collapsed into me for a hug. That's how he was, expressionless face, but showing love with his body and with words. Leaves and sand. But my body went stiff. I pulled away. I smiled reassurance into his eyes, not knowing why my body wouldn't let him hold me.

"Uh. Looka that..." Wendy bumped my arm—nearly spilling our Bloody Maries.

Wendy traced her finger across the curvaceous chalk-drawn belly of a pregnant woman underneath the words: *Pregnant Lady Special: drinks 2 for 1, all nine months!*

"I like this place!" She turned and exhaled a dry laugh.

The show was at Scum, a punk venue on the west side of Cleveland. I hadn't been here since the last show I played. Back in the black autumn before Georgie and I split up. I loved this place, where I'd spent so much time in my former life. There were two long rooms, one with a polished wooden bar and jukebox, the best jukebox in town. The other room was the main showroom, painted black with a mirrored wall at the back of the stage, and above the trim in the room, in the dark, were murals from back when this had been a gay dance club. The murals went unseen like shadows, but if you stopped and looked up, you'd see blue and black and dark red silhouettes of men having sex with men, men in cowboy hats with dropped pants and distant expressions, and women, too, lightly clasping long cigarette holders, and a lone figure in a doorway.

Scum was Cleveland: a mix of high and low, irony and passion. They sold MD 20/20 cheap, as well as a long menu of high-end microbrews. They'd built skate ramps in the show room and served locally sourced Mexican vegan food—cheap. The basement was a cave painted with cauldron images of long distorted breasts, anuses, elephants with penises for noses. The women's room had toilet paper and soap (rare for an underground venue), but the mirror wouldn't stay unbroken, and, for a while, a large mural called *Ghostfag* welcomed the women: black paint on red, a masculine person in a dress, looking over their shoulder running, sporting a five o' clock shadow and hairy testicles hanging out from under their dress as they run in thick witchy heels.

Scum was into international hardcore bands, not retro-punk or pop-punk, although sleazy punk was welcome, and anything far out. So, noise was welcome, too because it was loud and tangled, and quieter experimental music slipped in, too. The owner, Michael, was a surly guy known for his violence, his dark energy and his sharp humor. Everyone loved him for creating a venue/home for the weirdest shit/art/people that didn't fit into the commercial mold.

He had a crew of loyal kids, kids who'd jump behind the bar to help out when things got busy. Kids missing teeth from jumping into fights initiated by Michael himself against people bringing in outside beer or breaking speakers.

Quiet professors and early innovators of experimental electronic music could be found side by side with quivering street addicts bumping your arm for a dollar, just a dollar, to get a forty of Old English, or maybe crack, or the bus. And sometimes it *was* for the bus, you could get a forty of Old English at Scum for two dollars, but an RTA Day Pass cost five bucks.

That last show I'd played—I didn't know it would be my last. Until this night, Angelo's show. (And a bird shook constantly in my chest cavity all that morning, all that afternoon on Angelo's porch, and deep into this night.) In part because the last show I'd played had been a heartbreaker. Just as I was thrashing into the climax, my shit stopped working and I was muted. I writhed moaning on the ground, petting at the silver fur on my amplifier's numb, useless face.

I felt like a piece of shit.

People liked the set okay, seeing me cry and hit the thing. Hitting my guitar on the ground, *numb and useless.* I couldn't trust playing after that. There'd been a lot of malfunctions over the years, but I'd needed that show, I needed it to come out. (Two months after my *procedure* and bleeding through everything. *Something is wrong* was the mantra. I was sleeping on the couch at that point, and I remember trying to sleep that awful night, having to work in the morning.) The next day, I plugged everything in, and it worked fine.

Because there is a vortex at Scum: in the showroom with the black arcing skate ramps, and the dark mirrored wall. And there is a *shadowman* who lives there, and sometimes the player falls into the perfect trance, and other times the *shadowman* will tear the player down, so that she must build herself up again.

I told Wendy I wanted to set up my shit, that I'd be nervous until I got my amp and my new guitar and pack of cables, pedals, etc. into the showroom.

"Fucking Cher…it ain't worth it, Alice." Wendy followed me.

"You have a connection. Cher's great."

I saw the back of a fat head with a green Mohawk for just a second that looked familiar, then he was gone. All the people moved in layers of familiar, from these past dozen years I'd lived in Cleveland.

"We'll see. Sometimes I don't know if there's not more between us than just friction."

It was known that Angelo and I had quickly become close friends. People came up to me and asked me about line-up, etc. He texted me constantly to see how things were going, even before anyone was here. He referred to his guitarist as "a waste of sperm and egg."

Friends came in, but no Cher. Tom Orange, Henry, and Lucy, and more. Hugs all around. Mona Cost and Rocky from Red Liver, and Bill and Kerry from Noumenon Device. Arthur and Paloma. Murder and Juniper. Skin Graft, Dr. Quin, Collapsed Arc and Plague Mother. Bloodier Bloody Maries. No Cher.

It was only nine for a long time it seemed. The line-up was Noumenon Device first then Red Liver, then Angelo's band, then me.

We would wait until ten to start. Wendy and I sat at the bar. I tried to recall if this was the second or third Bloody Mary. They were too salty and very spicy hot. Thick. And they were dinner. Though my body was growing numb, I knew my mind would stay keen from that bird in my chest cavity quivering and waking me in anticipation of playing, and also of seeing Angelo.

(And this: I still hadn't told Wendy about seeing Billy and Mark—and that surely by now Simon knew I was alive.)

"It's just, Cher is what you call, high *mai*-ten-ence. That is, she wants to be wanting things, and keeping me waiting up and asking for her. But if I ask *her*, for anything, such as to just dig those long nails into this part," Wendy reached her arm back to her upper back, "this part that gets so sad, sore, from painting, just to dig a little bit, she looks at me like I asked her to suck a fart out my ass."

I caught a selfish glance of us between the crowded bottles against the bar mirror (what was this place fifty years ago, a bar... Or a hundred years ago, surely it was a bar then, for the factory workers just moved here, taking the streetcar down Detroit Avenue to visit their families in the old neighborhoods in the interior of the city, were there horses, too? Chickens in the yards, fresh eggs on the counter of this bar, this dark wood? And we were on Detroit Avenue, one of those ridges that had been Indigenous trails, and long before had once been the shore of Lake Erie, which was now a mile north and down from where we sat.)

Was this mirror here? A weeping mirror, melting sand.

I said, "She likes attention, that's all, she likes romance and drama. It's nice."

"Nice, but the attention, romance and drama only go one way!"

"I'll scratch your back, when you need it that bad."

"You don't have any nails."

She caught the bartender and asked her for two shots of Tequila, some special kind with gold flakes in it. I caught my own eyes again, my eyes like tiger eyes and my lips full and cheeks flushed, my high cheekbones stronger with age, I liked my face at thirty-four. I liked Wendy's face, too, the contrast of fast penetrating eyes, slightly hooded, strong features, quick to smile her gorgeous smile, but in this light, shadows made dark lines on either side of her mouth that frightened me.

"Here's to it, Alice."

"To dogs!"

We shot.

Goddamn! It was good. We picked limes off the napkin and sucked on them.

The heat was rising and the people sounds were getting bigger. Bar sounds of metal and glass and hominids chattering, some louder, speaking over others, an old Animals song weaved through it all.

I twisted off the bar stool and slipped into the mass, and there was Lucy in black. She hugged me and kissed me on the cheek. "Hey Margot, do you know when Angelo will be here?"

"Later, his guitarist..." My chest felt tight.

"It's okay, I know you guys talk all the time." She was breezy, waving away any awkwardness with one long hand.

Wendy pushed up between us, her whisky breath claiming me. "Who's this... hey. I'm Alice's girlfriend Wendy."

"Hey, Wendy my love, maybe you should go say hi to Cher." Cher was at the bar down a way behind Lucy. Smiling as she received a squat drink with an umbrella.

Wendy let go of my arm and pushed past Lucy, who said, "Alice?"

Michael came up to me, his eyes piercing though shadows. "Margot. It's after ten. Get shit started."

"I will. Good to see you, Michael, it's been a long time."

"Yeah," he grunted as he turned back into the crowd, elbowing a hipster in pink glasses.

Vibration, turning in the darkness to cover the small blue light. [whats happening?]

[Noumenon Device]

[be there in five]

Bill and Kerry of Noumenon Device were married, but they seemed to like each other. He built his own rigs: analog synths, wooden boards with rows of mini knobs and dozens of cables. She played synth, too, and did vocals. The story goes that they met in the middle of a performance piece over twenty years ago when she dropped a bucket of spaghetti on his head from the top of a ladder.

Their two giant wooden synths faced each other at an angle also facing the crowd. He sat, she stood. She was a small woman with clouds of frothy hair and her voice was low and frightening, sounding of reports, making dark witchy sounds. Bill focused on her while he worked his synthesizer.

We clapped and hooted for them as they floated their knobs down while the sound guy lifted the lights back up. There always seemed to be a purple light in the showroom, but it's hard to say if it's just a slanted memory.

I walked into the bar room with a long sigh as "Crimson and Clover" floated heavily in the air. I saw Wendy and Cher heading out the back door to the little parking lot where people go to smoke.

I turned then, Angelo smacked right into me and we were hugging. Warmth spread across my chest. The afternoon seemed like so long ago! We always met in relief and in smiling.

"C'mon…" he took my arm and jerked his head toward the bar. We copped a couple of Nascar nectars. I looked over to the back door, thinking of Wendy and Cher, and out comes green Mohawk from the men's room, wiping his hands on his jeans, and I realize it's Jeff fucking Vickers. Liz's brother, Mark's father. I'd glimpsed him earlier! But, this context was so screwy, it didn't register.

He walked up to the jukebox and put on Black Flag's "My War". He gripped both sides of the jukebox with thick hands and bopped his head.

I felt desperate to get Wendy out of there before she ran into him, but naturally, Jeff stood between me and the back patio.

I downed my drink and Angelo got us two more. He was saying something, and all I wanted to do was listen to him, but shit was on four sides. I saw Lucy sitting at the bar. She threw her head back and laughed.

"...morphic resonance?" Angelo was saying.

"Oh, what? Hey—want to go out to the front?" There was another patio out front facing Detroit.

"Okay, sure." He grinned. Then talked sideways at me as we headed out front. "It's this idea, some guy Sheldrake put out that humans are like subatomic particles, like material being moved by the subjective, consciousness, see there's a point when so many people have an idea that it's instantly communicated, instant paradigm shift." He put his hand on my arm, looked into my eyes and we understood each other.

"Oh, like, zeitgeist." I tried to hang on. All I wanted was to talk with him about these things, but my eyes followed a speeding car, and I looked into the street, I saw the street corners, and we were so close to Liz's house, cold spread across my chest, an ice flower crushing my chest, the bird and my breath, I felt short of breath, I wanted to *feel the smoke of crack hitting me there,* I felt my chest would never open again without it.

Even and especially here, this place I'd laughed and drank and played with friends who were faint acquaintances now, and it was layered, this whole city was layered now with that old music life and the life I spent waiting for crack alone. What is this life, I wanted nothing more than to breathe, to look into Angelo's eyes, to find *the spirit of this age* but more, I wanted to be alone in my room with Clarence and

235

the thick blue carpet. Maybe I'd come out of the cocoon too early.

He said, "Yeah, there are so many examples of this… "

I said, "Yes, the Spirit of the Age, transmitted from heart chakra, the seat of the soul, the individual soul, billowing out into the universal soul."

He looked at me. His eyes were work to look into. I put my hand to my chest and looked past him to the sidewalk, weeds grew through the cracks there. Knee-high stalks with rough green bundles of green for catching the sun.

"Go on then, ya fucking crackhead, go on!" came a voice from The Hawk, the old-man gay bar next door. We turned as a woman was shoved out the entrance, some eighties song fading fast as the barkeep closed the door tight after her.

"You got five bucks, honey?" The woman wore round glasses and hair slick to her scalp, radiating from her crown like she'd just stood up out of a pool. She sidled up to Angelo. He just ignored her and faced me more directly.

Cars went by fast. The funeral parlor across the street next to the furrier cast a cold white light, a false Moon.

"I might have some money." I reached into my pocket.

"Shit. I was talking to *him*. Not. You."

"All right."

The woman turned to him. "Don't trust her, son. She won't be true."

He said to me, "Do you want to go back in?"

"Yeah. In a minute, I have to tell you something."

The woman stood looking at us.

"You mind?" He said.

She chirped and turned away.

"Angelo, there's some people from when I was addicted, I might be in trouble with. And Wendy, too. And one of them is here."

He looked me steady in the eye. "What are you saying? Do you need

236

to leave? I can get you out of here."

I longed for it. "I can't, I've got to stay with Wendy."

"Are you sure? You're my friend. If you need to get out of here, or anything. I'll keep close to you."

"That means everything. Thank you. There's things Wendy doesn't know, and she'd be so pissed, so there's that, too. Angelo."

"Yes?"

"It's funny but. I'm as afraid of Wendy finding out as I am of them."

"Wendy should never get pissed at you. No one should. People in relationships don't ever need to get pissed at each other. I'm here if you need me."

I hugged him and wished we could stay like that. I couldn't say that Wendy would lock me away or worse if she knew I'd gone back to Liz's or ran into Billy. I couldn't say why I'd let her, why I half wanted to be locked away.

When we walked back into the bar room, "Ring of Fire" was playing, and Jeff was no longer in the room. Rocky from Red Liver said they'd be ready to go on in five.

Angelo turned to me, but then Lucy walked up to us.

Lucy glanced at Angelo, then hugged me. She stood back with her arms crossed and stared coyly at Angelo. He stood tall. She jerked her head at him as she packed her pack of long lady cigarettes. "Come on, fella, let's talk."

He put his hand on my arm. I noticed he had a peacock and a pigeon painted on his shirt. "I'll be back in a few minutes, text me if you need anything. Be careful." Then he followed her through the bar and out the back door.

I texted Wendy. [where are you – everything cool?]

In the main room, my hands shook, and my bravado melted quickly into shuddering guilt. As Red Liver played, my wretched mind raced, and I didn't see Angelo, which could mean just one thing. For him to miss two bands at a show he booked, he must be having an important conversation with Lucy. My hands were empty. After all those stinking drinks, how could I still feel so terribly sober.

Red Liver roared. Mona's dude joined the two women on guitar, and he was better than usual. Tense heavy metal guitar over the women shrieking and beating their gear, Mona in convulsions on the floor, lovingly giving her own feedbacking black and gold guitar tender kicks.

The door opened. I turned and Angelo walked in—with Lucy. I felt strange without him by my side. They held hands. That's good, good for him. I texted Wendy, [what happening now] He leaned over and looked at me, to see if everything was okay, I just shrugged. I asked them if they'd seen Wendy, and they said she was out back doing shots and bullshitting with anyone around her. Maybe Jeff had just slipped away, maybe it was nothing. Maybe he came here for punk and got noise instead and just left.

The crowd cooed. My heart hurt. There were a good number of people here, really, suddenly, maybe two dozen. I peeked above them and saw the begging woman from out front on stage, bumping her hip against Rocky's. Guitarist Eric looked a little pissed for a second but then stuck his tongue out and nodded.

The crusty punks in the crowd, the regular regulars, loved the woman, while the noisers weren't a hundred percent sure. People called her a crackhead, but obviously, she was drunk. I should know: I'd been the former and aspired to the latter.

Someone grabbed my arm like a purse. Lucy. "Oh jeez, M, what do you think of that." She whispered in my ear. Her breath smelled like green tea and honey, no wonder he wanted her.

The woman on stage raised her hands and swung her enormous

breasts back and forth. Rocky grimly drooled into her heavy gear.

"How are things with Angelo, then." I said. I was still shaking.

"He's great...a *wonderful* lover. A little clingy, know what I mean? He wanted to move in together right off. I'm like, not again, right? You know, give it three months and they're on you about leaving lights on, and when you walk in the room, they don't look up."

"I know. Maybe he's not like that."

"You can't talk to them about it. Then it seems like you're complaining, which is what they're waiting for, so they can tell you it's in your head, like, you present evidence, and they're like *you're still holding onto that, wow, what does that have to do with this?* Like tendencies don't exist, or you don't have a right to be upset when the relationship changes, when the passion fades, when they get controlling in subtle passive ways."

I didn't want to hear this. Now she was spitting in my ear. I never heard someone say it out loud. It gave me a chill deep in my bones. I knew I wouldn't live with a man again.

I pointed to the stage.

Lucy looked.

The woman had dropped her blue sweatpants and turned around, bent over and spread her cheeks. She swayed gently back and forth. Rocky and Eric looked distracted from the effort of ignoring it, while Mona had taken all her shit to the floor and was pounding and spitting circles.

"Gosh!" Lucy laughed a little bark and let her smile glaze over. She put her hand to her mouth.

What she'd said about living with men, as if it were inevitable. I'd been there with different men, such different men, but things always turned out like she said. But Noumenon Device. They seemed different. They seemed like best friends.

No word from Wendy. Angelo came back and handed Lucy a Nascar

239

Nectar, the same drink he'd handed me earlier. He didn't look at me. We were just the same to him, warm bodies. What mattered was who showed up. Who was available.

My heart was a stone sinking to my gut. That bird in there... something had drained the blood from my fingers. The naked woman's old man came in and dragged her off stage. (But not before some regulars got pictures that would grace the bar's Hall of Fame for the rest of the summer, to be sure.)

Red Liver finished with a pounding beat in isolation, the players panting. Our friend Murder peeled off a surprise two-minute set of high frequency shrill, shaking some punks from the crowd and pleasuring the rest of us. It was time for Angelo's band to play.

I'd heard Angelo's band's releases before, but this was my first time seeing them live. A beefy metal guy with a shaved head commanded a massive drum kit that looked over-the-top but thundered just right. Two other guys flanked Angelo, one playing bass, the other guitar, and Angelo had a sampler on a little round pedestal. They all had mics, but he did the lead vocals. He'd written most of the songs. The vocal dynamic was amazing. I'd grabbed another drink, a double shot of Jagermeister on ice, and my body warmed up again. I smiled, even though Lucy was up front dancing her ass off.

Angelo was my friend. Halfway through their short set, he said some words, some thanks, and he thanked me directly, looked me in the eye, then shook the sweat out of his hair, as they went back into a rumbling song. The bassist had traded out the bass for tape electronics that sounded like wild shrieks, moans and electricity.

I loved watching Angelo. He lifted his hands in the air and told the truth. He ran down the skate ramp into the crowd. Sexy. He just wore an undershirt revealing pictures on his body I'd never seen. And his dog tags. He had power—and I realized something about true power (I didn't think of Wendy): He manifested true power, which has nothing to do with oppressive power. I could feel it charging off his body, he had the power to liberate and empower others, and to express righteous anger in song. This wonderful loud sound. I wanted the power and was the power, too. *Potencia.*

When they were finished, he walked up to me, and we fell into each other's arms. "Great set," I said. "Thanks," he said, "Thanks for being here." He pulled his undershirt away from his skin to air it out. "Sorry for being so sweaty."

Lucy came up, and she wasn't sweating. With a cold smile, she said she was going out for a cigarette.

"I'll go 'wit-cha," said Angelo.

I watched him stride off with her. I watched the strength in his back, his songs still ringing in my head and jangling around his body.

They went to the front patio, and I went to the back.

They were all right there under the Moon: Cher, Wendy and Jeff Vickers, passing around a joint. My throat went thick. I wanted to hurt something.

Then Wendy jerked me all the way around.

She was shaking. "I got to go with him."

"What?"

Jeff patted me on the shoulder. "I'm real sorry about what my son did to you honey, that kid's *spoiled.* Always been a little shit."

Wendy leaned into my ear, "He doesn't know. Simon just sent him to get me. Damn… if you'd just kept your fucking head down. It was *bad* that he didn't hear about you from me."

Jeff coughed.

Cher looked at me, "Nobody's telling me shit. Where are they going."

Then Angelo and Lucy were there. I choked on cognitive dissonance—people from the crack days and the music days all here around

241

me. I wanted to grab Angelo and run.

"Jeff, what's Simon want with Wendy? He doesn't need anything with Wendy."

"I don't know hon. Mister Mysterious-o."

"Margot, what's going..." Angelo stepped up, but I shook my head at him.

Wendy said, "Oh, *you*, if she wasn't always trying to go out and see you, we'd be fine."

Jeff puffed up. "Who's this guy? You know Margot, my brother Billy likes you, he's a good guy."

"Well, that might be helpful later, but for now, hands off." Wendy put her hands on my shoulders.

Cher stood up. "I'm out. I'm done."

Wendy said nothing as Cher walked away.

Wendy clasped my hand. Then she looked at Jeff and Angelo. "Margot's my girlfriend, now, consider her with me. Got it?"

Then she looked me in the eye. Her eyes were bloodshot, and her voice hoarse. She told me to get a ride home, to sleep, we'd talk in the morning. She said she was sorry she couldn't stay and watch me play.

I hugged Wendy, and she bit my ear.

I jerked back, and then they tore off. I felt dizzy from people slipping away.

I saw a sign on the brick wall that said, "DON'T FEED THE CRACKHEADS."

Angelo and Lucy walked with me back inside. They said they'd give me a ride home.

It was time to play. I felt like that guy from *The Day of the Locust* with the big hands. I focused on setting up all the cables and plugs. The crowd had thinned. It was late. I was in the dark room, in a

circle again, but finally, I had my simple set-up set up and I played for
survival. Slow strokes building into bad electric buildings and

Wearing teeth *oh and calling cancer off of my shoulders*
slouching teeth the leopard bones mortal stones
take the can't hearing of this day—the hang
over threats
teeth senses to the sound of stones—the mortal stones
cancer candy called back and wanted
wanted for the last time one piece of lick—hate
the cancer—lick
jackals suddenly behind legs
but no one followed after all
just and only the jackals' breathing legs
tongue shadows
I know them
wanting for the last time one piece of lick—hate
August fell like two weeks of rotting wood
cold rot

December Jackals dressed like bolts behind me—if
If the rain felt underground could dress like night behind me
I am racing against collectors and money gods and cancer time
Sometimes December Jackals drink all my wine
and leave me with the suck of a bruised puncture sore
mmahhsssss and let them fall behind you

and a circle of light opens around me, I see other purple caves and
blind violets rise up just inside the front of me and I see Angelo in the
purple light *duende* and his face is the face of a loving bee.

There was that good *old* rush from playing that was like nothing else, and it was chased with more liquor. Wendy didn't text to say if she was okay, or when she'd be home. I rode in the backseat behind Angelo and Lucy, who seemed tighter than ever before. He said nothing to me about Wendy. We rode in silence.

But I'd seen him play, and he'd seen me play.

I didn't think I'd be able to sleep, but I did. I dreamed of my mother. It was the night before they left for Arizona, and she was telling me that I could come after them if I wanted, but they wouldn't be coming back to Ohio. Her red hair was faded and flicked with more white. She sucked hard on her cigarette. She said I was grown. She said it was my choice, but that she wasn't much of a phone person. It was like when a dead one appears in a dream, and suddenly the dream has dimension. I woke up in a sweat at four not remembering if that's how it had gone when they left, or if I just dreamed it that way. Back in sleep, her youngest face hovered in the wood over a stream in the parks by the house we all lived in together.

19

Mostly Animals

I woke wrapped inside a body. Holding a hand to my chest. I remembered it couldn't be Angelo, and my heart tore. Wendy. I looked to the door. I wanted to tear her hand off my body and run away from here forever. Then I remembered how she'd left with Jeff Vickers last night and I clutched her hand.

I'd slept with that door beyond my feet, the door that only locks from the outside. She is okay, and I am okay. We have survived the night.

I pulled her long cool hand to my lips. She moaned and pulled me in tighter to her, and Clarence by my head on the pillow, situated like a black hen, purred.

I felt her clothed body against my naked body, wearing what she almost always wore: blue cotton work shirt and jeans, both worn and soft, like my father wore when I was a young kid.

"Life..." she whispered in my ear after some time, "...Life is something like a web of errors. Like a web in your throat, swallowing cotton, or in the woods, a wet spider web wrapping around your bare ankles. But sharp. A web of briars. Like a person, an *actor* in this world, with perceived *agency*, becomes bigger than all the other ones, stepping on them, breaking them, and in this way *errs*." We were both awake now. She gripped me tightly. "With every move. Sharp wet grass, maybe. Mosquito bites on your ankles. Or in the morning, waking up to spider bites, so you know spiders have been crawling on your legs and feet at night. 'At night.' That's weird, like night is a place.

"So *Alice*, or the stranger, *Margot Jones*, life, is a web of errors. No meaning beyond that. Meaning is an error. Meaning will be weeded out eventually, maybe now. Drugs. See, we take drugs to feel *up* and also *peaceful*, at once, don't we? We put the drugs in our bodies to feel the *fire* like a button we can press. Rich people can go to a spa, poor people need drugs. But it's just stuff in the web of errors."

"Wendy—what's the deal. I should have gone with you."

"Cher knows, things I didn't want her to know. She's moving along."

I held both her hands in mine. Clarence stretched, dropped to the floor and padded over to his food bowl.

"Why, did you have to go out in the world, like that?" Her body radiated heat. She gripped me so my rib cage felt tight. "I could have kept you here, in this room. With your paints, and your yoga and your cat. You had to go out looking for *men*, looking for your old art fag friends."

She pulled one hand free and started fondling my right breast.

"It's like you've got some kind of *stink* on you that brings those toms around, that cross-eyed redneck Billy, and, that, psycho kid Mark, I cannot believe," she hissed, and I felt rage coming off her that seemed fresh and old, pre-memory, "that you went back to that APARTMENT where it happened!" She wrapped both my legs in hers.

"What happened last night, after you went with Jeff."

She caught her breath and held still. "Are you in love with that weird guy?"

"What? They're all weird."

246

"Your friend. Angelo."

"He's got a girlfriend." The heat in my body oscillated between sexy and suffocating, itchy. "And, also, he lives with his ex-wife. And also, I'd never want to live with a man again, they change. It changes when living together, it's practically a chemical change. I don't want to live with anyone, really, to be honest."

She loosened up and began to touch my side in long strokes down to my hip. "You know, those things, that's not what I asked."

"Too bad about Cher."

"She knew. She didn't need to know about my old job, to know I've been distracted with protecting you."

"That's what you've been doing—protecting me." I closed my eyes. My body was melting, opening under her touch. I almost laughed. "Well, I liked Cher. Angelo is a friend I love, I love him as a friend, he loves, but he doesn't need me, he's got Lucy to love."

"That's good, 'cause I have a plan, and it involves letting everybody go. But the cat. You just hang onto me like a baby chimp grips its mama, and I'll take you places, girl."

"Okay, Wendy. Oh—we need to give Clarence his injection today." She stroked me and my eyes closed. I heard a lawnmower rev up, somewhere in the neighborhood.

"At the end of the summer, we leave. New names, leave in the night. Free from those guys for good. We can go to Colorado, or California, or wherever. Where your folks live? Arizona. Yeah?"

I opened my eyes. I didn't want to take trouble to my family. I never wanted Simon to know where my family lived. "No, Texas. Wendy, what happened with Simon."

"We have to work for him, for a few months, for *free*. Bullshit. But then, you and me, vanish without a trace."

"What... that's insane. You know what? Fuck him. He doesn't really have anything. It's not like he can go to the cops. We can protect ourselves from one little man."

"He could tell Vickers what I did. He'll always have that. He could say, could say he just found out. He could say I had beef with the woman. They'd believe that. They love him now."

That didn't seem true.

She moved her hand to my inner thigh, but I froze. A steel wall rose up inside me, leaving me still wet, but cold. It was the same when Angelo hugged me yesterday. Closed door.

She sensed my sudden rigidity and pulled her hand back, and then sat up a little bit and started petting my hair.

I rolled onto my back and looked up into her face. I was damaged. Her eyes, so pale blue, I could never read them. Angelo's dark blue-green eyes moved like waters, but Wendy's eyes always seemed still and cold. They could penetrate, but not be penetrated. Yet, her forehead creased in concern. *Read her, read her, why can't I read her?*

I felt as if Angelo and Wendy were one person pulled into multiple dimensions and I was a being from a lower dimension who was trying to pull together the whole of the person I loved, the person who knew me, the person I knew. But then I felt shocked and alienated by this dehumanizing, solipsistic thought.

Wendy ran her fingers through my hair, gently pulling apart the tangles. Her smile was beautiful and convincing like a movie star's: you *believe* in its authenticity, even though it's perfect and always ready to shine.

"I love you Margot." She bent down and kissed me softly. It was when she said my true name to me, that I then felt like I belonged to her.

I reached up and touched her face. I stopped watching her and I touched her face. I told her I worried for her through the night.

"I just wished I could have seen you play."

"Ha. I'm playing again at the Spider Moon Fest in a few weeks.

You'll be there." I felt strangely soothed, as though things were settled. Angelo was with Lucy. And I was with Wendy. Cher was gone, and it was Wendy and me now. It was clear. But it was a superficial mental peace, helped along by exhaustion and the need to resolve a hangover. There was still a deep, painful nagging line running from my heart to my gut. I rubbed my hand there, to make it go away.

"Margot, we're meeting Simon this afternoon. I'm sorry, but we have to meet him, to work out the details." She sensed my fear and pulled me to her chest as she lay back, and I wrapped my arms around her.

We met Simon at an old castle by the lake. It was a mansion cut up and converted into a coffee shop and boutiques. Wendy said it had become his public meeting place. It was new, an old woman had lived there alone and recently died. I didn't even know the place existed, and to not know was strange, as if this castle had appeared by my lake out of nowhere.

Ostensibly, it was a just a hip new spot for scenesters and yups. But, there was something not right about the place. I promised myself to come back when I was free to explore the wandering balconies that wrapped around the first and second floor. Just to come back and look at the lake free and alone would be a miracle.

We were in the café situated in the parlor of the old mansion. The long windows fit tight and clean for such an old house. But the air was flat. The floor was embarrassing, you'd think in an old mansion the floors would be beautiful, built in an era when even humble homes boasted fine sturdy craftsmanship. But these floors were dark and warped and rough, and I didn't understand it. They creaked. And when we sat, our table kept wobbling. We were afraid for our drinks.

We had to wait. And meeting in a coffee shop instead of a bar didn't help our nerves. "Hey, how did they know you'd be at Scum last night, anyway?"

"Well, *Margot Jones*. Your name was all over the Facebook event. Goof-ass Facebook. *Angelo Qamar* promoted it well." She spoke as if she didn't trust our very names.

"So, how they'd know you'd be there?"

"Margot. They came for you. I talked Jeff into taking me instead."

"Oh, shit. Wendy." I went for her hand, but she pulled her elbows off the table and hid them in her lap.

"Just, be cool."

The place was empty. Wendy and I sat at our small round table. I had the feeling that there was a dining hall at the back of the house with a picture window overlooking the lake, and I wished we were there. The dreams of the lake lived inside me—the lake was a seat of power. But there were walls in the way. The windows by our table looked out over still, manicured bushes.

The only worker came over and asked if we needed anything. Her voice was loud and clear but stifled by the crazy floor. All sounds lacked resonance in this place. Her hair was natural, kinky and beautiful, her eyes were lined in dark electric blue.

"Hey, I know you..." She pointed softly to Wendy.

"Naw." Wendy picked up the menu.

"No—you're Barb's daughter, right? Natalie? I'm Sha'nee's daughter, Becca. How have you been? You meeting Simon?"

"You're wrong, hon, my name's Wendy." The way she pursed her lips, I could tell she wanted a cigarette.

Becca shook her head. "Okay then. Wendy. Well, can I get you a scone or, you?" She looked at me. I shook my head and held my mug of blackberry sage tea.

"What was that?"

She shook her head and looked at the door and Simon was there.

He looked strangely old, his face slightly asymmetrical and his color grey.

He kept his eyes on me as he floated over and sat to my right. He held out his hand, and I shook it. I realized with horror that his face seemed off because of a deep scar on his forehead that hadn't been there before. Wendy had been gone all night, maybe she'd sold me out after all.

He clasped my hand. "Margot, I want you to know, from the sincerest place inside me, that I am glad and relieved that you are still with us. I apologize for my rash decision earlier this year." I thought he was going to kiss my hand, but instead he let it go lightly. His lips and eyes looked dry. He placed his steady hands flat on the table.

"Simon, I apologize for hurting you." I only hit the back of his head to the floor, but my memory was distorted, did I hit him in his face, too?

"Shh, girl, you can't hurt me. Ha." His laugh was short and deep. He and Wendy looked nothing alike. The only resemblance was that her pale blue eyes and his light hazel eyes were both slightly hooded and seemed opaque, hard to see into, impossible to read.

Becca came over. "Hey Simon, you want some chai tea?"

"Sure, sweet baby. Wendy, you see I got our little sister working here? She's in school for environmental engineering."

Wendy nodded, her lips tight. Becca didn't look at her but smiled at me and walked back behind the counter. "Hard to keep track of all the kids our dad made. It's not like we grew up together..."

"I take care of all my sisters now, well, but baby Becca can take care of herself, that's for sure. Ha." Again the short deep laugh. He had changed since acquiring Liz and Sig's territories.

"Sweet Margot Jones." He took my hand again and gestured for my other hand. The table lurched a little as I reached over to accommodate his nonverbal request. Both my hands in his, and his hands were smaller than mine, dry, but warm. "That tea okay? We can get some milk and honey in there if you want."

He smiled at Becca when she set his tea on the table. The floor moaned as she walked away.

I shook my head and smiled, "It's good." I couldn't believe his forehead had such deep creases in it now. But then, I'd mostly ever seen him in the dark.

"Now, Wendy tells me that you and she would like to make amends for the time you all spent hiding from me, assuming the worst about me, et cetera. She says you would be happy to do some work."

"I am glad that it's all open now."

He did kiss my hands then and set them down.

"Well. Now, you're both going to work it off, over maybe three months?"

"Thanks, again, Simon." There was a twinge of fear in Wendy's quick smile. I was troubled by her deference to him.

"We won't prostitute ourselves." I said to him. His face changed. There was a brief angry silence where he looked at me as if I'd laid a chunk right on the table.

Then he leaned into me and said with quiet reptilian heat, "I don't need that. You think I would sell my *sister*? And I don't need you. I got some pretty young gals working for me now. You don't even know." He sat up and looked at me with loathsome pleasure. "Anyways, I want to keep you for myself. How 'bout you work yours off by spending weekends with me. Just me."

Wendy said to me, "Margot, I can back up whatever weekend story you want me to, for your friends, I'll back you up if you want to tell them you're doing some out of town job or something."

I was shaking from my core, like that day I smashed his head into his own floor. "No."

Simon sat back, crossed his arms and raised his eyebrows at me.

Wendy started to say something, but I held my index finger up to her. "Simon, I'll do some work for you. Just for the sake of peace and good feelings. But I'm not opening my legs, or anything else for you or anyone against my will ever again."

I took a sip of my tea. "I told people, people you don't know, people you wouldn't be able to guess, I told them exactly where to place blame if Wendy or I go missing or turn up dead. I've got triggers in this city and other places. Anything happens to us, they and the cops come for *you*."

"Damn Margot—you are full of horseshit. You are not making much of a case for yourself."

"Just see then. We go missing, just wait and see how long it takes for them to come for you. Have you ever been able to predict what I would do? No. You have not."

He nodded in short bursts. "Okay, then. HA. I've had some inkling of your tenacious integrity rearing its ugly head from time to time. Despite your general passivity. Okay, so, what then. Ya can't do any running around for me, 'cause you don't have a *car*." His foot tapped nervously, causing the floor to squeak.

Becca started towards us, but then she turned and went back into the kitchen.

"And I can't have you doing most other kind of work because you're too willful, and too motherfucking *crazy*."

"Simon, maybe she could help Billy with the…"

"No." he pointed his finger first at Wendy, then at me. It shook just a hair. He sat back and crossed his arms again, his eyes never leaving mine, nor mine his. "How about you *cook* something for me. Yes. How about you come to my house one night. And cook me some supper."

I nodded slightly.

"Cook me some *meat*."

We drove home in silence. Inside, I asked her what the fuck was that. She went to the kitchen. I followed her. She pulled out a half a can of beef stew left from her breakfast and ate it fast and cold.

"Why are you scared of him? What work does he have you doing? You made it out like the meeting would be for both of us, what happened last night?"

"Jeff and Billy told me he's changed. To look at him you can see it. They say he's into vulgar displays of power. They say he's gotten rough. Lizabeth Vickers was both our first times at taking things to that level. But for me, it was the end. For him, it was the beginning." She tossed the can in recycling without rinsing it and pulled baloney out of the fridge. I wanted to grab her skinny hips.

"You said the Vickers loved him."

"I say a lot of shit."

"Why wait till the end of summer, why not leave now?"

She handed me a piece of white bread. I shook my head but took it. She made herself a sandwich. "He gets off too much on the quick and nasty power that violence brings. It's a power that won't last, but in the meantime, we've got to be cool. Now he's got shit going on all over the Midwest, people everywhere. Bosses who last, like Liz and Sig, they do work for peace among the workers and the customers and everybody more than anything, you know. So, I see Simon running himself into the ground fast, then probably Jeff'll take over. Meantime, though, he won't let us move until we've made some gestures of concession to him. Or he'll do us in a big way. We're too high profile. We're too *symbolic* in his mind."

"He's fucking nuts. What about Johnny Maker? What does Johnny say about Simon these days?"

"How the fuck should I know."

"I just don't understand. I thought maybe Johnny kept him, from getting like this." I thought of that day in Burger King, how different

Simon was then, laughing with his cousin over Batman comics. Who was Simon really?

"Well, Johnny Maker and Simon are not talking. That bit I know anyway. Obviously Johnny is not into Simon's style these days."

"His style."

"You should have just gone along with him. What he means by 'cooking meat' I do not know. Fucking him maybe would have been a little friendlier." She slapped her phone on the counter. It had been bedazzled by Cher's niece.

"My mouth just said 'no' to him. My mind wanted to concede, but my heart acted through my body and said no."

"Well. You've done it for crack before, though I'm sure. And that kid Mark fucked you, and you didn't even know it right? I'm thinking fucking Simon on weekends maybe would have kept you alive, but I don't know what'll happen to you now."

"How can you say those things? You can't imagine how I feel, can you?"

She took her sandwich and left the kitchen. "I got to go to work. I'll protect you if I can."

"What's he got *you* doing? Wendy."

She shut her bedroom door.

Her door stayed shut. I picked her glittery phone off the table and gripped Johnny Maker's number. I texted him from my room.

Forty-five minutes later I stood in his apartment. He lived a half-hour walk from Wendy's, just around the corner from Scum. His carpet was dry and dusty, and the long old windowpanes beat in the spring wind, but his walls were full of life. As he made red zinger tea my eyes followed the lines of wild red, gold and black murals that covered the yellowed walls.

He hadn't questioned why I wanted to see him. When I arrived, I told him I was worried about Simon—he nodded and went to the kitchen to make tea. He had a single room with a kitchen and bathroom off of that—it looked like the apartment had once been larger, one of the quadruplexes built for factory families during the turn of the last century when they were moving away from tenements, but at some point, the front chunk of his apartment and had been walled off.

The murals—I thought of Angelo, and how Johnny and Angelo shared an aesthetic, and maybe sometime after all this shit was settled, we could all hang out. Because the murals were vivid like the colors of Angelo's house, and the shapes suggested mountains and the mountains were built from people, but it was an illusion because the mountains had faces and then the land on top was made from sunlight, but also plants—they were abstracted but suggestive, and so, also surreal, almost like op-art, but soft. The walls were saturated with color, green slithered through gold, sparks of deep blue popped in red—they created an environment, a fleshy forest that cozied the room. I thought of Maurice Sendak's *Where the Wild Things Are,* when Max's walls dissolved into trees and his room became the world.

The room contained only a stereo, a small table with a stained-glass top, stacks of books and a mattress on the floor covered with a beautiful quilt. I remembered Simon comparing me to Johnny, and I could see why—his room was a little like mine had been, but cleaner, more monastic. He came back and lit some incense on top of the stereo that sweetened the room with gentle patchouli before getting sucked out the open window.

Then he pulled the small table to the mattress, put the tea on it and gestured for me to sit. We sat. He didn't have music on, but the birds were loud. I felt old. This was the setting for a young friendship, but I knew I wouldn't be around here much longer.

"Thanks for having me over Johnny, with no questions, it's gracious of you."

"I know Simon's been crazy lately. If I were you, I'd get out of town."

I picked up the round china cup and smelled the hibiscus. "Why do they call you Johnny Maker?"

He laughed a low laugh and looked into his own red tea. "Well—when I was a kid, we'd drink Johnnie Walker, well, we drank it once or twice, usually we drank shit like Mad Dog, or Steel Reserve, whatever we could get our hands on, so... my name is John or Johnny, and often I'd ghost, but they didn't really have that word then, so they called me Johnny Walker, or The Walker, like, we'd be hanging out and I'd just *walk* off or whatever, and one time..." He smiled into his tea, "...one time we were tripping on acid, one of the first times, and they started in with that shit, like, 'We better make sure Johnny don't walk off on his own *this* time', and I said, 'I'm not Johnny Walker, I'm Johnny *Maker*!'" He smiled, looking into his cup, and gave a halfhearted wave at the walls, and some canvases piled on the floor by the books.

"That's cool."

"Naw, it's dumb, but it stuck."

"I wish I'd met you some other time, Johnny. I could look at these walls all day."

"You paint, too, right?"

"Some. Mostly animals. Beasts."

We heard children playing in the street.

"Johnny—is Simon mean? In his heart? I don't understand Simon, and I don't understand Wendy."

"You know, Margot—I don't like to leave this room. I go to work. I go for walks. But I'm not a social guy. I love my little cousin. Simon was a bright kid who got in trouble some, but smart, and I didn't think he was mean, no. I thought he was kind, but hard, you know.

Simon and Wendy, you know it's funny, her name isn't even *Wendy*, really, but that's her now. Wendy. Like, flying around with Peter Pan, like the woman riding the wind... Their dad was mean. But, they didn't even know him, they weren't raised by him. They were kind of rootless, especially her. At least Simon had a good mom, but Wendy's mom always treated her like a rat, always kicking her out, calling her nasty names. I know they were jealous sometimes of my parents, who were stable and nurturing. I didn't see Wendy much as a kid—you know, we got closer just a few years back when she moved back, and she and Simon were together all the time.

"I admired her when she was an activist, and we were started to work on some projects together, but then she got really into the idea of being a criminal, like it's 1920's Chicago or some shit. I'd tell her, 'This is not a movie.' But Simon—he was... I remember him as a little guy, you know? I can still feel the top of his head in my palm.

"Now that he's a killer, I won't see him anymore. He's come to my door, but I won't see him. I can't. You got to have boundaries, Margot. Most people don't even know shit about boundaries. Sometimes it seems like we aren't taught anything in this culture. Nothing about how to focus our minds or make real choices or even how take care of our bodies, or even feel with our bodies. Our *bodies*." He pushed up from the mattress and walked over to the stereo and put on Nina Simone. I closed my eyes.

I wanted to tell him my situation, but I was ashamed. Johnny Maker was a free person, and I had caged myself. How could I tell him Simon wanted me to cook him meat, and that Wendy was my lover but also my keeper? That I worked but had no money to run. That I felt bound to Wendy, but I felt free with Angelo. The whole thing was pathetic. I looked into the mountains on his walls. My vision softened a little and I could almost feel away out, but when I grasped, the vision snapped away.

"Margot—I can't make Simon not be a bad man."
"What are you going to do, Johnny?"
"Steer clear of the folly of ambition and the pull of bad men."

Clarence rubbed his cheek against my hand as I brushed him. He was plump from his saline treatment. I took care to avoid the place in between his shoulder blades where we'd given him his injection. He looked me in the eye. His eyes were yellow like the sentient Moon. Since we'd been treating his kidney disease, his fur had deepened and now shined blue-black like a crow.

I took an Adderall from a small clay box on my desk. I swallowed the pill with lukewarm water from the blue cup at my sink. I needed to get clear. I did yoga, but I did it too hard. Instead of clearing the crap out of my system, the postures clanged around me, my muscles spasming in echo.

My phone vibrated on the desk. I couldn't believe I'd left home without it. Angelo had texted six times. He wondered if we were okay. He wondered if I wanted to hang out tonight. I wanted to toss the phone out the window. I'd lied to Simon, naturally, about telling people to look to him if I went missing. I thought about telling Angelo. I thought about sending Noam an email. But, if I died, I wouldn't want them to make any moves. I wanted to keep them off of Simon's radar at all costs.

I picked up my guitar. I heard Wendy close the front door. The guitar felt good in my hands. I shouldn't even talk to Angelo. Simon would dig hurting people I loved. Wendy and I should run, shave our heads, change our names again. The leonine self-portrait stared at me, waiting for a true name.

I reached inside my gig bag and pulled out the sack of mushrooms Henry had given me.

I called Angelo.

20

A Secret Door

Then it was balmy night. Angelo and I sat five feet apart in the sand under the Moon. An hour ago we'd eaten Henry's mushrooms, and now we were in a space outside of place and a time outside of time. I smiled and gently traced circles in the sand. He kept checking his phone. Now his ex-wife Melissa wanted him. Fine. Because *we* were *here*. We were on the smallest secret beach, just under big rocks and trees.

Getting over to Angelo's to finish work on the flier for the Spidermoonfest had been a life-saving diversion. I wanted to tell him everything. I even said, "I'm so scared, everything will be all right, right, Angelo?" And he promised it would, but that's all I said. He was worked up about Melissa, who was camping with an old friend but had left him a note saying, "Dear A, we were good together. It's been years and we still suck. Let's get back together. I'll take you to dinner Monday when I get back. Love Mel."

"What the fuck is this? Who is she to me? She's the one who left, says she needed more space, then she comes here to my new place, says she needs a place to stay, just friends, and then we're barely friends. We don't talk. Nothing. And things are really working with Lucy—she's a cool lady." He was sitting bolt upright at his dining room table cutting out spiders and moons for the flier, while I sat to his right nodding and cutting. Breathing deeply to keep my heart steady.

"Are you sure it wasn't another Mel? JK."

"Nothing led up to this Margot. She's craahzy. *Craahzy*."

"Angelo, did you hear about that kid who was killed by the police? They didn't even suspend the cop. They drug tested the kid's body."

"Black children getting killed by cops all over this country. Always been."

We were drinking sleazy pink wine from a box. We hadn't eaten the mushrooms yet. When I showed him the baggie, he'd made a big O with his mouth and stowed them in a little drawer, suggesting we have a few drinks first. He had on *The Creek*, a shitty corporate radio station. Its tagline breathless and sexy: "We'll play *what the other stations won't.*" The commercials drove me nuts, but Angelo was in the mood for eighties music. Madonna would follow Men at Work, and he'd be happy, then a commercial would send me back into the dark box in my heart, where I knew we'd both be dead someday and not know each other anymore. Then a Foo Fighters song would come on and he'd slam the switch from radio to tape and say, *neeext*, sending harsh noise out the speakers.

"Do you love her?"

"What. No. What? Do you love your ex-husband?"

"Oh. No. I've loved people. Even people I've had flings with, or loved as friends. And my family. But Georgie... I loved who I thought he was, then who I thought he might become but didn't." I put the scissors down and pressed my hands into my thighs. "Okay, when I first was with him, I loved him, I was ready to love completely, but he only loved the way I loved him, he didn't love me. Or else he wouldn't have done the things to me that he did. And then I stopped loving him when I saw that. And it was early on. We stayed together for years after, and I felt dead inside because I thought it was *love itself* that wasn't real. I thought maybe, secretly, that men hated women, that men couldn't see women at all. So, sometimes I wake up grinding my teeth and catching my breath because I'm afraid he's still here. He never hit me in the face, there were other things he did. Our marriage was a corpse." *Shut up shut up shut up.*

Angelo had his hands in his lap now too. He was looking into me with both eyes. "That's terrible, Margot Jones." He reached over and patted my arm a little bit. "Echospore?"

I smiled. He got up and went over to the tiny chest of drawers on top of his stereo. I stole a long gaze at his form: his neck, his shoulders, his legs. His noble body.

He pulled out the baggie of mushrooms, and we ate them plain, and they tasted not bad. We washed them down with the pink wine. A man's voice from the radio, wet and sarcastic: "You bet there's places with no ads on the radio. *Commie* countries. 106.9 The Creek. Where *you* are the decider."

David Foster Wallace was right. Irony had been co-opted and weaponized. I told Angelo a story my friend told me about The Creek. There are prerecorded voices, no real DJs, just operators who facilitate the set lists. The gimmick of The Creek is they'll play anything people request. The fact that people seem to request the same Mellencamp, Meatloaf and Nickelback songs could be because people have been consuming that crap for so long that's all they know.

But no. One day, there was an error, and the automatic playlists couldn't be accessed. The poor fellow manning the shit panicked, so he found some sixties soul tune and played it while he figured out the glitch. The corporation called him, outraged that he would play something off the narrow approved list of songs.

Angelo shook his head and continued cutting out sea lions and seahorses from *National Geographic*. "Shit." He slammed the stereo to tape, and Dog Lady poured out.

"So, are you thinking of getting back with Melissa?" I regretted the Adderall and drank more wine.

"Naw. I just got with her because I was young and lonely and had just come back to Cleveland after being away since I was a kid. We were just married for a minute. I loved her, then. It tore me up when she left. But that was almost ten years ago, and I've met women since then, who have more passion, more ingenuity." He rubbed his thumb tip against his ring finger, gently examining a hangnail.

"Like Lucy?"

"Lucy. She wants to date me, but she doesn't want to be *exclusive*. Because we're not exclusive, she doesn't want to be, *intimate*. That's cool. She's cool to hang out with. But I want to be *close*. But I'm not in love with her, anyway. I don't know if I'll ever get to be with the love of my life."

"It's awful, isn't it." I smiled with lips that were going rubbery.

Angelo switched back to the radio, and "Young Turks" by Rod Stewart came on. Angelo went to shut it off. "No," I said, "I love this song." He looked at me sideways.

He said, "Hey, did you hear a woman was beheaded in Saudia Arabia for sorcery? Crazy." He peeled a panther from the letter M and slid it over a couple millimeters.

"Beheaded. Oh my god, no. Oh, why do they hate women so much? And magic?"

"They're fucked up." He pressed the panther.

"I can't take it—the sadism of it all, the cops, the Saudis, Bush, the corporations pumping cancer into the water and the air and the soil..." I put my tools down, looked to the tiny lobes of dust clinging to the whipping ceiling fan.

"Let's go to the beach."
"Okay. Yeah, let's go!"

We must have walked all the way to the beach. It felt like bicycles, but it was just walking. I felt fine. He sat and nervously texted with Melissa. I kneeled with the shimmering lake behind me, tracing big circles like wings on the sand on either side of me. The Moon was coming up. My stomach rolled gently, and I matched my breathing to it. Thinking in a flash that Liz's apartment building was just up the road from here.

The trees were breathing and they breathed all night. Urgency pulsed through my guts and my heart and wetness in my eyes and between my legs like love, like ovulation: profound fluttering peace.

"What do you say, Angelo?"

"I told her I'm tripping on the beach with you."

"Haah."

"She asked if you're my special friend."

"We should go in the water, mm, this air is velvet."

"I told her yes, you are my friend, and you are special."

I was sitting in a puddle of my own happiness. He sat five feet from me and looked into me with his boy's eyes.

"Margot?"

"Yes?"

"I don't mean to be, nosy, but I have to tell you something: I'm worried about you. You said you and Wendy were in some kind of danger? And, Wendy is controlling."

"I don't want to think about that now. I just want to be here with you."

He looked at me a long minute. "Okay. Oh, look..." He pointed toward large pieces of driftwood just in from the waves. He said they looked like animals. We saw they looked like beasts, and the trees were beasts, and we were beasts, and the waves were beasts, and the atoms were beasts, and we were all beasts in the living, breathing Creature.

We crawled toward the dark shapes of the driftwood animals in the sand. No moment of my life was ever so perfect. This Being crawling beside me and the World alive. The Trees breathing, the Lake breathing, the Moon watching, the Stars listening.

"What are you humming?" He said.

"*Om Mani Padme Om.*"

"I saw that today—I saw it written in black sharpie on the wall above the urinal at Marc's!"

We were now both kneeling, facing each other. The sand was a stomach, softly rising and falling with the breathing waves.

"Wow wow wow. Once. I was feeling so sad, and I was walking on that concrete path up there." I waved up past the elevations near us on the little secret beach, to the vaster higher areas of the park that overlook the lake and the more public beach. "You know, and I walked up the hill, and I was hitting the path so hard and trying not to cry, and I'd been fighting with Georgie, I guess, and then I reached the top, and I saw the water and the sky, and I thought, 'I love you' with every fiber. Then I looked down, and in the concrete were the words 'I love you.'

"Then, not long after he left, I was riding the bus, and I was feeling so sad," I put my hand in the sand between us, and I hoped Angelo would touch it, me, but he didn't, but his eyes held steady into mine, "...and I looked out the window, we were up there, over there, you know, on route two where the bus goes past the big beach, and written so big in the snow on the beach it said, 'I love you.'"

"This park loves you." The wooden beasts rose behind him, and beyond that the moonlit waves kissed the sand. And beyond that the city shimmered on the water.

"I love this park." The trees shivered.

I couldn't take it anymore, his eyes. I stood up and faced the lake that loved me. I'd stepped out of my shoes at some point and the pads of my feet melted into the sand. I stepped into the soft little lapping of the lake, and it was so warm for late May! This would be a hot summer. I wanted him to stand up behind me. I yearned for him to follow me. But the lake would be enough. I stepped.

"Hey. Let's go in, want to?" The water was up to my ankles. The breathless warmth of the water, perfect warmth.

I looked back at him and smiled with all the stars flickering inside me.

He sat with his knees up. I saw sadness in his eyes, and I wanted to drink it away. He looked at the lake. Fear moved over his face. "Naw, that's cool, I'm good on it."

I touched him with my mind and turned back to the black water moving under black sky. When we looked into Lake Erie, we saw different things. He saw the void, the rotting place, the nightmare basement.

I saw the Devi, the shaking Shakti origins, the place where jackals and hyenas can't reach, for now. I see the holy night sky melted down into moving first love, and last love, the holy *maa*.

I was up to my knees and my cotton dress felt like whispers, and I was about to pull it up over my body and off. I thought of *The Awakening*, maybe in the end it wasn't suicide, but dissolution into ecstatic oblivion. She left rotten tragic society for sacred communion with the Sea. *La Mer*.

"Margot."

I dropped my dress back over my thighs and turned around. "We have to go back to my house. Melissa needs some fucking confirmation number or something."

He had taken his socks and shoes off.

Angelo was about to join me in the water. Fucking Melissa.

"Okay. But, promise me we can come back out to this wonderful place."

Then we were in a taxi. Off the secret beach and into the cab, I tilted. I looked at Angelo against the window, and he seemed far. He didn't love me. I tried to focus on his face, but things were *timeshadowing* too fast, and I just saw a blur. I think he smiled, but it looked like a grimace. The cab smelled like artificial banana. My empty stomach rolled. The cab driver said things to us that I didn't understand. Angelo mumbled enough to him. The orange streetlights were awful.

Then we were in his house. Was the beach real?

The cab will wait, we just have to find the confirmation number.

I knew Melissa just wanted to get us off the beach, but I didn't care. I wanted to breathe again. My chest compressed. I lay on the floor and looked at his ceiling. Smooth swirls of paint. I thought of Wendy and the old tears came out of my eyes, down the sides of my face. Poor Wendy just wants to paint houses, she wants to be good. I remembered waking folded up into her beautiful limbs and her face all over me. Her face rising up before me, her mouth sensual, her eyes severe. I rolled on my side sobbing quietly as Angelo cursed and shuffled through boxes in Melissa's room.

Violet walked up and put her pointy little face to my face. She looked like a bat. My Clarence looked like a bear or an owl. She sniffed me. I sat up. I loved her. She looked at me like I was strange and backed away. Cats know when you're tripping. Then I looked over at Angelo's guitar, and there was a grasshopper, a big-ass green as grass motherfucking grasshopper playing its legs on the head of Angelo's guitar.

I looked at Violet, and then we both looked at the grasshopper. I laughed. *Are you the spirit of the guitar?* I said in my mind. *I love you! I love.*

Angelo. I whispered. *Look.*

HUH he grunted from the other room. He staggered in, sweaty and pissed.

You're on the floor? Let's drink some water. He nodded like the hominid he was, and we went to the kitchen.

I saw out the door that the cab was waiting. Who has money for all this?

We drank lukewarm tap water by the sink, and he stood very close to me. I smelled his chest through cotton, and he looked at my neck. I put my hands on my face, wondering if there were black lines where my tears for Wendy had dried. I put my hands on his chest and felt his heart racing. I couldn't look him in the eye. I looked at his chest and he looked at my eyes.

We didn't say anything. Then I said, "I think it's oppressive to trip inside, everything looks weird, all the angles of things look and mean and demanding."

Violet stood by us and meowed up, her young ears tilting back slightly. The grasshopper creaked from the other room.

"All is fucked up! *Let's gerrouutta here!*" He took my hand and out we went, no confirmation number, and I staggered with desire.

The cab ride back was easier. I felt peaceful. We held hands. I looked out the window at streets I knew well. Empty storefronts, Bela Buda with Rocky and Henry standing out front. The first apartment I'd shared with Georgie. We passed all of it on the short ride back to the beach. I didn't feel guilty. All the worst things I'd done in my life patted over me like foam hail and fell off, down into the black rubber of the cab. The guinea pig and other small pets I'd neglected as a child. The drums I was tricked into stealing to impress a guy who turned out to be a junky. Not calling 911 when Liz had been shot. Going back to her place. Nothing.

I knew these things, and I'd tried to burn them away, but now, in the cab, in early summer, with the echospore throbbing inside me and my Angelo beside me, I saw that there were other people involved in those things, other choices were made, it *was* a web, a *Yantra*, it wasn't all me. I was a child, for most of those bad things. I smiled. I kept my breathing even. I felt cool.

I smiled at the taxi driver, and he smiled at me. Then I stepped out and tripped and fell down hard on the concrete. The driver said something, but I was embarrassed. Angelo was there, he told the driver to go on. Blood flowered on my knees. I saw myself crying a little bit, but I stopped quickly.

Somehow, maybe there was a gate to keep cars out, but somehow we weren't dropped down by the beach, but up on the hill just west of the park under hard white streetlights. On the hill across from the rich people, the mansions, the hill overlooking the woods that veiled our secret beach. My smile was gross from crying, and I knew I looked ugly, and Angelo hugged me. I said, "We got to get away from these lights." We went and sat under a tree.

I'd felt my knees scrape, and the blood. The blood on Liz's mouth. Some people plain gone forever. Feeling nothing on their knees. I would cook meat for Simon. A plate of muscle, flesh.

Angelo lay on his back and looked at the stars and the tree. I looked north at the lake and the trees below. The sky and the lake moved together, two kinds of black. The skyscrapers downtown shimmered near enough against the water to the east. I felt like I'd come down. He talked about the forests of Malaysia, about the rules of going into them.

You should never bring meat into the forest, or it could draw the *harimau*, the tiger. You can't say *harimau*, or the other real names of

270

the animals, because that can draw them, too. You cannot bring an egg into the forest—that can draw the *orang bunian*.

Angelo searched the air with his hands, "…Sometimes people call the *orang bunian* fairies, but the word, it means, like, a deeper hidden place, but also sound…Yeah, they are the 'hidden people,' or 'whistling people.'" It came back to him. They live near us, folded into reality just a bit off from us. Look out for natural clearings. They look just like us, but they don't have that little crease above the lip, and they are beautiful. He touched his lip. Angelo knew someone whose cousin married an *orang bunian*. She went away with him, and then she came back.

He heard that a camper took eggs into the forest one night. In the morning, he cracked the eggs open, but they were empty. It was the toll of the *orang bunian*. The cost of going in.

I looked north into black water with the Moon to my back and whispered *Duende*. Sorrow welled deep from guts to crotch. I tried to listen for the Erie People. I tried to listen for Liz. My left thigh rested against his right side.

My voice was small. "I just found out about something, I can't believe I hadn't heard about it before, but Wikipedia. The people who were here before, the Indigenous people, they knew a deity called the Underwater Panther, the Panther is right there…" I floated my hand toward the dark lake. "I think that, I was with the Panther, in a dream…the Wildcat. The Night Panther…"

He said, "Yes, yes, yeah. I wanted to talk to you about that. Hey—dude, look." And I turned around. There was a one-way road that wrapped around the coast here, where life-size bronze statues of children played in the front yard of bulbous new mansions. Two living deer were standing in a yard. A doe and a buck. They looked around tentatively and carefully crossed the street to the grassy place where we lay, maybe twenty feet away on our stomachs. They looked out for each other. They stayed close. They walked along the grass down the hill into some trees.

We were like that for a while. Looking at the stars as the Moon rose higher. It was almost full. A pregnant Moon. I felt the shivering of coming down. Spirits began to recede back into the woods. But Angelo was still going. He described seeing colors in the trees, like magenta, with an urgent hard *g*. He said he longed for magenta in sober life.

Then we were on our feet and the trip came back to life. Angelo gestured to a thick oak and I touched it. "I know this tree."

Now Angelo said, "This tree is a living being. The plant life in our blood is responding to him. Can you feel it? Dude, look up, I can feel the stars watching us. Even the stars are alive!"

I could feel them. Sentience shimmered everywhere. We wanted to walk down to the little beach again, but we heard people laughing and talking down there, so we decided to go to the main beach instead. We walked down to the circular parking lot that had one path down to the little beach on the west side and one path through the woods to the large beach on the east side. The circular parking lot was a place to *park*, it was an overlook, ringed in trees, but through them lovers could see the lake and the city. It was the same place Simon took me that cold afternoon three months before, where I'd put him off and he'd grabbed my arm, paranoid that I was a spy for Liz. Now the circle was alive, warm and dark.

As we came down to the lot, I noticed how it was the circle lot had been carved into naturally circular landscape. I knew without a doubt that this had been a site sacred to the Erie. Though, Erie was a name given to them by their oppressors. I wished I knew the name they called themselves, I wished I could call it now. Surely it meant, "the

People." I whispered in the dark to the People.

We crossed the circle. We walked on a soft path into the woods. Angelo stopped to piss. He pissed through skinny trees down a hill, and the lake was vast down there. They're all here, beasts and creatures all around. I dropped my cell phone. It floated slowly down to the ground. Angelo was talking about a band from far away, saying, "Asia Pacific's the best..."

I smiled in the dark at his back. Everything felt beaten and happily worn. I had a flash then, of being in a plane, of flying over the Colorado river and watching the sun hit the water and flash along the curves, the sun in the water, curving like a snake, like a ribbon of light below. I didn't know if it was a memory of a dream of a vision of the future.

It was dark. The trees were tall and dark. It felt like the background of a creepy old cartoon: *oo ooo oo*. We were in the glow. We walked along the side of a hill with the bright Moon glaring down on us, bare on the dirt road. The lake crashing like a sea below.

We were in woods again, thicker, older. I knew these woods. The path twisted. I'd left things here, offerings, pumpkins and flowers. Angelo took my hand. We sweat as we ran slowly in the dark. I sensed he didn't want to linger here. Spiders and small branches hit my face, and I followed him into the dark.

I reached my arms around him and he held my hands to his chest as we stumbled over roots and stones. I could hear his breathing. And water running somewhere. There was a glow inside the woods, from the leaves, from the Moon.

We came out onto the sand again. We faced each other. We stood this way a long time, almost embracing, not kissing. Covered in a fine mist of sweat. There were no sounds. In a few long moments I felt sober again and shaking slightly. Terrified. *Let's move*, I said.

We walked across the longer beach and sat in front of the water, exposed on the huge bank of dirty sand. I looked west, but our little magic beach was veiled behind the round base of the circular lot that jutted into the lake. We'd failed to make it back there. We could only sense the smell of a fire and light dancing high on the trees swaying above.

Here, the magic had retreated, condensed into cold dew. Angelo sat with his knees to his face, his arms across them, his face hidden behind his glasses. The Moon hid behind the trees, behind us, and the harsh light of the highway and the awful sounds of cars crashed over the public beach.

The lake was inches, but could have been miles, from us. It looked wet and dangerous. Cold and polluted. I knew Simon would likely kill me. There was a way to see I had it coming. Something else was shaking inside me. I remembered when I first felt this way, when I first loved them. My parents: my mother smelling like pink lotion, her voice like opals, her hair like a lion, my mother sitting at the dining room table in her nightgown, looking into the *What*. My father, his hands smelling like warm ash, his smile rolling out of his eyes. They knew me, once. My brother, his long fingers, his palms wrinkly since birth, his feet, elegant like birds. Looking up at me. Telling me things. Precious stones in my heart, smoothed by old worry.

The thing inside my chest quivered then clanged. My eyes had been wet and filmy all night. Do all the people who love deeply carry this around all the time? This heavy awful thing? Beloved feet vulnerable, in peril against violet light.

Angelo was closed. Caged. I felt the sweat on my face. I looked away.

Do we carry this all the time, all of us?

I wanted to go home, but I felt exhausted. Home. This morning, in bed, I'd loved Wendy. Now, I dreaded seeing her again. I wanted to run, with Angelo, and be free.

I wanted to say something, but I knew he couldn't hear me. I said, "Angelo, I smoked crack so I could burn the fear, burn the white fear clear away."

I looked at him, and he looked at the lake. He didn't nod but turned his face fast toward me. There is a very slight asymmetry to his face that I loved. His wide eyebrows arched into tender points and his eyelashes beat softly. His neck was strong and curved gracefully into his back. "I know what you mean. It's the need to go beyond male and female, yearning for the union. It's seeing God in the creation. The need."

"That's it. You are, naturally tantra." I smiled away from his gaze, embarrassed.

"Want to head back?"

"Yeah."

We climbed back up through trees that had buzzed with life but were now silent. Going home to Wendy. I didn't want to go. He said he'd get another cab and drop me off. We were beat. I stopped on the path when we were under the bright Moon again. I didn't want to quite leave this world yet. I looked back at the *Lake Erie* once more. Stumbling, I pulled his arms around me from behind. I pulled his arms, and he held me awkwardly for a moment, and we saw the Moon on the water. I closed my eyes to find *Duende,* and the answer to Death once and for all. I whispered. Closed my eyes, looked to my third eye. *Lilac Wine* came back to me, filling me with its purple night song. He held me tighter then, bravely.

I turned around but wasn't brave enough to meet his eyes. We walked back along the dry path, through the hallowed patch of woods where he'd pissed, back onto the circular lot. I'd seen once, online, a postcard of this very place from a hundred years ago. Angelo called a cab. It arrived too soon.

He let the cab go in front of Wendy's. The power of the Moon filled the humid air. He said he'd just walk home from there. I wanted to ask him to come in, but I couldn't. He stood very near me looking into my face. I looked into his eyes and the Moon was there, too.

It was hard to find words, but he said, "Margot, if you are in danger, or you want to get away from her, you can stay with me anytime."

I longed for the violet and blue and magenta of his home. But I couldn't go. I didn't want to put him in any danger.

I had to stay by Wendy. Who'd saved my life. Who'd sacrificed herself for me. I felt her pulling on me from inside the house. What part of me wanted to go but was too weak, too afraid and guilty to leave her, to feel her rage and sorrow rain down on me? Something about my mother and being drunk too much, and my fucked-up marriage, something about loving the wrong way, that was too analytical and easily forgotten. I saw instead in a flash what love could be, with Angelo. I also felt the love that was devotion, steady loyalty jerked me back to the house. One love was freedom, the other bondage, but I was bound. "I can't."

"Okay, but if you ever change your mind." The veil of military stoicism lowered over his face.

I hugged him for a long moment and put my lips to his neck. Then he was gone.

Sober and awake, I tasted the salt from his skin on my lips and smiled with a thick pain in my throat. I laughed, thinking I'd tasted Shiva.

I thought, *as long as we can stay friends, as long as I can be close with*

276

him, and know him, I will be happy. Inspired. I wore him like a locket under my shirt against my heart, he was my safe secret, safer even because we couldn't be together. We would never take each other for granted, and we would always be friends, we would always be happy to see each other, we would always find each other. We would always keep this emerald night inside our hearts.

Clarence followed me into the pink bathroom. I sat on the toilet and urinated. I looked down at the deco design in the tile and it jumped. I laughed.

In bed, I got a text from Angelo: [*dua hati dalam gelora*]

[what is it?]

[two hearts in a wave]

I fell into a deep sweet sleep with Clarence in my arms.

Around three I woke because I heard Wendy come in. She slammed things around. I fell back asleep, but the sleep lost its layers of sweetness and went jarred and edgy.

21

June Knocks

I didn't dream. I was glad to feel the sun on my face before I opened my eyes. My gut went cold as I realized it was Wendy's arm draped around my middle. Everything that came with that heavy arm. I gently rolled over enough to check the time on my phone, and I saw another text from Angelo. My heart leapt, even with Wendy's body pressed to my back. I put the phone down. I wanted to save his words for later.

I opened my eyes, and everything felt right. My eyes were lubricated, my legs light. My mouth even, tasted clean but living, like the ocean. I was sober. No fear, no regret. Mushrooms had healed me. Maybe I didn't even need booze and pills. I felt that now I could see the mosaic from a greater distance. Clarence lay on my pillow, his fur gently touching my head, purring into my scalp. I thought, *yes, we're all beasts in one giant beast, a living creation, a creature.*

Light filled my mind—I could see clearly now. I loved Angelo. I would have to leave Wendy. This was wrong. I knew Angelo loved me. And I knew that there is love that is as open as us heavy, dirty beasts can muster, that we can be beasts with open hearts, lion hearts, but that there is a lot of fear in the world that can close the heart vents. Oxygen rusts the heart, and so it wasn't so hard to understand, really, that Wendy and I also loved each other, but ours was a sick love. I needed to let her go and move on.

I moved my legs and pain shot from my knees. Damn—they were bloody and the blood had dried. I'd fallen hard from the taxi. Pebbles and dirt had left long cuts. Fuck. It might scar.

I showered. I slathered my knees with ointment, and bandages covered the scratches.

I felt calm. I knew I'd have to leave town. I would talk with Wendy over breakfast. This whole thing with Simon, well it was obviously a set-up. He obviously wanted revenge. Maybe, and this was something I would not have considered before, I could even ask my brother for a little money to get out of town. I could work and then pay him back.

My heart lifted when I saw a text from Angelo. I shook even, as I pulled on my clothes. Savoring the moment before reading what he wrote. After I'd written, *I love you.*

Just [call me].

He picked up quickly. I know he could hear my smile.

"Margot, listen. I have to go out of town, maybe for a few weeks. I have to leave today."

"What. why? Is everything okay?" It took a minute to understand what he said, and then, I thought, *how wonderful. I can go too. This is how I will get out of town.*

"It's Melissa's dad. He's dead. I got to take her down to Moultrie, Georgia for the funeral, and then, I need to help her and her mom figure out everything."

Why you why you, why does it have to be you? "Sorry to hear it. That's good of you to be there for her."

"It's nothing. I have to go. I'll text when I can, though the town is so shitsburg that I don't even know if there will be reception."

"Okay."

"Okay. See you in a few weeks."

"Okay. Take care."

"Okay."

The line went dead.

Downstairs I waffled. I knew what I knew.

But what if I didn't know shit? What if he could tell how I felt about him and was trying to blow me off in this weird way? Or obviously, Melissa wanted him, or thought of him as her husband still.

Wendy came in and pulled out two mugs and poured us coffee. Coming out of me now, were the necessary but now joyless words. "Wendy. It's time for me to move on. I care about you. You saved my life, and I love you. But there's nothing for me here now. Simon isn't going to let me live. You have to know this, that I have to get out of town."

"Okay, let me just get a little more money together and we can take off."

"I need to go on my own."

Wendy exhaled and slammed her palm onto the counter.

"Listen, it's just what I've got to do. We got together in such a weird way, things can't ever really be equal between us."

"It's that guy. The fuck! Where were you last night?"

"I love you, but I have to go."

"I did you right, Margot. No one else is going to see in you, what I see in you. They see some loser, some drop-out slumming white girl, stuck in the grunge era or some shit."

"It sounds like that's what you see in me." I felt sorry for her for using such obvious manipulation. And in making me feel pity, it worked.

"Margot... I see you are *good*. You work hard. You have a good heart. Wait—you are a musician, a *hot* musician."

"Wendy. I broke up you and Cher. I'm going to take off, and maybe you can work it out with her."

"That's what you think of me? So little that you aren't even jealous? People see you as a middle-class tourist, as an empty vessel, you slum it with crack, with the black guy, with the dyke, then when you're done, you split with the white hipster guy."

These were the buttons. I hated being misunderstood. I hated being reduced to stereotype. "That's not true. Look, all I have are my authentic feelings. You know I'm not scene."

"It's okay. I get it. He's better than me, I know he is."

"I'm not going with him."

"You don't have to spare my feelings, Margot."

"No... he, ah, is taking off with his ex-wife." My voice broke. "I mean, her dad died, is why, but he's going to Georgia with her for a while." It hit me.

Angelo was gone.

I had no money, no car, nothing. Simon knew where I was. I was pushing away Wendy, the one person I had.

Suddenly I was crying again. When do these post-addiction surprise crying attacks stop? I wanted to hit myself in the fucking face like I sometimes did when I was alone.

She held me. I reached up and touched her hair, and she reached down and put her icy hand on my bare lower belly, turning me on like she always could. She whispered, "I know you're scared, I'll protect you. Please don't leave me." She said, "I never met anyone like you—from the moment I saw you, I was drawn to you." She smiled at me, and her smile was sly, but very close to my mouth.

I kissed her and wrapped my fingers in her hair, short and dirty with sweat, but so pretty. I remembered seeing her for the first time at Liz's, coming down like lightning, like a bad-ass heroine, or villain. And her face when she talked about the community space, and her comics and her dog dying, and all the good things turned to shit. Like a Cleveland blues song. And she pushed her belly into mine and I felt the heat. Maybe Angelo was too good, and he wanted to go away with his normy ex-wife. Wendy and I could just eat drugs and finger each other under the covers. We could run away. Change our names again. We could pull each other out from in front of the train and then find more trains, and rivers to swim in, too, too drunk, needing help. Saving each other, over and over. Forever in debt. This was a dirty love, but it was love, too.

June rushed in with full yellow awfulness. I received a couple brief, murky texts from Angelo the day after he left, and then nothing. I'd gotten used to texting with him all day long. We'd woven a thick rope, and we each held an end, and I hadn't even noticed we were holding on until now that it was worn down to threads and stretched over states.

Wendy was hardly home. She was distorted. She was forthright enough to say she was on something that helped her keep up and deal with what Simon had her doing, but she would not tell me what she was on or what she was doing for Simon. Her skin, always robust and golden, was now waxy yellow. Her cheeks sunk and she looked old. Her thighs got thin. How could her body change so fast? She wore long sleeves, even as sudden June days begat days longer and hotter, more like August dog days. The only AC we had was the unit in Wendy's room. The hottest summer I'd ever known. It felt like the end of the world.

Simon said he'd call on me when it was time for me to cook his meat. Wendy came home at all hours and said: "Simon says to tell you he'll be calling on you." I knew she was afraid of him, because she was viciously protective of me when it was anyone else. She resigned herself to Simon as if he were a force of nature. And yet, like a child with low agency but high determination, she plotted against him.

The days drained on. I walked past the community garden on my way to Bela Buda. Harsh brown weeds crowded Wendy's abandoned plot and pushed out into the common space.

My knees scabbed over but still hurt. They would scare, leaving angry slashes.

We breathed heavy wet air and were exhausted by long bright days. Wendy's paint truck sat in the drive. We lost jobs. I missed working with her. But she crawled in bed with me every night. My room had no AC, but that's where we always were, always my room, never hers.

She held me in the dark and said strange things in my ear about webs and worms and always our plan: *August... come August I'll sell the paint van and we head to Costa Rica. You got any people there? They got tiny monkeys at the windows in the mornings.*

I pulled her arms tight around me. We had no air. I was naked. Kicking off the sheet to expose my legs to the raspy window fan. But her arms were wrapped in a cotton men's shirt.

Wendy, are you shooting up? Maybe we should leave now. We could leave now, before he calls on me.

She wrapped her bare legs around mine, making rashy heat where our skin touched. *Don't worry, he'll let us go. August. We can get clean again in August. I need time, I've found a way to skim money here and there, not much, but by August, we'll have plenty.*

I held her hands in the dark. How could they be cold and dry in all this heat? She'd always been muscular, fleshy and vital, beautiful to me. *Wendy, we don't have to wait until August.*

We're just worms, Alice. Margot. It's a web of tissues and clay, and we're just worms getting by the spider. She laughed a cold dry laugh against my neck, and somehow, we slept.

I spent a lot of time at Bela, drinking with Henry and Rocky off the tap for free. Sometimes jumping in with people. We couldn't believe Bush would soon be out office. We didn't believe it—it seemed more real that he would suspend the elections. The Spider Moon Fest would bring the solstice and the long empty days would start to back off a hair. But July and August could only get hotter.

Henry asked about Angelo. It hurt my pride. I knew it was my ego that made me possessive of him. I tried to find my deeper self that had the wisdom to let go. I had to let him go. But when Henry asked about him, I wanted to smack Henry in his face.

The Spider Moon Fest fliers Angelo and I made blanched in the front windows. He'd dropped the finished flier in my mailbox on the way to Georgia, so I'd made copies and walked them around Lakewood. I just wished he'd knocked on the door that morning, so I could have seen him again before he left. I would have put aside my pride and asked to go with them.

I only felt good and strong and free was when I was alone in my room doing yoga and meditating and working on music. In the morning, I moved my body and stilled my mind. I could see clearly. I pressed my hands together and sang the *mantra gayatri* in a low close voice.

I knew I had to get away from all of this. I lost hours working, playing guitar and jotting fragments of notes, of visions from my night with Angelo. Partial lyrics and melodies and anti-melodies and ideas for paintings. I wanted to get away from Wendy and be alone and work. I would. I would get away. I knew in my heart I would see Angelo again. When I was alone it was clear to me that I didn't want to be with Wendy anymore.

But when she was around me, or I was out in the world living broke,

I felt trapped and sick and, so I drank as much as I could, and the clarity of morning disappeared. I wouldn't see Angelo, I wouldn't get away. When we were working, she'd paid me a little cash, but mostly paid me in booze, pills and food. Now that we weren't painting houses, there was still plenty of booze and pills, but no cash, and just a little food. Day-old French bread from a baker around the corner and punched-out peaches and oranges that she picked up dumpster diving behind the West Side Market.

Sometimes at night I found my drunken way back to my room to work on my pictures and sounds alone, and I was good again.

I'd winged it at Scum, and it had worked, but for the fest, I wanted my set to tell more of a story, a story with weight, dimension, layers. There was the guitar, which could do anything. It felt so good in my hands, pulling the strings out into different tones and screeches, and it could go dark and rhythmic or light and crinkly or sound like skin.

I listened to Leonard Cohen and thought of Angelo and our trip on the beach. I wanted lyrics to come from this, but I got no words, only colors. I wanted to build layers to pull me out of this stuck place, layers of harsh sound and cut melody, layers like the cold fear of waking with Wendy, shaking from booze, the hot fear that hit when I smelled meat cooking in the neighborhood, layered against the blazing core of knowing from my last night with Angelo, the knowing that *love is real*. That whatever he felt for me, I loved him for him, even if I never saw him again, I knew now that love is real.

I needed more noise. I needed a noise rig to add to my guitar and vocals. I borrowed some rock-and-roll pedals from Henry and strung them together. I still needed a mixer. I went to Bela to ask Henry if he knew anyone who could spare a mixer for just a couple weeks until after the show, but the bar was unattended. It was a hot afternoon, and the place wasn't busy, but there were a couple people standing at the bar, one guy in a sweaty beanie looking around like, *hey, where is the dude?* And the other huffing and puffing, muttering about how Bela can't afford to lose more business.

Suddenly Henry rushed in through the side door, his face was not red but covered in sweat. He waved his wiry arms around as if the customers were bees. "What? Okay, no, I mean, what do you want? Sorry, sorry." He took their orders, the first guy consoling and the second silent. Then, as he danced around pulling the levers and things for the espresso machine, he told the whole room that he'd been called by the manager of the community garden because his plants were stolen. "Cut! All my tomatoes and zucchini, just starting to grow, and the heirloom peppers, cut, cut to the stem."

Terrible, terrible, we all said.

"I'm going to find whoever took my plants, and I will step on his dirt-fucking neck!"

I ended up getting a mixer from Lucy. She was kind enough to come over to Wendy's. "These Behringers, don't last, but what else is there? Anyway, this was my old one, it's still okay. Just be careful with the input jack."

I was excited when I saw it. It was something I could hold and work with. She set it down on the dining room table where it sat like a puppy. "How you been, Lucy."

"Wrapped up in the fest. It's *effing* exhausting, Margot. You have no idea how much work it is. Handling the artists, finding them places to stay, it's too much. What's going on with you and Wendy?"

"I think we're going to move soon."

Just then, Wendy walked in, whipping hands through her hair. She smiled broadly at Lucy, almost giving her the eye, and I felt a pleasurable stab of jealousy arrow through me. She came over and twined her fingers with mine.

After Lucy left, I tried to take Wendy to her cool air-conditioned bedroom, but she pulled me outside to the painting truck. I realized I hadn't been in the truck or a car in weeks, not since we met with Simon. I was apprehensive, but she gave me a hug and said we needed to get away for the day and just be together. That since we hadn't painted in a while, we hadn't had much time together.

It was so normal I laughed.

We went to hiking in the Metroparks. We looked over the Rocky River and hiked up through lush oaks and maples to old Native American mounds that looked like gentle waves in the land. I couldn't believe I'd lived near the Metroparks for years but had never been to any of them before. The Metroparks are often called the Emerald Necklace because they are a string of forest wrapped around the city. For years I'd been tied up with Georgie and cleaning toilets and crack and Wendy, bad work and bad relationships had eaten up my life. I wished—I could come back with Angelo.

I tried to focus on Wendy, I tried to love her, even though things felt so wrong. We laughed more that day than ever before, just talking about people: about our customers and the things they'd wanted, *gradations of mauve to accentuate the voluptuousness of their walls*, and I told her about the Keith and Carrie and Karen I'd worked with at Autumn Villa, and the Maries, and she said Lucy's tiny, surgically-deflated nose betrayed her petty inner world, and we talked about the night, so long ago, when we were at that winter west side party, and obviously the Vickers shot up the house, and we didn't even know we'd come there to look for each other.

One night Lucy came into Bela with a new man on her arm. He had a toothy smile, rich brown skin and perfectly even dreadlocks. They were each exactly 3/4 inch in diameter. He looked exotically upper class. She whispered something in his ear with a dry smirk, and he leaned his head back and laughed loud.

When he went to the bathroom, she came up and gripped my arm. Telling me he's Myron, a cellist from Berklee, telling me when he plays the cello, he also plays little Indian bells with his feet. Asking me, "Isn't he super hot?"

"Yeah, sure! Hey, do you ever hear from Angelo?" I'd held back from asking her before, but he'd been gone weeks now, and I'd heard nothing. Not even on Facebook.

She jerked her neck back, looked at me sideways. "What about him? You know he's in Georgia with Sporty Spice."

"Ha! Yeah. Well, her father died, that's all. He said he doesn't love her anymore."

"Angelo wants a wife... I want a life. And Myron will be here all summer. *Margot!*"

"That's good."

"You're turning red!"

"It's this tea."

"You *like* him! You like Angelo. Okay. I can see it. But I thought you were a lesbian. Now."

"I like who I like. I'm with Wendy. Angelo is a really special magical person. But I haven't heard from him in almost three weeks now, not since the day after he left."

"Oh, Wendy's nuts and she treats you like shit! Everyone knows it! Angelo likes *you*. He *always* talks about you. He says little things, but lots and lots of little things. Like, 'Margot says reverb is like eyeliner', or 'Margot has a red dress like that', or 'Margot and I are blab la bla-ing whatever.' Go for it, girl! He'll be back. He needs someone to hold onto. He holds good." She winked.

She turned and joined Myron as the next act started up. They bobbed their heads to the circular saw.

I slid behind the bar, heart racing. I'd been there all day, drinking mint jasmine tea smuggled from home and sketching mandalas, water flowers, jellyfish and skulls. The air conditioning was sluggish, but better than nothing. I'd thrown down my beat-up mat in the hallway by the bathrooms and practiced yoga when I needed it. My friend Rocky was cool, a real cool scum noise artist, and she worked days now. She didn't care that I was there for hours, drinking tea from home. We talked some, but she was okay with us being quiet together, and I was grateful to her for that.

That night, when familiar faces began to show up, and Henry relieved Rocky (who I swear was wearing my abandoned green fake glasses as a headband to keep her long bangs out of her eyes), I hid behind the counter and shook out my face. Got drunk fast, re-acclimated.

Lucy was back. "Margot, good news!" She gestured to her Blackberry, "The grant came through! Between the grant and a generous donation from Myron's family, we'll be able to pay all the bands at the fest! You'll get two hundred bucks!"

"Oh, Lucy, that's great. Really." So many people were playing, she must have stacked up at least five grand somehow. Wow—getting paid, nice.

I drank some more. Tried to lose my body in the noise.

Henry was still pissed about his vegetables, going on about what he was going to do to the guy who took them. "I'm going to tear the hairs out of his head like threads out of a fabric, I'm going to cut off his toes with a wirecutter..."

"Jesus, Hen! Maybe it was just a hungry guy."

"No way. No fucking way. It was a sadist. Probably one of those

289

kids who've been throwing eggs. Lakewood is perfect, we have the beach nearby, the garden, it's cheap, we've got Bela, but there's people out there who want to cut us down."

I wanted to ask him again about work, but this was not the right time, obviously. He told me before the owners weren't hiring, but he knew so many people, I figured maybe he knew about some work. I hardly had any clothes that were in one piece, and I guess my confidence was shit—I hadn't made a resume in so long. I didn't have a car or money for a bus pass—my dream was that maybe he knew of some business around here that was hiring. But there was nothing—they were calling it the Great Recession. People with master's degrees were competing for my old job cleaning toilets at Autumn Villa.

I just patted him on the arm. I made a silly face to cheer him up.

Henry said, "Hey, Jeez, I'm sorry, Margot. How are you, hear yet when our pal Angelo will be back?" It was just something to say to me. He had things he said to people. He worked the counter, while I poured myself something pale and bitter from the tap.

"Don't you remember? I don't hear from him. I don't know anything."

Back at home, sometime after midnight, came a pounding at the door. I froze. Beveled glass shook as a woman knocked, and I couldn't hide. She saw me and pointed. I opened the door to a woman with heavy short hair cut into a reddish-brown helmet, a woman with deep creases by her mouth who filled out a blue t-shirt like a muscled young man. She looked pissed, but then she smiled with red rubbery lips. Her eyes were the brightest blue I'd ever seen, not like Wendy's, but rather dark, dark blue. "Hey, where's Wendy? Wendy around?" She popped her head around me, looking into the house. Her scratchy voice and aggressive forehead promised some kind of action.

I smiled despite myself. "Well, she's asleep. She's been working nights a lot."

Wendy stumbled out. "Bitch!"

"Horse Face!"

The women embraced. Wendy's face lit up with her old vitality, and I felt jealous that this woman I'd never seen before could invoke that power, while Wendy had been fading in my presence for weeks, aside from the day in the woods, which now seemed like a dream.

Wendy introduced me to her friend June. Her old friend from when she first moved back here. I tried to figure out whether this was an activist friend or a criminal friend.

"I thought you were in Buffalo?"

"Naw, that shit's over and done now. I'm in the 216 for good, maybe."

"Yeah, whatever."

"Wendy, is she cool?" June's breath was short, as if she'd run all the way from Buffalo.

"Yeah. Oh, yeah. June, this is my girl, Margot." Wendy thrust her hand in my direction, and there was a beat where I felt June readjusting her expectations.

"Okay, good. You girls want to make some money, cause, guess what? I got a plan."

"Oh shit!" Wendy smiled and pulled her hair with both hands, somehow reminding me of Billy Vickers, but this time, the enthusiasm was jarring rather than infectious, like someone trying too hard at a rock show. "Naw, dude, come on, let's have some *coffee.*"

"Yeah, ha! *Coffee.*"

By coffee, I guess they meant weed laced with meth, so they smoked in the kitchen while I made myself instant coffee from the hot water spigot. It was a hot night. The fan beat, and I remembered a hot summer spent sitting in front of a tv with Noam on the floor of a stranger's house, stomach knotted until the distracted babysitter would take us back to our folks, but also, the first summer Georgie and I lived together, when I loved him, and we ate cold Chinese on the porch of our first place, but then, he'd always want to go back into the tv, leaving me to look at the stars alone.

June explained. "Hey, you guys know like, ten to fifteen manhole covers are stolen in Cleveland a night?"

Wendy jerked her head back, "Bullshit. And hey, that shit is got to be, like fifty pounds or some shit."

"Yeah, but look. You can't just take a manhole cover to a resale shop, but there's drug dealers who'll swap it for drugs in the middle of the night, and then they have ways to melt it down and shit. I heard somehow it gets to China, then, they make it into shit and sell it back to us!" June was drumming her hands on our kitchen table, caressing it.

Wendy shook her head. Opened the refrigerator and then shut it. "Wha-at? I thought everything coming out of China was plastic. So, what, we have drugs, and then we have to sell those, or what? There are people in this town who are already selling the drugs, you dig?"

"Wendy. Wendy. Wendy. Wendy. You've got the truck, okay, and the three of us are strong, right? I got my own. Connections. I'll take care of the drugs. You guys work with me, you get a clean cut. Don't worry, no cops going to fuck with three white women at night, right? On the west side?" June settled into one of our kitchen chairs.

"Unless they want hand jobs." Wendy leaned back and put her hand to her mouth. June handed her a cigarette and lit it.

June looked at the fridge then back at Wendy. "You got any sandwich stuff? Like...no, hey fuck you, that is nasty! Cop hand jobs. You are a buzzkill! Naw, fuck that! Want to be such a *pussy*, you can be the look-out."

"Come on, June, shit, settle the fuck down. What are you really here for?" Wendy paced from the stove to the sink, flashed her eyes at me.

"Wendy, what's wrong with you, bitch? You look so skinny." June had finished her pitch. Now she saw Wendy, gripping her elbows, wearing a black turtleneck with the neck cut out in this ferocious old-time heat.

I licked my lips. "June, I'm in, I'm down if you want. I need some fucking bread." My voice sounded imposter, overly earnest.

June smiled. "Manhole Covers! Right on! Tremendous! Well, there you go, Wendy, your girl's got more in her sack than you got."

"Margot, you just be cool. I got it." Wendy smiled sick and sarcastic, and I sat on the floor. I sat on my feet and lay back, my head on the floor, looking at the front door in the other room, and then over at June.

June smiled at me with her twinkly blue eyes, and I liked it. I loved butch women. I needed money. I needed it bad because I had to figure out a way to leave on my own, without Wendy. Fuck Simon and his meat. And the Spider Moon Fest. I had to get out of Ohio soon. Angelo was gone, Wendy was turning her back to me every time I tried to get close, and I still had no idea what she was doing with Simon.

"Okay, I'll call you, Margot."

"June, shut the fuck up. Leave it alone, Margot. I give you everything you need."

The next night I went to Scum. I wasn't booked, but I had to play, so I jumped on to my friend Paloma's set. I'd never jumped on like that before, but I had to play.

When I got there, the touring band was playing, so I slipped in without a drink. It was a little late, but still early for the headliners to be playing. Maybe they had to get back on the road that night.

I didn't know the band, Mystic Breach, but as soon as I walked into the dark room, I felt swallowed up. People get burned out at this latitude as the solstice nears, and the crowds in June are always thinner than in May or April. That night there were maybe half a dozen, Paloma, Rocky, Murder, Mona and Lucy among them.

Mystic Breach didn't care. They were a force. Later, I would realize they were a bit like The Birthday Party, but that night, all I could see was them. The vocalist and the drummer both beamed with the power of glamorous androgyny, long hair and mystery. The drummer was a beauty with a sad long face and long straight blond hair, and the vocalist wore scarves tied around the top of their head and long bushy black hair sprang out. They had muscular arms and a tender mouth. The bassist and guitarist worked hard. The music and the lights throbbed together. Noise acts were on the bill, but headliner Mystic Breach was more like garage torch music, and I loved it. The bodies working hard on stage, bodies that had been on the road for weeks, bodies that gave off a sweet stench that filled the open room.

Sober with raw nerves, tears wet my dry eyes. And the singer with their heavy blue rhinestone lidded eyes, met my eyes and cried, too. Then the drummer, leggy, with an elegant aquiline face, walked slowly from behind her kit in platform heals. The singer passed their mic to her and helped her down off the stage, then they hopped up and replaced her behind the kit to support her song with thudding, plodding simplicity. The drummer strutted slowly around the room with her deep Nico voice, singing and meeting eyes with us six or so in the crowd. At the end, she took a bow, and I wanted more.

I almost forgot I was sober, but Paloma came up and squeezed my shoulders and passed me four drink tickets. Pretty generous considering the low turnout and that I'd jumped on. But somehow, the bar seemed so far away. Getting a drink, the negotiation that would require, and then tossing out the empty, holding onto my gear, getting another one, and I'd have to scrounge for change for the tip.

I wasn't up for it. Instead, I was just feeling, feeling so much, more than since I was a kid. I could feel my body.

During the last few bars of Taboo's set, I remembered Angelo getting me drinks, and sure, that's why going to the bar alone seemed so hard, and I felt a tear in my body from my groin to my mouth. I suddenly longed for him like I'd never longed for anyone in my life. I thought of my mother, holding onto her in a pool when I was a very young child. Pressing my face against her skin, her black bathing suit, the afternoon sun shifting behind clouds on the water, me just wanting to stay against her skin.

How could Angelo be so far away? How could he ever have been so close. I texted that I missed him. I almost texted that I would take him up on his offer to stay at his house, but I imagined Simon showing up there one day—anxiety seized my throat as I tried to push down images of Angelo bound and tortured by Simon and his crew. I forced myself to exhale.

The text didn't go through.

When I was with Wendy, I did want to be with her. But whenever I was away, I thought of Angelo. I thought of Wendy pacing around the house and felt sick with a heaviness that was laced in slick fear, and gave way to deep, resigned pity.

I talked with the vocalist while they tore down and we set up. They said they hated touring in the summer, that they preferred to travel in February because that was the magic time. Most people feel bored and depressed in February, but that's because we've all forgotten that it is the quickening of the year. They said where they were from, which was Maine, they call that time of year the "thaw within the thaw".

February—I don't remember much of what came right before

295

February, the night Mark dosed me. Something had started to thaw within me then.

Henry walked up. A few more people came in, but though my body was nervous, my shoulders tight, etc, my mind was clear. I hadn't played sober much, but I'd been surprised to discover that setting up is more difficult, but playing is easier, when you'd think it would be the other way around.

Henry said, "Guess what?"

"Yeah?" I passed a patch cable to Paloma. She was going to do tape manipulation and stuff with contact mics and seashells, and I was going to do vocals and guitar. I left my little noise rig at home so it wouldn't get fucked up before the Spider Moon Fest.

"Remember how my vegetables were stolen?"

"Uh, yes." I'd thought that might be the thing to push Henry over the edge.

"Well, I got a call today. It was just children! This group of kids goes to the garden every year to collect vegetables to donate to the food bank, and there is a plot designated for it, but someone made a mistake and let the kids just cut plants from anywhere in the garden!"

"No kidding!"

His shift in perspective was quite radical. For days he thought men had come and cut his living food from the earth, had stolen plants he'd been nurturing for months. He'd been rambling sick revenge fantasies involving hot pokers. Now he discovered it was children taking them for hungry people.

Paloma smiled, her black hair falling over her cheekbones, and we began.

The sun moves sideways not down into these small, quick nights. Angelo is in Georgia but I feel him here, and I live in Wendy's house but she is gone.

Gone most hours, and when she is here, she is gone. I am in Wendy's soft bed but she is hard. Angelo is kind and loves sweet smells enough to steal away flowers as a boy, even as he drew muscular warriors tearing each other apart to sell to the other kids so he wouldn't have to steal Marvel comics. And later tapes. We are men and women. Wendy is the brutal woman and Angelo is the nurturing man. I am mother and father inside myself. Wendy is hard ice but so weak, her once strong arms are now sticks: but I know her heart is good, because her heart is damaged by loving soft things in a hard world, her dog dead from cancer that could have been treated if she'd had money and her neighborhood that went to foul mush like a diaper box under heavy rain. Angelo loves hard and stands like a soldier because he was a soldier and is now a warrior for good things, for love and art, and now he is gone with another woman. When he was here, my heart felt light. Wendy is recklessness that I want, I can't help it: the criminality and speed, but always with heart! With the hope of heart. Angelo is all heart, but I can't really believe that he would love me and love me unconditionally. I don't want it to go bad. Now that he is gone, my heart is pressing down. He was here—I can taste the salt on his neck from that night by the lake—but now he is gone. I can't save Wendy. Angelo can't save me. But he opens up the artist inside me. He is my cosmic trigger. They are all real in the world, and they are also parts of me.

For three and a half weeks, I waited for Angelo. I experimented with telling myself he was an acquaintance I wouldn't be seeing again. He was alive in my heart anyway. I imagined a life with Wendy. I kept thinking of going off on my own, but then NO came up like a wall in my mind. This was the first time in my life I didn't have my own money, for one thing. I was afraid of the sensations of complete whole-body *feeling* like I had started to feel the night at the Mystic Breach show. Only in the morning, in my room, when I was on my

297

mat, only then could I *feel* with the safety of being the observer. And Wendy kept at me, just when I'd get to sleep, she'd wake me up, over and over again through the night. The long June days seemed all ON and no OFF. The pills and booze kept coming. Adderall, Xanax, cheap bourbon, expensive vodka, heavy IPAs at Bela. I was getting all turned around.

Just a year ago I'd been painting in my room and partying with Tasha. The days went inside out then, too, but I had my own place and a job. Had I grown at all the last year, or just gotten sicker? Was all of it, getting off crack, meeting Angelo, performing again, for nothing? I was more hooked than ever on whatever was around. There was something though, some shift inside that I could almost grip.

22

The Dinner Table

The Wednesday before the Spider Moon Fest, I woke to a text from Simon.
[Tomorrow night: you bring filet to my house. I have everything you need to cook it.]
I didn't have money for filet. Wendy was up and gone.
June never called me about the manhole covers.

The last I'd seen June was the night after the show I played with Paloma. She and Wendy were smoking more of those speedy joints, and I was drinking Red Bull and vodka. I got on a riff about how solipsistic Facebook was, and I somehow thought June wanted to talk about it, but later I was embarrassed at how my drunk head had made me oblivious to her obvious disinterest. Wendy smoked cigarettes that night, and she kept looking at the window above the A.C. unit and smoking and June kept looking over at her, then me, maybe wondering which one of us would leave first so she could be alone with the other one.

I hated the flat silence of Wendy's first floor bedroom. It was so like the room in the house that was shot up the night of the winter party, with the same type of bare dresser and bare bulb in the ceiling, not painted anything but apartment white, even though this was her house and she was a painter... and where were her comics? She'd never showed them to me. Had she trashed them, or had she made it all up? It felt too late to ask.

Hating the silence, I filled it with dim brilliance about writing ex-lovers on Facebook and how the interaction was like talking to yourself, and how did it affect us, being able to reach so many people, but really by only writing alone and consuming photographs, not in person. *In person.* Physical. Wendy and June were slightly older than me. There was a generation younger than us as big as the baby boomers that would maybe not ask these questions because they were born into it, so I asked them of the white paint, the bare bulb, the women with pin eyes and sweat, the strange lack of music, the blue cigarette smoke. The smoke burned me out.

I went out into the torso of the house, which was hot and muggy for the lack of Wendy's window unit, but more alive. I stood on the dry hardwood floor I'd over-mopped. I wanted to be alone, but I was lonely, so I went back. Opening the door, I braced for them fooling around, but no, they were in the same postures: June with heavy shadows under her eyes, holding her thick arms, not smiling, Wendy with legs crossed at the window, licking her dry lips. Killing time. How was this different than crack, anyway? I forgot what I was going to ask them about, but I wondered for a long minute, about how many people we all knew that we didn't know we all knew? None of us had significant online presence. We were invisible people.

Wendy seemed to pick up a story she'd been telling June before I came in, her words rolled over me and slowly made their way to my ears: "... 'Member that big old bitch Fred I told you Simon capped back in the day? You know—that summer when we had that laundromat thing going?"

"I guess. Oh, yeah."

"Fred's brother shows up the other day, packing, and I had to take care of him. Fuck—he was bigger than Fred!"

"No shit!"

"Motherfucker tried to headbutt me with that big dumb towhead-head of his, but I went like this," she jerked to the left, "and capped him right here," she put her hand to her guts just under the ribs.

My head was hit with grey fizz. "Wendy—wait, I thought you meant, you said Liz was the first for you and Simon—"

She was in my face. "I don't know any motherfucking Liz. What the fuck girl. Cut your tongue out before you say that name again."

I glanced at June, who winked at me. Hands in her pockets, grinning like a leprechaun. "Wendy."

"Shit girl." Wendy pushed back and looked me up and down, smiling. "Simon's been in this game since the mid-*nineties*, slinging dope since he was twelve years old. You think he never saw any blood till you came along? Shit."

"Why—but when did you—?" What about her dog, the comics, the storefront—what was true, what was make-believe?

She stepped up to me again and cupped my face in her hands. "I told you that so you wouldn't be scared. You were so shook up after, you-know-who, bit the big one."

"But you said he'd changed, after, and that he's more dangerous now."

"Maybe he *has* changed." Her breath tickled my cheek, her lips close, her eyes dancing around my gaze. "Maybe it's *you*, Margot. Maybe you change people for the worse. Maybe you make people sick."

My heart whipped in my belly. I stepped back from her as she slid her finger from my neck to my hip.

"But, Johnny Maker—Johnny said it, too, he said Simon's a killer now." Maybe now was the lie, maybe she was fronting to impress June.

Her flashing eyes made me flinch, thinking she'd be at my throat again, but she stood back. "You saw Johnny. When did you see Johnny Maker, girl?"

I glanced at June, who watched with interest—I wanted to say I could see who I wanted, but that would make me sound like a teenager.

Wendy pulled up her shirt, showing me her holster for the second time. "We protect Johnny from the shit. He doesn't know everything, dig? Don't go to him again. For his sake and yours."

I was going to vomit.

I looked at June, "I—am going out to the porch. But please, call me about the hubcaps, okay? Really. I need to stack up some cash of my own."

She worked her face in contempt. "What?" Turning to Wendy, "Give me one of those."

Wendy's shoulder jerked as she passed a cigarette.

"The hubcaps."

"Hubcaps. Oh—you mean *manhole covers?*" June's grimace began to twitch into a mean smile.

I whipped my hands around, backing out the door. "Yeah, yeah, sorry, duh, I said hubcaps, but I was picturing manhole covers. Yeah. Please, call me."

She looked at Wendy. "Hubcaps!" And laughed a dry laugh, looking around for a chair, she looked at the single bed behind Wendy, then worked her way down to the floor with stiff knees in stiff trousers.

Wendy did not join in the joke. "Margot. You don't go anywhere without my okay. You belong to me." She stood still, her flat eyes on me, her hand on her gun

When June spoke again, she spoke to the lonely wooden floor in front of her crossed legs. "Hubcaps."

I walked to the library to look up filet. I wished the pepper spray weren't expired. I wished I had a gun. Wendy had a gun. Why do we have to put up with this shit. I could be bringing raw meat to my execution. I printed out directions, I printed out costs. My hands shook and would shake for days.

I had no help. I'd been a vegetarian most of my life. What are *tapers*? I didn't understand the crazy costs per pound, and I was more confused leaving than when I'd gotten to the library. I called Henry, but he didn't know much about meat and started asking too many questions. I saw there were prices per pound, but nowhere did it say how much a filet weighed. I saw filet was part of a tenderloin, but no way could I afford to buy more than I needed. I wished Wendy had let me work on the houses alone. I was down to five dollars.

I knew I didn't have anything but my guitar to sell. I asked Henry if I could work Bela that night for tips only. He could have a night off. I ended up getting eight bucks in tips. I hoped that with the five I had, I'd have enough to get the meat.

I didn't tell Wendy that night about Simon's text. I don't know why. She'd made up with me after that night with June, chasing me through the house for a tickle-fight, wrestling on the living room floor, covering me with quick kisses. But the image stuck: standing under the bare bulb with her scary pale blue eyes and a hand on her gun.

When she came to me in the night before I was to go to Simon's, we didn't have sex. I pulled her arm tight around me and gripped her hand to my chest. She fell asleep with one leg draped over mine, and I lay there with my eyes open and dry.

I took a walk up to Giant Eagle in the morning. We were having a heat wave. Humidity coated my arms and my legs. The cold air conditioning hit my body like a swimming pool, and I was glad enough to cry. I had just enough money. The white paper package was heavy in my hands like the flesh it was. Pink water seeping at the corners. Then, I realized it would be bad to walk this meat back home in forty minutes of ninety-five-degree heat. How would I get to Simon's house later, anyway? I stood in the store, my mouth open, a little stunned with a sour chill in my stomach. Slow motion, subterranean desperation, seeing only execution at the end of the long day.

"My—god! Margot! *Strawberry Shortcake*, is that you?"

I turned slowly and there was Tasha pushing samples by the fish.

"What's up Hollywood?" I walked to her, and she jumped up and hugged me. I held the meat out from between us. She was still so soft to hug and wore the same glasses, but she'd grown her hair in, and now wore it natural and short.

Distracted, I couldn't think of how to talk, how to be with her. "What you got?" I said, forcing a smile. I gestured to the little white paper cups on her table.

"Crap, no one wants it. It's like some kind of half-diet cola. The diet people don't want it, and neither do the regular people. What you doing?"

"When you get off your shift?"

Lucky thing: She was done in an hour and I could cop a ride. I moseyed the store. I stopped catatonic again for a minute in front of a product...it was hard for me to understand. I read the label maybe nine times. *Artificial Tears.* What does that mean? The light in the aisle went kind of yellow, and the floor tilted, had I been here before?

Tasha's car smelled like chewy cherry candy. It was new and got cold

304

fast. Good for me and the meat.

We caught up fast. It just took a few minutes to get to Wendy's. I wanted more time with Tasha. Her wide smile and cool fuzzy hair made my heart sway. When I knew her before, she'd shaved her head and worn long blond, pink or blue wigs. I told her I liked her natural hair. She said she learned a lot in Marysville.

"You still with Jesus?"

"Yeah, he's my guy. Actually, I'm a UU now that I'm out. There's more space for nuance on the outside."

"Cool."

"Margot, I heard things about you! I heard you were dead, man. First, I heard it was an overdose, then I heard it was Simon. Then I heard you were alive!"

"Tasha, are you tight with Simon these days?"

"No girl, I avoid that man like the plague, he's gone full-cray. I smoked some buds with him when I first got out, but he's not the same dude as before. I don't hang with Billy either now. He's sweet but trouble, always trouble with that boy, same old."

"Tasha—you and Billy were busted getting me clothes…"

"Margot, I already told you to be cool about that. We loved you, but you told us not to, we were just into it, we were doing it for fun, to be tough, it wasn't your fault. We did that shit all the time, anyway, it was just a matter of time."

"I love you, Tasha!"

"Ah, Margot, I love you, too. You know who I *have* been kicking it with…"

"Who?"

"Johnny Maker. He is the finest guy around. You know it's true! That man is awesome."

"He is. You are wise to be hanging out with him. Done with girls, I guess?" Johnny Maker. I felt a little jealous, wishing not for the first time that I'd met Johnny before I'd met Simon and Billy and Liz, but I don't know how I ever would have met him without them. That's how it goes. It was good he and Tasha were hanging out. I hoped they stayed together and away from all this bullshit.

"I am a wise woman. And as much as I love other wise women, I was only gay for the stay. I can't help it: I love man body."

"Tasha. I need to tell you something, please. Don't worry, but if anything happens to me, know that it was Simon who did it, okay? Just in case."

"Margot, what's wrong, what's going on, are you okay?"

"Please don't worry, but just, if anything happens to me or Wendy, and it won't, but if it does, tell whoever gives a shit that it was Simon who did it."

"Wendy! I loathe that fucking psycho! She's a dick! I heard something about you staying with her, but I couldn't see it. Wendy? Why Margot? She's fucked up."

"I don't know."

"Look, Margot, Simon's gone crazy, for real. Last summer, he was a nice chill dude, I know it. Somehow, he did the work he did while still being a down-to-earth, kind person, but something has snapped. Shit's gone to his head. He's seen too many of those Al Pacino movies. But *Wendy*. She's always been bad. Now, don't turn your back with *Wendy* around, 'cause she is deep crazy. For real, she'll fuck you. One time she told Cher she had appendicitis, said she was down at Metro getting the shit removed..."

My smile was getting stiff as I thought of ways to disengage.

"Turns out she's just up in Detroit with another woman, but she still cried to Cher about non-*extant* medical bills, just to get some money and sympathy on top. She's always pulling crazy shit. She lies."

"I hear you, T. She saved my life once, though. I never knew anybody well who wasn't shit-storm crazy underneath."

"Oh whatever, Margot. Yeah, well I get it. She is real sexy."

Wendy showed up late in the afternoon. She saw the meat in the refrigerator.

"Did he call on you?" She strode into my room, shooting off sparks.

"I don't know how I'm going to get there. We haven't been working." I moved slowly through *Surya Namaskar*, breathing with a hissing sound in my throat.

"Here's for a cab. I wish I could take you." She put money on my desk. I didn't thank her. I hadn't really seen her in days. She peeled off her jeans and I caught a whiff of cheap raspberry perfume with old coffee underneath. "I fucking hate tight jeans. I'm gonna throw these out right now."

"So, he's paying you, then?" I held bridge pose and began breath of fire.

"Well, he's working me too hard not to. I told you too, I'm finding ways to skim extra." She sat on the bed, wanting me to stop moving, to give her attention. She squeezed the jeans in her lap and blew her bangs out of her eyes. She wore opaque blue shadow with glitter. Was she hooking? I couldn't imagine her doing anything like that.

"You don't seem worried then, that I might not be back tonight." Invoking Kali, I stuck my tongue out, closed my eyes and crossed them at my third eye. The fire in my belly grew.

"Don't worry, Alice, Simon just wants to be close to you."

It was too much. I pushed up into cobra, then back into downward dog and up into mountain pose. Standing over her. Sweat all over my body. "Shame me. Kill me. Rape me. You think he wants to 'be close to me?' You're blind to him. Why you say that name. Don't call me that name anymore. It's creeped out. I feel like *Alice* is some little girl you shook to death or something."

"Simon promised me he wouldn't hurt you. I think he just wants one last chance to get with you."

"You are okay with that, then."

"Hey, at least you just have to do one night with him to get right. I have to work all hours of the night and day doing shit you would not approve of, believe me. But soon, we'll be out of here, we can do whatever we want. August."

"You make me feel like a ghost. Look me in the eye for once." My sweat fell on her sleeves, but her blue eyes couldn't seem to focus into mine.

"I am."

"I can't see it."

She broke her diffused gaze. Looked out the window. "You think you might want to get back with Simon? He's a big man, now."

"Are you fucking kidding me? He's a sociopath. No. I'm either with you or on my own, can't tell what the fuck is going on."

She stood and pulled me close. Whispered in my ear. "Good. Cause I want you here with me. I need you. You've opened up my life. You'll relax, I'll make you feel so good. Better than those nasty men who just want to jerk off in you and then roll over. We'll get out to Colorado by fall, baby-doll."

I wanted to leave sooner. I wanted to leave now. But she was bent on August for some of many unknowable reasons. "Why are you letting me go tonight?" I pushed away, trying to look into her face again. "Don't you love me?"

Wendy let her mouth open, then shut it and tilted her head.

"I love you, Wendy. Don't you love me?"

"Oh Margot, you're so naive. You with your good middle-class teeth. You're such a good girl, aren't you." She sucked her teeth and sneered, glancing at my chest.

"Alright then, what the fuck am I doing here. I wish I'd left with

June. Or anything else but here."

"Wait, you don't understand. Forget it. Yes. I love you, you'll be okay. Simon's okay, he's my brother, you know? He knows—how much..." she waved her hand between us, and then wrapped her arms around me.

She felt like a scarecrow. Her brains were more scrambled than ever. Crazy Wendy. Her head smelled like that fake berry stuff. I generated a fresh new skin of hatred of Simon for making her do whatever the fuck she was doing. I also stepped into the shadow of hatred for her because she'd fed herself to him, and now I would feed myself to him.

Simon called through the cheap apartment door for me to come in. The meat felt like a severed hand. I walked into the living room where I'd beat him months before. I gagged on the smell of chemical powder fragrance vacuumed into the new carpet. He sat there, at his small round pine table. Hands folded, legs spread. The table was already set for one with a large carving knife in front of him. As if I'd walk in with a tray of prepared food.

My hands shook.

"Go on, Margot, get in the kitchen and make me that fillet. I got some bacon for you to wrap it with."

I was relieved he'd left a simple recipe on an index card. Online, I'd found so many different ways to cook filet mignon, and so many involving elaborate sauces, but not a simple recipe like this. All I had to do was wrap the bacon around it, add some coarse pepper and bake it for twenty minutes at four hundred degrees.

Opening the raw meat, I was overcome by nausea. That night came back, and I pushed aside a dream that the bacon Simon had made the next morning was from parts of Liz: white soapy fat and gummy red muscle. I picked up the filet. A black cow's black eyes flashed in my mind. I felt faint. I bit my tongue and quickly wrapped the bacon around the filet.

He came to stand behind me. I didn't like his newly shaved head. Now he was just all edges and scars. I slipped the filet into the oven.

I washed my hands. "Simon, do you want a salad or some potatoes or something?"

"Naw, just the organ meats."

"What?"

He nodded at the fridge. I opened it and there was a large glass bowl of organs covered in saran wrap.

Suddenly he was behind me. I jumped as he grabbed the back of my arm. He had the knife in his other hand. "You know how to make those?"

"Where are they from?"

He laughed his new short dry laugh. "HA. A cow. Dummy. What you think, those are *Sig's* organs?"

I hated myself for shaking. "Hey, can we put on some music, or something?"

He got up in my ear and said, "Just sauté those organ meats with onion and butter. Arrogant bitch. Before I slip this knife up in your guts."

The onions were precut. The only knife in the area was the one he held. I moved fast. His anger fueled my anger and cut the fear.

Purple veiny things danced with onions and butter in his expensive flat wok.

I piled it all on a wide painted plate he'd left out. The meat covered wild brown horses running. My throat went tight.

I set it in front of him. There were tapered candles, but he left them unlit. He'd returned the knife to its proper place in between the plate and the spoon, though it was larger than a steak knife, grotesque. "Do you want me to do the dishes, now?"

"I got a maid for that. Just get me a big glass of milk."

For just a second, I thought I might be able to leave.

But after I put the milk in front of him, he grabbed my wrist and pulled me forward. He pointed the knife at my throat. "Now you just get down on your knees down there by my feet like the dog you are." He pulled my arm toward the floor and then pushed me off balance. Not once did he look me in the eye. I got down, shaking still. "You don't need to beg. You just keep your eye on my boot while I eat, lest I kick you in your bitch face with it."

He ate slowly. Chewed with his mouth open. I heard every bite. He gulped cow-milk down, chasing the heavy meat. It takes a long time to chew through so much sinuous tissue. He tore through the complex chains of amino acids, proteins grown into fine elaborate structures supporting the movement of life.

Finally, I heard him scraping the last bites off china. A piece of some kind of organ meat fell to the floor by his foot. "Well, Margot, you done good, that was some good meat. I know you'd rather poison me, you weird fucking witch. Margot. You did so good. You can eat that bit there on the floor, it's okay, honey."

I shook my head, and moved to get up, but so fast, he gripped my hair close the scalp with his left hand, the knife to my throat with the right. Tears sprang like juice.

"No, bitch, eat it."

I froze, my mouth too dry. He shoved the back of my head down until my face was shoved into the organ meat and carpet. I bit the meat. I chewed it. He yanked me back up. I almost lost the meat, but he commanded me to chew it, and swallow it, and I chewed with no saliva. *This could be the last thing.*

For just three seconds, I saw us both from a distance of four feet, and I felt fine. My life, the experiences and people, seemed rich enough, a

311

full universe. I was ready to die.

The organ meat went down my throat like an egg through a snake, dry and nearly whole despite the chewing. Inside I went still, but my body shook. Tears wet my cheeks.

He exhaled and released me. I felt my mouth, my scalp. He looked away with a faint smile. He was spent.

"Go on, get."

I moved to stand up.

"No, crawl, crawl out of here, bitch-dog." He stood up, over me, with the knife. I turned and crawled to the door on hands and knees, exposed. Once I was close to the door, he stormed over and pulled me up into a strange embrace. His face was an inch from mine. He still didn't look me in the eye, but at my forehead. Just like his sister. "We are square, Margot Jones. But don't show me your face again. I see your face, again, and it's the last time."

23

Soham

Out the door, slogging down the stairs, sobbing. My face contorted. Why didn't I feel the relief I'd earned? My body shook so hard it was difficult to walk. A pale globe hung in the stairwell, which smelled like chlorine and the meat I'd cooked. I'd see him around every corner until he killed me. In every dream. Meat. Tinged with the taste of floral carpet powder. Breathing was hard. I raged in my heart at Simon, at Wendy, at Angelo even, and most of all myself. I couldn't believe the fucking sun was still out there, exposing everything.

I stood at the landing, wiping my face with my skirt. Waiting for composure to call a cab, not wanting the cabbie to think I'd had a lovers' spat. I had no lover.

The front door swung open and there was Billy.

He was beautiful: golden hair grown out over his little foxy eyes. He looked like Robin Hood.

"Whoa there, Margot... good to see you girl! What he do to you? That sadistic little ferret! I know he's a shit, honey, I know he's a shit. Come on, I'm get him, I'm sick of working for his nasty *azz*."

"No, I gotta go, let's go, Billy, let's go."

He looked down at the package in his arms, something he'd brought for Simon. "Fuck him, wanna go swimming?"

We stripped to our underwear and dove into Simon's pool, the same pool where I'd swam with Tasha and the Vickers just a year ago. Tasha had been the pool manager then. I forgot to ask her where she lived now that she was out. She wouldn't have come back here. Maybe she was in Johnny Maker's room right now.

The sun finally slipped away, and it was just me and Billy. I opened my mouth underwater and rinsed out the organ meat. My breasts felt light. The chlorine of time away. I cried a little bit more. It was a happy cry, finally. The Sex Pistols and Bikini Kill blazed through my brain, and I relived the encounter at Simon's on my knees with the meat in a whole new way, like *fuck it, I am freer in any given moment than Simon will ever be.*

Billy whooped and dove. "Feel better, girl? Feel better, Margie?" It felt fine. But his sweetness, his kind male body, made me miss Angelo more than I had since he left. More than I knew. Slicing deep into the water, there was silence, and I felt light.

Billy was staying in the penthouse of Lizabeth's apartment building. Now Jeff's apartment building. I wondered why Liz hadn't stayed in the penthouse of her own building. Until I saw it.

"Mark's not still downstairs, is he?" We walked into a foyer/mud-room area like I'd never seen in an apartment before.

"Naw, back with his mommy and daddy out in the 'burbs. Fucking loser. I should have killed him that day, girl."

"This place...what the fuck. Haa. Wow." The entrance opened into a giant red room with windows looking out over the oaks and the blackness of our lake beyond. The secret beach where Angelo and I had tripped was just past those trees.

Walls had been partially torn down, leaving chewed plaster of Paris and the internal structures, wires, boards, the connective tissue. It wasn't safe: possible lead paint, potential for electrical fires. Water dripped somewhere. The dark red wallpaper looked like it was from the nineteen-forties, the same elaborate design as in the hallway on Liz's floor. The large penthouse was one floor up from her apartment and the old man's apartment and spanned the area of both.

"Want some dogs?" Billy walked through the darkness into a kitchen, spilling yellow light through a dark dining room. I followed slowly. Touching the dark woodwork. Liz's woodwork had all been painted white, like most places I've lived. Rentals so often had thick white paint over wood. Wendy and I had removed some in renovation—it was a pain. Strange to see the original wood here, I wondered how long it had been since someone lived here.

"Forgot—you're veg. Think alls I got is some 'spistachios." He popped his head around holding a dark blue tin. I smiled and took it. I wasn't hungry.

"I used to live here, in this building. Did you know that? There was a management company, I had no idea that Liz owned it. That we shared a roof the whole time."

"No shit. Small world—small *Cleveland*."

I looked for a bathroom. There were two. This place—it would be too expensive to fix up, too expensive to rent. In the bathroom, I drank water from the tap, making a cup of my hands. I was so thirsty, and the water was cold and metallic. I slipped my wet bra and undies off and put them on the radiator to dry. My eyes looked as dry as they felt, eyeliner just a shadow trace after the crying and the swimming. My eyelashes short and translucent. I looked into my bare brown eyes.

"AARR! This *sheeit* is so goddam good! I couldn't be veg. I fucking love hot dogs!"

I had to get out of here.

He came up behind me in the hallway, I felt dizzy, wasn't sure which way was where. He had a hotdog in his mouth, and another in his hand, and he hugged me. I laughed despite myself.

He lit some candles and pulled out a box of beer and a flask of dark liquor, and we sat in the empty dark living room, drinking fast. I panicked for a moment, reminding myself of what he knew and didn't know about Liz's murder, and what he thought he knew. "Hey Billy, I want to say again, I'm so sorry about Liz. I was getting tight with her... she was a good woman."

I felt Lizabeth's ghost. I imagined Liz as a teenager holding baby Billy, her cheeks full, her red mouth open and sarcastic, her eyes keen and her hands warm on his little body. She would have dressed sharp, and she would have showed her cute, chubby legs under smart plaid skirts. Her hair would have been dated even then, bleached and teased, but I saw her in expensive amber sunglasses. And she must have even been a baby, too, once. I saw Lizabeth walking in stiff leather baby shoes, smiling a huge, wildly gaping, oval, hominid smile, innocent of language, of subtext, just thrilled with independent locomotion and thriving on the delight of other beings, witnessing with love and wonder, creating an ecstatic feedback loop...

"Ah," he lay out on his back. The Moon came in and made the light around him blue. "She was the oldest, and I was the youngest, and she was like a mother to me."

I swallowed bready beer and my eyes felt soft. "I know. She said you were like a son to her. I needed a mother, too, believe it or not at my age, and I went to her... Did you guys ever find out for sure who..."

"Girl, would you believe one of Sig's? That's when we knew the old man had to go." He clicked his zippo and whipped his hand, "Him and Liz went so far back. Shit." His voice broke, just a little.

The whisky and beer were working on me. I was floating and clean. Billy and I were suspended in this place. Sig dead. Wrong. It was all wrong.

"First, we thought it was the Puerto Ricans, makin' a move, but Simon come to find out, old *Sig* called it, must have been old-timer's disease, I guess. No reason for him to do her like that. There was only one thing we could do, then."

"I remember Sig." The man had garnered respect and had seemed kind and discerning. I rubbed my hands together. "I have a hard time believing it."

"Me, too. Well, I could say at least us and Simon and the Puerto Ricans are all working together now, that's what Jeff says, you can't deny it's good to have *peace*. But tell the truth, I fucking hate Simon. He's just too *mean*. Takes the fun out of the shit."

I thought of Wendy, of holding her skinny body. Of her plan to go out West. And I stayed quiet.

"Fuck. You never know for sure."

"Yeah." I lay back and looked at the ceiling. He'd turned on a fan that whipped the summer air, fresh from all those open windows, the lake and trees shimmering out there. It was still hot. I lay my arms out, palms to the sky I couldn't see.

"Wish I had a boom box in here, girl, we could listen to some Floyd," he smiled, and his eyes wrinkled as he looked at me, tracing my inner wrist with his finger, "...like that one time."

I smiled back with my head, but my body tensed up. I felt I was being disloyal to Angelo. Even though Angelo was with his ex-wife, and I slept with Wendy every night! Heart dissonance. Wendy who fed me to Simon. I pulled on the whisky bottle, there wasn't enough of anything to give me a break from all this anymore. Even here in suspension, my talking-self reared its ugliness in my ear.

Eerie, Erie here. Okay.

Billy stretched out on his belly and grabbed a little black overnight bag. "Wanna get high?"

My body clanged a sour note. I wished for him to just pull out a joint, but he pulled out his pipe and a little sack of rocks. He sat up into a cross-legged seat and stuck his tongue out as he started fitting the shit together.

"No thanks." He must have forgotten the winter already, the night that seemed so long ago when he told me to stay away from crack. When he told me to make a choice and fight for something. Maybe for someone like him, crack was safer in the summer, more acceptable in the party atmosphere of June, like how people say social drinking is okay, but drinking alone is not okay, a position I could never relate to.

"Hhn." He took a hit and the cocaine crackled. I remembered how his voice got nasal when he was high. I'd felt so loose, and now so tight. I thought of being here alone with him, him high. I remembered what he was like high. Fun Billy disappeared. He'd shut the blinds and peek between them, paranoid, get mad, stomp around. I imagined him forgetting about me, pacing all night while I tried to sleep on the floor. Everything was shit. I reached out my hand and he passed me the rock.

The night went fast. We talked for a quick hour or two, licking dry lips, and I heard the birds begin their wild song. When the sky moved from black to purple, and the movement of the black trees and fleshy waves became visible, he put his hand on my foot.

I did feel like fucking, rocking and swinging. No one would know. But I didn't want take off my clothes and be naked with handsome

Billy, I didn't want to kiss him, I didn't want him to take me away anywhere, I wanted to stay with myself. I realized, in the warmth of his hand on my foot, that I would not be going home to Wendy. That I had no home there, that my home was in my own body.

Before, I would have been scared of rejecting him, of him sulking and guilting me, or even forcing me, but I wasn't afraid. It wasn't the crack that gave me courage. The high was already wearing thin; if anything, the crack provided the small bit of fear I felt, a residue of fear from the pulling back of crack's fleeting yellow power.

I put my hand on his hand and looked him in the eye. He was looking at my leg, his tongue touching his upper lip. I said, "Billy, I want to be your friend." I touched his face, I said, "Billy—I want to be your friend."

He rolled over onto his back and moaned. "Not the friend zone!"

"Oh Billy, I just can't. I just don't want to have sex right now."

He looked up at me with a heavy mouth, then smiled, "Sex? I was just looking to make out, maybe cuddle a little." He groaned. "Okay, shit, girl, okay. Well. I'm not a piece of shit like Mark, you know, I'll take my time. Gawd!" He stood up and walked around the room, shaking out his legs, seeming simultaneously frustrated and relieved. "I'll take my time. I'll win you back!"

"Billy—I like you. I don't know where I'm at with love right now, I just know I need some time alone with my body."

The sky was moving into trees, and the lake was just beyond. I had to go out and get in it. I wrapped my arms around myself and closed my eyes, the eyes buzzed, and I dreaded coming all the way down—maybe it would be easier if I were outside.

Billy plopped down across from me and started rolling a cigarette. "Well, I could say something about how we both want some time alone with your body, but I won't!"

Beyond Billy the sun flooded Cleveland, the sky, the trees, the lake, all filling with light. The only leaping thing left in me was a desire to disappear into that lake. The sun touched the city, our city. And the oaks. And the birds, hundreds of birds, we were in the treetops and the birds were screaming. I wanted to die in all that pure joy.

I told him I needed to go to the lake, and he nodded, seeming tired at last, and gave me the entry code, which of course, I already knew.

Then I was down the stairs and out the door and running on rubbery feet. I almost got hit by a black SUV at the strange intersection of West Avenue, Lake Avenue and Route 2. I was down the hill and down the wooden steps to the beach where Angelo and I had seen creatures in the driftwood, where the trees and Moon and water spoke, whispered and moved with us, and where he almost stepped into the water with me, before he was called away.

Now I stood alone on the beach and the sun stood tall on the water. The same water, then black, was now frenzied in a mad textile of hungry dark blue and grey waves. Laughing waves. The trees rose up the hill behind me. Gaudy McMansions were planted at top of the hill, where we had seen the deer. The sky opened in front of me, endless. The same driftwood creatures slept in the sun. All of it, all of me, imprinted with experience.

This was the day before the solstice, the day before the Spider Moon Fest. I stepped into the water. The sand was dirty but smooth. I stepped a bit deeper into dark, bubbly muck that accepted and held my feet that often cramped from years of housekeeping and hairdressing. I wrapped my arms around myself and closed my eyes. Holding myself, I looked into the bright red pulse of my lids.

Holy air, cold water, warm muck.

Everything had worn off, worn away. I was raw again, sober. The light, the day. I felt a welcome splinter of wood in my heart, the pulse

320

of an oak. Expansion—for a moment I glimpsed the I Am written in the sky, the Lake saying it plainly—the dark waves not to be feared because I was the water. I Am. The truth, the realms, the web—all of it was real, living mystery. I'd walked through the Red Door into the Forest to the Sea, and now I was the Fool.

24

The Casino

I slept until three on Billy's piles of sleeping bags. He didn't touch me. Instead, he paced, creating movement in my dreams. I shot up in a panic. I'd never called Wendy, never told her I was okay. I grabbed my phone. Nothing from her. Nothing from Angelo. Fuck it. Billy shuffled in and offered the pipe again, and I declined. I hoped it would be out of my system by tomorrow night, not wanting to be going through withdrawal at the Spider Moon Fest.

Simon and I were square. I was free! I had nothing to fear.

I told Billy I needed to get back. I needed to practice for the show tomorrow. I plucked a pistachio shell off my shoulder blade.

"I'm not letting you go that easy! Come on, I got to make a run down to Parma, come with me, come on! It'll be fun—you'll get a kick out of this place." I didn't want to face Wendy anyway. I had to get mentally prepared to tell her I was leaving. Anyway, I had nowhere to go. I'd kill some more time hanging out with Billy.

I took a shower and slipped into my now dry bra and undies. My eyes were so bare now they looked like a stranger's. I'd worn heavy black eyeliner for the last twenty years. I looked close to the mirror deep into the brown eyes. Yes, I filled up the eyes, it was me in there, always me.

Parma's never far, but it always feels like it. It's the quintessential American suburb built during the brief era when working class people lived like middle class people. Two generations from the tenements they had become homeowners. Parma is vast and cut off from everything. It sprung up fast after World War II. The fragile, suddenly expanded, middle class filled miles of cheap little boxes in rows and rows. It was a good time for workers, but Parma also was a textbook example of racist white flight from urban Cleveland. While southern black working people moved to cities like Cleveland after the war, white people began to leave. Factories left the black neighborhoods first, and racism only deepened in white enclaves like Parma. Now, the main streets are clogged with cars and all the businesses have neon signs last updated in the seventies. Off the main roads, Snow and Pearl, neighborhoods repeat endlessly.

When Billy said we were going to the "Casino", I'd assumed it was the name of a bar or a nickname for a bar. Like the women's bar Wendy and I went to a few times, called the Nickel *or* The Five Cent Decision. But here we were, pulling off a main drag, slowing down as, one after the other, Billy scanned for a certain house.

"'Ap! There you go. The one with the duck." He jerked back into a spot down the street a little from the Casino: a one story-house half-brick and half-white siding with a plastic goose in sunglasses out front. It looked like any of the other houses. If anything, the lawn was cut shorter, but there were no flowers, no bushes.

We walked in the side door and right down into the basement. Billy was in a certain mode: hyped up and macho, so he stomped along ahead of me. Dread hit as I realized I was craving crack. It comes back so fast. And the shame... I should have counted all those crack-free

323

days.

Once in the dark basement, I felt shy. It was a small half-finished basement, but at least two-dozen people were packed in. Mostly middle-aged white guys and a few pretty young girls. They looked sedated. Billy tossed me a beer, winked at me and jabbed an old man with his elbow, and they laughed. I popped open the beer with the intention of downing it fast, but instead, I just held on.

There was a 52-inch plasma screen broadcasting a boxing match. A skinny black man with curving black lines tattooed on his shoulder plowed into a dark blond, white guy. Red spit shot across the screen. The tv was turned up as commentators talked like auctioneers. *The Creek* was also blaring out of a boom box, commercials for "pre-owned" vehicles and pop songs by reality tv stars competed with the fight. I was not used to *this* kind of aural bombardment. Circular saws, natural distortion and feedback loops, I was used to. But this made my head spin.

The main man introduced himself to me as Cozzi. "This is why we've opened up the Casino today honey, the Soto/Murphy match. See, that young Soto is fighting for his dead father. Big game. But you should have seen the Vazquez/Marquez match last March. That was something, *Magnifico* Vazquez. Wow." Cozzi was a stringy man in an undershirt. He wore dark glasses in the dark basement. White scars littered his arms. They might have been from cigarette burns. "This is just my house, rest of the time." His voice was all dried out.

Billy made his rounds, shaking hands, sipping on a Budweiser, smiling like a golden retriever. A large poker table dominated the room. The loudest men sat at the poker table with cigars, holding their cards and talking dirty. Small round tables were scattered around the room with more men who played in silence. What they played, I don't know. There was one broken booth in a dark corner packed with teenagers, both boys and girls, laughing, being lazy with the cards.

Cozzi saw me looking at them. "Those kids are just here to buy weed. They're from the neighborhood, they just stay 'cause they know it's cool here. Those guys," he gestured to the men at the massive poker table, "They're not fucking around. They're the hard hitters. They're here to bet. You should see these guys come Super Bowl, they bet on everything from how long the national anthem is going to be, to which team's going to win in the coin toss." He smiled and touched my arm.

A girl came up from nowhere and handed us each a red cup of something. "Rum and coke," Cozzi said, taking my still full beer and tossing it into a recycling bin. He thanked the girl. He stood a little too close to me. "So, honey, you with Billy? You Billy's date tonight?"

I laughed nervously and sniffed the rum-heavy drink. I wanted to drink it, but I thought of paint thinner. "We're friends. I live with somebody." I was hungry, looking around for pretzels or something, but there were no snacks in sight.

"Okay, okay, I see. I didn't know Billy had such nice friends…" He rubbed my arm with his eyes on the screen and walked over to a folding chair facing the match. "Ouch! Looka that spook *swing!*"

I cringed. This was what it was like to be in a basement full of white gamblers in Parma.

I had to urinate. Billy was sharing a joint with some of the teenagers, while simultaneously swiveling around in time to exchange insults with some old men at top volume. He shared a fixed grin with the Cheshire cat.

I went a little dizzy. The pale girl with the braid who'd handed me my drink walked past. "Hey excuse me, where's the bathroom?"

She stopped, looking a little confused. "Upstairs, I guess? They mostly just piss out behind the garage, but I'll show you."

I followed her up the tight stairs. Her legs shined strangely coming out of her denim shorts. Getting onto ground level was a relief. The house was quiet: a kitchen that looked un-lived in, nothing on the counter but a blue glass pitcher, a living room with just one couch. I couldn't even hear the subterranean cacophony. "There you go." She pointed to a hallway. "I got to get back down there, okay?"

I slipped into the bathroom and scooched down my shorts. It was hot as fuck. I urinated with my eyes closed. Pissing felt good. I looked at the red cup on the sink. What I really needed was water.

I let myself think of Angelo. We'd tripped nearly a month ago. I had believed that he would be back for the Spider Moon Fest. That was stupid—he was in another world. He was with Melissa in a small town in the Deep South. He was such a responsive person, so attuned to whomever was in front of him, he probably had forgotten all about this world.

I opened my eyes. In the dull light I saw nine nude pairs of pantyhose hanging around the shower, one of them stained dark with blood. Women don't wear those anymore, especially in the summer. Maybe lawyers do, but not regular people. The girl, though, the one I followed up here, it hit me that she was wearing nude hose under her daisy dukes—were all these hers?

I wasn't in a hurry to get back to the smoky basement racists. I poked around the tiny hallway, hoping there would be some pictures or something to entertain my starved brain for a minute, but nothing. One bedroom door was closed, the other door was open, probably Cozzi's room. The bed was just a mattress on the floor, but oddly a cheap, overly ornate headboard loomed over it. Wasn't he afraid it would fall on him? I felt my skin prickle at the fear of someone surprising me, but I didn't really do anything but look into the open room. There was not much in the room, just some shoeboxes, overflowing ashtrays, a green dresser and a 1992 Cindy Crawford poster by the window with closed blinds.

A *meow* made me jump out of my skin as a young Russian Blue cat skipped out from behind the small green dresser, knocking a full ashtray over as she crossed the room, and ran past me. I turned with a smile and faced the other door, the second bedroom. But this door had a lock on it from the outside.

My heart beat faster as I touched the cheap particleboard and pressed my ear to the door. I didn't hear anything at first, but then I heard a faint whimper or small voice... I strained to listen more closely. Someone grabbed my arm. It was Billy.

"Oh, Billy...hey." I smiled, relieved.

"The fuck you doing up here?" His face was close to mine, his breath sour. "Why you get out my sight, girl? That's not a safe thing to do, and you know Cozzi works for Simon now." He pulled me into the living room.

"The fuck, Billy? Back off, man. What's behind that door?" I whispered.

"Don't worry about it."

"Billy, please."

His face softened. "Ah, sweetie, come on girl, you know. That's where the girls stay. I fucking hate it."

"What...those girls, with the red cups?"

"Dammit, girl. You live with Wendy, right? I thought you knew."

"Wendy... what? What."

He exhaled, took my hand, and sat me down on the couch in the bare living room. Tissue curtains hung still at the picture window. I thought of my grandmother's house, like this one, but packed with stuff and now far away and long gone.

"I hate it, Margot. Simon says it's business, a natural evolution, but it crosses a line with me. You know, there's always been women willing to work the streets, sell ass, women who are addicted to the shit who need to supply their habit with quick cash." He tapped out a cigarette and lit it. "Well, since Simon been boss, he started doing like some other folks, organizations, he's moving away from the street ho-pimp thing, but not really into fancy escort/strip club shit, but into this thing where the girls stay at a house, or several houses, and the men come to them. He's got a couple more small rooms in the basement. Sometimes the girls get to sent to other places, other cities and other girls come here. So no one gets attached. Sometimes they make pornos, for the internet, I guess. He says it's all profit this way, and under the radar, too."

"Like, a bordello?"

"No baby, like *all profit*, like the girls don't get paid. Well, they get paid in food, water, and drugs."

I sat up. "The door's locked… you don't mean they're *slaves*."

"I can't believe you *live* with Wendy, and don't know this shit."

I felt like I was going to get sick. In a flash I wanted crack but breathed away the craving while it was tiny. "Why do you keep saying *Wendy*. What's Wendy got to do with it?"

"Dang, girl, I should have left you at home." Home. He got close and quiet. "Okay. Used to be, guys, guys maybe like me, but *not* me, would, in this kind of a set-up, become boyfriends with teenage girls, get them hooked on drugs, feed them love, talk them into running away, and then keep them in houses like this. But these situations evolve like all business evolves. Capitalism *is* like a virus, Margot. Bosses discovered that what works best now is when an older *woman* befriends the girls. They trust the woman more. You get a better breed of girl, who say, has the self-respect to know that older guys are dangerous, thus girls with better hygiene, teeth, etc.

He rubbed my arm. "But Wendy, well, you know she looks cool, and she's tough and charismatic. Shit, you should know, word is you're with her due to some Stockholm Syndrome shit. Simon says she saved you from an accident or something, housed you, up, and that's how you got to be bosom buddies. Lucky for you, you're hanging out with me again. Bitch is crazy."

"You are saying that Wendy is luring children into being sex slaves."

"Shit. We don't exactly call it that. *They* don't call it that—I'm not involved. Directly. You know, shit's all over. There's lots in Toledo. Look it up on the internet! Shit. They advertise in the back of *Scene* magazine! It's a big social problem, girl, around the world and in Ohio, too!" His grin turned nasty, "Wendy *loves* it, though. She's a sick chick. She loves fucking with people, turning on them. Surprises, you know. Here she is, Simon's paying her big money this summer to go around cultivating these little hotties, who are nice and clean but not so upstanding that people would be surprised if they ran away. It turns the bitch *on*, Margot!"

"No, if she's doing it, it's because she's forced to." I thought of the lock on my own bedroom door. I'd pushed away the memory of her locking me in the room, it had just become a silver circle on the door, I'd forgotten about the lock.

Billy took my hand. "Why—why would she *have to* do anything."

"She's been miserable since she's been working for him."

"The misery ain't from the work, it's from that crank/heroin cocktail she's been shooting."

"Hey Billy," I stood, shaking, "I got to go. I'll see you."

"Oh, honey, I'm sorry, baby, I thought you knew."

"I'm going." I walked into the kitchen, and he followed me.

"No, I'm not letting you go that easily, Sweet Pea!" He tried to get playful and grab at my waist.

I turned and took his face in my hands. His eyes looked back into mine, at least now, not when he's high on crack and his pupils are points, but now, his eyes looked deeply back into mine. "Billy, you've been a good friend. You got to know this: Simon killed your sister."

He pulled back. "Naw. How you know that?"

"I was there. I was silenced, so. I couldn't tell you. They almost

329

killed me, but Wendy hid me away, threatened me. But fuck Simon. He did it, he killed her, Billy." Relief hit me like water dropped from a high place.

"I *knew* it." He spun around and smashed the blue pitcher to the ground. "Fucking *knew* it! *Dang*! First thing I said to Jeff when we found out, but he was like, 'No, no. We need to investigate.' But wait—he wouldn't *deign* to do the deed himself, tell me, he had Wendy do it, right? Of course, she was his muscle then, sure."

"No, no, it was some little guy I've never seen before, you know, that was Simon's first hit, so he probably commissioned an out-of-town dude. But I saw it, so that's what he meant by Wendy saving me from an accident—he wanted to kill me, sent her to do it, but she saved me instead. She took care of me and got me clean." I was disgusted with Wendy, but I was still bound to her in some way after all those nights together, after everything. I couldn't feed Wendy to Billy in the heat of the moment.

"I see through you. Even by that bullshit account, she *knew* about it." He got up in my face, he gripped my arms too hard then let go and punched the fridge behind me. "Fuck! Shit!" He turned to me with tears in his eyes. I shook, almost laughing, his grimace matched my shock inside. "You break my heart, Red, why'd you go with *her* and not me? Anyways, I don't know if I can protect you from Jeff when he finds out."

I put my hands over my face. "Oh, Billy, baby, I've got to go."

He took my hands off my face and kissed them, his lips shaking, his eyes looking into mine, then behind me. "Shh, it's okay. We'll get them, but I'll keep you safe."

I had to get out of town. I had no money, nothing. I wasn't even wearing eyeliner. The Fest was tomorrow—maybe I could get that two hundred dollars from Lucy early.

I followed Billy like a dazed child. We were in the basement again.

Billy turned and hissed, "Stick close by me, I'll finish my business, then we'll split. Got to get to Jeff's and tell him." My mouth was clenched as I tried to grasp how to even understand the present moment. It was as if a giant cheap coin flipped behind my eyes, one side shooting out crippling branches of guilt, the other side, rage, pure rage. The girls stood here in this room. On tall shoes, in clear pantyhose. Suddenly, I could see them, everywhere.

Billy whispered, "And don't say a word about the girls right now or Cozzi will shoot you, no hesitation."

The party was louder. Drunker. The teenagers who'd come for pot and stories were gone. Cozzi slumped in a lawn chair. His head lurched, and his lit cigarette touched his arm. He jerked back up. An old guy walked past me and winked, murmured, *"Narcoleptic."*

A man from the table called out, "What says this next round lasts less than eight seconds?"

I exhaled, feeling faint.

"What you got?"

"This nickel baggy and your momma's box!"

"Fuck you—five bucks."

I looked into the face of the nearest girl, long brown hair parted in the middle and tied into low loose braids, thin lips painted cherry red, long nose, many freckles. I waved feebly at her, trying to figure out how I could get these girls out of here. She would not look at me.

My phone vibrated in my little shoulder sack.

I watched Billy working the people, impatient, eyes flashing. His suspicions confirmed, he was eager and hungry for the blood of Simon X and Wendy O. I waited till he got Cozzi over to a corner, where they were doing whatever he'd ultimately come here to do, and I turned for the stairs.

"Hey, GIRL." He was sharp. I bolted. He was fast and caught me on the stairs, caught my legs, and I fell forward, hitting my forearms on the steps. He gripped my sides hard. I said, "Let me go, I'm gone."

"Come on, hush-it, we're going to Jeff's, I still have that package for Simon was due last night, remember?" He was hissing in my ear, breathing Budweiser and rage. "You and me, we go to Jeff, and then we all go deliver the package to Simon." He held me like a canine, his paws kneading me, his breath on the back of my neck. The room was quiet, except for that "Jack and Diane" bullshit coming off *The Creek*.

"Come on, Bill, what the fuck are you doing." Cozzi was standing behind us.

"No, no, I'm sorry, Margot." Billy's voice was hoarse. He loosened his grip, but still held me, stroking me softly, he let his head fall into the hair at my neck. A sound rose up from deep within Billy's guts, an ancient howl, the old-time grief howl, for a second his lips vibrated at the back of my neck and he gently tore off me and stumbled up the stairs and out the door.

I stood up on shaky legs and followed him up and out without looking back.

Smacked by the wall of wet heat and glare. How could the sun still be stretching out this day? The sun's awful rack.

Billy mewled and kicked his car.

"Billy, I've got to go."

"I know." He fumbled around with bags and opened his car and fumbled around a little more while I stood there, thinking maybe I should just walk off. Then he pulled out some bread and asked for my hand. He counted out ten hundred-dollar bills into my palm. "It's not much, but it'll get you out of town."

"Billy...wow."

"No, I do have to. Margot." He looked up and squinted at the bright sky. "I wish it wasn't like this. On the inside or on the outside, either way, there's no choices in my life. Run. I'll smudge the money. I'll tell them you ran."

I ran until the sun turned red. Until the pain in my hip from sleeping on the wooden floor faded away. I ran squinting because my sunglasses were gone. I ran until I didn't know if I was back in Cleveland, or still in vast Parma, or going the wrong way into some farther out suburbs. First, I zigzagged, hoping to veil my movement. After slowing my pace down, my mind rose back up with all its angry desperate talking, and it occurred to me to keep the sinking sun to my left, as north was the way to the lake, the way to Lakewood, the way home.

I called Wendy. Nothing. Straight to voicemail. My stomach lurched. I sweat out the dying itch for crack until it was gone.

I took Pearl on a bridge over a highway, 480 I guess. Then to get away from a main road, I walked a little while east, then west, mirror maze of sun on waning storefronts, I found myself finally heading north on Fulton Road. Eventually I came to the Zoo. With my meandering, it had taken me nearly two hours to get here, and I knew it was farther still to Lakewood. My mouth was dry. I held Billy's money tight and sweat into it. I'd call a cab. I was afraid of someone taking the money. Where would I take the cab? How far could I get—I racked my mind for anyone I knew maybe in Toledo or Detroit…I wouldn't want to bring trouble to anyone…

The sound of complex birds from warm places burst from lush trees, birds with a world independent from mine. I wanted to sit on the big rock by the panda sign. I could leave everything, but I had to get Clarence. I looked at my phone. Nothing from Wendy. I wanted to be done with her, and I didn't want her dead. I didn't know if these things were possible.

I held the phone and squinted against the long west where the sun refused to go down. My body was slick with heavy sweat. My phone buzzed.

[the Moon is rising after midnight and it looks backwards and wrong – the Moon misses you. I think about the night at the beach] Angelo's text was from two weeks ago, and it was broken.

Then another came in: [boring as fuck.. the only venue is a country bar with a dj on Thursday nights] and another [driving me nuts...but she's grieving. I hate grief it's so incomplete]

The vibrations piled on top of each other as texts came in, waves of texts, cascading texts: [haven't heard from you hope you're okay] [if Wendy did anything to you...she's already on my list] [...I dreamed of you last night on the beach...I can't take it...I love you][Moultrie GA is hell on earth and hot as Satan's soggy balls]

My hands shook and the texts kept coming. [...I'll keep texting in case you are getting these and can't get back to me...maybe it's my phone. I have to keep touch somehow. Most people don't even have internet down here—can you believe? Mel's mom says no long distance on her landline. I've never felt so alone, but I'm thinking of you and missing you...] Finally they stopped.

The last one was from early this morning, maybe when I was standing on the beach in the sun: [okay hon, we're getting into Kentucky now. I drove thru the night, now Mel is taking over and I'm going to zzz. I'm turning off my phone to conserve battery, but I'll call when I'm in Cleveland. Take care. <3]

I read over them again. He thought of me. He loves me. Angelo Qamar is coming home to Cleveland.

The phone buzzed again, it was a call, it was him, and I dropped it. The battery slid out onto the hot asphalt.

I fumbled the phone together and called him back.

25

Children of the Mountain

The heavy sun finally settled into a magenta puddle as Angelo pulled up. His eyes were on me before he stopped the car, before he jumped out. His eyes: shining and alive in his otherwise fixed face. He pushed his cool dark hair back and touched his glasses, but left them on, moving fast, to me, reaching to get the door for me, catching me instead in a sharp, heavy embrace. I wanted to apologize to him for being such a nasty person. Not ready to be his friend. Unfinished, damaged. My face was bare. I gasped instead and became newly aware of my body, so dependent on animal breathing.

He put his lips to mine then, and our tongues grazed an electrical second, then I kissed his mouth, and he kissed my lower lip. Lips shaking, I held him, pressing my face into his shoulder. I closed my eyes and reveled in dimensions unfolding within the dark pocket of my soul. We were together in the dark, secret inner place.

On the way back to Lakewood, we fell quiet. The safe feeling of riding next to him was intoxicating. I looked out the window and touched my fingertips to my mouth. He glanced over at me a few times, maybe expecting some explanation, but I was silent. Smiling. He told me about Moultrie, Georgia. *"That's* the sticks." He said Melissa was at the apartment, but she would be moving down there, soon, to stay with her mother. He said she felt more like a sister to him than ever. They'd driven her mother's car up here instead of flying back. The whole way up, they battled over the radio, and she shot wads of wet paper at him through a straw.

He said he thought of me every second.

I told him life up here without him was not life at all.

I couldn't get Wendy on the phone, so I asked Angelo if we could swing by her place to get Clarence and my stuff, and if I could stop in at his place for a bit. I knew they'd be coming for her, or us, but I had to get Clarence out.

"I didn't hear from you—I was worried."

"I didn't hear from you. I understand now. I have to leave town tonight. I have to figure out how—plane or train, I don't know. I have a grand."

He didn't ask why. He looked ahead.

When we got to Wendy's, I told him he should wait outside.

Relieved the painting truck was gone, I felt my heart in my throat as I grabbed beige plastic grocery bags from under the sink and headed up to the powder blue room. Purpose cleared my eyes and it was easy to see what I needed and what I could leave. I collected my toothbrush and gear, I poured Clarence into his carrier.

My head was cool, but my heart was beating so hard that my hands felt tingly, and I had to keep forcing my chest to take in more air. I needed food and water. Okay.

Okay. I worked to get my guitar over my right shoulder with half a dozen tiny bags looped over my left arm and picked up the carrier in my right hand. I turned and was face to face with the painting of myself as a lion. Shit. *Shit!* I spat out the word and then felt bad for

Clarence, who didn't like hissing sounds like that. I thought about leaving the painting, I didn't need it. But I didn't want Wendy to have any talisman, any totem. I gingerly pulled it off the hook and down with my chin and inner forearms and worked my way downstairs and through the house with the painting in front of me and all the things I needed in each hand or draped on each arm, all in one lousy, breathtaking trip to the front door.

I set Clarence's carrier on the porch while I loaded up the other stuff in Angelo's red car. Just as I turned back to go get him, Wendy pulled up in her painting truck.

The cicadas screamed.

She saw me, and I saw her, and I walked back for Clarence. Only halfway up the drive, she stopped the truck and hopped out and was up by me on the porch. Anger hopped off her wiry shrunken muscles. She wore an undershirt, and I could see for the first time how much weight she'd lost just these last few weeks. I could see the track marks.

What the fuck had happened that night I played at Scum when she went with Jeff Vickers? That was the night she changed—who was she really?

I imagined her, wearing feather earrings and blue eyeliner, skinny, hip and blond, picking up misfit girls in the few dingy malls out in the poor suburbs on the east side. Or maybe going out as far as Youngstown, Toledo, Canton. She would be so cool, maybe even playing music I'd given her. Smiling at them as if she could see their genius, their spirit, their teenage hearts that had been so misunderstood and underappreciated. I thought of these girls shot full of cheap dope, getting raped. And Wendy maybe getting off on it. The rage pooled vast between my eyes.

Or maybe Billy was lying. He was too earnest to lie, but maybe he was wrong.

Wendy's eyes never met mine.

337

I said, "I went to see Simon last night."

The picture window behind us framed lamplight sprawling warmly on the couch, making things seem normal. Like it was time to come in for dinner. Time to return to the old family circle around the fire to share bread, wine and stories.

She put her hands up. "Just, I'm almost done doing this one thing for Simon." Her voice went nasal like Billy's did when he was high. "Please, tomorrow night. It'll give me time to skim a little more bread and get our affairs in order. I can come see you play? We'll talk at the show. You're right, we can leave town, we can go. I'll pack some things." She leaned close, her lips touching my ear. "We'll go away after the show tomorrow night, right after the show, okay? We'll go up to Kelly's Island, and figure all this out, okay?"

"You know what? Don't you fucking baby talk me, motherfucker! I'd like to fucking terrorize you. I know what you did. I know about the girls, and I'm gone, you read me? Gone." I spit the words in her face.

Her face collapsed in grotesque understanding. I stood there a few seconds longer than I wanted because my knees were liquid. Then, suddenly, I was walking down the stairs.

"Margot."

I thought of her gun and turned. She was so small. Even standing on the second stair. "I don't know you."

She looked beyond me, at Angelo's car. "I know where he lives." She bit her lip.

I looked at her and I saw nothing. Maybe she had a gun somewhere, but no wits left, no strength in her arms, no drives beyond survival. I said, "Hey. Hey."

"What."

"If you show up at his house. I will kill you."

Back at Angelo's, Melissa was cooking grilled cheese and baked sweet potato fries. It smelled so good I felt sick. Angelo said I could put my things in his room. His room was neat. Only meaningful objects existed there. A green Army-issue trunk. Pictures of an older and a younger blond woman on his dresser. They shared his eyes. Must be his mother and sister. On his nightstand was a shell I'd given him. I sat on his bed and let my gaze fall into the white wall.

He came in, turned on a little fan. "I know some people like fans. I'm used to the heat. I know you're veg, so I made you a grilled mushroom and tomato sandwich instead." I held his hands and looked up into his eyes, and he looked back.

We three sat around the table. The table was still littered with scraps from the Spider Moon Fest flier we'd made the night we tripped, the night before he and Melissa had left. He hopped up and stacked the loose ends and lit fat red candles. Melissa didn't wait to dig into her two sandwiches. She'd gotten a deep tan, and her hair hung lank over her shoulders as she ate fast, looking at her plate.

"I'm sorry about your father."

"Well," she said between chews, "...we weren't close. But, that's worse in a way, but thanks."

Angelo sat down and we ate. For once, there was no music. We were all tired, and quiet. The tomatoes juiced into the warm bread. I'd last eaten pistachios sometime in the night. My face mashed into the floor at Simon's flashed in my mind...but I was in a different place now.

I wanted to hold Angelo's hand, but I thanked him instead for the food.

Melissa set her elbows on the table. "Margot. Angelo talked about you constantly. Kept bitching cause his phone didn't work."

Angelo blushed, turned his face to stone and took his plate to the kitchen. I looked at Melissa and smiled. She shrugged.

I looked up the Greyhound schedule for Cleveland to Flagstaff, afraid I'd have to wait till Monday, wondering already if I should fly instead, but could I bring my guitar, or? Fuck it—I'd have to leave everything—but Clarence? I hadn't flown in years and years, a last-minute flight might be more than the money I had, I really had no idea.

But then I saw there was a Greyhound leaving before dawn. The next bus from Cleveland to Flagstaff left downtown at 4:30 AM. If I didn't make that one, which I would be wise to make, there was another one at 8:40 AM, and another at 6:25 PM. All around two hundred fifty bucks. I had no idea it was that easy. I could be at my parents' house by Sunday night.

I told Angelo mechanically that I'd have to maybe sleep a couple hours and then get up around two-thirty to catch a bus downtown to the Greyhound station. Then I'd be gone.

He said he'd take me. I said, no, please. He'd just driven up from Georgia, he needed sleep.

"I can't go to sleep with you here and wake up with you gone. What the hell is going on? Who are you afraid of?"

"I don't want you to know anything about it. I wish I could stay."

"I can give you a ride. I wish you didn't have to go."

Later, in his room, I felt sleepy and calmer than I should have.

I'd taken a long bath and wore a long black slip. I was afraid they'd fight, but instead old wide-headed Clarence groomed baby Violet as she rolled onto her back, neat little paws in the air. The cricket sounds came in on velvet air through the window. Angelo opened his trunk. He showed me his photo album. People he'd lost. He showed me fliers from his bands in Malaysia. He showed me action figures, medals and passports that had traveled the world with him. Then he put them gently back into his trunk and locked it up.

"You're here, in my room." We sat side by side, watching the still trunk.

I took his hand. "I like your style."

We got under the covers then. We didn't kiss. We lay on our right sides, spooning. I held his hand to my chest. The cats were curled together on his pillow, while both our heads rested on mine. I'd never slept with a man like this. The shared heat welled up into sleepy, wide desire. We eased into dreaming, and gently woke up, his hand still at my chest, in the morning. He put his mouth close to the skin on my back and said, "You're my best friend." We kissed again and our mouths felt clean like children's mouths, even after the night.

The night was over. "Fuck. Fuck! I set my alarm for 2:30 pm! Fuck what an asshole!"

He nodded and snapped out of bed in military mode, his dog tags making their gentle sound. "Don't worry—you're here, no one came, everything is fine. I'll get you to the station to catch the 8:30 bus." His body was beautiful. He wore underwear with little legs and he kept his front from my view, but his back was handsome, and I ached for him. I didn't want to leave this bed.

While he was in the shower, I fell back into sleep for just a minute, just enough to catch one last threshold dream. I dreamed I was running, and the motion of the running changed whatever shades of black were before my eyes and soon a woman shimmered into view. Before the woman came into full focus, I saw the night behind her, and the full Moon, and I saw the woman was floating above a vast black ocean. She was cocooned within a flaming bush, or maybe it was a cave of spouting water, rushing against gravity from the sea. Alligators snapped at the edges of her glowing organic mandala, roses

341

flipped out of the ocean, too, and clams and lilies. Then She came into focus. Her mouth turned slightly in a relaxed Shiva Buddha smile, her eyes calm with ageless peace and wisdom, white candles sprouting from her crown. She had four arms: one hand in *gyan* mudra at her heart, and in another other a trident, another hand brandished a sword, and the fourth lifted in *apana* mudra with index and pinky fingers raised into the swirling air. She sat in a lotus on top of a lion within the water and flames above the black ocean. She had long black hair, dripping earrings, necklaces, bare breasts and soft pants, she had a special tantric seat. Her third eye was shining, bright and aware. She hovered there, all stillness, all movement. And then, she was so close, her face in my face, and then my eyes were open.

I will stay and play the show. Breathing Beasts in the Creature. Ten thousand wings flapping against the doors of eternity.

No, I could not stay. I had to go. I shouldn't even go to my parents. I should go somewhere I'd never been, where they'd never find me, or anyone I loved.

26

Spider Moon: The Cost of Going In

I stood up. Awake. I looked at Angelo's animal cards as I heard the shower turn off, and more water run in the sink. He'd collected packs of these cards from the same Remarkable Thrift where Wendy used to work. The cards were from the late seventies, and he remembered them from his hazy early childhood days. He was buying back the world of his childhood one pack at a time.

The Thick-Legged Flower Beetle (shiny black creature investigating a violet pink flower with a soft green background), the Sunbeam Snake (coiled like the Cuyahoga on sharp bluegrass), Australian Kangaroo Mouse (brown with white bellies, standing on two legs with worried hands, shadows on sand the same color as their backs, low light casting small shadows), Black-Tailed Godwit (long beaks in long grasses and low sun), Jack Dempsey Fish (1970's blues and greens in water with water plants), *Structures*: Echinoderms (called Serpent Stars, red branches spreading like veins, fingers, neural pathways), and beloved *Major Biomes*: Equatorial Forests of Southeast Asia card (lush living primeval forest, where sweet Angelo had been lost for a time). The greens moving to browns moving to pinks and oranges and the misty blues of the skies at the time of our births long gone.

He came out of the shower with a thin faded peach towel wrapped around his lower half. I wanted to look at his body, but I felt shy. He had used his body in his life, and now he held it straight and proud. Radiant. He flicked on the radio, combed his wild hair straight and slipped on his glasses. Some Nickelback crap played. He swatted the radio off. He said, "Listening to this shit is the equivalent of eating a worm waffle with whipped cream on it, and other unhealthy things...like artificial honey."

I wore a red sundress and red lipstick. On the drive into downtown Cleveland, we picked up tall cups of black coffee and sunglasses for me, and because I couldn't see him again anyway, I told him everything. I told him I'd smoked crack with Billy. I told him I cooked Simon meat. I told him Wendy killed Liz. And that now Billy knew. I told him about the girls, about Wendy luring them.

I don't know what I expected from him, maybe empathy, but instead he went inward, and I felt anger. He began driving too fast, cursing at people who weren't using turn signals.

I wanted these last moments to be nice.

His jaw was clenched while he drove.

"Are you mad at me?" I hated the whimper in my voice. I gripped my right hand in my left. How many times had I said that to Georgie, and other men, in my life.

"No."

It didn't take us long to get downtown.

He was double-parked, so we just had a few seconds.

He turned to me. "I'm sorry, I just wish you'd never met her. I wish you'd met me first instead."

"Me, too."

Angelo put his finger in Clarence's carrier, and Clarence rubbed his cheek on it. "So, is there an extra fee to take pets on the bus?"

Embarrassment waved over me. I hadn't even checked to see how much extra it would be to take Clarence on the Greyhound. "I...don't know."

"Margot. Wait. Is there any way you can stay?"

"I love you, Angelo." We kissed.

Then, too soon, I stood alone in the station. Not alone—with Clarence. I gently set the carrier on the floor so he would have steady ground. I looked into his wide face and into the primordial light of his yellow eyes. I'd left my leonine self-portrait in Angelo's room.

I turned and his car was gone, of course. I thought, maybe, I could go back and work things out with him, and then maybe, we could go away together. Maybe we could take a plane... that would be the quickest, safest way out. We could leave this afternoon. But the thoughts were draining from me like sugar from the blood. It was good he had the painting. The only version of me safe to stay in Cuyahoga County. My future had to be alone, like before when Georgie had left. I had to start over clean and not involve Angelo. Maybe I'd go to California instead. I walked with the lopsided pet carrier into the line, just beneath the sign that said *Pets Prohibited*.

I took a cab to Bela Buda. The festival started at noon, but Henry and Lucy and her new guy were already there. Henry let me put Clarence and my stuff in his apartment above the venue. I told him I'd left Wendy. He smiled but was distracted by the big show. Downstairs, Lucy draped webs from the lights, as she directed the men to move around tables and chairs. It was *hot,* but her black bob moved cool and shiny as ever, even as she wore a black trench coat. I had no shame asking Lucy for drink tickets, and she poured five in my hand: very generous considering there were as many as two dozen bands playing. Fake spider webs hung still in June light.

I was numb with no plan. I had no idea if the thousand dollars I had was enough to get a same-day one-way plane ticket to Arizona. With a cat. I was down the cab fare, so less than a grand. If I went to Arizona, would Simon know people to track and kill me there? Could my family be hurt? Or—if I went somewhere no one knew me, how could I get by with no money? I told myself the Vickers and Simon would be going after each other, that they wouldn't care about me.

I wanted out of Ohio, but instead, I sat in a booth. I needed energy but couldn't eat, so I fingered a packet of Sudafed in my pocket, not really feeling it but needing something.

As soon she saw my gear on a table, Lucy hit me up. I left the pills alone. Breathing shallowly without a smile, she wiped her slick hair out of her eyes and handed me the schedule, asking if I'd make sure the parking lot was ready.

Out back, the first acts were setting up. The small parking lot for the people who lived above Bela was transformed into a concert venue with a makeshift stage of wooden pallets and a heavy-duty extension cord leading from inside the building to a PA. I wondered if Lucy had a permit. I hoped it wouldn't rain. They sky was grazed with dirty clouds, but you never could tell.

The schedule was insane:

noon-2am

Inside:

Thursday Club/Fragments collab, Contamination Diet, Murderous Vision, XTerminal, Moth Cock, Dead Peasant Insurance, Andrew Coltrane, 9 Volt Haunted House, Angelo's band, some dudes from the Rubber City Noise Cave, me, Dog Lady, Clan of the Cave Bear, Gomorrahizer, Self-Destruct Button, A Real Knife Head, Glacial 23,

Witchbeam, Orange Luna Temple Lull and Tusco Terror.

Outside:

Fascist Insect, Plague Mother/Lucy collab, Mona Cost, Ilsa, Rot Ton Bone/Rob Resch collab, the Family Chapter, Robert Turman/Aaron Dilloway, Baat, Jerk, Paloma, Arthur, Iron Oxide/Henry collab, Collapsed Arc, Flat Can Company, Noumenon Device, J Rod, Flux-monkey, Ann B. Klorox, Skin Graft, Cunting Daughters, Relentless Corpse and Red Liver.

Sets would alternate between inside and outside every half hour for fourteen hours. Relentless. I was glad to have sunglasses again.

When I came back in, Lucy was directing some young guys on the best placement of a wooden lunar mandala. "Hey Lucy, do you know when Angelo is going to be here?"

"Oh, he texted and said he wasn't able to make it. Yeah, I was really surprised. Just back in town, and he had been so psyched on it all spring..."

I stepped outside and called him. The sun was already high in the sky.

"Are you okay?"

"No pets on the bus, so I had to come back. I wanted to come back. I thought you'd be at Bela, I felt stupid, so I didn't text. I figured you'd be here early."

He was silent and I kicked my shoe into the ground.

"You shouldn't be there. It's not safe."

"Angelo. I don't know what to do, so I want to play the show."

"What if Simon's killed the Vickers and now he's coming for you?"

The sidewalk sparkled. The world was too real. I'd been raised on 1990s Quinton Tarantino movies, but this was life, this was real, who

347

cared about me?

"Without the Vickers, Simon doesn't have much of a crew, really. I think...if anything, the Vickers probably caught him by surprise. It's probably, all over now." My stomach lurched. I started toward the gas station down the street to get a can of Coca Cola.

"Just stay there. I'll be there in five."

The sound check sounded like electric rain. I drank brown cola fizz in Bela's shadow and watched the shadow dissolve as clouds blotted the sun. I felt strong, endless. I wanted to play. Angelo's red Honda Civic came round the corner. I followed and he slammed out of the car and walked to me, direct, focused as always.

He saw me as I was and not as something he needed. He took my hand and we walked to the wall and held onto each other. I kissed his neck and he whispered, "Let's stick together."

"Okay. Let's go upstairs and use Henry's computer, I need to see if there is a plane out of Cleveland, if I can afford it."

"I don't think he has a computer, but let's go, I'll go wit'chu."

Henry had gone out to pick up some cables for one of the Michigan guys, whose car was busted into at a gas station while he'd gone in for smokes and road food. Luckily, they just made off with his cable bag, not his gear bag. We'd have to check Henry's computer after he got back. We got some beers and the show started.

A few sets and beers in, I felt euphoric in the way of the drunken afternoon. I felt safe. Even after the monster I'd unleashed, there was lightness of being just from being free from Wendy. Now I wasn't

348

afraid of anything. I'd never seen how beautiful this place was, not really. It was as if another Margot were on a silver bus heading west, and another Margot had died in Simon's apartment two lifelong nights ago, and this Margot was the one who got to stay for one more show.

Good people filled the space. People I'd known for years, people I'd missed. I was saying my secret good-bye. Mona Cost let a violet velveteen cloth fall over her as she fell to the ground at the end of a hurricane set. We clapped, we howled. She clawed her way out, long hair stuck to her cheeks in muggy sweat.

As we made our way to the outside stage for Contamination Diet, Angelo took my hand. I wasn't sure if *sticking together* meant for the day, or if he wanted to fly away with me, but his hand felt good.

"I'm—processing all the shit you told me earlier, still processing. Where the fuck is Henry?" He scratched the back of his neck. We squinted in the white solstice sun and Contamination Diet roared.

Then clouds clotted up, so Lucy had the next three acts play inside. I clung to the edge of the bar by the men's room. The corner I'd spent so many hours over the years. From here, I could watch the whole room. Through the spring Angelo had often stood by me there too, our forearms touching, sharing a beer. I bit my cheek and thought of Wendy and Simon. I surrendered into the feeling I most cherished: suspension inside a noise set, an abstract song, surrounded by warm people I cared about without having to talk to.

Thursday Club/Fragments scattered the floor with gear. The four men crouching through the sounds like organs in one body. Small piercing sounds, and then rough stones grinding, revealing their crystal shine, *blind violets rising into shivering growth at the bottom of a deep well.*

Our wild goat friend's purple paintings lingered scarlet and torn blue, long after the thirty days the owners usually kept work up. It was too hard to undo the damage he'd done by nailing expanses of wood into the walls. And so, as people played, and the solstice sun wore on, the sun's light shifted over thickly painted leaves with fairy faces inside. Shadows lingered over painted shadows, veiling secret red doors.

Angelo whispered, "Hey, Henry's back, let's go!" The guys playing on the floor looked at each other and then in one motion slipped the volume on their mixers down. We let the silence sit for half a second, and then we clapped and howled. I recognized certain voices, people who had been making the same whistle or *yeah* after a set for years. I missed them suddenly that last day more than in the time I'd been away smoking crack with Lizabeth Vickers.

"Okay." I saw Henry behind the bar now crowded with loud people.

Then Keith from Cheap Kiss walked in the front door! He spotted me right away and walked over. Keith looked shy in a Black Sabbath t-shirt with his pokey straight hair sticking out from under a brown and yellow Cleveland Browns cap. A thick, pretty woman led him to me by the hand. I shook my head and had to laugh in agitated surprise. He gave me a delicate little hug and introduced me to his new girlfriend. "I'm used to seeing you dressed in scrubs not in...red. Wow! Margot, we came to see you *jam*. I saw this gig on Facebook." Keith gave me a thumbs up. "Hey, Cheap Kiss is playing *Peabody's* on the 13th! I'll invite you. You should come out."

I looked for Angelo, but he must have been moving through the crowd to get to Henry.

I looked at Keith and his new girlfriend. "Yeah, hey you guys seem happy." I'd felt rubbery and a little confused even before I saw my friend from Autumn Villa days.

Keith took off his Browns cap and held it at his belly. "Yeah, Margot, please, I know divorce is hard to talk about, but Carrie and I hadn't

350

been happy..."

"Oh Keith, no, it's okay. This is good for you. Divorce saves lives—it saved mine." I squeezed them both, only to see Mark Vickers outside talking with his father, Jeff. My buzz dropped to my uterus like a stone, and my mouth went sour with beer. My hands were empty. I excused myself, hoping Angelo would stay inside, but he followed me to the front door.

Lucy stood on a chair and whistled. "We're going to have a fifteen-minute intermission, and then Jerk will play outside—the skies are looking clear!"

Angelo caught me halfway out the door, "Where are you going? Rocky's working the bar now, she says Henry ran upstairs, let's go up..."

"I know, hang on, it's Vickers."

"Fuck." He followed me outside.

Humidity hit us like a wall. The air was sweating. Jeff came up to me. "Margot, honey, how are you? Did you play yet?" And then he hugged me in his wrestler arms. He held me at arm's length and looked into my eyes, and I saw what seemed like kindness in his. I'd never seen him in daylight before. His eyebrows and eyes had a sweet hangdog look, and his ever-neat green Mohawk made him look like a dad.

I exhaled and looked into his doggy eyes. "Jeff—"

"Sh' sh' sh', honey, Billy gave you some money, right? Along with that gift comes the further gift of not having to think about those people anymore. You don't have to worry about Simon and Wendy anymore. But it would be best if you moved on. After you play, you just get on, okay?"

"Okay."

"I know you didn't do nothing but good by our family."

"Okay."

"I know it and I appreciate it."

"Liz was my friend. Billy, too. And—"

"But we're just wondering where she is, 'cause she isn't at home. You haven't heard from her have you?" He glanced at Mark, who was staring into the street, smoking a clove cigarette, bored as always.

"Wendy?"

Jeff shook his head and looked at Angelo. "That bitch Wendy did a number on her, man."

"Jeff, no, I took off from her place last night. I don't know where she is. I'm done with her."

"Are we out of here? This noise shit all sounds the same and I'm tired." Mark kicked a bottle cap into the gutter.

Jeff looked apologetically at me. "Too much fucking Grant Theft Auto. I told his mother." A car slowed behind him. "Well. Margot." He held out his hand, "Here's wishing you the best, hon, and I wish I *had* gotten to see you perform. Maybe someday when the air..."

"HIPSTERS!" Eggs tore out from the slowed car. The car squealed off. My belly was hit. I put my hand to my dress, laughing because it was yolk and not blood. Jeff and Angelo were spared, but egg dripped from Mark's quiff. Angelo chased the car down the street.

"Poor kid," Jeff put a finger on my belly and yolk stretched between us before falling to the concrete, "You've been through it. I'd hate to see anything else happen to you. If you hear from Wendy, call Billy, right?"

"Right. Yes."

"Then you'll clear out after this show?"

"Yes."

"Things'll be messy around here for a while, Margot. Don't want you caught up in more shit, okay? Trying to keep Billy out of trouble, too."

"Okay, yeah Jeff thanks."

He winked and flicked the egg from his finger then grabbed Mark and they were off, Mark grumbling about how he was so *not* a hipster, etc.

Angelo came back and looked at my belly. "Lost the fuckers."

"Let's go upstairs, find Henry."

"Are you hurt, are you okay? Those eggs can hurt people. Once, they got Henry in the eye."

I wanted to grab him and squeeze him, but I didn't want to get egg on him. He kissed me on the lips and said, "I can't believe I can kiss you."

Henry was stoned as fuck, and it took him a minute to understand we needed a computer. I went into his tiny bathroom, stepping around two cat boxes and dodging spider plants. I rinsed egg off my dress. I put as much of my face and head under the cold water, too. The pleasure was deep. In the mirror, my hair sprang back away from my face, my heavy black eye makeup bled darkness exposing small red eyelashes. I put on fresh lipstick that had half melted in my small shoulder bag.

I didn't know how to read what Jeff had said. The Vickers were not opaque like Simon and Wendy, they seemed to wear emotions pretty plainly, but they always had some agenda, something they wanted. Did Jeff think I knew where Wendy was, and he was threatening me? Or not? He clearly wanted me to leave town, but I didn't really know why.

All I knew was Wendy was still out there.

I came out and Angelo said, "Come on, he doesn't have a computer, but Rocky does. She's staying next door. He's going downstairs to trade off with her." He grabbed a couple apples from Henry's counter and bit into one. Noise buzzed our feet through the floor.

Rocky's apartment was a sticky hot room cluttered with boxes, a desktop computer on crates, and a mattress with worn Smurf sheets. Her old desktop was so yellowed from cigarette smoke the screen was hard to read. We waited for it to dial up. Her hair was glued into lazy spikes and she wore thick and sickly pink foundation that didn't cover the cystic acne underneath. "I can't wait until we get some fucking broadband in this town. Not that I could afford it, anyways. I've only been here a month, but I'm having to move back in with my dad. I just can't make any fucking money. I'm a piece of shit in a toilet world."

"You're young, go home. It's okay. This is no time to be young or old in America."

Angelo handed me an apple.

Rocky stepped back and gestured to a web page she'd pulled up with all kinds of flights listed. I looked at flights to Phoenix and flights to LA. I had no idea how cheap flights were! Well, at least cheap if you have almost a thousand bucks in your wallet. "Fuck, Angelo, I can totally afford to get out of here."

I looked at him. "I can take you too, if you want."

He nodded. "Check about cat fees. And taxes."

Rocky lit up an American Spirit and said, "You can use your debit card to pay on there, too. I think."

"Shit. I hope it'll be okay if I just show up with cash. Shit. I'll need a taxi, too."

Angelo crouched next to me. "I'll take you."

I still wasn't sure where I should go. California was nice and far, and the weather was good to be homeless in, which was likely since I could not afford to live there. I wanted to go to Arizona. I wanted to see my parents and my brother and his pregnant wife. I just wanted to protect them from any shit I was in, but I wasn't sure if I was still in shit. I had a feeling I was.

I wasn't even sure if Angelo was going with me. I grabbed a beer off the tap and left some bread on the counter for the tip. The sun was still out, but it was heading west. The next flight to Phoenix was 1:45 AM, and the next flight to LA was 2:10 AM. I knew if I were smart, I'd just go to the airport and wait, but I wanted a little more of the show. I could see—I was in love, and I loved this crew, and I had to go. It was like seeing in color for the first time and having to be so fucking precious about it or else it would be torn to shreds, burned up, just a few sweet glimpses.

I wished for a groggy minute that I hadn't had any beers, that I'd stayed clean for the day, but that was impossible. I didn't know how to do that.

Noise came from out back—Jerk was starting up, one of my favorite bands of all time. Angelo and I ran out the back door.

Halfway through Jerk's set, the cops came whirling up. And then the rain came down. We wanted to grab gear and run it under the nearest shelter, but we were afraid to run with cops around. After all, they shoot children. Big fat drops of rain, smelling like asphalt. The trees shivered. Henry came out with a tarp—he'd unplugged the PA from inside. He had it all wrapped up. Jerk was pissed.

NOISE VIOLATION. Henry asked the cop, "What about those kids and the eggs? Where are you then?" The cop pretended not to hear, and Henry didn't say any more.

Now all the bands would have to play inside, and the show would have to be over by midnight.

Lucy was unflappable. She put on her real estate agent smile and a little black rain cap and announced two bands would set up at once, and performers would just pull off, each following each all night.

No breaks. Seven-minute cap, ideally. Aim for it. I copped a vodka Red Bull. In the last few minutes of rainy quiet before the four-hour barrage of nonstop noise, Angelo asked me if I wanted to split.

"Are you going with me?"

"I was going to ask if you'd sit in with us next month." His face was stone.

"I wish I could." I looked at his shoulder. He had a life here, his band.

"Can you trust them?"

"I told them about Simon. That's worth something."

"What if Wendy shows up here? What if Simon is still out there?"

"I think they got Simon. She must be hiding out."

"You should go now."

"I want to play first. I want more time with you."

Then we were knocked out by the wave of Fascist Insect playing. And then Skin Graft. Wave after wave of harsh and strange sounds. We stood in our corner by the men's room, drinking and drinking, but our eyes stayed sharp. Then I closed them with my tongue pressed to the roof of my mouth, my eyes came together in a dark womb at the third eye. Noises filled the space with dynamic agitation.

I checked my phone and found a text from Billy: [Hey girl, dont worry—your safe at the show, your safe for good now, we took care of them. I hope your new life is better than this one. Love, Billy]

"A golden ticket," I said to a painted unicorn with a white goatee, its paw settled in the lap of a golden lady.

I was drunk, and I didn't feel anything beyond minor relief that we were safe. I didn't think about how they "took care" of Wendy. Joy drained, and I wanted to be alone. I wanted to leave, but I was drunk, and I felt afraid to leave the warm nest of friends and go out into the night. Alcohol felt like family, but it was dangerously numbing. It was summer, but the night was sharp. We had our artificial light.

Believing in survival was easy. Future was a birthright. In True Night, I would have to face what happened, and I'd have to figure out what comes next.

In one corner, Dog Lady's set wound down to the ground, to a sweeping, breathless finish, and we exhaled and raised our hands. In the corner by the window, Angelo's band erupted with feedback lightning. He said something in his mic about his friend, his Rose, and his eyes grazed mine. Then he turned to a simple drum kit with his sampler on a stand and made this rhythm that was of the deeper part of earth. A waltzing ¾ time: da Da DA da Da DA, but slow and red. The analog drums and sampler smeared together in expressing this *Durga* triple heartbeat. He'd stripped his band down to three. His fellows added one at a time: warped tape shrieking, modular synthesizer clashing with feedback loop. Blips, scrapes, rising and falling. The set rose. Halfway through, Angelo staggered the rhythms, and the sampler emerged from the physical drums with a strange new voice. Angelo took the mic and over all that noise, screeched four even lines of grind vocals. Then Tom Orange jumped in from the north, made a single trumpet blast, and the players went silent.

We roared. It was a set for the ages. Angelo staggered out from behind the set and fell into my arms. We breathed cheek to cheek, and desire wrapped around our feet, slithered up our core. "I'll go with you, baby, let's go."

"Oh, Angelo. Look, we're okay, Billy texted and said it was safe to stay. I want to play. It's safe. To finish."

"Okay, yeah, you're right! I mean, if anything was going to happen, it would have happened by now. Everything is good!" He smiled.

My set kept getting pushed back. My phone stayed blank. Nothing from Wendy. Wendy was gone. The clouds made the night come prematurely. Then they split apart at ten revealing strange red brightness. The crowd swelled to its fullest, and then it went dark. People were tired and drunk. Mumbling with grouchy affection. Bela Buda, with the wet bodies and storefront glass, started to feel like a terrarium.

Angelo and I went out for air. I thought for a minute of Tasha and Johnny Maker. I wanted things to be good for them. The clouds had fully cleared, making the sky perfect black, with one star, or was it Venus? And the full Moon was rising, after the longest day, in the east. Fat, golden, and low. Coming from our secret beach, to Lakewood, the Moon was coming to the show.

Lucy came out and looked at the Moon with us. She looked at Angelo with a touch of lusty regret, and then asked me again, "Nine Volt needs to go on next, something about a babysitter, would you mind, Margot, maybe going on a little later?"

Eventually, it was time. Keith was long gone. I'd been in a drunken noise trance these last few hours, but nerves shot up again. The crowd had thinned out. Only one or two weirdoes were left to play after me, but I had to hustle because it was closing in on midnight, thirty-six minutes. My fingers trembled as my mind sharpened. I used the line of electricity to focus when I set up: plug the extension cord into the wall, then the power strip, then the amp and mixer, then the mic and tape decks into the mixer. I'd brought a second little amp to plug my guitar into because it seemed to get lost when mixed with two tape decks and vocals. I might be better off plugging into the PA, but I trusted my amp's special hum and partial tube distortion.

Angelo stood up front with his arms crossed. Henry brought me a vodka martini and winked. "Show us your A-game!" The people stood, many hadn't seen me play at Scum, had never seen me play, or hadn't seen me play since I fucked up a year and a half ago. I did a jerky little soundcheck, downed the martini and closed my eyes, finding the psychic center.

I played from my sex, my core, *Shakti* moved up into my heart, lungs, out my arms, hands, and out my mouth. I grunted and *out, out out.* There was Angelo. A silver Moon cord connected us, and I returned to the dark, hidden room of our souls that I'd glimpsed when we kissed in the street the day before. I saw two mummified Dravidians, lying in each other's arms, dark hair and candlelight. I saw that they were alive but sleeping. Us. Wendy leapt into my mind's eye, I moaned, I pulled the strings. She was on a white horse, white lightning. She compelled me. But then she flattened into a slick vodka ad in a perfumed magazine. Her blue eyes painted ice.

Beyond these visions, a haunted house unfolded, and I climbed narrow stairs into occult rooms. My mother worked there, her shoulders hunched up into stone, grooves in her bones from decades of bra strap. But the rooms led into halls and it smelled like benzoin, an old ship, and near the kitchen, with the fire, and the pot, I put my hands out to the Creature: blazing like a tree made from the kitchen fire, eyes flickering off every point, consuming nothing but the night *Duende.* Drinking night sky. Creature was a slow burn paradox: burning away hyenas and jackals, burning the white fear clear away, and burning the white fear clear away *was* a slow burn paradox: Creature was both smaller than this room, and infinitely large. Creature put a hand to my heart, I felt the burning as wet, salty touch. My eyes closed within my closed eyes, and a golden disc emanated from that soul place, just behind the heart. The disc expanded in perfect concentricity. Welled out from my chest, into the vivid living world around me.

My eyes flicked open. Ungrounded hum. I flicked the volume down on my mixer. A daze.

Wendy in the crowd. Yellow bandana, torn faded jeans, tight on her spindly legs. Clapping dull air between cupped hands.

Angelo wrapped his arms around me. "That set was beautiful."

"Wendy's here." Why had Billy said she was taken care of? All the expansiveness evaporated, and the looseness I usually felt after a show, was filled up with tight dread. My sweat turned cold. "I... blacked out during my set... was it okay?"

Henry and Rocky piled onto us. I felt like an athlete. I stroked and clenched the money in my small bag, making sure it hadn't slipped away. I saw Wendy through the front window now, smoking a cigarette with Arthur, Paloma, Mona and Murder, laughing a broad horsey laugh. I could leave out the back. I held Angelo's hand. Moth Cock sauntered up to the PA and started low but got high fast. Iron Oxide had asked to go last, but now looked at the clock and crossed their arms, afraid there wouldn't be time for their set. In a flash, I realized I'd wanted two things all along, since before Georgie, even back in the shadows of the yellow house on twelfth street in Canton: Big Love and Big Freedom.

I wanted to grab Angelo and slip up to Henry's, but instead I walked out the front door. Arthur and Paloma embraced me, gave me wide, sparkling smiles, complimented my set. The Moon climbed. Now pointed, paler, brighter. Wendy hesitated for a minute, and then pulled me in for a hug, kissed me hard. Her saliva drenched with Camel cigarette, reminded me of Georgie, and I pulled back, wanting to spit, but she held my arm tight. "I really liked that Margot. I've never seen anything like it, but I liked it a lot."

"Wendy, you got to get the fuck out of here."

"Whah?" She looked around and laughed hard. "Why's that, baby?"

Angelo said, "She'd done with you."

Arthur and Paloma exchanged a look, and he started to say something to me, but I said it was okay and they went inside to get a drink, leaving me outside with Wendy and Angelo. We could see Moth Cock jamming through the window, one sitting like Pan poised with a flute, his hair a cloud. It was a quarter till midnight.

My head was dizzy with guilt about my rage that she was still alive. I was a monster. "Wendy, you have to leave."

"Sure, baby, we'll leave, but is there going to be an afterparty?"

"No. Angelo, Henry's back at the bar, let's go."

Wendy grabbed my arm. "Okay, I just want to have a drink with you and your friend here before I take off, okay? After the noise is done." She pulled me close. "Maybe you can tell me why fucking Vickers came to my house last night pounding my fucking front door half off the hinges? I took off out the back. I've had to hide out at June's mom's house all day. The fuck, Margot. Can't reach Simon—he could get us out of town."

I pulled her chicken claw off my arm. "That's your fucking business. I saw the girls. I saw the bloody pantyhose. —I saw you kill Liz. I was there, but I didn't kill her. You killed her. I couldn't do anything. You killed her. You took those girls. You locked me up."

Angelo stepped up in her face. "You need to go."

"Hey, fuck you, kid. Okay, what the fuck ever. I'm out." She walked quickly down the street.

I saw what I wanted in Angelo's eyes: eyes the color of the living oceans: blue infused with the dirty green of life.

Inside, Henry was pouring rounds and rounds. Iron Oxide took a while to set up. We went up to Henry and said we had to split now. He tossed us his keys.

It was after midnight when we came back down with Clarence. Iron Oxide was just getting started with their dank thudding weirdness. We still had to pack up our gear. Henry crossed and uncrossed his arms at them, afraid that the cops would back and do something worse since the music had gone past midnight. Lucy was carefree, finally, at a round table crossing and uncrossing her legs at her new man and others, talking almost over Iron Oxide, who moved into a bendy dirge.

I wondered about the lock on the door of my room at Wendy's. Had she kept someone in there before? I wondered if there had been an Alice. I wondered if anything she'd ever told me had been true. My stomach turned, the light in the room went sick and the whole city felt off.

After the set, people got loud again, wanted more to drink, but Henry was beat. He turned the high lights on, announced last call. Angelo and I stood by the wall, our eyes dry. Maybe we felt safe lingering in our private public space. By a quarter till one, the place had cleared out. I said mental good-byes to each of the people as they filtered out in happy little clusters. I wished I had more time with them. We loaded up Angelo's car. Despite all we'd consumed, we were stripped sober and exhausted. Clarence sat in his carrier behind the bar. We'd have to leave soon to make the flight.

Lucy and Rocky hugged us and went upstairs to smoke weed and watch *Blue Velvet*. It was just Henry, Angelo, and me. I knew we should leave, but the street was frightening. I wished we could stay there forever, as Henry locked the front door, turned off the neon lights, turned the interior lights low. Forever in that warm space. He lit a bowl and passed it to Angelo, who took a quick hit, but then said we had to go.

A knock on the side door.

Henry sucked in his hit and smiled, "I'll get it, I think it's this girlie."

He flicked the volume up on Glenn Branca's "Ascension" as he swung the door open.

In a flash, Simon was through the door and in my face. "You mangy cunt. Told Billy Vickers I killed his sister." He went for his gun, but Wendy pulled him back. Even with her recent withering, she easily outweighed him by twenty, thirty pounds.

"Hey—what the fuck, I told you it's not her fault!" She pulled on his arm, smiled back and forth between him and me. "Come on, we got to go. Margot. Simon's coming, too, we're going to Florida."

I pushed away from both of them. "No, I'm going on my own, I'm done. You brought those girls to him. You didn't have to. Like I didn't have to tell Billy. But I did."

"Margot, we're going to the airport now." Wendy stepped close.

Simon pulled his arm free. "*We're* going to Florida, but this bitch is going straight to Gehenna."

Before Simon could pull his gun, Wendy grabbed my arm, whipped me to her, and had her gun on him. "I'm leaving. Taking Alice with me." She pinched my flesh. "You should have just come with me earlier, Alice. We don't need his money or his bullshit."

Just then, the side door jerked open. In walked Jeff and Billy. Simon and Jeff pointed guns at each other. Wendy jerked and pointed her gun at Billy. Billy looked at me and Wendy, then at Angelo, who stood just out of my sight. I wished Angelo would run, but there was nowhere to run anyway, the front door was locked. Henry hid behind the bar.

"Simon, Wendy," said Jeff, "you go on and lower those guns, now. We can work this out."

Billy clenched his jaw in Wendy's crosshairs. He looked at me. "I'm so sorry, girl, we knew you'd draw her and Simon out. You should have left yesterday." His skin was red and wet with sweat.

Simon's voice was quiet with cold rage. "I am looking at you Jeff Vickers. Crazy. Stupid. Hill-jack. Suburban mall-punk redneck. I'm looking at your face for the last time. I am done with your stupid white trash family. I end Vickers." He steadied his aim. Wendy stood back, behind him, gripping my hand.

She was smiling.

Then Simon turned and shot Wendy in the chest, in the belly, three times, then one more. I heard the fire, but would only understand later. Her body whipped back slapping the ground hard by the front door. I was down there by her side, though the memory of my movement was lost.

My face was wet, but I don't remember crying. I held her face, seeking life. Angelo came down beside me, wrapped his arms around me. I touched Wendy's face. There was nothing. So quickly, there was nothing. She was warm. Her blood was wet. But there was nothing behind her face.

I heard the men's voices behind me, distant, like how I've been told people leaving their bodies in hospital rooms hear the voices of the medical staff. My body was moving, my hands on her face. My hearing was cold, somewhere else. Simon's voice was steady: *How's that Vickers. My sister for yours.*

Angelo and I crouched by Wendy, the front door was two feet from us but locked...I could still hear the shot.

Simon, Jesus Christ... Jeff's voice was high. *Your sister...*

I heard the sound of a steam-powered machine—it was Henry hyperventilating behind the bar. Simon had his gun on Jeff again. His hand was shaking. His voice had changed. "Jeff—I hit Lizabeth because she wouldn't let me grow, she kept stepping on me, but we were making shit happen..."

Wendy, her white hair splayed out like a star crown. Never to ride into a room again. Never chasing after anything again, not women, not justice, not control. She was a predator. She was dead. Smells rose from beneath her, feces and urine.

Seized, I turned and looked into Angelo's eyes again. He was right there, crouched behind me, his hands ready to steady me, help me up.

364

With my eyes I said *we have to go now.* He nodded.

Simon's control was slipping. He was losing Jeff. Jeff was waking up. "You've lost it Simon—this is sloppy as fuck. We are not in Cleveland—this is Lakewood. Cops will be here any fucking second." He remembered us, cowering on Bela Buda's black and white linoleum. Jeff said, "Margot. Get up. Get out of here."

Simon sneered. "Hah. That's why you need me, Jeff, you're too soft. You can't leave loose ends."

Simon swiveled his gun toward Angelo. I leapt, covered Angelo with my body, we fell to the ground, there was a single shot. My eyes pinned shut. I held him. I felt nothing. Had Simon shot Angelo? I wanted to take the shot. *Awaken the bones.*

Police sirens. Vickers' desperate voices. My voice, a low wail: *no, not you, not you, not you.* Angelo's body moved, alive, alive, he put his hands on my face. I opened my eyes. I saw no blood. I touched his chest, his stomach, no blood. He was saying *get up, get up, we've got to get out of here.*

Then I was on my feet. Simon lay on the ground behind us. The one shot: Jeff had shot Simon. Blood soaked his shirt. He was dead. His face. Henry popped up from behind the counter. "Margot, you guys go on, I'll tell the cops everything but leave you guys out of it." I sensed him bagging things up behind the counter. I looked up, and the Vickers were gone.

I would go, but Simon's face stopped me. A death mask. The scar on his shaved head was naked and vulnerable. A spirit flickered across his face. A child with bright eyes. My legs wouldn't work. I fell to my knees at that face.

Henry and Angelo hauled me up, and soon, Angelo and I were heading back to his house. Clarence mewed from the back seat. A jerky weight settled in my chest. Angelo laughed mechanically.

Had I been inside the whole thing? Or outside of it? The Moon was high, but still watching with a Mona Lisa smile.

I fingered the dried egg on my dress.

Angelo looked straight ahead and laughed. He wore a manic joker smile. Oak trees swayed in front of endless doubles. A raccoon climbed like a human from a thick branch onto a second-floor porch. With one hand gripping the wall, she turned her head and looked down at us. Her eyes steady as the night, penetrating.

27

Meet Me Holy in the River

P ulling my clay body up the short stone stairs to Angelo's front door took effort that frightened me. Once inside, he zipped around, slashing his fingers through hair wet with sweat. His rushing hurt. He seemed to not see me anymore. Did he regret promising to leave with me?

"I'm ready, so whenever." I blinked my dry eyes.

Violet padded out from the shadows to greet us. Angelo turned fast and took my hands. "I'm so excited."

I exhaled. Felt like I'd slipped my dress off over my head in that dark lake after all. "Yes—you want? Let's go. I mean, I think we missed the flight. What about…" I waved a hand at his purple lights, his plants, his blue sparkling fabric.

"It's okay. We'll make more. I want to be with you. Always."

Melissa clomped out from her room and stretched, revealing a Felix the Cat tattoo on her taut belly. "How was the show, assholes?"

When the sun met sky again, we were just reaching Dayton, Ohio. Dawn opened behind us, transforming the whole of the sky instantly from black to darkest blue. This was the time of day when cats most like to play. I reached into the back seat and let Clarence and Violet out of their carriers. They poured around the grey fabric, sniffing at invisible things. Angelo's small red car was filled to the top with hurried bags of our stuff, our gear, Angelo's trunk and his backpack. I wouldn't have believed it possible. If we drove through, we would reach Flagstaff by tomorrow, but we won't drive straight through. We will zig and zag around, stopping in motels, hopefully with pools, to rest, to stretch our bodies and to be naked together.

In twilight dawn, the trees along the highway looked silver. We were the only car on the road. I rolled down the window. The air was new and carried the promise of gentle wet heat. My brother's wife will have a baby. I thought of Liz. She listened to the ghosts of the North Coast. Now we were leaving the land of her ghost. The land of the Erie.

The land of the Erie and other people with lost names who lived between the Black and Grand Rivers: it was their mounds Wendy and I visited, their beach Angelo and I dreamed on. The earliest people left centuries ago for other land—their ancestors must be out west somewhere. Later, the Erie were brutalized and absorbed by the Iroquois during the Beaver Wars, not long before white people pushed into Ohio.

My own family had not been in Ohio a hundred years ago, and in forty-five minutes, the last of my family would vanish from Ohio.

Angelo slipped a Tusco Embassy comp into the tape player. The air crinkled and then swelled with sound. The cats chirped. We'd been awake for nearly twenty-four hours, helped along by sleazy energy drinks. I slipped off my flip-flops, put my feet flat on his dash and my hand on his leg. *Awaken the old-time bones.* I said, "Angelo, death is a bend in the river of life. We try to dam the river, dam ourselves, stuffing our senses, or faces against it with any dull thing around.

There is pain in animal life. But, we can swim in the river—you know, if we had a baby, I think I'd feel like a baby with a baby inside me, and a baby inside that baby." *Meet yourself in me. My love.*

He said, "The river is death, the river is life."

I asked him to pull over because I wanted to drive.

We stood on the shoulder for a minute, holding each other as two or three cars thundered past. A shadow hit my gut when I thought of Wendy and Simon dead, the reality of their bodies on the floor of Bela. I knew I wasn't done with all that had happened. Something of their bodies would always be with me.

I thought of the girls in Cozzi's house, and I wondered why Jeff and Billy let me go knowing that I knew about the girls, and if they'd end the operation now that Simon was dead, or if I was being naïve in hoping they would. Angelo and I could not be free as long as those girls were not free.

As I clicked my seatbelt words flashed in the center of my head: *Simon is not dead. Simon is alive.* I shook my head, blinked my eyes.

I pulled out my phone, texted Henry: [there's a house in Parma on T—- Street, off Pearl with short grass and a goose with sunglasses. Trafficked girls are in there—tell the cops, the media, whoever, please]

He wrote back right away: [ok. Best to you and A. Bela is closed for a few days—everything's over, but, that guy Simon is not dead—they took him in an ambulance.]

Simon is alive.

I pulled back onto the highway, and the sun quickly filled the sky with light. Now, we needed stories of the future we could create with love and intention. We needed a fucking break. We needed happy schemes to get us on the road, to get us to whatever work was out there for us.

"Henry says Simon is alive."

"Okay. It's okay."

I tossed my phone out the window

Angelo touched the back of his hand against my thigh.

I said, "I think—I want to quit drinking, quit everything that blots out awareness. Life."

He said, "Okay. Me, too."

We told each other stories. We told each other that we will find the musicians. We will find friends wherever we go, because we can find the musicians. We will find my family. We will keep our hands on each other. We will tell each other about our love in everything we see. We will carry water in the dry heat. We will come into *bhujangasana* facing a new sky. We will paint animals on our walls. We will learn new trees. We'll try being sober, except maybe for mushrooms. We'll open a venue in our house and have a baby. We'll find groups that fight sex trafficking, and we'll join their fight. We will put our hands and feet in that other dirt. Red dirt. We will breathe together. Again, the sky opened up.

THE END

Acknowledgments

I have a lifetime of beings to thank for coming to this place of finishing my first novel.

Teachers, friends, family, ancestors, plants, animals, elements, trans-dimentional figures of mystery... Is it pretentious to independently publish a book and then have a long acknowledgments page? Well—I have nothing against the magic of pretending and my heart is filled with gratitude.

Thank you to my husband, Mitchell, who has supported and inspired me since the day we met in 2009, months after I started the first very different version of this novel that included farming potatoes in tires and time travel to the year 2078. Mitch not only awakened my heart and materially supported me, he also helped edit *Beasts and Creature* and cooks dinner for us every night.

Love to my daughter, my heart, my Rose, Abigail, who was born months after I defended a version of this novel as my thesis in 2013.

Thank you to my mother, who gave me life and a belief in fairies, ghosts, Avalon, silver cords and stillness, and to my father, who shared a lifetime of ideas and stories with me as a friend. My mother was one of the first readers of this book, and my father once posed the question, "Am I the sender or the receiver?"

You both have loved and respected me my whole life, and I am eternally grateful.

Thanks to my brother, Wyatt, for being my dear friend since age three and my long-running noise comrade. I send love and blessings to him and his magickal wife Laurie, AKA noise artist Yohimbe. Check out their label Evidence Tapes on Bandcamp.

Infinite love to my darlings: Ellie, Leona and Veda!

Gratitude and so much love to all my noise friends and collaborators, including Kristen Drake, Bbob Drake, Pauline Lombardo, Stephen Petrus, Sarah Husher, Ryan Kuehn, Kyrie Gentilcore, Tom Orange, J-Guy Laughlin, Jose Luna, Nate Scheible, Jim Matzorkis, J.T. Whitfeild, Jeff Curtis, David Imburgia, Scott Hosner, Robert and Bethany Resch, Grace Harper, Vincent Masters, Cynthia Piper, Mike Collino, Bridget Quinn and Roman J. Thanks to David Russell Stempowski for inspired collaboration over the years as well as for the art and cover design for this book.

Thanks to all the musicians/bands mentioned in the novel, and any I might have missed. You can find many of them on Bandcamp. Although, some of them were made up.

Please dear reader, keep in mind this is not a nonfiction book about Cleveland Noise, and the perspective I bring is not expert and comprehensive, but rather partial and weird and pulled together from shows spanning 2006-2012 as well as pure invention. I recommend the 2010 movie *City/Ruins: Art in the Face of Industrial Decay* if you want to learn more.

Special thanks to Paul Schlachter and his venue Now That's Class, which inspired Scum. I'm grateful to Paul and his crew for providing a home for all the weirdos and misfits, all the best stuff. NTC has recently closed after fifteen years. Paul has wisely passed it on to the brilliant and ethical Emma Jochum, who has changed the name to No Class.

I am grateful for all the venues, mostly gone, especially Bela Dubby, our other home for five years, and also the 71st Door, The Yellow House, the Embassy, The Black Cat Factory, the Green Room, Mahall's Twenty Lanes, The Happy Dog, Turnup Records, All Go Signs,

Tympanum, the Rubber City Noise Cave, Ben Osborne and Voice of the Valley and more. Deep gratitude and respect to the late Pat Hanych of Pat's in the Flats. Pat hosted all kinds of underground music with joy and equanimity for decades.

Thanks to WCSB, WRUW and the wonderful DJs for playing noise and experimental music. Gratitude for the Audio Visual Baptism series. Thanks also to No Rent, Unifactor, Alien Passenger, Hanson, Hermitage Tapes, Everyone Else Has A Record Label So Why Can't I?, A Soundesign Recording, SKSK and all the noise labels. Also, the band Mystic Breach was inspired by a band called Taboo from Maine.

Thank you to my teachers, especially the brilliant wonder-worker Clemintine Guirado, whose grace and intelligence has been an engine of support for the long haul. I am grateful for the NEOMFA consortium and all my teachers in that program, in particular my thesis committee: Imad Rahman, David Giffels and Christopher Barzak—all gentle, wise and insightful. These professors are each beautiful writers, and I am so grateful for their time and feedback. Thanks to Ted Lardner for the courage to seek truth in wild dreams, texts and textures, and to the late Gary Engle, to Robert McDonough and Mark Lewine, John Hoyt and Fredlee Votaw.

Thank you to my yoga teachers: Michael Curtis, Rhonda Kuster, and the late Psalm Isadora. To Nicole McLaughlin-Lublin for providing Firehouse Yoga—a place that honors the loving inclusivity and experimentation of yoga. To our friends at the FLOW. To the writers of the sacred texts. To the teachers who liberated my heart: the late Ram Dass. The late Thich Nhat Hanh. Helen Hamilton. Eckhart Tolle.

The natural, loving awareness of yoga pulled me out of a depression 20+ years ago; it is yoga that saved this book from a tragic ending.

Thanks to writers, living and dead, who helped me love the art of the novel, especially when I struggled with its relevance: Jen Beagin,

Jennifer Egan, Kurt Vonnegut, Joyce Carol Oates, Mary Gaitskill, Ken Kesey, Zora Neale Hurston, Kate Chopin, James Baldwin, William S. Burroughs, Joan Didion, Stephen King and Joy Williams.

Thanks to Reedsy for offering excellent support for writers.

Thanks to Jackie, Bobby and Tom.

Gratitude to my family, including my Papa the poet, who helped me with school, my other beloved grandparents, and all my magickal aunts, uncles and cousins. Love to my husband's family in Texas and here in Ohio.

Thanks to Black Sun Lodge and its members, past and present.

Thanks to childhood friends who I don't see any more outside of dreams, but who taught me a lot about love: Keely, James and Eileen.

Thanks to any other friend along the way who hasn't been mentioned here. It's an oversight—every friend, and most enemies, in my life helped bring to fruition my first novel. This is a novel about true friendship.

This is a novel about power and love.

Gratitude to my body ancestors and to the ancestors of this land.

Thank you to the Spirit and Spirits of nature who are the greatest teachers of love, truth and power. Thank you Moon, Earth, Oak Tree, the Oak Man, the Black Ram, the Rocky River, Lake Erie, all the cats and dogs I've loved, Red-Tailed Hawk, Sun, Durga, Squirrel, Maple, Crow, Cottonwood, Cuyahoga River, Nimishillen Creek, Meyers Lake, the Great Yogi Shiva, the Gayatri Mantra, Sky, Plant Medicine and the Flying Yak.

Again, gratitude to Sweet M, my love forever.

I encourage support and donation to the Renee Jones Empowerment Center in Cleveland, an organization that helps survivors of trafficking and sexual assault heal and rebuild their lives, as well as empower the community to work against trafficking and violence. rjecempower.org

Please check out more of David's work: drsdesigns.net

If you'd like to connect with me, please check out my website: amandarhowland.com